# TO SLIP THE SURLY BONDS

BOOK TWO OF THE PHASES OF MARS

Edited by
Chris Kennedy and James Young

Theogony Books
Virginia Beach, VA

Chris Kennedy/Theogony Books
2052 Bierce Dr., Virginia Beach, VA 23454
http://chriskennedypublishing.com/

Publisher's Note: This is a work of fiction. Names, characters, places, and incidents are a product of the author's imagination. Locales and public names are sometimes used for atmospheric purposes. Any resemblance to actual people, living or dead, or to businesses, companies, events, institutions, or locales is completely coincidental.

To Slip the Surly Bonds/Chris Kennedy and James Young -- 1st ed.
ISBN 978-1950420513

*For all who have taken to the skies to protect the ones they loved...*
*and never returned.*

## Preface by Christopher G. Nuttall

When I was in my early teens, my grandma had a friend who had a keen interest in the American Civil War. He owned a small library of books on the subject, he was always interested in discussing the conflict...and he simply couldn't understand why I preferred reading *The Guns of the South, How Few Remain* and even *Stars and Stripes Forever* to books that covered actual *history.* Alternate history, I loved; real stories, novels set during the *real* battles and the *real* aftermath of the conflict...not so much. I wasn't sure I could put it into words, at the time, but it was true. I was always more interested in alternate history novels than *real* historical fiction.

In some ways, they were often more interesting—and more informative—than pure historical fiction. *The Guns of the South* works, at least in part, because it allows us to see how a post-independence might have developed...and why we, looking back from nearly two hundred years in the future, would regard the Confederate States of America with horror. It also allows us to see how the influx of new ideas changes the conflict, both technological—the storyline revolves around time-travellers introducing the AK-47 to General Lee's armies—and sociological. How does a society react if it discovers that its descendants passed (will pass) a stern judgement on their ancestors? And it also touches on issues—logistics, for example—that are rarely so clearly defined in more *accurate* historical fiction.

On one hand, the core of alternate history has always been to look at how things could have been different. The flow of history runs, if I may borrow a concept from Dale Cozort, through a series of floodplains and valleys. The former are the moments when a single different decision may change everything; the latter are the moments when there can be little real change, whatever happens. A small adjustment in the opening days of the First World War, for example, may change everything; no amount of adjustments will save Germany from defeat in 1918, once the Allies gained a significant technological and material superiority. These choices are both defined by people—the leaders on both sides of a conflict, in particular—and the resources available to them. The latter constrain the former and alternate history allows us to see why.

Indeed, it often sheds new light on history. The Battle of Moscow was decisive, I believe, in the sense that it probably represented Germany's last chance to win World War Two outright. The Battle of Midway, on the other hand, was not. The balance of power—economic as well as military—was so badly stacked against Japan that an outright Japanese victory at Midway would not have changed matters in the long term. Midway was not the battle that doomed Japan. Japan was doomed by the decision to go to war. But Japan was caught in a vice and, again, alternate history lets us see *why*. Many decisions that—in hindsight—have been branded as foolish (Hitler's march to Stalingrad, the Athenian expedition to Sicily) make a great deal more sense when one looks at the issue through their eyes. They were, in many ways, the best of a set of bad options.

But, on the other hand, alternate history allows us to enjoy wars—and everything from romance to detective fiction—in a very different world. The panzers never drove through Dorking during the march to London, but alternate history allows us to imagine that they *had*—and consider what sort of world they would have made, if Hitler had invaded Britain in 1940. Those of us who enjoy speculating about how alternate wars might have gone—from an Anglo-American war in 1930 to a NATO-Warsaw Pact war in 1970—can study the forces and options available to the leaders and try to form a coherent whole. Or, for that matter, a second USA-CSA War in

1890. How different would American history have been, I wonder, if the CSA had gained its independence?

And those who use alternate history as a setting for stories can pull together a vague background, then let the story flow. My own interest in alternate history began when I was very young, when I stumbled across a book called *Invasion* (Kenneth Macksey). Written as a campaign history, weaving fact and fiction together into a seamless narrative, *Invasion* sought to portray what would have happened if Hitler had tried to invade Britain. (Spoiler alert: he won.) My interest grew and sharpened as I developed both a passionate interest in history—thankfully, I didn't get much history at school; that would have killed my interest stone dead—and haunted charity bookshops and libraries for alternate history books. I found it fascinating, to the point where—in my late teens—I founded an online alternate history magazine, *Changing the Times* and spent far too much of my time browsing alternate history forums. I enjoyed asking 'what would have happened if'...and reading the answers. I had some good times, back then. We all did.

And then I became a writer myself.

Alternate history can be a tricky genre to write in. There will always be people who will argue—rightly, wrongly, does it matter?—that you got it wrong. There will always be people who will insist that the purity of your timeline is more important than story-telling potential. Yes, Hitler probably *couldn't* have successfully occupied Britain; it's still a pretty good setting for a story. (You can still get a pretty interesting flame war going on a number of alternate history forums by asking if Hitler *could* have succeeded). There will always be people who will have issues...

...And that isn't even *touching* the people who will accuse you of having a hidden agenda, of whom the less said the better. Seriously. Don't give them even a moment of your time.

A good alternate history background flows from a single change, with the consequences neatly thought out and slipped into the text. In some cases, it looks at an immediate change—i.e. a fictionalised version of what happens when Lee *doesn't* lose some orders before Antietam. In others, it looks at the long-term effects of a change—i.e. a story set in a world where Britain won the American War of Independence years ago, with the characters living in a very different world to our own. In some cases, it deals with the fantastic—time travellers, aliens, random acts of 'alien space bats'—in others, it asks pointed questions about what sort of world might be created if things were very different. But in all cases, a good alternate history story rests on the characters, rather than the background; these are the people who live in the world the alternate historian made.

The stories in this volume are all alternate history, focusing on air power and air combat. In some cases, the story follows an evolving shift from established history, as we know it; in others, the 'point of divergence' is in the past, only hinted at in the story. In all cases, they focus on how the world we live in could have been different. We may not live in the best of all possible worlds, to coin a phrase, but we do not live in the worst either.

I enjoyed these stories. I hope you do too.

Christopher G. Nuttall
Edinburgh, United Kingdom, 2019

# Contents

\* \* \* \* \*

# Friends In High Places by Joelle Presby and Patrick Doyle

*"Do thank that very charming Rear Admiral Fiske for his encouraging words. It shall greatly reassure my dear sister-in-law to know the Aide for Operations has made me the promise that my nephew shall not go on one of those dreadful escort ships. He's to do something with aeroplanes instead.*

*Did you know that a Russian princess has taken up flying? It must be a much safer occupation."*

-Excerpt of a letter from the desk of the Second Lady of the United States, Mrs. Lois Irene Marshall

\* \* \*

*January 1915, Port of Hamburg, Germany*

"Chief Hays!" The surprise of hearing a familiar accent so soon after disembarking in Germany startled me.

Europe might be in the midst of their Great War, but an American abroad had time to speak for a few moments with a fellow countryman. As long as it was truly only a few moments.

My young officer charges had multiplied from the nephew of Vice President Marshall to now include a half dozen sons of successful businessmen and even one senator's son. I personally had suspected half of the men's families of terminal ignorance on the subject of aeroplane safety and the other half of a more cold-blooded calculation. The political value of a war hero weighed against the risk of losing a family member shouldn't come out ahead, but if they were valuing a dead war hero against a reckless young pilot just as likely to crash into some Stateside barn on a dare if left at home...

The well-dressed and older gentleman with a pile of his own luggage waved me down and, with a reluctance that I hoped didn't show too clearly on my face, I stopped.

My charges were halted too, so I wouldn't lose track of them if I also paused. Lieutenant Marshall and Lieutenant Thompson stood outside a dockside bar waving energetically up at an aircraft fitted with pontoons now soaring overhead, bound, according to pier-side gossip, to embark with a German cruiser and serve to extend a squadron's observation range.

The rest of the Americans in our group would be inside the bar.

The gentleman abandoned his baggage to his escort and waved delightedly at me.

"Sir, I don't believe—" I started to form my regrets.

I tried for politeness in acknowledgement of the bespoke tailoring of his clothing but also firmness because this man, for all his upper-class Boston accent, was not my responsibility. *And darn it all,* I reminded myself, *as a United States Navy Chief Petty Officer, it was high time I herded my new band of officers past the dockside bars and got everyone to work.*

The gentleman stood a few inches under six foot, boasted a well-groomed beard, and favored me with an expression of absolute delight. Behind him trailed an underling who earned a second look from me and a salute.

A U.S. Navy commander in a crisp uniform with a look of much exhaustion on his face made the tracings of a salute back at me, and I dropped my salute as neatly as I could manage. The top three medals the officer bothered to wear indicated he'd served well and been amply recognized for it by senior naval leadership.

"Tell the ship to wait for us, Edmunds." The older man waggled a hand in the general direction of the busy dockside and not towards any specific vessel.

"Yes, Ambassador," Commander Edmunds replied.

Any sailor could see the already outgoing tide and mark the emptying piers though. *No ship's captain worth the title, whether military or commercial, would be pleased to waste the ocean's gift of easy sailing,* I thought. *But maybe for a senior enough passenger, he'd wait an extra dozen hours or so for the next tide.*

Edmunds gave the ambassador a blank look with the skepticism of his expression only showing through a slight wrinkling around the eyes and did not scamper off to deliver any such message to the, presumably, waiting vessel. But he did incline his head politely.

"Ambassador," he said, "I see you've already recognized Chief Hays, who you'll remember was present with the Marshall boy during that Kamerun incident." And I noticed that the gentleman was immediately distracted from remembering to repeat the foolish order and instead allowed the officer to direct the conversation. "Chief, this is Mr. Belmont who has been serving as our ambassador to Germany for these last few years."

"Sir," Edmunds said to Belmont. "We really should be making our way to the ship."

"In just a moment," the ambassador said. "I really must have a chat with the chief."

The commander quite obviously did not sigh. He turned and whistled to catch the attention of a pair of roughs wandering the docks and gestured for them to take charge of the gentleman's luggage. Some German spoken faster than I could follow resulted in the men hefting trunks between them and hauling them off.

The aircraft with the pontoons had vanished from view, but Thompson and Marshall continued their discussion. From the way Thompson's hands moved this way and that, I was certain aviation was still the subject of their discussion.

Lieutenant Marshall, tall, of neat dark hair and a striking physical similarity to Vice President Thomas R. Marshall, leaned in to listen with rapt attention to Lieutenant Thompson's tales. Thompson came from a southern family and had flown on dirigibles and was eager to study the workings of aeroplanes with their impressive speed and, perhaps, military utility as observer units.

I dragged my attention back to the man in front of me.

"My pleasure, uh, Mr. Ambassador," I said. I had no idea what the proper mode of address was. Now twice assigned as part aide-de-camp and part keeper to the Vice President's nephew, I wished there'd been some sort of instruction manual on handling these people who'd never speak to me in the normal course of events.

Commander Edmunds gave me a sympathetic smile.

"We really should be making our way to the ship, sir." He gestured beyond to where the porters now carried Mr. Belmont's trunks across a gangway.

He had my sympathy.

A returning overhead engine's eager roar drew matching hoots of delight from nearly everyone around us. The seaplane buzzed overhead, and even Mr. Belmont grinned up at it.

"Those the ones they were considering embarking on the armored cruisers?" I asked, not willing to let a source of information go.

Commander Edmunds nodded. "So the Germans say."

Mr. Belmont squinted at it. "Is that what they intend to do with those? I wouldn't know. German military secrets, I suppose."

"An extended observer, I understand. Just the one pilot instead of a whole zeppelin aircrew, so it's easier to make accommodations for them onboard," Edmunds replied. "They haven't, at least yet, attached any rig for bombs aboard the aeroplanes either. So a tradeoff to be sure for the military utility of it all."

"Bombs?" Mr. Belmont snorted. "What a ridiculous notion. Good thing you're escorting me back Edmunds, or you might give these Germans far too many ideas."

"I suspect they'll have plenty of ideas on their own, sir," I said with as much mildness as I could infuse in the words. People swirled all about us on the busy waterfront and most, if not all, were Germans. This was Germany after all. And some would surely have proficiency in English. Likely no one would repeat what I said and make my officers' lives more difficult for it, but I saw no reason to risk offensive words against the host nation.

"But Mr. Belmont, your ship does seem quite ready to depart," I reminded him.

I could see the fine passenger liner was ready to pull away from the pier with tug boats and line handlers all standing about waiting on a last few elite or perhaps even a single final important passenger to get onboard so they could go before the tide turned, and they'd have to waste coal powering out against the currents instead of with them. Commander Edmunds favored me with a grateful smile and gestured Mr. Belmont again to the ship as if another hand wave would be enough to shift him.

"It'll wait," Mr. Belmont said with complete confidence. "I could hardly go without stopping to congratulate the very fine sergeant here."

"Chief." Commander Edmunds corrected while I tried to keep up.

"Congratulate, sir?" I was baffled. Certainly my lieutenant had survived his Africa assignment, but I'd been honest in my report back to higher authority about what exactly we'd done during the defense of Port Doula.

"Yes, of course congratulate!" Mr. Belmont patted my shoulder. "The whole Marshall family is delighted with you! Well, our esteemed vice president didn't say as much directly, of course. You know how he is, always hoping for Mr. Wilson's recovery. As we all do, naturally.

"But a young war hero relative will be ever so useful for the next presidential campaign. I do hope you enjoy going to all the fine Berlin parties. The Kaiser, bless him, doesn't throw many these days, but the younger set can have quite a good time."

"Uh, thank you sir." I didn't expect the lieutenant would attend all that many parties. The orders had said, 'Make a close study of German military aviation.'

Over Mr. Belmont's shoulder, the bar's door opened, and Lieutenant Junior Grade Roberts popped his ruddy blonde head out long enough to call out something that drew the other two lieutenants in after him.

If Marshall, Thompson, and the rest were settled in at the bar for a while, I would've liked to head on down past the commercial shipping docks to see if I could get a good look at the other piers which might hold some of the German naval fleet.

The ambassador looked at me expectantly.

"I, um, don't expect to attend parties," I said.

Mr. Belmont laughed. "You sound just like those admirals!"

Commander Edmunds gave his charge a concerned glance which only amused the ambassador more.

"Sir?"

"My understanding is the young lieutenant requested sea duty following your tour in Africa and certain esteemed persons felt he was too important to risk on assignment onboard a naval escort," Commander Edmunds explained.

"It would've been an absolute waste." Mr. Belmont shook his head. "I heard those Navy boys were almost going to give him that assignment, too. Ridiculous the level of pressure required to make them see sense. And after that masterful piece of work in Africa, too!"

"I'm afraid I don't understand, sir." I remembered quite clearly that Lieutenant Marshall had telegrammed asking for a follow-on assignment instead of resigning his commission. Yes, there had been a mention of sea duty, but he'd been more than a little intrigued with aviation, and I was almost certain he'd mentioned that as well in the message.

"You didn't tell me he was so modest Edmunds." Mr. Belmont continued to beam at me.

"I'm sure Chief Hays does all he can to help his officers, sir," Commander Edmunds said.

"Help? This far beyond that." He turned to me. "You are a master!" He clapped me on the back. "I heard it directly from Lois Marshall, herself, who had it from the young lieutenant's own mother. Excellent job keeping the Marshall boy close enough to get a bit of the glory from that nasty business in the African colonies. Be a different story if he'd been in that mad cap boat loaded up with explosives, of course!" He chortled at his own joke, and I firmly kept my face as blank as I could manage.

Commander Edmunds' face matched mine.

The boat in question had in fact included both myself and Lieutenant Marshall in the crew.

"I can't imagine the guts of those natives getting on the thing. But I suppose their lives are wretched enough that it doesn't take so much bravery to risk them."

I supposed quite the opposite, but it wasn't my place to say. I made a polite listening noise and said, "Sir, what was it you needed? Your ship needs to depart soon, I believe?"

Commander Edmunds gave a small shrug to indicate that it didn't much matter how long it took to shift the senior man.

The ambassador in turn looked at the ship with a sense of glum, and I guessed from his gulp that I was facing a man prone to seasickness who'd like to delay his departure as much as he could.

Mr. Belmont finally squared his shoulders looking resolutely at his luxurious passenger liner.

"Well, I must be off." He patted my shoulder one more time. "You keep it up. You get the slightest hint that there's a change on the front, and any vessel flying American colors will load you both up for the next trip to the States."

"And the others?" I inquired. I'd been led to believe they were all fairly well-connected young men.

"Ah, if you can." Mr. Belmont shrugged. "Some boys'll run wild on any continent they find themselves on. Others matter quite a bit more. The president's own nephew." He smiled. "Gotta keep that boy of ours safe. Bright futures ahead for that one!"

"Vice president's nephew." I corrected automatically.

"Maybe, maybe. There's an election coming you know. Reason I've got to endure the sea voyage after all. People to speak with. Caucusing to do." He waggled a hand to indicate a great deal of other items too long to bother with listing.

"Then let us not miss the tide sir," Commander Edmunds said. "It would prolong the trip," he added, which had the desired effect of causing Mr. Belmont to pale, gulp, and turn resolutely towards the vessel.

The ambassador waved over his shoulder a farewell to me, and off he went.

"Just what assignment did the Navy give our Lieutenant Marshall?" Commander Edmunds asked.

"Flight duty," I said.

"Ah." The commander murmured, "In dirigibles?"

"Aeroplanes," I corrected. "Experimental aeroplanes."

"Hmm. Very safe."

"Sir." It was as noncommittal an agreement as I dared make. "I believe someone told his family that only the zeppelins held bombs and someone might have thought that meant an aeroplane was safe.

And possibly there'd been some concern regarding mines and sub-marine attacks if he'd taken the positions being bandied about."

"Good luck with that." The commander gave me a nod and hurried after his ambassador. His chuckles did not fill me with a great deal of confidence.

At least the naval service had not, this time, sent me with any instructions implying that they thought aviation was safe and easy. Perhaps it was less important to them than shipbuilding or the training exercises the fleets of the Atlantic and Pacific were engaged in. They had to prepare in the event we one day were sent to join in the great war and support our allies. But with our German allies fighting our French and British allies, it was anyone's guess who the United States ought to be fighting anyway. My best guess remained that our nation would stay out a while longer at least. Though it was clear my little group thought it inevitable that we'd come in on the German side soon.

The mess in the African colonies certainly implied a level of duplicitousness on the part of the French and British colonial administrators, but our politicians back home had accepted the apologetic responses to that. And at least for now, Germany still held her territories on the southern continent. But those distant wrongdoings had little immediate impact on the war on the European continent. They did, of course, impact what the locals of that continent thought of the colonizer governments and a certain former colony over in the Americas had begun to notice as well.

Lieutenant Thompson waved me down from the bar's open window.

"Hays! I say, Chief Hays! Come have a tankard of beer with us." A brimming second mug appeared in his hand before he finished calling out.

I entered the bar, and Lieutenant Marshall lifted up his own mug in a cheerful toast to our safe voyage.

"Roberts can go get us the train tickets," Marshall was saying. "There's a three-week flight observer course we all probably ought to enroll in which'll let us get up in the sky before the war is all over. The pilot course is three months, so." He waggled a hand indicating it might extend beyond the timeframe of the conflict.

"Some ought to take the pilot training," Thompson said. "We should learn what they do differently. I'll do it if no one else wants to."

"Oh I want to, too. We both should." Marshall said, "Not much value in learning how to take notes in German about whatever the infantry is doing when we could be flying an *Albatros* instead."

"Or one of those scout monoplanes." Thompson clinked his mug against Marshall's in agreement.

Roberts looked back and forth between the two lieutenants. He was most junior and least confident. His blinking blue eyes reminded me of a pet bunny trying very hard to become a hound.

"I'll do the observer training," Roberts volunteered. "Somebody else can do the flying; really, I don't mind." He patted his pockets to locate the group's travel funds. "I'll be right back with our train tickets."

*I could be Lieutenant Marshall's observer,* I supposed. *I couldn't lose track of him if I were in the same aircraft all the time.*

"Do you suppose he knows that the monoplanes, *Eindeckers* I think I heard them called, don't have an observer seat at all?" Thompson said.

"He can join in with the ground crews and stay with Chief Hays," Marshall said. "Tell me again what you've heard about the new *Eindeckers*. One set of wings instead of two, of course I know. But also a bit faster and more maneuverable than even an *Albatros?*"

Lieutenant Thompson, who couldn't have actually seen either German aircraft type himself yet, drew in a breath to share his rumors.

*But what had Marshall just suggested? No way would be I staying behind.*

"I'll be entering pilot training too," I said.

\* \* \*

*'' T he man's a commissioned officer for God's sake, did you expect the Navy to give him orders to sit at home and knit? Most of the boys begged off and took orders home after seeing a few Germans crash. How was I to know he wouldn't be one of the quitters?*

*"And if you do 'take a ship over to speak to the boy yourself,' you might indicate to him that we'd appreciate a bit more specificity in the technical details of his reports. 'Dashingly beautiful machines' is all well and good but helps develop our own aviation industry not at all."*

-Excerpt of a letter from the desk of Rear Admiral Bradley A. Fiske, Aide for Operations to the Secretary of the Navy

\* \* \*

*April 1915, The Skies Above Germany to the East of France*

Despite my misgivings, I had to concede that flying these crates around had grown on me…a bit. That said, I didn't have any illusions about my longevity in the flying business.

The warmth of Spring at ground level chilled to a fine frost at altitude and my wool gloves could stand to have a few holes darned shut. The *Albatros*'s engine growled in a constant thrum my ears had grown near deaf to over the last three months. The wind tore at my face, and I pulled my hat down more firmly and tucked in an edge of scarf threatening to pull free.

Poor Roberts seated behind me didn't need the shock of my scarf striking him in the face while he was trying to see to make notes and practice his navigation.

The shimmer of little streams embroidering the patchwork farm country below rolled on in a comfortably familiar landscape we'd flown over countless times now. But Roberts had a devil of a time recognizing any of it.

It probably didn't help that we were flying with a loaded rifle strapped in next to him. I had no gun as pilot, so it'd be up to him to shoot anything that needed shooting.

And good luck to him, because he'd need it.

Marksmanship in the sky might quite reasonably include prayer as much as practice. Our speed gave him eighty knots of wind to struggle against while attempting to hold a rifle steady. An enemy would not be flying alongside like a kite being towed for target practice but instead would be maneuvering or possibly even diving towards us and shooting back. Roberts might get a few seconds in which a target was close enough for him to reasonably hit anything, and he'd need nerves of steel, too, and buckets full of luck to actually hit something.

I put higher chances on the German observers, Shultz and Hoffmann, riding with Lieutenant Marshall and Lieutenant Thompson just ahead. But they'd probably miss anything, too. The German Leutnant Boelcke leading our little air convoy had more experience in the air than anyone else we'd met and much of it was much, much closer to the front than we were now. The French had taken to arming their observers with pistols and Boelcke had been having his own observer fire back with a rifle. But today he was flying an *Eindecker,* which of course had no observer to use a handgun or anything else.

Our *Albatros* aeroplanes soared over the countryside quite as powerfully as the good luck bird they took their name from. Canvas stretched tight across a set of wings below my cockpit and another above. The engine rumbled below my feet, drowning any noise the propeller whirring in front made. Lieutenant Junior Grade Roberts huddled in the seat just behind me. The edges of his maps sometimes tickled the back of my neck as the wind tore at them. The implied warning that shooting at an *Albatros* would rain misery down on the enemy struck me as quite appropriate.

Ahead, Lieutenant Marshall drove his plane up to spear through a wisp of cloud off to my left. Shultz gesticulated from the back seat and wiped one handed with dramatic motions at his goggles.

Leutnant Boelcke flew in the *Eindecker* at the very front of our group. He shot bolt straight towards Douai with none of the darting here and there of my American lieutenants. The greater power of his engine opened the space between him and us, but he'd glanced back from time to time and would angle up and down to slow enough for our slower aircraft to catch up whenever he judged the distance too great.

Lieutenant Thompson, in the fourth aircraft with another steady German, Leutnant Hoffmann, angled his plane off to my right as if he was going to go through a much larger cloud bank well out of our way. Hoffmann reached forward and thumped Thompson on the head. The aeroplane returned to its proper course.

Marshall threw back his head in laughter inaudible over the sounds of our engines and the roar of the wind.

We'd seen aeroplanes crash during pilot training. An important strut could break. An engine could quit. The propeller could sheer off—especially on those aeroplanes with a pilot-operated machine gun. None of our current aircraft (thank heaven!) had one of those.

We already learned a few useful things to take back home with us. *If only I could convince Lieutenant Marshall to go before our luck ran out*, I wished.

On second thought though, *perhaps I shouldn't hope just for luck. The flight instructors had frequently drummed on the tables and declared: 'The cemetery is filled with lucky pilots. Don't be lucky, be good.'*

Tattered map edges slapped against my head. I twisted to look behind in case my observer needed to signal something and got my goggles knocked crooked by the wind for my trouble. I straightened them.

Roberts' hands shook more than could be explained away by the chill of altitude, and I could see his lips moving in a half chant. He wasn't paying me any attention and from his stricken expression, I knew what he was saying to himself. It was the flying instructions being repeated over and over.

*One. You must focus your attention, all of it.*

*Two. You must always have a landing spot in mind that you can glide to if your engine quits.*

*Three. You must keep track of the time so you don't run out of fuel.*

*And finally, most of all you must know where you are so you don't accidentally come down on the wrong side of the lines.*

The chief instructor did tend to go on like that, but who am I to argue with someone with nearly 60 hours flying these machines?

I suppressed a quiet laugh at what that handful of hours experience meant when spent in the sky. There were ten-year-olds a plenty who had sixty hours at sea and it meant nothing. But flights came in short bursts with days or weeks of preparation before and after in an attempt to make the lightweight craft less dangerous to fly, but still there were crashes. So much so that perhaps the man who hadn't broken himself and hadn't broken his plane was more than lucky. Perhaps he was good.

The wind filled my lungs with a crisp air somehow more exhilarating than breathing was on the ground. We flew northwest, the sun flashing off the clouds but not blinding us too much. We were to deliver our aeroplanes to an aerodrome near the town of Douai. Boelcke had arranged an early takeoff exactly so we'd not be flying blind into a setting sun, a fact for which I was grateful. Our four machines, an unusually large group of aeroplanes, were haphazardly strewn about the sky in a rough diamond with Boelcke in front, Thompson to the right, Marshall to the left, and me in the rear.

I flew a bit higher than the rest while the cloud cover remained sparse enough for me to see everyone. I liked the idea of more time to set up for a glide if some part of my aeroplane failed me.

Thompson pulled his cap off and waved it in the air only to get thumped again by his observer. The energetic young man and his serious back seater made me laugh. They'd be buying each other rounds at the little tavern closest to the Douai airfield after we landed and joking about whatever this newest in-flight argument was about.

The other aeroplanes had shrunk with distance. I'd been gradually climbing without noticing it. I pressed the stick forward gently to level out.

Reminded to focus on my own flying, I checked the gauges. Rotations per minute for the engine hovered about where they should be. Nice oil pressure. The time on my watch told me we were about half way to Douai. I double checked the fuel level: eh, it matched well enough. I tapped the glass and the needle wiggled up to where it ought to be. *We should make it but there wouldn't be a whole lot extra.*

Boelcke dropped altitude to clear a few clouds and banked to the left and then to the right, examining the countryside for landmarks. He adjusted our course a few points to port, or rather to the left.

Fencing and scattered tree lines broke up much of the deceptively friendly countryside into plots too small to land on. The furrows and ditches between the new plantings would challenge the *Albatros*'s wheels and struts. I kept track of the larger fields and pastures spreading out here and there beneath us. A nice fallow one would pass beneath us in another minute and would slip away out of gliding range not too long after. I scanned for another.

A glint in the distance flashed. I wiped at my goggles with the end of my scarf. The sun did tricky things with church steeples and farmhouse roofs, but I peered hard. The flash shone above the horizon in a patch of sky clear of all clouds.

I waved my left hand without turning and pointed at the spot where I'd seen it. My observer neither tapped my shoulder in acknowledgement nor thumped my head. I batted awkwardly at the edge of the maps and still got none of the responses I needed.

Thompson and Hoffmann's aeroplane flew almost directly in line with the odd flash. *Neither showed signs of having seen anything. Maybe there was nothing to see?*

I turned in my seat and Roberts finally looked up. He glanced at tiny scattered farmhouses far beneath us, turned gray, and tried to bury his head in the maps again.

"That way," I yelled, gesturing back towards the flash.

Roberts, wide-eyed, gave me a thumbs up and pointed not beyond Thompson's aeroplane but beyond Boelcke's towards Douai. Then he looked at the ground again, his clenched hands shaking hard.

I faced forward and pulled hard on the stick to climb. Sunlight on the wings could make such a flash. I cursed. I'd looked away. Now I had no idea where to find that aircraft again. Marshall, Thompson, and Boelcke all flew straight, seeing nothing.

Maybe there was nothing to see?

A tiny black speck appeared just above the horizon in front and slightly right of our formation. A little bug framed by the wide blue sky. The front was that way. But so was the airfield at our destination.

Except there'd be no reason for a friendly pilot to be streaking directly at us. The dark thing—a flying aircraft, I was almost certain—didn't seem to be maneuvering and was moving roughly in the opposite direction of us. The dot hung in the sky, growing larger and rising higher above the horizon now; I assumed that meant an aeroplane at a higher altitude, though I couldn't tell by how much.

I pointed and yelled. I couldn't go any faster. The *Albatros* engine went the speed it went or it was off. I could make slow left and right turns to reduce my forward movement, but that'd be pure cowardice. It would leave the three other aircraft flying on ahead, still unaware of the coming interceptor.

I couldn't help myself, I looked back again and waved to Roberts to point out the intruding aircraft. He attempted a smile and waved back as if I were trying to have a pleasant chat midflight. I turned again to Boelcke, Marshall, and even Thompson: none of them saw it.

No one pointed. Not one of the observers attempted to signal anything. No one made any attempt to communicate the presence of another aeroplane, and not a one of them was looking back at me. I had no wireless to signal them with and shouting into an 80-knot wind over the drone of the engine was futile. I couldn't hear Roberts from own my back seat, let alone someone in another aeroplane a hundred yards or more in the distance.

I looked back to the right to find the black dot but saw only a vast empty sky.

I suppressed a surge of panic.

*I shouldn't've looked away, except of course it would've been very nice if someone else in our little formation could've looked around and paid attention to my waving arms to all be alert to the danger.*

Scanning the horizon, I saw nothing above or below. *It shouldn't have been possible to disappear.* Then I realized it: *my own wings could blind me!*

I pushed the stick to the left which raised my right wing slightly to reveal the sky behind it. *There it was!* I felt momentary relief, but I would not look away again. I would not make the same mistake three times in a row. Though even while I promised myself that, I realized it no longer mattered.

The spot had grown into a French single-winged *Morane* too large at its closing range to be lost even in the wide expanse of the sky.

Its engines must've been shrieking down on us, but it dove utterly silent under the sound of our own racket.

It grew giant. Propellers and nose angled straight on. *All the whole sky and did he mean to ram me?*

But no, I could see a bit of the *Morane's* tail. The Frenchman had a different target. It fell on the closest *Albatros* from above, with Thompson blinded by his own upper right wing.

Hoffman threw his hands up seeing it at last. A split second later, the German was reaching for his rifle.

The front of the *Morane* flashed with bright sparking.

If it were burning, shouldn't there be smoke? And the propeller would be visible instead of that blur if the engine had given out...

*God help us, that was machine gun fire! And on a single-seater aeroplane! How the devil had the French done it?*

Then everything happened at once, and I didn't even have time to swear.

The *Morane's* dive dropped it underneath Thompson streaking by far too close for either aeroplane's safety.

Hoffmann fired his rifle, tracking the French plane as it fought to pull up.

Thompson jerked my way and slumped over the stick pitching the *Albatros* down as it began the slowly increasing left turn of a propeller-driven aeroplane with no living hand on the controls.

Hoffmann sighted his rifle and returned fire as the passing French plane buzzed under their aircraft.

The *Albatros* turned and turned. In the moment when it faced back to Douai again, I thought maybe Thompson might yet manage to land it, but the downward spiral continued and the pilot didn't move.

The French plane shot up away from Thompson's erratic circling. The floundering *Albatros* threw the German observer this way and that and still he tried to find the French aircraft for another shot.

And I saw what Hoffmann could not see: the aircraft dropped.

Dodging Lieutenant Thompson's plane seemed to have the spoiled the Frenchman's interest in taking a shot at the rest of us. The *Morane* hung in the air for a moment as it banked towards a heading to France.

Marshall's *Albatros* streaked across the sky with Shultz twisting to fire at the fleeing Frenchman.

In the silent skies, I could only imagine Shultz's rifle fire.

*Crack! Crack!*

I jerked in my own seat to see that Roberts, face white with fear, had his gun up and was shooting as best he could even with the poor angle I'd given him on the target.

*Crack-crack-crack!* I dove forward. I had more altitude that either Marshall or the Frenchman. I could close and give my terrified gunner a chance to hit something too.

Roberts swung the barrel of his rifle over my head and down following the *Morane*, now passing under our plane. It banked into a left turn and fled to the southwest.

The Frenchman lifted his face to stare directly into my eyes in the split second our planes passed each other. He gave the smallest shrug as though acknowledging the insanity of war as my observer shot at him. The distance opened, and Roberts would need a miracle to hit the now zig-zagging Frenchman.

Lieutenant Marshall's aeroplane roared beneath us. I threw my body against the stick to roll right, straining against the guide wires. He buzzed past, wing tips mere feet away. Oblivious to the near collision, he leaned forward against the biting cold wind, focused entirely on catching the *Morane*.

Shultz gave an exaggerated shrug at the foolishness of pilots and touched his temple in an ironic salute.

Marshall's *Albatros* and the *Morane* shrunk into toy planes in the distant sky.

Boelcke's *Eindecker* circled well clear, and I could imagine his exasperation at being the only unarmed aeroplane in the fight. I half expected him to produce a brace of pistols from under his jacket and bring down the *Morane* all on his own. But instead, his aeroplane tracked over the spot where Thompson's *Albatros* met the earth.

The Frenchman realized too late that his zigzags had let Lieutenant Marshall close to nearly on top of him. And worse for the *Morane*, we had the advantage of altitude.

At the last moment, Marshall pulled out from his dive and slalomed over the Frenchman, letting Shultz rain bullets down on the enemy aeroplane while its own machine gun pointed uselessly at open sky. The *Morane's* nose began to lift and turn that deadly barrel.

Roberts and I were closing, but still too far to be of any help.

The French plane slowed.

It hung in midair for a fraction of a second and began to drop.

We closed fast, but it was over. The Frenchman hadn't begun an engine powered dive to regain speed and circle around to strafe us. This was a mere glide. A motionless propeller betrayed his complete loss of engine power. The *Morane* drifted with gentle corrections down towards a long fallow strip of farmland.

One lucky shot in that hailstorm of bullets had actually struck the Frenchman's engine! Lieutenant Marshall followed alongside and above the stricken enemy plane, and I trailed him. Boelcke settled in behind us. My nerves kept me scanning the sky, but no other aircraft appeared.

Shultz secured his rifle. Marshall kept his *Albatros* over the *Morane* and pointed with increasing agitation at it.

The wounded French plane maneuvered with lethargic slowness, angling only towards the open farmland with no power left for skilled evasion. It glided heavy and slow, now an easy target for Marshall's observer. Shultz shook his head and finished doing up the straps to secure the rifle for landing.

Boelcke behind us might not be able to read those jerky movements well enough to know Marshall was furious, but I knew my lieutenant.

The French plane maneuvered gently to angle towards the flattest-looking field. A railroad cut a neat line through the friendly German countryside, and the growing toy-sized buildings nestled beside the tracks suggested a train station.

People spilled out of the buildings ogling up at us.

The *Morane* touched down with expert lightness, bumped along the rutted earth, and rolled to a stop.

Lieutenant Marshall and then I made safe, if less skilled, landings. I coasted to a stop and unstrapped from the airplane. Boelcke followed, shutting off the *Eindecker's* engine and climbing out.

Soldiers from the train station ran toward the French plane, while curious onlookers gathered around all of us.

Boelcke stripped off his scarf and gloves while assuring them all that we were German allies and only the *Morane's* pilot was a Frenchman. I pulled off my own helmet and let the warm air restore feeling to my frozen skin.

The French pilot, first to land, stayed in his aeroplane fussing with the controls. My eyebrows went up. *His wood and canvas contraption might have broken speed records before the war, but he was grounded now and stopped. What did he hope to do?* I wondered.

*Oh.* The man hefted a wooden strut broken from his own aircraft and battered at the cockpit gauges with it.

Boelcke yelled a command to the soldiers in the crowd, and the man was wrestled from his airplane before he could do more than crack the glass on his oil pressure gauge.

I climbed from my plane, setting my boots down on soft warm earth.

Lieutenant Marshall pressed through the crowd, and I hurried to follow.

Two soldiers held the Frenchman and the rest kept back the curious farmer's family and examined the *Morane* with Leutnant Boelcke.

Marshall strode forward, sweeping off his helmet and goggles to hang by their straps, and unbuttoned his coat to reach his revolver.

"Sir! Lieutenant Marshall!" I shouted into the commotion, but if he heard me, he didn't look up.

The German soldiers holding the still struggling Frenchman saw but looked back and forth to Boelcke and their own senior officer, uncertain whether to restrain their captive for Marshall or to defend the man against an obviously enraged American pilot.

"Achtung Leutnant!" Boelcke yelled. "Leutnant Marshall!" The crowd hushed, and the senior German pilot's ringing command voice broke through.

Marshall's rising hand froze, and Boelcke waded briskly through the crowd and soldiers. In mixed German and English he said, "Das pistole: Put. It. Away!"

Lieutenant Marshall looked at Boelcke, then me, and then at the revolver in his hand as if he'd just woken up. He holstered the weapon and stood perfectly still in a pose I'd seen on more than one naval officer expecting to be publicly harangued by a superior for an infraction he hadn't been entirely convinced was wrong.

But Boelcke brushed straight past.

"Mr. Hays," he called over his shoulder to me. I could never convince these Germans to call me 'Chief' or just 'Hays' as a mere enlisted man. "The propeller." He pointed. "Most interesting. It is, how do you say?"

"Armored," I said.

I marveled at the construction. Creases on the metal plates lining the backs of the prop blades left shiny divots where bullets had struck. I spun it by hand. The sluggish movement would reduce the aeroplane speed but also, oh, the pings had deformed one of the blades. "He was lucky to be able to land."

"Maybe. Maybe," Boelcke acknowledged.

And the machine gun, I examined it, and did my best not to let color flood my cheeks. The French *Morane* mounted a 7.9mm Hotchkiss. The American gunsmith lived in France and had set up his factory outside Paris decades ago, but that hardly made it less embarrassing since it had been built for supplying the frogs during the Franco-Prussian war.

"Normal gun," Boelcke said.

"Nothing special," I agreed.

"Suffisamment speciale," the French pilot said, and clapped his mouth shut tight again when not just Marshall, but Shultz too glared at him with red-rimmed eyes.

A German officer consulted with Boelcke and took control of the situation, detailing a few men to guard the French plane, others to take the French pilot away toward the station and to disperse the crowd. The *Morane* was to be studied with detailed reports to be sent to several of our own German gunsmiths trying out machinegun-mounting techniques. The pilot would go stay with some landed gentry relatives if he would give his parole.

I walked to Lieutenant Marshall, who sagged in his overly thick flying gear. I shrugged off my own heavy jacket and encouraged him to do the same.

"My American friends," Leutnant Shultz said. "If you please, keep watch on our aeroplanes." The German's English had started quite fine and only improved on being paired with Marshall as his observer.

Shultz made a slight nod in the direction of the farmhouse barn's hayloft where two boys stared in open fascination at our aircraft, and one seemed to be measuring the distance to jump on the upper wing of my *Albatros*. The soldiers assigned to the *Morane* were little better, turning the propeller this way and that as they'd seen me do.

Shultz gave a small shrug as though apologizing for his country-men's fascination.

"Mr. Boelcke and I must go to the telegraph office in the train station to send in reports and make arrangements for all the aero-planes to be collected."

"Of course sir," I said, locking eyes with the boy in the hayloft who abruptly found a need to retreat into the shadows of the barn. We obeyed Leutnant Shultz's request.

Or I did. Marshall turned his back to stare at the point on the horizon where Lieutenant Thompson and Leutnant Hoffmann had gone down.

Lieutenant Junior Grade Roberts followed Marshall's gaze and gulped.

"Chief, I, uh, I should make a report too," he said and hurried after Shultz towards the train station. I was pretty sure Roberts would be on a nice safe boat to America as soon as his family could get his telegram and answer it, and I was glad to see the brave little rabbit go.

Walking ahead with the soldiers and Leutnant Boelcke, the downed enemy pilot was waving his hands energetically trying to explain something. His German was even worse than mine, but I gathered that the Frenchman was as shocked as the rest of us that rifle fire had succeeded in bringing an aeroplane down.

Roberts's quick strides had him at the back of the crowd, and he blended in out of sight in moments.

"You saw this coming," Marshall said to me.

I hurried to salute having forgotten my manners, and my officer batted my hand down.

"Never mind all that. Tell me about the beginning of the engagement. When did you spot him? And how the Devil did he manage to shoot down Thompson and Hoffmann without destroying his propeller? Could he have done it again? Or could anyone, do you think?"

The French pilot was being peppered with much the same questions in German. I replied with much less hesitancy than they did.

I hadn't seen this coming, not really, but I wondered if maybe an admiral had at least suspected it could happen.

\* \* \*

*"Absolutely! We must have a full series on America's First Flying Ace in the papers immediately. If the other side can claim the munitions ship* Lusitania *is an innocent commercial liner because some fools took passage on it, we can call our favorite war hero an ace.*

*"Oh, and see if Rear Admiral Fiske will make some sort of arrangement with the Germans about a medal. It's the least he can do after causing Lois Irene such distress."*

-Excerpt of a letter from the desk of the Chairman of the Democratic National Committee, Mr. William F. McCombs

\* \* \*

*August 1915, Douai Aerodrome at the French-German Front*

The engineers who examined the *Morane* found a frozen fuel line and bullet holes. Officially, the credit for the capture went to no one. Unofficially, Leutnant Shultz and Lieutenant Marshall had yet to buy their own beer even months later. And even better, the weaponry on the French plane had proven inspirational for arming the remarkable single-seater *Eindecker* aeroplanes.

Marshall and I soared, each in our own *Eindecker*, on our second flight in the new machines.

The wonders of better and better gear made flying almost comfortable. My face had frozen again with my wool scarf not quite wrapped thickly enough on the warm morning before takeoff. Engine oil splattered at me in searing droplets, whipped over the small windshield, but my goggles and scarf saved me from the worst of it and icy wind chilled any burn instantly. A length of silk around my neck protected my skin from chafing against the cold-stiffened collar of my flight jacket.

Lieutenant Marshall and I had flown for about an hour already. The controls felt light, turning so easily compared to an *Albatros* with half as many guide wires to throw my strength against, and the whole sky opened up with no upper set of wings to block my view.

The openness brought back a sense of how truly fragile we were in the sky, and I'd convinced a harness maker to construct some straps to secure us to the aeroplane seats. Most of the pilots rolled their eyes, but when Boelcke accepted them, everyone else did too.

Even better, we each had one of the new machine guns installed. Much like the Maschinengewehr 08s, which of course I remembered from the Port of Doula in Kamerun, these were Spandau LMG 08s—air-cooled in the chill of altitude instead of water-cooled. And Fokker's clever timing belt made the gun fire in bursts between the propellers.

We hadn't used the guns on each other of course, but we'd taken practice targeting dives and done every other tag teaming maneuver we could think of. Leutnant Boelcke planned to go hunting in the twilight this evening, and Marshall and I were going with him.

We turned now, low on fuel and tired, towards Labrayelle airfield just outside Douai.

Where smoke rose in the distance.

I stared, rubbed the surface of my goggles to clear them, and looked again. Black streaks smeared ugly lines in the bright blue sky.

The heavily trenched front could not move so fast in just an hour for Douai to be shelled by artillery. The infantry, poor souls, would do well to move ten feet forward and take another trench without it be wrested back immediately in that time. To have moved over ten miles and now have field guns in position was impossible. And yet something, multiple somethings, burned.

Lieutenant Marshall hand signaled that he'd also seen it.

I nodded in an exaggerated motion to say, 'Yes, I see it too and understand.'

We dove for speed with Marshall leading. First the Douai cathedral spire and then the buildings of the town emerged, undamaged but eerie in the emptiness of their streets. My sense of dread grew as the smoke wisps darkened into arrows narrowing at the horizon just southwest of Douai, pointing at Labrayelle, at our own airfield.

Tiny flashes peppered the ground followed by dirty puffs sometimes spreading into fires if a grounded aircraft or a cache of fuel caught flame. The smoke over the airfield fogged the sky.

Marshall waved for my attention and pointed upward with urgent jerks of his arm. A moment later his machine began to gain altitude. I dragged the stick back to follow him up and held pressure on the rudder to counteract the *Eindecker's* natural inclination to twist left and follow the spin of its propeller.

The desperate struggle for altitude ate at our previous speed. Our engines rattled on in ear-splitting growls, but the pressing rush of the wind weakened.

Specks above the horizon swirled through the billows of smoke. We climbed with increased desperation into the thinning air and blazing daylight. Marshall leveled out and pointed down.

A half dozen aeroplanes circled below us. A few alternated taking a dive to release tiny specks and then climb again. Less brave ones scattered their bombs from altitude with no effort to aim.

Not one looked up at the blinding noon sun to notice us.

Marshall picked a target, pushed his nose over, and began a shallow dive. I followed.

The leather straps pushed against my shoulders keeping me with my machine rather than floating out of the cockpit. I fervently hoped these suddenly very important straps did their part and held me in.

Staying with Marshall required me to focus every ounce of attention I had on his craft. His wing bent, and I must bend mine immediately too.

But this did no good, I realized. I was too close to watch for danger without becoming a collision danger myself.

I climbed and added gradual s-turns to slow my forward progress until his machine was another hundred feet ahead. Continuous stick and rudder adjustments kept me in position behind him.

I stole a look out ahead of the lieutenant's machine now that I had a little more room to maneuver. A fine mist of engine oil covered the little windscreen at the top of my cockpit, but better covering the windscreen than my goggles. I leaned out to get a better view.

The enemy aircraft continued their bombing runs oblivious to us still.

Marshall angled towards one of the non-diving aeroplanes. It circled unaware of any danger. The double wings weren't right for a *Morane*. And the paint, oh, these were the British *B.E.2c* biplanes! Two seaters, but the one in front of us held only a pilot.

The British pilot reached down, paying no attention to the sky above his upper wings, and lifted up a bomb.

I realized why the observer and his seat were gone. They'd made room for the weight of the bombs and the fuel needed for a long flight by doing without a second crew member.

The British pilot lobbed the bomb over the side in the direction of our maintenance crew's tents.

Marshall's hand came up to prime his Spandau machine gun.

I itched to do the same, but my barrel pointed far too close to his *Eindecker*.

The rat-a-tat of his attack was a long vicious growl louder even than our engines.

The *B.E.2c* banked to lift his wings even as Marshall's *Eindecker* raked him with machine gun fire. The pilot brandished a pistol and fired it, not at the lieutenant, but at me!

I released my hold on the stick in shock and my *Eindecker* turned immediately to the left. Even that reaction was more than a second too slow to matter.

Shaking, I took hold of myself. No one had ever looked me square in the eye while trying to kill me before. At once terrified and furious, I longed for a target of my own and cursed the orders keeping me glued to the lieutenant's side.

My arms ached from an hour of forcing the guidewires this way and that in close maneuvers, but I'd let them ache ten times worse and be happy for it if I could shoot at someone bombing our home.

People boiled out of the tents below. One lone *Eindecker* rolled around burning aircraft onto the airfield and launched into the sky.

I pointed my nose ahead of the Lieutenant Marshall's aeroplane so I could catch up to him. He aimed for another Brit heading to the southwest toward Arras. This bomber flew in a straight line and seemed unaware of the lieutenant stalking him.

Another rat-a-tat announced Marshall's next attack. Realizing I was catching up a little too quickly, I pulled back on my stick to get above them both and slow down.

The pilot of this second biplane must have seen the lieutenant fire from hundreds of feet away. It would've taken a miracle to hit anything from that distance. All that Marshall had accomplished was to alert his target.

The lieutenant flew closer and fired again.

The British pilot jerked his bomber left and right in a desperate erratic zigzag that made my back ache in sympathy, and my eyebrows lift in slow understanding.

Marshall didn't fire. He closed.

The enemy's wild evasion had slowed him so much he became almost still.

Marshall released a single burst dead into the British machine. The biplane propeller stuttered and stopped as smoke wafted off the engine.

Lieutenant Marshall, still moving faster, came alongside his victim to hold position next to him.

The smoke grew thicker and flickers of flame emerged. The fire crawled towards the cockpit.

Marshall waved his arm at the man, pointing downward. He needn't risk a field or sheep pasture landing. A mowed well graded airfield waited beneath him. And he must land immediately!

The man stared out at nothing.

"Land for God's sake!" I shouted uselessly into the wind.

Marshall fired his machine gun at nothing, and at last, the British pilot looked up and saw the urgent gesturing down towards the airfield.

Too slowly, he started to descend. Lieutenant Marshall followed him down.

The flames licked over the biplane more quickly now and I knew there would be no escape for this British airman. The fire engulfed the fabric and frame of the 2-seater, burning its way to the cockpit. I looked on in horror as the engine fell away, the wings folded upward, and the flaming fuselage plummeted earthward.

Marshall broke off even as Leutnant Boelcke joined us in the sky, dodging around the falling wreckage of aeroplane.

A deadly dance ensued as other German pilots found the remaining unburned machines and launched after us. The former attackers became the attacked and Fokker's guns proved every bit as deadly as the British bombs.

\* \* \*

*"I do believe Rear Admiral Fiske is quite as stunned as the rest of us. As for 'Our Boy,' I say if the man wants to fight, let him fight. And for the United States, I see no reason to overturn President Wilson's past decisions. He kept us out of the war, and if America would like to continue that they shall be free to say so in the coming election."*

-Excerpt of a letter from the desk of the Vice President of the United States, Mr. Thomas R. Marshall

\* \* \* \* \*

## Joelle Presby Bio

Joelle Presby is a former U.S. naval officer who was born in France but not while it was occupied by Germany. She also did not serve during the Great War. She cowrote The Road to Hell, in the Multiverse series, with David Weber. She has also published short stories in universes of her own creation, Charles E. Gannon's Terran Republic, and David Weber's Honor Harrington universe. Updates and releases are shared on her website, joellepresby.com, and on social media through MeWe, Facebook, LinkedIn, and Twitter.

https://www.mewe.com/i/joellepresby
https://www.facebook.com/joelle.presby
https://www.linkedin.com/in/joellepresby/
https://twitter.com/JoellePresby

\* \* \*

## Patrick Doyle Bio

Patrick Doyle graduated from the University of Minnesota in 1993 with a degree in History, a commission as an Ensign in the U.S. Navy, a love of flying, and no pilot slot. Pat's desire to be a pilot won out, and he left active duty back when peace was breaking out in the mid-90s to eventually become a commercial airline captain at a large regional airline. As a member of the Navy Reserve, and with the downturn in the airline industry in the 2000s, he resumed his Navy career, serving in various active duty assignments. He recently returned to the airlines as a Captain and simulator instructor teaching the next generation of commercial pilots how to throw themselves at the Earth and miss. In his spare time, he writes, travels, and designs games. He currently lives in Minnesota with his wife, Linda, and son, Matthew.

# # # #

# In Dark'ning Storms
# by Rob Howell

31 March 1915

The band started playing the moment they could see the famous mustache rise above the deck. The normally bright eyes over that mustache were hard and black. They flicked from the officer at attention in front of him to a group of men clustered at the bow of the ship. He turned to the officer, "Permission to come aboard?"

Captain Washington Irving Chambers of the USS *Langley* saluted. "Yes, Mr. President."

"Thank you, Captain Chambers." Teddy Roosevelt returned the captain's salute. "And I'll thank you for dismissing this band. We have too much to discuss for all the normal formalities."

"Of course." He glanced at his executive officer. "Dismiss the welcome party."

Commander Pope Washington saluted, turned to the band, and commanded, "Welcome party, dismissed!"

The band and honor guard saluted and left.

President Roosevelt gestured at the men who had followed him aboard the *Langley*. "Have you met Admiral Fletcher?"

"No, sir." Chambers saluted the Commander-in-Chief of the United States Navy's Atlantic Fleet.

"I apologize, Captain," said Admiral Frank F. Fletcher. "These aren't the circumstances in which I had hoped we'd meet."

"I understand, sir. I appreciate you coming to see us personally."

"President Roosevelt has convinced me that your project has great potential. I have, of course, seen all the reports that suggest the *Langley* is a waste of money. However, I remember my time with the Bureau of Ordnance, and I had to see what you're doing here before we make any decisions."

"Thank you, sir."

Chambers turned to the other admiral and saluted. "Welcome aboard again, Admiral Mayo."

Admiral Henry T. Mayo returned the salute. "Captain Chambers, you look like hell. When did you last get some sleep?"

"Last night."

"How many hours?"

Chambers looked embarrassed. "Two, sir."

"And the night before?"

"Even less."

Roosevelt shook his head. "I appreciate your dedication, but we're going to need you to have a clear head."

"Yes, Mr. President."

Roosevelt gestured at the last person behind him, a civilian. "In any case, you've met Mr. Curtiss, I'm sure."

"Yes, sir. Welcome aboard." Chambers held out his hand.

"Thank you, Captain," replied the spare man with deep-set eyes.

The President tugged down his vest. "Now that the introductions are over, let's get to it."

"Yes," agreed Fletcher. "I read the report from the yard, but I wanted to come see the damage myself."

"If you'll follow me." Captain Chambers gestured, and they walked to the bow. Several men in cheap suits and loose ties pointed at various things. A number of workmen bustled around. The bulk of the damage had been to the forward starboard strut holding up the flight deck. A temporary replacement had been fitted to hold up the undamaged wood planks of the deck and sheets of plywood had been laid to cover the scorched, damaged portions.

"I'd like to hear your description of what happened."

"Yes, sir. We were trying out the new bomb racks for our BE.2.cs. When Lieutenant Bronson started to pull up to fly, the left-hand bomb fell off the rack and landed on its fuse. It exploded, as you can see, and flipped the plane over the bow. We assume both Bronson and Lieutenant Welsh, riding in the front seat, were killed instantly."

"We can hope for that small favor, Captain."

"Yes, Mr. President."

"What engine did you have on her?" asked Curtiss.

"A Liberty L-8. We've needed the extra power-to-weight ratio for increased payloads. With those, the BE.2.cs can even carry the short Bliss-Leavitt Mark Sevens. Without an observer, of course."

Curtiss sighed and ran his fingers through his hair. "I worry about those."

"What do you mean, Mr. Curtiss," asked Roosevelt.

"Well, Mr. President, thanks to your efforts getting appropriations for aviation in general, we've managed incredible advances. The Aircraft Production Board has done great work these past five years. Those Liberty engines wouldn't have been available so quickly without it, nor for that matter the aerial torpedoes. However, I wonder if we're going too fast."

"With all that's happening in Europe, I don't think that's unwarranted," said Admiral Mayo.

"I don't disagree, Admiral. However, my first guess at what happened here is the power of the L-8 and the acceleration these pilots have to use to lift off from the *Langley* torqued or twisted the airplane's wing, which was originally designed for an engine a third the horsepower. That twisted wing then caused the rack prototype to release the bomb. I'll bet anything that the engineers designing the new racks didn't take that into account."

"Makes sense, Mr. Curtiss," agreed Chambers. "We've been adding and upgrading these birds since we got them, and they bear little resemblance to the original ones we bought in 1913."

"We're pushing the mechanics as well," mused Mayo. "We keep accelerating their training, but we're expanding naval aviation so fast they almost have to learn on the go."

"Then we should slow down the program," stated Fletcher.

"With respect, sir. I disagree," blurted Washington. He looked as startled as anyone at his presumption in this assemblage.

"Continue, Commander Washington," directed Roosevelt.

"Well, Mr. President…," he hesitated.

"Too late now, Pope," said Chambers with a smile. "But I have an idea what you're about to say, since you've said it to me often enough during these past months. They'll want to hear it."

"Yes, sir." The commander straightened. "Mr. President, I was on the *Maine* at Santiago de Cuba."

"You were?"

"Yes, sir. I was sent by Captain Crenshaw to lead the lifeboat party to safety." His eyes dropped. "I was the highest-ranking survivor."

"But only because Crenshaw ordered you off the *Maine*?" asked Fletcher.

"Yes, sir."

The admiral's mouth tightened. "And how does that inform you in this instance?"

"Sir. I'd have gladly followed Crenshaw into that, even knowing it was to our deaths. We knew at that moment the rest of the squadron needed time to reform against the second Spanish squadron."

"Yes. Fighting Bob's report made that clear."

"Well, Admiral, if the *Langley* had been there with these aircraft, the *Maine* would have survived."

Fletcher glanced at the President and then back at Washington. "And why is that, Commander?"

"At any given moment we have over twenty BE.2.cs fit to fly. We have over a hundred of the Mark Seven torpedoes in our magazines."

"Are you saying they would have sunk the ships in that squadron, Commander? Yes, they were Spanish, but there were two battleships and two armored cruisers in that group."

"Probably not, sir, but they didn't have to *sink* them. All they'd have had to do was slow them until the rest of the squadron could reform. *That*, Admiral Fletcher, *that* we can do. Right now. With the training Lieutenant Commander Ellyson has pounded into them."

"Those that have survived, at least," said the President.

"Yes, sir." Washington paused. "Sir, we've all heard the nickname. The *Langley* is 'Teddy's Toy' to every newspaperman."

"And congressman."

"Yes, sir. But it's the 'Covered Wagon' to us. It's not been that long since people went west to the frontier in covered wagons and many of *them* died along the way. We're taking the navy to a new frontier on this ship. They might scoff at 'Teddy's Toy,' but didn't they scoff at Jefferson for the Louisiana Purchase?"

"Out of the mouths of babes," murmured Roosevelt. "They did, Mr. Washington."

Fletcher stared at Washington with narrowed eyes. "Are you willing to risk your career saying that to congressmen, Commander?"

"I've never forgiven Captain Crenshaw for sending me away, Admiral."

The commander of the Atlantic Fleet considered that for a long moment. "Very well, Mr. Washington, I'll take your words into account."

The group glanced at the damage.

"Shall we continue this in my briefing room?" suggested Captain Chambers after a bit.

"I don't need to see any more," said Roosevelt. "Do you, Admiral Fletcher?"

"No, sir. This confirms what I expected to see."

Once in the briefing room, an orderly provided coffee for all the visitors as they settled in.

Afterward, Roosevelt continued. "This is becoming one hell of a mess, especially if Mr. Washington here is actually prescient."

"Sir, the *Langley* suffered only superficial damage." Chambers leaned forward. "You saw the initial repairs. We made those before reaching port. If we were in a battle, we could have still launched and landed our aircraft. Now that we're here at Newport News, the shipwrights say they'll have her repaired in just a couple of weeks."

"That's not the damn point and you know it."

Mayo leaned forward. "Sir, we've had far fewer casualties in 1915 than we had in 1914. This was the first fatality since January and that was caused by ice."

"I know, I know, but your little mishap here happened the day after the *F-4* sank and every congressman is girding up their loins to correct mistakes in previous appropriations bills to 'protect our valiant young men.'" Roosevelt snorted. "There's only about two of them that know anything, but they're about to cut your funding to the bone unless we can do something to prevent it."

"What do you have in mind, Mr. President?"

Roosevelt leaned back. "I hate to say it, Admiral Mayo, but I don't have any good ideas. I wish we could have used the *Langley* during the Tampico incident."

"That was barely a month after you first visited us. We weren't ready. It would've been worse publicity than you have now," interjected Chambers. "Far worse."

"I know, Captain," said Roosevelt in a clipped, testy voice. "I was merely thinking that had she been available at that time, you could have proved the *Langley*'s usefulness once and for all. Non-believers like Admiral Fletcher here might have even been convinced."

"Don't be too sure, Mr. President," snorted Fletcher. "Many other admirals own positions far more entrenched than mine. I'm much more likely to look favorably on something like this given my time with Ordnance. I often think every officer should spend some time there."

"Be that as it may, Admiral, I can't think of anything we can do now to prove just how valuable the *Langley* and those who follow her will be." Roosevelt sighed. "But we have to do something."

Mayo considered. "All we've done is sail her around Pensacola and up the East Coast to Virginia. We've never sent her anywhere else."

"Where do you propose to send her?"

"Mexican Coast?"

Roosevelt shook his head. "The Mexicans are still angry about the Tampico Affair. I'd rather not press them."

"Fair enough," agreed Mayo. "However, I'd rather not send her into the Mediterranean right now. Not with the battle happening at Gallipoli."

"The Philippines?" suggested Chambers.

"That'd be a possibility." Mayo's face turned grim. "However, thanks to General Wood, we don't have a big enough base in Subic Bay to properly support her."

"I doubt Admiral Howard would thank you for sending the *Langley* to the Pacific Fleet anyway," said Fletcher.

"Also, I'm not prepared to send the *Langley* all the way there without at least a torpedo boat squadron to escort her."

"I think we can agree we'd want her to have some escorts, wherever we send her." Fletcher smiled. "But that, at least, is no real problem. The *North Carolina* was scheduled for a training mission anyway and there are three squadrons of torpedo boats in Hampton Roads waiting for an assignment." The commander of the Atlantic Fleet thought for a moment. "And if I remember correctly, the *Nereus*, a collier which would have been a sister of the *Langley*, and the

*Culgoa* are currently unassigned. That's sufficient escorts and supplies for a decent cruise."

"That's an idea." Roosevelt mused. "And I think I can make it better."

"What do you have in mind?" asked Mayo.

"You've all heard of Frederick Palmer?"

"The correspondent who's been just about everywhere? What, the Boer War, Boxer Rebellion, Greece, Philippines, even the Russo-Japanese War?"

"That's the one. He sent me a letter after the Mexicans released him from jail. He's looking for a good story. We could send him with the *Langley.*"

"Hmmm. And if he writes about the challenges facing the crew and the pilots, maybe he can sway public opinion."

"Exactly," said Roosevelt. "He won't sugarcoat any mistakes, but he's seen enough to know what's what."

"A good, honest reporter would be better anyway," Fletcher agreed. "That leaves only one question. Where do we send her?"

"The only option left is the Atlantic, Mr. President," said Mayo.

"The Germans have been more aggressive with their submarines. I'm not sure that's a good idea." Fletcher shook his head.

"Sir, we've been practicing with our subs in the Caribbean. Ellyson and his pilots have scored their fair share of successes, and he thinks aircraft might be extremely valuable fighting submarines. Again, it's something we have much to learn about, but the possibility is there. Wouldn't it be better to learn that now, when we're still neutral?"

"That makes sense, Captain," agreed Fletcher.

"Gentlemen, we are *not* sending the *Langley* out to fight German submarines," growled Roosevelt. "I do not want American young men to get anywhere close to that madness on the Western Front. My time as president is short, I don't want to run again, and I certainly don't want to leave my successor involved over there." His face twisted. "Especially if *Wilson* runs again."

"No, sir, that wasn't my thought," responded Chambers. "I meant if a submarine did approach us, our planes and a squadron of torpedo boats wouldn't be their easiest target. Besides, we're still painted white and are clearly neutral. I assume the *North Carolina* and the other escorts are also still white."

"They are, Captain," agreed Fletcher. "If you stay out of the Kaiser's new exclusion zone, there should be no reason for the Germans to threaten you."

"Agreed. That would risk 'Teddy's Toy' unnecessarily."

The President grimaced. "Getting the *Langley* sunk would essentially eliminate all money for naval aviation."

"I understand, sir. However, having the *Langley* perform flight operations on that side of the Atlantic would be a major step forward."

"Mr. Palmer's reporting certainly would influence Congress." Roosevelt's mustache bristled in his anger. "Those short-sighted fools."

"Yes, Mr. President," agreed Fletcher.

"Very well. Captain Chambers, do you completely understand what you have to do?"

"Yes, Mr. President. I am to push the limits of the *Langley* as much as possible without involving myself in naval skirmishes between the Germans and English. I'm not to risk the *Langley* over-much, though I am to make sure Mr. Palmer is impressed."

"I don't envy you, Captain Chambers," said Admiral Fletcher.

"Admiral, in the officer's mess, just two decks down, is a wall with over forty names after adding Bronson and Welsh. Every man on this ship understands the risks. We all know what we're doing is difficult, and we all know we could be the next name painted on that wall. Yet, still, every single man on this ship chooses to remain. They believe in what we're doing." Chambers shook his head. "I won't deny this will be a tough mission, but I'd rather try to complete it with these men than any other job you could give me."

Roosevelt suddenly grinned. "Far better to dare, is what you're telling us."

"Yes, Mr. President. Jones, Farragut, Crenshaw, and all the other great heroes of our navy's past deserve no less."

"Well, Captain Chambers, with you and Commander Washington here," the President nodded toward the executive officer, "I'll admit to much more optimism than when I boarded my 'toy.'"

* * *

28 April 1915

"The plan was to harmonize sailors, officers, aero-plane mechanics, and pilots into a force so ho-mogeneous that flesh and blood became machinery, with every crewman aboard the USS *Langley* working together with that sort of efficiency; but human elements older than the United States Navy, which had given warriors cheer on the march and fire in battle from the days of the spear to the days of the quick-firer, hampered the practical application of the cold professional idea worked out in the conscientious logic of the academic cloister.

In more traditional branches of the navy, there is a sentiment and association among the sailors. Their tradition is based upon memories of Old Ironsides, Mobile Bay, and yes, the *Maine*. If they were not proud of it, they would be unnatural fighters.

The members on the *Langley* are not immune to that sentiment and association, of course. Indeed, the second-ranking officer aboard the *Langley* was on the *Maine* at Santiago de Cuba. However, the machinery they are trying to learn and embrace is so foreign to many of these boys as to be much like the very top of the unconquerable Mt. Everest. And yet, like that soaring peak, they are seeking to lift our eyes to the heavens.

If you, dear reader, often peruse pages such as this across the country, then you are likely to have learned of their defiant efforts to reach the sky from the sea. What sentiment and tradition these men have is often of death, as can be seen by the somber mural in their officer's mess. Upon that wall are listed those who have perished to achieve this dream, and we have all too often mourned the fate of these heroes.

It is the sad duty of your correspondent to inform you that yesterday, these crewmen had to emblazon that mural with yet another memory. Lieutenant, j.g. Richard Caswell Saufley, while attempting to land his Royal Aircraft BE.2.c upon this selfsame *Langley* suffered an engine failure and his aeroplane fell as a stone into the cold, gray waters of the Atlantic Ocean. Despite speedy reactions by Captain Washington Irving Chambers and his doughty crew, the plane sank with Saufley's body before anyone could reach it."

- Frederick Palmer[1]

\* \* \*

Early Morning, 1 May 1915

Chambers stepped onto the bridge.

"Captain on the bridge!"

"As you were," replied Chambers. He glanced around. His command might not have been necessary. The bridge crew had barely responded to the announcement. He had never seen them so lethargic.

"What's our position?" he asked the navigator. Upon the response, he replied, "That should put us about one hundred miles south of Brest? About ten miles from the exclusion zone?"

"Yes, sir."

"Have you the course laid out for when we are forced to skirt the zone?"

"Yes, sir." The navigator rolled out the map. "When we get to this point in approximately an hour, we'll change course to 350 to skirt the zone."

"Good." He turned to the bosun's mate at the voice tubes. "Please call for Commanders Ellyson and Washington join me in my briefing room."

"Gentlemen, we have a problem," Chambers announced when they had gathered.

"Yes, sir," replied Ellyson. "Saufley's death seems like the end."

---

[1] Palmer, Frederick. *Our Greatest Battle* (New York: Dodd, Mead and Co., 1919), 42-3.

"True, and while I understand, we will correct it. We're not going back to Norfolk with our tails between our legs."

"Agreed, sir," replied Washington, straightening a touch. "What did you have in mind?"

"We have little to lose at this point. Therefore, we are, as of this morning, going to commence full aeroplane operations. We're going to push the sailors and air crews on the *Langley*. We're going to log flights everywhere we can. We're close enough to France we can fly over their coastline. We'll do the same to Cornwall and Ireland when we get there. Then we'll loop back and surprise the Danish in Reykjavik."

"Is that legal?"

"I'll radio ahead and warn them we're performing maneuvers. And then, once we've done all that, we'll make a visit to Halifax. Mr. Washington, when we get there, arrange for as much shore leave as possible. Their little funk notwithstanding, the men have performed admirably, and I doubt we'll have the opportunity to reward them once we return home."

"Yes, sir."

"Once we leave Halifax, we'll sail along the coast, making surprise bombing runs over every American base we can."

"That'll get you cashiered!"

"Likely so, Mr. Washington, but we both know my career is over once this jaunt is completed. Might as well earn my way out of the Navy."

The two commanders glanced at each other.

"Very well, sir," said Washington, his eyes filled with doubt.

"Make sure Mr. Palmer has complete access to everything. I want him watching us refuel those planes, and I want you ensuring that refueling process is fast and smooth. Just like we would have to launch for an imminent battle."

"Yes, sir."

"And you, Mr. Ellyson, will tell your pilots they're in for the hardest time of their lives. They're going to fly every day. Some will likely die. We've danced around this issue too much to doubt it, but those who survive will be the best pilots in the world anywhere."

"Aye, air, sir!" snapped Spuds, his eyes bright. "And we're flying over the exclusion zone?"

"Yes, Mr. Ellyson. I want you to find and play tag with every ship in the area, be they English, French, German, or Japanese for that matter. I want everyone to know we can cover something like 8,000 square miles at a time. The U-boat commanders are welcome to try and shoot you down. At least then you'd have an excuse to fly bombing runs at them."

"With live bombs?"

Chambers shook his head. "I think not, Mr. Ellyson. It's not worth getting into the war, but it is worth putting the fear of God's angels into those commanders. And for that matter, any English and French captains that get upset."

The two commanders laughed.

"I'll get right on that," agreed Ellyson.

"Do that. I'll want a formation flight over Brest when we get to our closest point. At least ten aircraft, including one of the radio aeroplanes. Arrange for Mr. Palmer to be in an observer seat for that flight. Come to think of it, get him up as often as possible."

"Yes, sir!"

"Get to it, gentlemen. I want this crew so angry at me that they forget they're about to get tossed away by Congress."

The two commanders saluted and left the room, almost bouncing in their excitement.

*Now all I have to do is forget I'm about to get tossed away by Congress.*

\* \* \*

Early Morning, 7 May 1915

"**D**amn this fog!" growled Ellyson. He stood on the bridge of the *Langley*. "We're not doing anything until this lifts."

"Agreed, Commander." Chambers gestured ahead of his ship. "You can't see her, but the *Terry* is about ten thousand yards ahead of us, making sure we don't run into anything."

"Hope her captain knows what he's doing."

"Admiral Mayo has high hopes for Commander King. He'll probably claim him for his staff as soon as he's reassigned from the *Terry*."

"Good." Ellyson snorted. "Guess I'll just gather all my pilots and observers and we'll go through the list of ships that are supposed to be in the area. If this pea soup ever leaves, maybe we can find them all."

"That's a good idea. I know the *Partridge*, a boarding vessel, should be around here. Also, the radio telegraph picked up messages from the *Juno*, a British cruiser, saying she was heading back to Queenstown."

"We'll find those, no problem."

"Check with the navigator and radio telegraph men; they'll know more."

"Aye, aye."

Ellyson went to both, scribbling down the list, and then assembled his pilots to show it to them.

"Gentlemen, we're going to find all of these ships, especially that one." He pointed at one name. "I want all of you to review the silhouette books."

The aviators gathered around a table and began swapping the silhouette books back and forth. Ellyson stared at boarding vessel silhouettes for about ten minutes, but he was too restless to properly focus.

"Spuds, get the hell out of here," Lieutenant Melvin Stolz, his observer, finally snapped.

"I need to memorize this."

"Why? That's what you have me for. And frankly, you're driving us all mad right now."

The other aviators laughed and nodded.

Ellyson shook his head. "Fine, I'll go up and yell at the fog to clear off."

"Excellent decision, sir. Glad you thought of it."

With a bark of laughter, Ellyson left the room and went onto the flight deck. He glared up a time or two, but mostly stared forward and watched the gray waves roll towards him.

Suddenly, he realized he could see more ships. He glanced up. The sun had definitely started to burn away the clouds.

"Enough waiting, by God!" He stormed down to the hangar deck. "Get every plane ready to go. The weather's clearing, and we'll launch as soon as we can."

The hangar burst into activity, and Spuds almost ran down the steps to the other aviators.

"Get ready, gentlemen. The weather's clearing, and we've got flying to do."

"Heaven be praised," snapped Stolz. "I thought my eyes were about to become permanently crossed."

Half an hour later, the fog had completely cleared off. The Atlantic was as smooth as it ever got and was the blue that caught the soul of every romantic nautical poet. Ellyson climbed into his BE.2.c with Stolz in front of him. Two more BE.2.cs waited behind him to follow.

Spuds accelerated and with a pleasant sigh of relief, he felt air catch under his wings. He pulled back on the stick and brought his plane into an ascending spiral. He waited until the others formed up on him, then headed them all northeast at an easy fifty knots some eight hundred feet over the water.

He yelled to Stolz. "If we're right, the one we want should be about thirty miles that way."

"I'll keep my eyes open. If she's there, she's the biggest thing around, so we should see her easily enough."

"Four stacks."

"I know, I know."

Spuds grinned. "At least I remembered that silhouette."

Stolz laughed, but kept his head swiveling back and forth from either side of the twin-bladed propeller, periodically staring through a pair of binoculars.

"Spuds!" Stolz pointed. "Is that smoke over there?"

Ellyson squinted through his goggles. "I can't tell, but we can certainly check it out. Send the signal for course change."

"Aye, aye." Stolz raised the appropriate signs and waited for confirmation. "Got it."

Spuds did not say anything but banked the BE.2.c slightly to the west.

"It's definitely smoke, sir."

"Agreed." Spuds thought about accelerating, but they'd be to that pillar of smoke soon enough and while this might be the prize, she wasn't the only ship out here.

"That's a lotta smoke, Spuds."

"Might be our fish, Melvin."

"Yes, sir."

As they approached, Stolz muttered, "One, two, three...Four! Four stacks, it's gotta be our baby."

"Yes!" agreed Ellyson when he got closer to the four-stacked ship sailing east. "It's definitely her."

"If only the 'Covered Wagon' were that big," Stolz said with a laugh. "The book said she was almost eight hundred feet long. I'd sure like to land on a deck that long."

"It'd make it easier, wouldn't it?" Ellyson banked the B.E.2c around. "Shall we give the passengers a thrill?"

"Absolutely."

Spuds zoomed across the liner, with the other two following closely. He then banked around and approached from the stern. The planes flew at about two hundred feet along the starboard side of her, waggling their wings. Passengers lined the rail, waved their handkerchiefs, and lifted their drinks at the aeroplanes.

Laughing, Ellyson continued east toward Ireland.

"That took a goodly amount of our fuel, sir. We should think about heading back to our five hundred feet of deck in about thirty minutes."

"That'll still give us time to get to Queenstown. The *Juno* is supposed to be there. Send the signals to the others.

They soared over Queenstown, then zoomed over the *Juno* berthed at Haulbowline Island. They continued south into the Irish Sea.

About fifteen miles southwest of Queenstown, Stolz yelled, "Spuds! To our left, is that a submarine?"

"I don't see it but signal the others we're going to check it out."

Moments later he banked the BE.2.c over the spot Stolz pointed out to give his observer a clear look.

"It's definitely a submarine, sir. And it's submerging. I think it's German."

Ellyson's eyes sharpened. "It's right on the shipping lane to Queenstown and all the ports in the Irish Sea."

"What about the liner. They wouldn't sink her, would they?"

"They shouldn't, but the Germans have been talking tough about this exclusion zone. We've to get back to the *Langley* anyway and Captain Chambers will want to know as fast as we can get there."

Ellyson pushed his throttle ahead as fast as he dared, given his fuel level.

Fifteen minutes later his seat harness yanked him back as the arresting gear caught. The deck crew began pulling his B.E.2c into place.

"Stolz, get everything organized down here. I'm going to Chambers." Ellyson jumped down and ran up to the bridge. Breathlessly, he saluted the captain. "Sir, I believe we have a potential issue."

Chambers eyebrows went up. "What is it, commander?"

"There's a ship about thirty miles away, bearing about 030. I think it's our big prize."

"Well done, commander."

"However, about forty miles ahead of her, ten or fifteen miles south of Queenstown, is a submarine. I think it's German."

Chambers' eyes widened. He pulled out a map. "You're saying there's a U-boat in the path of the *Lusitania*?"

"Yes, sir."

Chambers stepped over to the radio telegraph station. "Mr. Howell, please send, Attention RMS *Lusitania*. This is Captain Chambers of the USS *Langley*. Submarine activity detected ahead of you. Please take appropriate action."

Startled, the communications officer complied. After a moment, he turned back. "Sir, Captain Turner asks our location."

"Send it back."

Howell complied. Then he leaned back with a wild look on his face.

"What did he say?"

"Uh, sir, he said, 'If you are where you say, you cannot possibly see a submarine in any position along my path. If you can see a submarine, you apparently have no proper understanding of navigation and therefore are more hindrance than help. Please refrain from bothering me in the future.'"

"Save me from arrogant old men who haven't discovered we're in a century of many wonders!" snapped the captain.

The bridge crew stared at Chambers.

Chambers continued, growling, "Please inform Captain Turner that we are an aeroplane carrier and that we do, indeed, possess the ability to see things along his path. I should not have to remind him that he is responsible for approximately two thousand people. Even should we not possess that capability, it behooves him to pay attention to the warning."

"He says he believes he has things well in hand. He says his ship was designed to be too fast for any submarine to catch."

"Captain Turner, this is not a drill. Please take evasive action and prepare for a torpedo attack."

"He replied, 'doing such would disturb those chattering monkeys unduly. I am unwilling to listen to that chattering on the word of some bloody colonial who is at best a poor sailor and at worst a danger to his crew.'"

Chambers took a deep breath. "Very well, Captain Turner. Understand that I will hold you personally responsible if any of your passengers are harmed from your inaction. Should, of course, you yourself survive." He shook his head. "Mr. Howell, record any future messages from him, but don't bother me with them unless they are relevant."

"Understood, sir."

The captain turned to the bosun at the speaking tubes. "Please inform Commander Washington I need him in my briefing room immediately." He turned to Ellyson. "Come with me."

When Washington entered the room, Chambers said, "Commander Ellyson, please explain the situation to Mr. Washington."

"Aye, aye, sir." He complied.

"Mr. Ellyson, what do you suggest we do?" asked Washington.

"I take my BE.2.c with three other birds out, all with full bomb loads."

"And do what? The United States is still neutral. Are you suggesting we attack the U-boat in contravention of the President's desire to stay out of the war?"

"As we were reading up on the ships in the area, the references said the *Lusitania* carried something like two thousand people. If the U-boat does decide to attack her, it could be worse than the *Titanic*."

Chambers looked troubled. "Commander, I have to think about this."

"With all due respect, sir, we don't have any time."

The captain shook his head. "Yes, we do." He led them out of the briefing room. "Mr. Howell, please inform the rest of the squadron and all other vessels in range that we have spotted submarine activity in the area." He turned back. "Mr. Washington, where's the wind coming from?"

"Wind out of the northwest, heading 330."

Turning back, the captain said, "Mr. Howell, you will then signal, not radio, all the other ships of the squadron that we will be turning into the wind imminently."

"Aye, aye, sir." The lieutenant at the communications station turned to his equipment.

"Pope, have the navigator plot a course to where Ellyson saw the *Lusitania*. Then would you be so good as to order four planes, including Commander Ellyson's, fueled and armed with live munitions? Also, make sure Lieutenant Chevalier's radio-equipped plane is ready to join them."

Now it was Commander Washington's turn to raise his eyebrows. "As you command, sir." He snapped the orders across the bridge.

"Thank you, sir," said Ellyson and he turned to leave.

"Not so fast, Spuds. We have about ten minutes before the planes are ready to launch. That gives us a bit of time to determine our course of action. Mr. Washington, what do you think?"

The executive officer pondered for a moment. "Sir, I think we have to seriously consider sending a flight to assist the *Lusitania*."

"If we attack the U-boat, we may very well have committed this country to this God-forsaken war. Given the casualty reports from the Western Front, if we attack that boat, we might be putting the lives of hundreds of thousands of American boys on the line."

"That's true." Washington grimaced. "However, didn't we get sent out here in order to show we could operate away from the American coast? To tell the world what we could do? What better way to do that than to dissuade the U-boat from attacking the *Lusitania*?"

"Yes, sir!" Ellyson turned to the captain. "I don't have to attack the U-boat directly. Between the four armed birds in the flight, we'll have twelve bombs. We can simply use those to herd the U-boat away from the *Lusitania*. We needn't attack the Germans, just drive them off."

Chambers tapped his fingers together. Eventually, he replied, "Thank you, gentlemen, for your words. Go make the preparations, and I will give you a decision when you are ready."

The two commanders left and Chambers went back to his quarters. There, he took out his bible, pulled out a folded piece of paper, set it to the side, and turned to Psalm 104. Then to Psalm 107. Then he unfolded the piece of paper carefully. It had yellowed, which was not surprising, since his mother had sent it to him nearly forty years before. In her delicate script, the first words were, "Eternal Father, strong to save."

Someone knocked at his door.

"Come," commanded Chambers.

Commander Washington leaned in. "Sir, Ellyson's flight is ready."

"Lieutenant Chevalier?"

"Ready to go as well."

*I can't not act.*

"Please inform Mr. Ellyson he has my permission to continue. He is to do all he can to prevent the U-boat from attacking the *Lusitania* up to and including attacking her directly if no other attempts succeed. He is to keep us apprised of all that happens via the radio. And may God have mercy on our souls."

"Aye aye, sir. For what it's worth, I concur."

"Thank you, Commander Washington."

Washington saluted and left.

Chambers stared at the page. A single tear dropped on it, blurring "brethren's shield."

\* \* \*

Ellyson barely waited for the other planes in the flight to launch. He yelled back to his observer, "Relay a heading of 040, height 600. Tell them not to worry about formation but to extend our line. Two go to my left. Two to my right. Make sure Chevalier is next to us. They're to go as far as they can and still see signals from the next plane over. We want to cover as much sea as we can."

The signals went out. "You're going to owe them some beers, Spuds. They're not exactly happy with you."

The pilot laughed harshly. "They'll get over it, especially if we get the *Lusitania* to safety. Now keep your eyes peeled."

"Will do, Spuds."

The five BE.2.cs flew at about six hundred feet over the ocean. The line stretched about a mile in length.

"Sir, I see smoke, bearing 350."

Spuds looked where his observer was pointing. "Good eyes, Melvin. Relay that down the line."

"Aye, aye."

"I'm going to wheel around the ship, then start zig-zagging across its path."

"Relayed."

Spuds turned slightly. Presently, he saw the tips of the stacks. Given the wake behind her, the *Lusitania* had just turned.

The gaggle of passengers welcomed him again. This time, their revelry seems hideous and horrible.

"Have Chevalier explain who we are and remind Captain Turner of the submarine activity."

"Aye, aye." Wryly, Stolz added, "Probably just as well we can't receive radio telegraph signals ourselves." Then he lifted the complex series of signals.

Presently, a sailor on the *Lusitania* came out on the foredeck of the liner and waved.

"Tell the others, I'm going to swing over the ship and then we'll begin our search pattern." After a moment to allow the message to get to the other planes, Spuds guided them over the *Lusitania*. They swung back and forth several times before the far-right plane started flashing signals.

"Sir! Lee's spotted a submarine on the surface approximately eleven thousand yards away."

"Heading?"

"110."

"Are they in range of their torpedoes?"

"I don't know, sir. We never got briefed on that."

"Yeah. Was just hoping you had an encyclopedia handy."

The observer laughed grimly. "If their torpedoes are anything like ours, he can't be too far out of range if he launches at the lower speed."

"If he does that, the German torpedoes can't be that much faster than the *Lusitania*, right?"

"Probably not. Ours wouldn't be."

Ellyson sighed. "That's probably why Captain Turner was so sanguine about the possibility. The submarine commander will have to get closer. Ours have a maximum range of about three thousand yards at high speed. We'll just try and keep the sub about five thousand yards away. Order the flight to close in. Tell Chevalier to report the location of the sub to both the *Lusitania* and the *Langley*."

"Done, sir."

"Tell the others we're going to circle between the U-boat and the *Lusitania* at about two hundred feet. Let's make sure the sub sees us. Maybe they won't want to tangle with us."

"Won't she just submerge?"

"Probably, but hopefully we can still see her shadow. It's a bright, clear day, after all."

"We could just go bomb her now. She hasn't reacted to us at all, yet."

Spuds stayed quiet for a long moment. "We can't, Melvin. We don't even know if it's German or not. We have to wait for it to attack before we can do anything."

"Yeah, that's what I thought you'd say."

"Make sure everyone knows to keep watching that sub."

"Signals sent, sir. Chevalier reports radio messages sent as well."

The commander didn't respond, but put his plane in a slow, fuel-conserving circle between the *Lusitania* and the submarine.

"They see us, sir. Looks like they're preparing to dive."

"I'll keep us banked as much as possible. Tell the other pilots to provide observers the best sight lines possible."

"Yes, sir."

"When she's submerged, tell me if you can or cannot see her shadow."

After a few minutes, Stolz responded, "She's completely under, but on a day like today, I can probably see her shadow fifty feet or more below the surface."

"Good. Has she changed course?"

"Yes, sir. Looks like she's slowed and is creeping to an intercept route ahead of us."

"I'm going to spiral overhead. Tell the others to go ahead of us. We'll try and keep a line between the *Lusitania* and her."

"Aye, aye, sir."

After about five minutes, Ellyson asked, "Has she moved away?"

"No, sir, I don't think the sub believes we can see her, or maybe doesn't care."

"Blast! Have Chevalier send to the *Langley* we need a relief flight. We can stay out here for another half hour or more, but we're going to need help if he doesn't go away."

After a moment. "Signal sent and confirmed."

"Let's get her attention. Send to Lieutenant Mustin to do a bombing run. He is to drop one bomb at about four hundred yards ahead of the sub."

One of the BE.2.cs curved around gracefully to fly ahead of the sub.

"Bomb released, sir!" announced Stolz.

A moment later, they heard the sharp crack of the bomb exploding on the surface of the ocean.

"Any change, Melvin?"

"No, sir."

"Damn his soul." Ellyson looked to the west. "The *Lusitania* is just coming straight this way. Send to Chevalier to warn that idiot of a captain we're over a submarine, maybe he'll do something smart."

"Radio telegraph message sent, sir."

Spuds stared at the liner, willing her to shift course or do something, anything. Nothing happened.

"Stolz, tell Mustin to do another run."

Afterward, the submarine and liner were still headed for each other.

"By Christ! Hang on." Spuds twisted his controls, and the BE.2.c dived towards the shadow beneath the water. At the very last moment he pulled up, yelling at Stolz to release two bombs.

Behind him he heard them explode and he twisted around.

"Still no change, sir."

"Tell Bellinger and McIlvain to drop two of their bombs each right on top of the shadow. Then they are to circle above it."

The shadow continued to settle into what would be a perfect shot if the liner did not adjust.

Spuds thought for a moment. Finally, he yelled to Stolz, "Signal Mustin and Chevalier to keep on my tail."

"Confirmed."

Ellyson pulled the stick around and aimed his aeroplane at the *Lusitania*. A few minutes later, he dove right at her. If the earlier pass to cheer the passengers had seemed close, this one was insane. The three planes went across the liner's bow right in front of the bridge windows.

"That got their attention, sir, but…"

"But what?"

"They seem angrier at us than worried about anything else."

"Tell Chevalier to keep sending the warning."

"He is."

Spuds kept flying around the *Lusitania*, but Stolz's assessment proved correct. A number of officers appeared on her deck, waving them away. One even had a revolver, though Ellyson never saw him fire it.

He looked over. The planes over the sub seemed far too close. Not even a mile away.

*The sub is well within range.*

"Signal to all planes, we'll drop our last bombs right on top of the sub. Follow me."

After a moment, the flight regained its formation and Spuds led them down. Whatever inexperience these pilots might have had when they left the Newport News shipyard had long since been trained out of them. Each put their bombs directly on top of the black shadow.

But nothing changed.

And then something did.

"Sir, I have a track in the water!"

"What?"

Ellyson banked his plane over and there, to his horror he saw a line on the water heading directly for the *Lusitania*.

Six hundred yards away.

Five hundred.

"Melvin. I wish you weren't here."

\* \* \*

8 May 1915

"It has always been the great heart of our men, beating as the one heart of a great country—simple, vigorous, young, trying out its strength—on the background of old Europe, which appealed to me. It is the spontaneous incidents of emotion breaking out of routine which revealed character.

Yesterday, a flight of aeroplanes landed on the *Langley*. The aviators of that flight stepped down from their amazing examples of human ingenuity and technology. They did not move quickly off the deck, as they usually did. Instead, they simply stood and stared at each other. I cannot tell you for how long, for I too was mesmerized. I do not know if a single word was said among them, but the fellows, at some length, went below decks. It was also their wont, as they left the deck, to laugh, shout, and show with their hands the incredible aerial maneuvers they could achieve, and indeed inflicted upon myself. This, too, they did not do on this day.

It is but ten days since it was my sorrowful duty to report the death of Lieutenant Richard C. Saufley. It was yet another in what seemed to be an endless string of deaths for little gain in the field of naval aeronautics. The very recent addition to the Navy Hymn by the poet Mary C. D. Hamilton that asked, "Lord, guard and guide the men who fly through the great spaces in the sky," seemed in that ancient time, but ten days ago, a desperate plea for clemency as they lifted their way to assured death.

Today, I have learned more of the great hearts of our men, for there was to be one more aeroplane in that flight. In peril in the air, these aviators certainly are and will be, yet this they offer, and willingly, that others may live. That plane, piloted by Lieutenant Commander Theodore G. 'Spuds' Ellyson accompanied by Lieutenant Melvin Lewis Stolz, through great skill and bravery, prevented an attack by a German submarine on the RMS *Lusitania* by intercepting its torpedo with the incredible feat of diving their plane into the torpedo headed for the liner, knowing they would die, and saving perhaps as many as two thousand souls. It is possible, as I think of it, the more than two score deaths accrued by these, the bravest and best of our great country, is but the price to pay that we become greater than old Europe has ever been."

Frederick Palmer [2]

\* \* \* \* \*

---

[2] Ibid., 478-9.

## Rob Howell Bio

Rob Howell is the creator of the Shijuren fantasy setting (www.shijuren.org) and an author in the Four Horsemen Universe (www.mercenaryguild.org). He writes primarily medieval fantasy, space opera, military science fiction, and alternate history.

He is a reformed medieval academic, a former IT professional, and a retired soda jerk.

His parents discovered quickly books were the only way to keep Rob quiet. He latched onto the Hardy Boys series first and then anything he could reach. Without books, it's unlikely all three would have survived.

His latest release in Shijuren is *Where Now the Rider*, the third in the Edward series of swords and sorcery mysteries. The next release in that world is *None Call Me Mother*, the conclusion to the epic fantasy trilogy *The Kreisens*.

You can find him online at: www.robhowell.org and his blog at www.robhowell.org/blog.

# # # # #

# Perchance To Dream
# by Sarah A. Hoyt

Near the destroyed village of Cappy, by the bank of the Somme, where the river flowed due west, a muscular young blond man turned on his camp bed inside a stone hut.

Despite the rain falling outside, sending tendrils of dampness through every crack in the old walls, the hut was almost too warm thanks to the blaze in the fireplace. The blaze itself was a sign of the occupant's importance, since wood in the French countryside—long martyred by the marche and countre-march of armies in the conflict the world called the Great War—had grown scarce.

Manfred von Richthofen, youthful leader of Jagdgeschwader 1, flung the woolen blanket from him and turned again, this time lifting his arm above his head as though to ward off some threat. The scar on the side of his head, imperfectly hidden by the short blond hair, seemed to pulse, livid.

"No," he whispered.

He was not speaking of the distant thrumming of artillery that served as the devil's lullaby to a countryside devoid of innocent sleepers. He'd heard it too much over the last three years for this, the

Kaiser's latest and desperate push to victory, to disturb his sleep. And the flapping of the tent-hangars, like housing for prehistoric beasts, was a true lullaby. For beneath those hid the planes of the Jagdgeschwader 1, his very own flying circus, the source of his glory and, more importantly, a source of comradery, of hope.

And yet Richthofen's sleep was agitated, perturbed by dreams that marched beneath his eyelids. In the morning, sitting on the side of his bed, rubbing the place on his head where an old and never perfectly healed injury sometimes spit up fragments of bone, he couldn't remember anything of the dream.

No, that wasn't true. As he pulled his coveralls over his monogramed gray silk pajamas, a single memory came back, sharp edged, like a fragment of ice on the surface of a deep frozen lake, like a fragment of bone emerging from the flesh.

It was a pamphlet, white and crudely printed. It showed a picture of a flower-covered grave, and beneath it read in English:

*To the German Flying Corps.*

*Rittmeister Baron Manfred von Richthofen was killed in aerial combat, on April 21ˢᵗ 1918. He was buried with full military honors.*

The memory was so sharp that Richthofen stood, fastening the coveralls, staring ahead, as though the pamphlet hung there, in mid-air, in front of him.

*It's just a dream*, the Red Baron thought. *A strange one, but still a dream.*

"No, Moritz," Menzke's voice sounded, with just an edge of exasperation, as he tried to prevent the Deer Hound-Great Dane cross from rushing the Rittmeister and bowling Manfred over with exuberance.

The orderly carried a ewer Manfred would know was filled with cold water. Manfred woke enough from his thoughts to brace against the dog putting his paws on Manfred's shoulders. Managing, just barely, to stop his face from being licked, Manfred managed a half-laugh, "No, Moritz," he said. Then, scratching at the dog's ears as the animal fell to all four paws and squirmed in happiness, "How is my little lap dog this morning?"

But even Moritz couldn't distract him from the nightmare.

Moritz was dry. And Richthofen, looking out his window, could see that the pervading rain that had dogged them for days had finally lifted to reveal a hazy sky. Great wisps of fog drifted across the airfield, like fingers searching out something.

Chances were that later on the fog would burn out, and the sky would clear, revealing good hunting weather. Which they'd had rarely enough of in this wretched place. He should be eager to climb the sky in his red plane, but something felt wrong.

Where had that damnable note come from to invade his dream? Why now? What dormant thing in his life had kicked up that shard of fear to put horror in his night and confusion in his morning?

It wasn't that he thought himself invincible. Oh, once perhaps, long ago, when he watched the enemy flyers go down in flames and thought that he was too good, too lucky for such a fate to befall him. But since the crash that had left the scar on his head, it had become far too personal, far too possible. Richtofen knew that like the many men he'd shot down, he was mortal. He knew very well that not all crashes ended in an awkward landing and being taken prisoner. He paused again, absently petting Moritz, where in his mind the flames that had almost consumed him before he could land and escape were felt anew.

For a time, he got ill every time he shot someone down, and only the greatest of will power could keep him flying and serving his country in the air.

Menzke poured his water in the basin, and Manfred splashed it on his face, welcoming the cold as a reviving shock.

*I should shave*, Manfred thought. Before his wound, it would not have been a question, as he was a fastidious man. When his thought was in disorder, it was doubly important that he present himself as ordered and in full control. Catapulted into command at the age of 25, he maintained the respect of his men by behaving as though he were someone apart. That included appearing impeccably dressed and shaved, whenever humanly possible.

*No, instead I will have breakfast*, he thought. *I can shave after the mission.* He knew lately—since his wound in October of the year before—he'd relaxed a little, and might sometimes be seen to drink a little too much, or stay up too late, with his companions. But he no longer had the courage some of his men had, who decided to forego breakfast in order to fly as early as possible. They'd return from the hunting, ravenous as hawks. The ones who returned.

Manfred had never understood how anyone could cheerfully face death on an empty stomach. Facing death, surely. He did it every time he flew. But not on an empty stomach.

The thought of death brought the image of that damnable note again. The problem wasn't even being aware of his own mortality, but being aware of his people's mortality. So many of those he commanded had died. He thought of his friend Werner Voss, now gone. He'd promised Werner's father he'd come over and hunt during his upcoming leave. Normally the prospect would cheer him up, except he felt as though it would never happen. As though it were a dim and distant prospect, something he could not quite reach. And it brought thoughts of Werner, and the other youths who had been his friends and crashed down in fire and blood.

Manfred shook his head to the inner voice, wiped his face, and gave Menzke, standing by anxiously, the slight head shake that meant he wouldn't require warm water for shaving. The orderly silently retreated, stepping outside of Richtofen's quarters. There was a single, precise knock on the door, as if the next visitor had been waiting for this precise opportunity.

"Come," Manfred said. He knew it who it was, as his adjutant, Karl Bodenschatz was his customary morning visitor, usually with a cup of warm chicory to replace the coffee which had lately been in short supply. In fact, Manfred had not tasted coffee since he'd been home, recovering from his wound. And even that, procured at who knew what expense by his mother, had had more than its normal proportion of chicory embittering its taste.

Bodenschatz looked immaculate as he usually did, but his face was unusually grave. He handed Manfred one of the cups he carried, and absently used his free hand to pet Moritz who'd come nosing around him for his morning greeting. "Rittmeister," he said, just the one word on handing the cup over.

The formality while in quarters was preserved between them, even if Bodenschatz was one of Manfred's remaining friends and the one scheduled to go hunting with him in the coming leave.

Manfred's acceptance was an as perfunctory, "Danke," but his eyes searched his subordinate. "Out with it, Bodenschatz. What troubles you?"

There was a half-embarrassed chuckle and a click of the tongue. "Nothing troubles me, Rittmeister. The air should clear, and the weather should be fine for hunting a Lord or two."

Since the Royal Flying Corps had initially been composed mostly of noblemen, the Germans had referred to them jocularly as "Lords." The phrase "hunting a Lord" was often used by Manfred himself, but the joke rang hollow today. In fact, every flyer he'd downed alive and taken prisoner had been a splendid fellow, the kind that might have become friends with Manfred, had Manfred met the man during his visit to England before the war.

It seemed to him the scar itched, and he rubbed at it. There was something to that. A scrap of dream, reaching for him like the fingers of fog outside. He made a sound, not quite a snort, expelling air through his nostrils. He was not usually given to foreboding and second thoughts. *You are becoming an old woman, Manfred von Richthofen,* he told himself severely. *Lothar would laugh at you.*

He knew this was true, too. Though Lothar, himself becoming an ace of some renown—though a hunter of rage, not of brain like his older brother—at the moment lay in a hospital bed, recovering from injury. He shook himself.

"And yet you are troubled," Manfred persisted.

"Nothing to speak of, Rittmeister. Only…" Bodenschatz took a sip from his cup, as though to hide his expression. "Only I saw a fresh column heading towards the front this morning."

And Manfred understood. Bodenschatz had been infantry himself. While Manfred's own time on the ground had been limited, Bodenschatz had had experience of the front in a more prolonged and fraught way. He felt for those going forth into the mud, the barbed wire, and the ubiquitous stench of death.

"I know," Manfred said. "I know." He didn't say what else he knew, because he couldn't say where the certainty came from. He'd started the war sure that they'd be in Paris in no time, and in fact had burned with fear Lothar would be ahead of him in both honors and glorious moments. The certainty they'd lose, and that the Kaiser's last effort was just that, and utterly doomed, had come from nowhere. He'd tried to dismiss it as the result of his head wound, but he didn't think that was it. He thought it was rather the things he saw from the air, the comparative strength of the forces, the churned and desolate ground between, covered in the unrecovered remains of dead men.

Bodenschatz gave a half-hearted laugh, as though recovering himself. As though he too understood the words that Manfred hadn't said, and must distract himself from them lest they come out and raise despondency and fear. Both of them were too loyal to do that. "Well, at any rate, they somehow knew who we were, and they asked about you and told me to tell you they'd be looking to you for protection."

Manfred smiled.

"They always ask," Bodenschatz said. "They always ask for you, and seem comforted you'll be flying above, protecting them."

"Well, it is certainly better than what they used to say, when I was doing my milk and eggs delivery," Manfred said, referring irreverently—as always—to his time as a courier. "Which was, *God punish the Englishmen, their artillery, and our flyers.*"

"I'm not sure they don't still say it, Rittmeister. Except, of course, for you."

Manfred opened his mouth to protest that he was just a flyer, like other flyers, but that note from his dream rose before his waking eyes again:

*To the German Flying Corps.*

*Rittmeister Baron Manfred von Richthofen was killed in aerial combat, on April 21st 1918. He was buried with full military honors.*

In the dream, that note and the grainy, black-and-white picture of a flower-covered grave had been dropped over the airfield. Would they bother doing that for any other flyer? No. Obviously not.

Manfred didn't know how, or when it had come about, though he knew the Kaiser had used him for propaganda—oh, with Manfred's full consent and the aid of Manfred's slim autobiographical volume—but there was more to it than that.

In this war of slow attrition, flyers stood out. They got to survey things from above. They were free of the mud—though not of the death and blood—the ground fighters endured. And most of them lived charmed and all-too-short lives.

It was the daring and the risk that had attracted Manfred. But he'd stayed alive despite the risk. Most flyers died with maybe ten kills to their count. He had over 80 kills. Most flyers, before he'd first painted his plane red, had tried to be as inconspicuous as possible, hiding against the sky, so they could take the enemy by surprise.

His style, his flamboyance, the touch of old-fashioned, unapologetic knighthood—the tradition of fighting in the open and boldly, laughing in the face of danger—that clung to him; the way he treated downed enemy flyers like equals temporarily on the other side; the way he looked for his fledglings and young flyers, all of it had made him a legend not just to his own side but the other side as well. The double-edged quality of being used for propaganda was that you become a pivotal point of the war effort.

In his own case, and for himself, he'd done very little. Surely, yes, the English airmen were a danger to those in the trenches, both because of aerial bombardment and being the English artillery's eyes in the sky.

But yet Manfred was a single man, and his death would not win or lose the war for his side.

The scar itched again, and some other thought, a memory from the dream, perhaps, tried to rise. It didn't manage to reach his consciousness, no matter how much he frowned, attempting to retrieve it. It was like trying to recall where one had left something, and thus it retreated further and further the more he tried. Something about his importance to Germany. He was sure they'd lose the war, yes. He'd been for some time. Staying alive would make no difference. But he still felt there was something, something to his life and death that—No, it was gone.

He gave an uneasy shrug and put his now empty cup down. "As well I have some breakfast," he said. "While waiting for the weather to clear."

Bodenschatz nodded, though he looked trouble.

*Probably only because I'm having strange reactions this morning,* Manfred thought.

"I had a nightmare," he said finally.

"Oh?" his adjutant asked.

"I can't remember it," Manfred hedged. "It just left behind an uneasy feeling."

"Ah," Bodenschatz said, but didn't sound reassured.

They crossed the muddied field side by side, Moritz gamboling beside them, splashing water from puddles as he jumped them like a cat.

The mess hall, another long tent, was loud with young voices, alive with the smell of coffee—or yet more chicory, but close enough—eggs and marmalade.

Silence fell as Richthofen entered and all eyes turned to him.

"Good morning, gentlemen," he said in way of greeting. He didn't require formality here, and there was no more than a moment of silence, before the loud discussions returned. The Red Baron took his place at the table, asked for tea instead of coffee, and was grateful at the warm bread. So often it was coarse and made with who knew what, but this morning it felt and tasted like real bread.

*I'll have to compliment the cooks*, he thought, looking over his flyers. His cousin Wolfram was waiting eagerly for Manfred's permission to fly the hunt for the first time. With an air of dread he hoped did not cross his face, Manfred nodded at the young man, an indication he'd be allowed to join the dawn patrol. Just as he did, there was an uneasy prickle behind his eyes, the memory of Wolfram getting in trouble, of having to rescue—And just like that it was gone.

*This is getting ridiculous*, Manfred thought angrily. It would not be unusual, of course, for the young pup to get in trouble. They often did, despite all the rules Manfred laid down, the rules that had come to him from Oswald Boelcke. And often the trouble the young pups got into was fatal. But—

*Yes, Lothar would be laughing at me a great deal by this point*, Manfred thought. He ate his breakfast, smiling at the young men's jests, then thanked the cooks for the meal. Leaving the mess tent, he then strode out into the field to inspect his plane. The scarlet *Fokker Dr. I* had been wheeled forth from the tent-hangar.

*Please don't fail me today*, he thought, looking over the plane. It still looked new, being the replacement for the one in which he'd crashed, proud and red. He knew the young men in the trenches would be looking for that red dot above them, and he would not fail them. It was for them that Manfred had ignored the pointed "suggestions" that he he take a safer post at the rear. With his aircraft being so visible and well known, that route would be the same as his being killed, his disappearing.

*The men need to know I am alive, flying above them and protecting them.* He looked at the clearing sky, then towards his quarters. Menzke would be gathering his flying gear there, waiting to help him dress—with the unobtrusive ease of long practice—in coveralls, jacket and boots.

*I need to shake off this dread and lead my men*, Manfred thought as the orderly set to his task. He continued trying to rally as he walked back toward the flight line. On his way to his plane, he found that Leutenant Richard Wenzl had lain on a stretcher while the squadron waited him. Seeing their leader coming, several of the younger pilots tipped Wenzl out, with a sly smile, as Manfred passed by. The men laughed, and as Wenzl climbed back on the stretcher, Manfred stopped to tip him out. His men's laughter and shouted jeers rising behind him,

Manfred went and stood by his plane, looking back at the gathered pilots with an air of, "What, did something happen?"

*At least they are all in good spirits*, he thought, the laughter reaching a crescendo. As sunlight began to fall on the gathered assembly, Manfred looked up and realized the cloud cover was rapidly burning off. There had been reports of the Englishmen being more aggressive about trying to attack German fighters on the ground.

*We must climb soon*, Manfred thought. As always, the familiar need to be aloft, to be above, to be flying started to course through him. Utterly irrational though it was, he felt safer in the skies than down here, where they were sitting ducks for any English bombardment. So perhaps not irrational. The skies, after all, had been mostly safe for him, save for one incident.

*I am not going to let this funk come back!* He turned to speak to his flyers, but heard Moritz whine and turned. The poor dog was struggling towards him with a heavy plane chock tied to his tail.

*Ah, Wenzl's revenge*, he thought, grinning. *Or perhaps Wenzl and some of his friends' retribution.* He grinned. This was good, as it was obvious they were in great spirits, and great spirits increased their probability of survival.

"Come here, you silly hound," Manfred muttered. He knelt to free Moritz and petted the animal, this time receiving a couple of unavoidable, grateful licks to the face. He stood, looking over his men, and felt suddenly grave. It was if, for a moment, he saw the passing shade of Oswald Boelcke standing in the back row, gazing at him sadly.

*That...that was odd*, Manfred thought. *Surely a trick of the wound.* Shaking his head, he suddenly felt as if whatever dark thing was reaching from his dream, the Dicta Boelcke were the way to avoid it.

"It is a beautiful day to fly patrol," he said, informally, to scattered chuckles. "You're all anxious to fly and sure of victory, as indeed am I. But it's been awhile due to this abominable weather, so please indulge me in a quick review of the dicta Boelcke."

The chuckles died down. All eyes turned to him, and he stood, petting Moritz, whose panting seemed suddenly very loud.

"So, to begin," Manfred said. "Always try to secure?"

"An advantageous position before attacking," the men answered, initially with some hesitance then with a strong common recitation. "Climb before and during the approach in order to surprise the enemy from above, and dive on him swiftly from the rear when the moment to attack is at hand."

"Very good," Manfred said. "And, try to place yourself between the sun and..?"

"The enemy," the men finished, and added, with well-schooled harmony "This puts the glare of the sun in the enemy's eyes and makes it difficult to see you and impossible for him to shoot with any accuracy."

"Do not fire the machine guns," Manfred prompted.

"Until the enemy is within range and you have him squarely within your sights."

"Attack when the enemy least—"

"Expects it or when he is preoccupied with other duties such as observation, photography, or bombing," the men continued, the recitation almost resembling a chant.

"Never turn your back—"

"And try to run away from an enemy fighter. If you are surprised by an attack on your tail, turn and face the enemy with your guns."

"Keep your eye on the enemy and do not allow him to—" Manfred started, realizing he was grinning like a proud father.

"Deceive you with tricks. If your opponent seems damaged, follow him down until he crashes to be sure he is not faking."

"Foolish acts of bravery only bring death!" Manfred shouted.

"The *Jasta* must fight as a unit with close teamwork between all pilots," his men replied. "The signals of its leaders must be obeyed."

"Attack in principle in groups of four—"

"Or six. When the fight breaks up into a series of single combats, take care that several do not go for one opponent."

Manfred nodded. There was a feel something in the rules was very important, but he couldn't think what. He always tried to follow them, at any rate.

"Very good," he said. "Let's keep it in mind as we bag our Lords."

The last line was delivered with a sense of feline anticipation, a feeling which only grew as Manfred saw the telephone operator running from the communications shack. The Baron knew what the man was going to say before he gasped out his report.

"There are several English planes at the front."

Like that, the levity and laughter, the boisterous good humor of the flyers vanished, replaced by determination. The men rushed to their planes.

"Wolfram," Manfred said, treating the young man with the informality of family. The simple name arrested his cousin's headlong rush. Manfred knew the dream had involved Wolfram, and though he didn't believe in dreams, at least not as harbingers of fate, he thought perhaps his mind was trying to warn him of something, "Wolfram, obey the dicta, and stay clear of engagements, please."

"Yes, Rittmeister," Wolfram answered, seemingly obedient before plunging headlong towards his plane.

*I hope that he's not giving me a child's simple promise to a parent before engaging in dangerous games,* Manfred thought, frowning, before he climbed his own plane.

Shortly thereafter, his kette of five planes took to the skies, followed quickly by the rest of the Flying Circus.

It was a quick journey to the front. Adjusting his goggles as he closed with the trenches, Manfred scanned the surrounding sky. The men on the ground counted on him to keep the English off their backs as they massed for the Kaiser's great push. He would do just that.

*These clouds haven't all burned off,* he thought. The wisps of white were gradually thickening, breaking up lines of sight. Looking he saw a passing flight from Jasta 5. Counting, he saw that there were only three of the aircraft from their fellow unit.

*That won't do,* he thought. Gaining Wenzl's attention, he signaled for the man to join up on Jasta 5's small formation. Waggling his wings, Wenzl led Weiss in a reversal to turn and join up with the trio of aircraft. Looking back, Manfred quickly took stock of the four other pilots still with him on his patrol: Wolfram, Scholz, Karjus, and Wolff.

*Pups are always the most likely to get in trouble,* Manfred thought to himself, justifying why he kept a close eye on Wolfram. In reality, something about the young man bothered him, something irrational and probably rooted in the unremembered nightmare.

The quintet followed the Somme, climbing to 10,000 feet before the trenches became visible. Putting his fighter into a shallow bank just on the German side of the lines, Manfred began to search their assigned sector. Just past Cerisy, a hamlet on the banks of the Somme, Manfred spotted the enemy. Or, at least, a gaggle so large he was fairly certain they were British.

*At least my eyesight has not failed me, even if my nerves are trying to*, he thought. A great part of his exceptional fighting prowess was not his ability as a pilot—he'd never been more than adequate, and knew it—but the vision which let him distinguish in a vague glimmer against a bank of clouds the presence of aircraft. That same vision now told him that the gaggle was British, apparently eight of their Sopwith *Camels*, lazily circling just on English side of No Man's Land.

*Let us begin*, Manfred thought, then signaled his subordinates. From below Manfred there echoed the shellbursts from a battery of anti-aircraft guns. He ignored it. Unless you flew straight at them, the anti-aircraft were like an act of God: unavoidable, unlikely to be directed particularly at you, and a sign of bad luck if they struck you down. The best a pilot could do was hope it missed. Far more pressing were the enemy aircraft right here, up in the sky, with them., while you kept your eye on your enemy right here, in the sky, close up to you.

As if they'd been conjured from his thoughts, sudden movement and sound attracted Manfred's attention.

*Damn these clouds!* He realized poor visibility had caused him to miss two Camels attacking Weiss's all white triplane. Cursing softly at the loss of time, Richthofen wheeled his formation in a wide left turn, climbing, and prepared to single out a Camel on the edge of the melee for an attack. Out of the corner of his eye, he saw the original eight enemy turning suddenly towards his flight.

*Well, this is about to get interesting,* he thought. *But we will have an altitu...*what is Wolfram doing?!

The pup had separated from the rest of Jasta 11, chasing some target that Manfred could not yet see. Then there was close-in jostling and shooting as his four remaining craft merged with the two, then eight more *Camels.* Fire passed close by, well too close to him, and Manfred jerked reflexively.

*I cannot tell if that was the English or someone shooting at the English,* Manfred thought, growing concerned at the chaos. Then he was too busy dodging and turning, the numbers preventing him from going over to the offensive. Despite their numerical advantage, the English were too clumsy to draw blood, while the Germans were too worried about getting possibly swamped to do so either. Two more *Camels* joined the fray, but ironically the increased numbers worked against the English as Manfred's Jasta began working like a team versus the Englishmen flying as a dozen individuals.

That was, until the Jasta 5 flight joined the fray. Even as he was starting to gain an advantage on an Englishman, the five additional *Fokkers* disrupted Manfred's command of the situation. The sky was suddenly filled with tracers once more, the Englishmen's rounds creating thin white threads that crisscrossed in every direction. Still, the Fokkers outnumbered the *Camels,* and he watched as the advantage grew with a *Camel* falling out of the sky with an obviously dead pilot at the controls

Manfred looked around to select a target, simultaneously proud of his men for not breaking the dicta by rushing at the same plane and frustrated none of the Englishman would cooperatively separate away. Then, with a sudden rush of nausea, he realized Wolfram was in danger. Above his cousin's gaily decorated plane, with its purple wings and silver fuselage, a *Camel* hovered, diving on Wolfram as the latter stooped on a pair of Englishmen.

*No*, Manfred thought as he saw the *Camel* plunge, guns blazing. He only remembered to breathe again as the Englishman's initial burst missed behind the *Fokker*, the man having failed to lead Wolfram. Wolfram, suddenly aware of his danger, plunged into a dive with the *Camel* in hot pursuit.

"Never try to run away from an enemy fighter. If you are surprised by an attack on your tail, turn and face the enemy with your guns," Manfred whispered, whipping his fighter around. The pup had forgotten.

He saw Wolfram level off and head towards Cappy, but the *Camel* was in pursuit, spraying bullets in all directions. Then it was suddenly not spraying bullets at all, but following a determined course away.

*He has run himself out of ammo or jammed his guns*, Manfred thought, following almost instinctively. He had selected his prey. He'd take this daring *Camel* who had attacked Wolfram.

The Englishman, unlike Wolfram, had kept looking around. Therefore, he saw the scarlet triplane diving on him and doubled his efforts to escape. Firing an initial burst that the *Camel* just barely evaded, Manfred cursed and continued to close in.

*I will not waste any more ammunition firing at long range*, he thought angrily, closing. He knew the *Camel* was disarmed. Or at least, it wasn't turning around to face him. Instead, it was attempting to zigzag in escape, which meant that Manfred would slowly gain on him.

Manfred was prey to excitement he hadn't felt in a long time. Forgetting caution and misgivings, he stayed on the plane's tail. He forgot the ground flitting by behind him, forgot danger, forgot the very real possibility of death. This was the glory of fighting in the air: the chase, the heady flight, the air rushing past, the feeling that one was above it all.

The enemy was obviously trying to decide whether to land behind German lines or stick with his kite long enough to cross back over English lines. Manfred fired again, and once more the man ahead of him seemed to have a preternatural sense of when to zigzag. Even though it caused the Red Baron to miss, the maneuver also killed some of the *Camel*'s speed, leading to Manfred closing the distance some more.

The trench system flashed by under them, barbed wire and ugly jagged cuts in the landscape. And suddenly Manfred became aware of another memory from the dream. A voice in his mind, not his own, one with a distinct English accent saying something about chasing an enemy behind the English lines and getting cut down by anti-aircraft fire.

Almost imperceptibly, he became aware of his surroundings again. He realized he was about to cross the lines. He heard anti-aircraft fire up below, still too far to inflict damage. But not too far. Another two seconds and he'd be upon them.

He ceased firing and started climbing, watching the *Camel* fly on, lower and lower.

Better the Lord escape to fly another day than for Manfred to be brought down in flames, riddled with fire, or whatever other dark fate hung upon his half-remembered dream.

A sudden burst of fire behind him made him aware he had now become a target of pursuit. And that he'd become completely isolated, far from his own flight.

*Foolish acts of bravery only bring death.*

Well, at least he wasn't going to run. He turned around, facing the enemy and letting out a burst of machine gun fire, which was returned. There was a brief impression of some strikes on the enemy craft, and he heard canvas ripping on his own craft before the two craft were past each other. Manfred reversed course, seeing the *Camel* follow suit.

*So, you accept my duel then*, Manfred thought with a haughty smile. The planes circled, two hawks in a deadly fight. He was so close he could see the other man's pose, hunched intent over control and machine gun.

*You're a brave one*, Manfred thought as he tried to circle behind for advantage. The *Camel* somehow managed to hold the turn long enough for his own triplane to shudder in warning of an impending stall. Manfred side slipped out of the turn, lowering his nose to regain some airspeed while risking a quick glance for his original prey possibly circling back in. His quick glance told him that it was merely him and the single Englishman, now less than a thousand feet over No Man's Land.

Once more the duel was rejoined. Manfred quickly realized that the two men and their aircraft were evenly matched, and neither was going to turn for home. While the stiff breeze blowing out of the west gave Manfred some advantage if he turned to run, he quickly realized that this *Camel's* pilot was able to eke enough speed out of his aircraft to make that a difficult proposition. Likewise, Manfred was able to use his triplane's slim maneuverability advantage to keep the *Camel* from gaining a decisive upper hand.

As the sweat poured from his body and his arms began to burn with the onset of fatigue, the vision of that cursed pamphlet with the image of a grave and the announcement of his death floated before his eyes. And suddenly, as though broken forth by the burst of battle, he saw what would follow, or at least what had followed in his dream: the defeat of the Kaiser's push.

That part was no wonder. Manfred had thought this last, desperate, crazed attack would fail. Not that he could put in words why, but in his stroke of clairvoyance Manfred realized it would be scarcity of supplies, ammunition, and men that would doom the Kaiser's last gamble. The best of Germany's youth would die at the front, leaving the nation with the dregs, the boys and the oldsters. In the end the trenches would consume the new advance as they had consumed others. With the Americans looming, the war would become one of attrition. Germany, surrounded by hostile countries and consumed by blockade, would almost certainly lose.

*The dream showed me the future*, he thought, even as he fired a snap burst that just missed his adversary. *It will be a nightmare. The French and Englishmen will be vengeful.*

The *Camel* somehow whipped its nose around, the pilot nearly stalling it to bring the twin guns to bear. It was only Manfred's own catlike reflexes and the *Fokker*'s maneuverability that allowed him to twist mostly out of the tracer's path. Still, he heard several impacts and looked back to see a brief bit of smoke back near his tail as the canvas tried to ignite.

*Germany will perish*, he thought. The country would be despoiled, made to pay for a war that was only partly its fault. It would be doubtful that the Kaiser could keep his current amount of power, or indeed the throne, after such a spectacular defeat.

Once more the *Camel* was briefly in his sights, the Englishman having made a narrow mistake. Manfred fired, seeing bits flying off the Sopwith's top wing and more canvas rips down the fuselage. Then the two fighters were past one another, Manfred immediately whipping into a climb to separate from his foe to the north. The *Camel* followed suit. Dimly, Manfred heard cheers from the German trenches.

*We are a proud people*, he thought. Sure, they'd be defeated and broken, but they wouldn't lie still very long. He had the awful presentiment—the dream had made it a certainty—that as soon as another generation grew up they would again engage in battle. That fire and blood would once again consume Europe.

*Just as certainly as I will die here if I continue this fight*, he thought in a sudden realization of his own fatigue, *so Germany will if she rises again.* His own lands, pressed close by the eastern enemies, would be destroyed. But more than that, an entire way of life would be cast into doubt, destroyed.

Just as the men on the trenches cursed their own flyers, who were, in their minds, above them both socially and physically, and cared not for their plight, so would the people who'd fought and died and suffered from this defeat come to view the war. It would be seen as having been a game of Lords, an unjust and heedless fight between battle-mad barons heedless of what it did to those on the ground, the lower classes who had paid in blood, treasure, and humiliation for what the nobility thought a grand fight.

*'Nothing good comes from the peasantry feeling like they've had enough.'* His history tutor's words echoed in his ears. The last century, from the madness that had begun in France to his nation's own aborted revolution in the 1840s, had been a constant reinforcement of such lessons. Even now, the Russians were in the middle of such a convulsion.

*What if that happens in Germany?* he thought. Then again, his reflexes saved him, as a different *Camel* came slashing into the duel. Manfred whipped around on the interloper, firing a burst that saw a torrent of strikes into the enemy's machine guns and cockpit. The Englishman never recovered from his attack, slamming into the ground just before the German trenches.

*Where is the...oh no*, he thought, seeing his long-term duelist having positioned himself between Manfred and the German lines.

*Never turn your back and try to run away from an enemy fighter.*

Sure. He never had. And he wouldn't again. But behind the Englishman he could see three more *Camel*s attempting to move towards blocking his escape. Thinking back to his duel with Hawker, Manfred realized this was how the English ace had died.

*My men can criticize my decision only if I'm alive*, he thought. Sometimes the best option was to disengage. This close to the English lines, the odds against him would only get worse. For the first time in many fights, Manfred felt a sense of being in imminent, immediate danger. Dodging his original opponent's attack, Manfred circled upward then made for the German lines as fast as he could. The *Camel* pilot belatedly reversed, attempting to catch Manfred before he got away.

*Dammit*, he thought, as his engine suddenly began running rougher. There was a sudden burst of fire, and his seat splintered. Manfred kicked his rudder, and the *Camel* turned away before overshooting given the *Fokker*'s sudden loss of speed. Looking forward, Manfred only then realized that some fire must have holed his engine, as there was a horrible streak of oil along the *Fokker*'s nose.

*I have to get away*, he thought, suddenly feeling faint. He reached to where bullets had torn into his seat, touched his flight suit, and had it come away with a shade of crimson that matched his fuselage. He didn't as yet feel pain, but he knew he'd been hit.

*I cannot afford to die of this!* his mind protested. There was a sense he was very important for Germany, very important to avert the future his dream had shown. That future of more fire and blood. The future in which Europe plunged into a fight again and again, till all the things that had made it great, the things that had made it the primary world civilization were destroyed, and his own lands fell under the same sort of madness now consuming Russia.

With a rush, he realized they were passing over the German trench system. He was now behind his own lines, and his own anti-aerials were firing at the *Camel*. Manfred felt as though a haze was upon his thoughts, as a haze descended on his vision. The engine was now certainly in its death throes, and he had maybe 150 feet of altitude. Flames began shooting out of the nose in front of him, and Manfred had visions of crashing down in fire.

*I have to bring the aircraft down, safely*, he thought. It flashed into his mind that at least the dream couldn't be right. He might die, but it wouldn't be the English burying him. It wouldn't be the English sending that damnable pamphlet to his people.

*Not important*, he thought, sighting one of the many supply routes that ran towards the front lines. Carefully, he controlled his descent into a road cutting through a muddy field. He was aware of the *Camel* still on his tail as he made an awkward landing. At least the *Camel* wasn't landing. Just following him down, Manfred guessed, to make sure he wasn't faking it. Or perhaps the pilot of the *Camel* had also been hit by the anti-aircraft machine guns.

Manfred didn't care. His blood thundered past his ears with a sound like a rushing train, and he knew his heart was straining, which told him he was fast losing blood. The thud of his wheels was a welcome relief as his vision went cloudy. The plane bumped on as he instinctively shut off his engine, flung off his goggles, then pulled on the brake lever to try and bring the *Fokker* to a stop. With a roar, the *Camel* flashed close by overhead, then slammed into the ground ahead of him.

*Is the Englishman mad?* Manfred thought, as his conscious tried to fade. Through the enveloping darkness, afraid that the enemy would approach and—against all rules of gentlemen—put a bullet in his head, Manfred reached for his side arm. Then there were was a man climbing into his cockpit, a voice speaking in German.

"Easy, Rittmeister. Easy. You're among friends."

He was aware of being helped—pulled, to tell the truth—from the plane. Opening his eyes brought him confused glimpses of many men, of uniforms. He asked only, "The *Camel?*"

"Captain Roy Brown has been taken prisoner, Rittmeister."

\* \* \*

It wasn't till days later, fully conscious in a hospital, that Manfred's brother informed him either one of his defensive bursts or one of the German anti-aerials had so damaged the *Camel* that it had no chance but to land.

"I would have liked a chance to meet the man," Manfred observed, his arm in a sling.

"Well, if he hadn't been so fixated on trying to bag the Red Baron, the man probably would have had a chance to meet you again once you recover," Lothar observed. "That is, if you ever got over the embarrassment of trying to run from him."

Manfred fixed his brother with a silent glare. Lothar, after a few moments, broke away from the gaze while mumbling an apology.

"It occurred to me," Manfred said, candidly, "that being so famous, partly because the Kaiser made me so, I was needed. For...for the war."

*If I tell him what I was really thinking, they'll lock me in an asylum,* Manfred thought. The grave covered in flowers in his dream had been so jarring that its significance had eluded him. Until he lay in a hospital bed, able to think. It was then he had realized that he was as famous—and respected—on the other side as on his own. He knew that from his encounters with the men he'd taken prisoner.

*The newspapers they've shared with me only confirms it*, he thought. Several of the English papers were trumpeting his wounding and shooting down. Of course, they were far less triumphant in discussing the fact that he'd managed to, counting Roy Brown, take two of their pilots with him.

Lothar looked at him dumbfounded.

*Lothar has never been a thinker or a planner*, Manfred thought. *That is fine; I will do the planning for both of us. For Germany and for Europe itself.*

"Now you won't be able to avoid taking a backseat in the war," Lothar said, scoffing. "They'll put you in as an inspector at the rear. What with the shattered shoulder to recover from."

It was the sort of scoffing and teasing they'd engaged in as boys, each striving to be stronger and more visibly brave than the other. But Manfred was no longer a boy.

"Yes," he said. "That is likely."

He closed his eyes on Lothar's expression of incomprehension, of not knowing what had changed. Manfred didn't either. Except that whatever warning his mind had tried to send him in that nightmare had hit home.

He'd be alive after this war. And try to make it the last great war to ravage Europe.

Before worse happened.

\* \* \* \* \*

### Sarah A. Hoyt Bio

Sarah A. Hoyt was born in Portugal and lives in Colorado. Along the way she's published over 32 books (around there anyway. She keeps forgetting some every time she counts) she admits to and a round dozen she doesn't. She also managed to raise two sons, and a countless number of cats. When not writing at speed, she does furniture refinishing or reads history. She was a finalist for the Mythopoeic award with her first book, and has won the Prometheus and the Dragon. To learn more about Sarah and read samples of her work, visit http://sarahahoyt.com.

# # # # #

# Trial of the Red Baron

# by Richard Fox

London, England
January 5th, 1919

The last time Flight Lieutenant Edmund Wells walked the halls of Holyport, there hadn't been as many armed guards. Wrought iron bars over each and every window cast slanted lines across the marble floors as Wells strode past a pair of soldiers who clicked their heels together and saluted as he went by.

Wells reminded himself to walk straight, even though the heavy briefcase in his left hand was doing everything it could to make him lopsided. He stopped in front of heavy oak doors, their handles bound by chain and a padlock the size of his fist.

A guard standing next to the door offered Wells an impeccable salute.

"Fine morning to you, sir. Lord Newton gave strict instructions that the prisoner's not to be visited by any but the Red Cross," the guard said. "Seems this Hun is right popular—or notorious, if you ask me—with a lot of folks and prisoners of war can't be bothered as such. I'm to turn away anyone and everyone that comes to see him. Rank regardless."

"You're doing a fine job, Sergeant." Wells jabbed his fingertips into a small fold on the outside of his case and withdrew a piece of paper. He handed it off to the guard and waited as the man read.

"Right unusual, but ignoring a written order from Lord Newton is a sure way to be reassigned to another camp on some bitterly cold Scottish island." He handed back the note. "The prisoner's been nothing but a gentleman since he arrived in May, but you've any problem just start shouting, and we'll come most ricky tick."

The guard drew a key from within his tunic and opened the door.

The prisoner's 'cell' was almost opulent by any well-to-do Englishman's standards. An oak desk with piles of paper, tall bookshelves along the walls and a window (barred, naturally) affording a view of London. A pile of unopened packages were stacked in one corner, enough that Wells could have climbed atop and nearly touched the ceiling if he'd been so inclined. On the other side of the room, cured meat, sausage, cheeses, and candy sat in wash baskets. All German goods, by their packaging.

The prisoner, wearing a grey uniform and tall riding boots, faced out the window, his hands clasped behind his back. Another man, slight of build and in a simple uniform, stood beside the desk, holding a tray with a steaming tea kettle and chipped cups.

"*Du bist früh, Herr Schmidt,*" the prisoner said.

"I'm afraid I don't speak German, my apologies," Wells said as he walked up to the desk.

Manfred von Richthofen, infamously known around the world as the Red Baron, half- turned toward Wells. With 80 victories, Richthofen was the top scoring fighter pilot ace of the entire Great War. Almost of his victims had been British, which made it unsurprising that he'd been shot down and captured in their sector a few months before the Armistice. His face was stern, eyes set like every strict military commander Wells had ever come across. Noting Wells' rank, the German fully turned to regard the new arrival, his bearing stiff. Wells noted an unfolded map of Germany on Richtofen's desk. Large swaths of Prussia, the baron's homeland, were given over to the proposed state of Poland. One town was circled in pencil, an arrow pointing to it.

"Is there something I can do for you?" Richthofen asked with a heavy accent.

"Flight Lieutenant Wells, pleasure." He extended a hand, but Richthofen remained still. Well pulled his hand back and gave his brief case a pat. "Seems my arrival is a bit of a surprise. You've not heard?"

"Heard what? I know the treaty negotiations at Versailles have stalled, but prisoners of war are being returned to their homelands," Richthofen said. "Yet I, and many other officers and British citizens of German heritage, remain here. Your hospitality is noted, but I have no desire to stay in your jail a moment longer than necessary."

Wells felt a tinge of dread as he prepared his next words. *Anger is a normal first reaction*, he thought.

"I'm your solicitor, and your barrister, for your upcoming trial, Baron. I'm sorry word of this didn't reach you sooner." Wells gripped the handle of his case tighter, ready for an outburst.

Richthofen touched a hand to the map on his desk, then swept it beneath an unopened pile of letters. He motioned to a chair next to Wells.

"Please, sit." Richthofen went back to the window.

As Wells sat, he noticed a long scar across the back of the prisoner's head, wide as a coin in the middle and tapering to points close to the ears. Wells had served in His Majesty's military long enough to know a bullet wound when he saw one.

"This is all a bit of a surprise to me as well," Wells said. "The military commission was called a fortnight ago. Seems things are in a bit of a rush." He opened his case and removed a notepad and pen, uncovering a thin book with a red biplane and German words on the cover.

"I see you have my autobiography," Richtofen said. "I thought you were my lawyer, not an admirer."

"I thought it better to get to know you before we met," Wells said. "Seemed appropriate. A chap translated much of it for me."

"There are few things I regret from the war. That pulp rag is one of them. I had pilots to lead, battles to fight; I didn't have time to truly share my entire life's journey on the page, and at 25 the idea of having an autobiography wasn't my own. The German Ministry of Intelligence and Propaganda thought it would help boost the public's morale. That and all those blasted cards with my face on them."

Metzger set down a cup of tea and saucer for Wells, complete with several sugar cubes.

"To more important matters. What am I charged with?" Richthofen asked.

"Violation of the Hague Treaty of 1907, specifically Article 23, killing an individual who no longer had the means of defense. You're to be tried under British law as you're in our custody," Wells picked up his tea, but set it down as the trembling in his hand threatened to spill.

Richthofen gave off a chuckle.

"Since when are soldiers to be tried for murder simply for carrying out their duties?" he asked. "I killed a great many individuals during the war. Am I charged with all their deaths?"

"There is only one such incident at issue, a Sergeant Reuel Dunn. Is the name familiar?"

"No," Richthofen said quickly. "You're in the Royal Air Force but you don't have your flight wings. Are you aware of how air combat occurred over the front lines? I did not stop to exchange pleasantries with any English plane I saw. We simply did out best to try and kill each other."

"The 2nd of April in '17," Wells said. "Seems you forced a Sopwith down behind your lines and then—allegedly—fired on the aircraft while it was stuck in the mud, killing Sergeant Dunn."

"That was what you call 'Bloody April,' yes? I shot down many planes that month. But firing at someone on the ground, I do not recall."

"As your solicitor and barrister, we share attorney client privilege. I'm not familiar with Germany's laws, but anything you say to me is confidential and will only be used to better prepare your case."

Richthofen ran his fingertips along the scar on the back of his head.

"My memory is not quite what it used to be." Richthofen looked at Metzger and spoke with him in rapid fire German.

Wells dropped a sugar cube into his tea, watching the two converse. Wells was bringing the tea to his lips when Richthofen snapped his fingers. The teacup bounced against Wells teeth painfully, and a drop of tea fell onto his tunic.

"Now I remember," Richthofen said, "a two-seater. The plane landed in a muddy beet field and when I flew over to note the location for my report, one of your men in the rear seat fired on me with his machine gun. I looped around and returned the favor. This is what I'm to be charged with? Trading bullets?"

"There is some dispute as to the events of the day. Were there any other witnesses we could call in your defense?"

Richthofen shifted his weight from foot to foot.

"Lothar, my brother, flew with me that day, but he was already on his way back to our base when I was shot at. Voss saw…but Werner is dead."

"He was something of a rival of yours, wasn't he?" Wells asked.

"I did not have 'rivals,' Mr. Wells," Richthofen said angrily. "I had comrades. Brave men who would have died for me, and I for them. Voss was a hero, and a good man. Now," he composed himself quickly, "the trial begins tomorrow morning, doesn't it?"

"Yes," Wells said, surprised. "How did you know?"

"I swear it is always raining on this blighted island of yours, but the weather is starting to clear. This privilege between us, it extends to written documents?"

"Certainly."

Richthofen sat at the desk and began writing a letter.

"Give me a moment," the German said. "Please finish your tea. I have too much."

"I wasn't aware that prisoner rations included such fine leaves or actual sugar," Wells said as he took another sip.

"They don't. The Red Cross delivers packages to me from Germany almost daily. Metzger is still sorting through yesterday's post. Do you know the conditions back home, Mr. Wells? Your navy keeps up a blockage even though the fighting has ended. Food, food that starving women and children need to survive this winter, is held back from them by your government."

He stopped writing and looked up at the English officer.

"Do you know what it is like to return from the frontlines and see children, little more than skin and bones, in cardboard shoes running through the streets?" Richthofen asked. He picked up a handful of letters then slammed them back to the desk. "Conditions are even worse than my last trip home, but still people send me food through the Red Cross. I've tried to get word back to Germany that this must stop, the food should go to the needy, but your government censors every word of my letters home."

Richthofen returned to his writing.

"You know where the Swiss Embassy is, yes? You're to deliver this letter to Mr. Schmidt as soon as you leave here."

"Attorney client privilege does not extend to espionage," Wells said as the color drained from his face.

"The fighting is over, and I have no intelligence worth sharing with my government. Besides, Mr. Schmidt is with the Red Cross. He will see my requests finally delivered back home." The baron looked up and cast a guilty glance to the pile of boxes over Wells' shoulder. "Will you do this for me?"

"I." Wells cleared his throat. "I suppose I could swing by the embassy. But what of your case? How will you plead?"

"There is something you must understand." Richthofen signed the letter with a flourish then folded the paper. "There is no trial. There is only theater."

\* \* \*

Wells looked at his reflection in the glass window of the Old Bailey, where Londoners had faced justice since the 1700's and adjusted his wig. Down below, he saw a sizeable crowd along the road leading to the guarded entrance where Richthofen would arrive. The entire front rank of spectators carried cameras, and a pair of motion picture cameras flanked either side of the door.

There were signs in the crowd; BLOODY RED BARON and MURDERER stenciled on more than one poster, braced on a wood frame waved aloft.

"Think this will take long?" a gruff man asked from behind.

Wells smiled at the King's Counsel, Jameson Mort, an older man wearing the same style of robes and wigs.

"My client's yet to arrive," Wells said. "I'm sure we're in for a full day before the judges."

"Lord Newton expects this business to be handled promptly," Mort said. "Any grandstanding or needless delays will not be appreciated by those in Parliament."

Wells' smile widened.

"Sir Mort, are you suggesting we do anything less than our full duty as agents of the law? I'm aware that this is the first ever war crimes trial held under the authority of the Hague treaty, but that I'm acting as solicitor *and* barrister is odd enough to warrant a review of the judgement by the Supreme Court, no matter which way the case decides. Is the tribunal of judges, instead of a jury of peers, also done for the sake of expediency?"

Mort levelled a finger at Well's chest and made a phlegmy snort.

"Be quick about this," Mort said. "Your boy's arriving."

Shouting from the crowd carried through the window. A lorry with barred windows pulled up to the gate. A pair of bailiffs went to the back of the car and unlocked the doors. Each grabbed ahold of a handle and paused as camera's flashed. A man in a deep blue suit stepped onto the road and gestured to the film crews.

"How did Richthofen know there'd be a media circus?" Wells asked himself.

The doors open and Richthofen, his wrists and ankles bound by chains, came out of the lorry. Even from his high vantage point, Wells could see the German wore a chest full of medals, a gold and enamel blue Maltese Cross at his neck, the *Pour Le Merite*, Prussia's highest award for valor. Richthofen held his head high, staring at the assembled crowd with contempt as cameras flashed around him.

A tomato sailed out of the rabble and struck the side of the lorry. A bailiff hustled Richthofen into the courthouse.

Wells turned around and looked over the courtroom. The seating area was full of reporters and men in military uniforms. Even with winter's cold, the room was heating up from so many packed bodies.

He made his way to his desk situated next to a metal cell big enough for one person with a wooden stool inside.

Mort's desk held very little in the way of paperwork, which struck Wells as odd. He expected the prosecution to have a mountain of evidence prepared for this trial. Wells had passed the bar in the last year, and what limited courtroom experience he had led him to believe that Mort either didn't take his role seriously…or he was supremely confident of the outcome.

Cameras flashed as Richthofen came in through a side door and was placed into the cell. He looked regal and carried an air of contempt.

Wells hurried over and leaned close to the bars.

"This is madness," Wells said. "I don't know how it is in Germany but in England the accused is innocent before proven guilty. We've already grounds for a dismissal."

Richthofen shook his head slowly.

"Let this play out," the baron said.

"I'm beginning to think everyone's having a laugh at my expense," Wells said. "This is a trial, not a ten-penny show on the West End. They can sentence you to death, Manfred. You must take this seriously."

"All rise!"

Three judges in far more ostentatious wigs than Wells and Mort came into the courtroom and took their seats behind a tall bench. The judge in the center banged his gavel and set a pair of spectacles onto his nose.

"Be seated. Hauptman Manfred Freiherr von Richthofen," the judge said, "of the Imperial German Flying Corps, you are charged with violating Article 23 of the Hague Convention of 1907. Specifically, that you did, on the 2nd of April last year, kill one Sergeant

Reuel Dunn while he no longer had the means of defense. How do you plead?"

Wells rose to his feet.

"If it pleased the court. The defendant will—"

"Not guilty!" Richthofen shouted. He sprang to his feet...then turned to the camera and raised his bound wrists as high as he could. Camera bulbs popped like rifles along a trench line and several military men in the audience began shouting at the baron.

Wells felt his cheeks burn with embarrassment as the judge hammered his gavel, demanding order in his courtroom.

Richthofen returned to his stool and gave Wells a wink.

"There will be silence, or I will clear this courtroom," the judge said. Calm returned in short order.

"Counsel Mort, call your first witness," the judge said.

"The state calls Second Lieutenant Algernon Warren to the stand," Mort said.

A tall man in his early twenties and a uniform so crisp it looked as if it had been sewn that morning took the witness stand.

"Lieutenant Warren," Mort said, "I understand you've just been freed from a German prison camp. Thank you for your service. I do hope you were well treated."

The judge levelled his gavel at Wells before he could voice an objection.

"It's good to be home," Warren said.

*Sounds like an educated bloke from money*, Wells thought. *That's not going to help our cause.*

"Tell us what happened on the day in question."

"We were to conduct a photo reconnaissance over Vimy Ridge," Warren began. "I flew the Sopwith while Sergeant Dunn manned the rear gun and carried the camera."

Warren's face scrunched in concentration.

*Can't tell if he's trying to recall what happened or rehearsed testimony,* Wells noted.

"We'd just crossed the front lines and come through a cloud bank when Jerry, excuse me, the Germans, attacked," Warren continued. "Sergeant Dunn took a bad hit to the shoulder that first pass and collapsed into his seat. He never had a chance to fight back."

Wells heard the rattle of chains as Richtofen stiffened.

"Second time around the Germans took out my instrument panel and holed my gas tank. My engine quit, and I managed to glide to the ground where a mud puddle stopped my landing before my plane could roll into a canal. I turned around to help the good sergeant. He'd been hit in the back of his shoulder and down his arm, but it wasn't too bad."

*So, by his own admittance, the sergeant was still capable of wielding a machine gun,* Wells noted, jotting a note to himself.

"I was about to apply a bandage when we heard an aircraft approaching. I looked up and there's that bloody baron diving right for us. He hit Dunn again, this time in the stomach, and put a fair number of holes in my flight suit. Then the last of the fuel in my tank caught fire, and I had to pull Dunn clear."

*But you didn't suffer any burns or wounds yourself?* Wells noted again, writing another note.

"I got him to a dry spot and then he looked up at me and said, 'Think I'm done.'" A melancholy smile touched Warren's face. "Sergeant Dunn...ever the joker. He lost consciousness a few minutes later. German soldiers took him to a field hospital and me to a prison. I learned Dunn died of his wounds that same day."

"This must be difficult for you, Lieutenant." Mort turned to the audience and asked, "Did you or Sergeant Dunn fire your weapons after you landed?"

"No, Counsel. We knew the gig was up after we landed well behind enemy lines in a dead plane."

"Did you try and signal to your attacker that you were out of the fight?"

"I was too busy trying to patch up Sergeant Dunn. By and large, the German pilots were known to be a sporting lot. I didn't think they'd decide to use us as target practice, especially not one as famous as the German propaganda machine had made Richthofen."

"No further questions." Mort looked at Wells. "Your witness."

"Thank you." Wells adjusted his robe and remained behind his desk as he stood up. "Lieutenant, for those of us who've not served in the air corps, how can you tell your fellows apart while in the air? I imagine it's difficult when more than a few dozen yards away."

"It's not called the fog of war because things are damp. It was quite difficult," Warren said. "Whenever there was a spat in the air, we had to work out the details after we landed."

"If it was so difficult telling other British planes apart, then how do you know that the defendant was—as you allege—the man who fired on you and Sergeant Dunn?"

"Because after he was done *murdering* Sergeant Dunn the pilot flew right over the top of us," Warren snapped. "That plane was red. Bright red. There's only one fighter in the whole war that was so garish, and that was his!"

Warren's finger was like a weapon as he pointed at Richthofen.

"There's a simple explanation why he's called the Red Baron."

Cameras flashed again, capturing the accusation.

*Well, walked right into* that *one*, Wells thought, keeping his face passive even as bedlam erupted. *I just established the witness' credibility for the prosecution. Good show, I'm sure this will be mentioned as a shining example of idiocy in every law textbook for decades.* Despite his outwardly calm demeanor, Wells struggled for a moment before managing to speak again.

"Lieutenant, clearly this was a serious incident. You surely reported this to the Red Cross once you were sent to detention."

"No, I did no such thing." Warren shifted in his seat. "The guards knew who'd shot us down and were quite keen to remind me how lucky I was to have survived the encounter. To level such a charge while in German custody would have been something of a death wish."

There were murmurs around the court room at that.

"These are Huns we're talking about. You know what they did to Belgium, killing any civilian they could get their hands on if it pleased them. Whatever treaty protected me as a prisoner could have been just another scrap of paper to them if I tried to expose the truth about that hero of theirs."

"Then when did you bring this incident to light?" Wells asked.

"During my…" Warren frowned, then looked down at his knees. "During my reintegration after I got out of the prison camp. Yes. I told everything to the intelligence chaps then. No need to fear retribution."

*Ah, now we get to the coached responses*, Wells thought. He stepped around his desk and was about to approach the witness stand when Richthofen tapped against his bars. The defendant motioned for Wells to come over.

"Your honors, may I have a moment to confer with my client?" Wells asked.

The judge nodded curtly.

Wells went to the cage and leaned close to speak with Richthofen.

"The witness is lying," Wells said, "Let me get to the bottom of this."

"Of course he's lying, but that's not what's important," Richtofen replied, then continued as if he were speaking to a simpleton. "We are not here for justice Mr. Wells, we are here for a show. For the theater of it all. What will be in the papers is his accusation. The brave war hero back from captivity to balance the scales for his dead comrade. Press him too hard and his entire story comes apart."

"Exactly my point." Wells seethed.

"Your jackals can't have that. Oh look, the man in the blue suit from my arrival is speaking to the judge. I wonder what they're talking about?"

Wells looked up at the bench, and indeed a man in a blue suit was there whispering in the judge's ears.

"No more questions to Warren," Richthofen said. "He's suffered enough."

"I'm the one that's passed the bar examination here, not you," Wells put his hands on his hips. A dozen cameras flashed, capturing the moment of disagreement between client and counsel.

Wells' hands shot down to the side of his legs.

"Good." Richthofen winked at him. "Very good."

"Does my esteemed colleague need more time?" Mort asked.

"No. No further questions of the witness," Wells said.

"Then the prosecution wishes to enter into evidence—" Mort picked up a water logged and mud stained log book from the table and opened it to a place marked by a red silk ribbon, "—the log entry of one Second Lieutenant Charles Etienne deBerigny, dated the 2nd of April, 1917. Which reads, 'Warren and Dunn forced to land behind enemy lines. Observed all-red Albatross firing on grounded aircraft with crew still inside. Men listed as missing in action, likely dead.'"

Grumbles went through the crowd. Wells heard more than one utterance of "Murderer."

"Your honors I must object," Wells said. "Why are we reading from a logbook and not receiving this testimony from Lieutenant deBerigny?"

"Because deBringny died in a crash at the end of the same month," Mort snapped. "This evidence corroborates testimony from Lieutenant Warren and there is no reason to doubt the authenticity of the entry. I doubt deBringny knew this would become evidence in a later trial."

"The log entry doesn't state if the defendant was fired on before he engaged Warren and Dunn. We have no way of knowing what else deBringny, or anyone else in their squadron, saw. There is no context for this information, and it must be rejected as hearsay."

The judges conferred amongst themselves for a moment, then the judge in the center picked up his gavel and leaned over the bench.

"This court will adjourn for five days to give the prosecution an opportunity to locate other witnesses that can corroborate the log entry." He banged the gavel, and the three of them exited out a door behind the bench.

"Yes, as expected," Richthofen said.

"Bloody hell," Wells said to him, "I don't know how hard you hit your head when you crashed behind our lines, but you need to focus on what's happening here. This isn't going your way; you're aware of this?"

A guard came to Richthofen's cage and fumbled with a key ring.

"Come see me in two days," the German said, "and bring all the newspapers you can."

\* \* \*

Wells dropped a half dozen newspapers onto Richthofen's desk. He was on the front page of every single one. Pictures of him in irons with protestors to his back, in the courtroom cell, and with him sharing the unfortunate moment with Wells.

Richthofen picked one up and scowled. "I should have worn my Iron Cross."

"You're lucky this case isn't tried in the court of public opinion," Wells said. "Just look at these headlines, 'The Red Baron shows no remorse when confronted with his victim.' 'Bloody Red Baron defiant in the face of justice,' and that's not even from the tabloids."

Richthofen skipped over the front page and opened a paper. He flipped through several pages then tossed it back onto the desk.

"I can speak English much better than I read it," Richtofen said, his tone unflappable. "What of Germany? Any news?" he asked.

"What does Germany have to do with your trial? Here, in London?"

"Is there anything about protests, the armistice negotiations at Versailles?"

Wells slapped a palm to his face, then looked at Metzger standing nearby with a tea tray. "Do you speak English at all? Can you explain to me what's wrong with your officer?" Wells asked.

Metzger's bushy mustache twitched, then he raised the tea tray a bit higher.

Wells held up two fingers and sat down at the desk. He mumbled thanks to Metzger when he slid a cup and saucer with two sugar cubes to him.

"I need to know what's happening in Germany," Richthofen said.

"There were wire reports of massive protests. Not the usual goings on with the Communists or Socialists, the whole body politic.

Seems your trial has touched something of a nerve back home," Wells said. "Your brother, Lothar, was arrested at a zeppelin hangar with a few other pilots and well-armed men in civilian clothes. The press thinks he was going to come here and break you out. Hence the doubled guard outside your door and around the walls."

"Lothar, always thinking with his heart and not his head. What of Versailles?"

"The German delegation has walked away from the table." Wells took a sip of tea. "The French are demanding we and the Americans march with them into the Rhineland. I daresay your trial was timed very poorly."

"Do you think your country wants the war to resume?"

"God no. Millions dead. Poor lads without arms and legs across the Empire, and for what? Belgium? Your Kaiser's gone and fled the country. Most of the German army's in the streets fighting each other with sticks and bottles. Think they could organize a defense before Cologne was full of our former colonists?"

"Tell me, Mr. Wells, did you know of me during the war?"

"I spent much of the fighting laid up in a hospital after taking shrapnel in Palestine. Didn't have the chance to read much German propaganda, sorry," Wells replied, his tone cold. "When you were captured was a different business. I'm sure everyone in the English-speaking world saw the photo of you standing next to your wrecked plane, surrounded by smiling Australians."

"I did not seek fame during the war, but the Ministry of Intelligence and Propaganda found a use for me beyond my role as a fighter wing leader," Richtofen explained. "The eighty planes I shot down were nothing compared to the carnage along the front, but what I was made to represent; the knight reborn, a modern-day Siegfried, was more valuable to the war effort. Could you imagine if your King Arthur were arrested for stealing the sword from the stone?"

"Preposterous. There'd be riots in the streets…" Wells set his teacup down. He frowned, then narrowed his eyes at Richthofen.

"Germany is now angry. Angry enough to do something foolish. But she is also hungry, and your navy's blockade continues while negotiations are stalled," Richthofen said, "and Germans continue to starve. If your leaders thought they could humiliate Germany into a treaty by putting me on trial, that was a mistake."

"Richthofen, I understand you were something of a big deal back home, but you're in England. You're on trial *in England.*"

The German looked at him, a haughty smile on his face.

"None of your clout matters to the judges, and if we don't mount a better defense, I don't think this well end well for you."

"How well do you know your von Clausewitz? It is time for the *schwerpunkt*, to strike at the heart of the matter," the German said. "This is what you will do the next time we are in court…"

\* \* \*

Richthofen sat on the witness stand, feet chained to the floor, his hand cuffs locked to an iron ring embedded in the wood at waist level. He kept an almost regal air, like he was a baited bear with no fear of dogs.

"And then what occurred?" Wells asked.

"Tracers went up the side of my cockpit. I felt more than one round hit my aircraft's frame. Then I looped around and saw the machine gun on the downed Sopwith still firing on me."

"You're sure it was from the ground? Not another plane?"

"I've charged machine guns before. I know who was shooting at me. So, I fired off another fifty rounds that put a stop to the attack. Once I saw the pilot drag the observer from the plane, I returned to my home base."

"Why not fly off once you came under attack? Why engage?"

"I had come to know the English by that point. Spoken with men I'd shot down, even dined with them on occasion. They were gentlemen," Richtofen said. "All the others who survived their landings knew well enough than to keep fighting. If I'd left that one alive, I feared he would fire on the German soldiers that would come to collect them or fire on my fellow pilots when we passed by."

"Just to be clear—" Wells nodded to the tribunal, "—Sergeant Dunn had the means to resist when you fired upon him."

"Shooting at another person with an automatic machine gun is a bit more than 'to resist.'" Richtofen sneered. "He decided to keep fighting, and he got what he wanted."

An angry rumble came from the crowd.

"No further questions." Wells went back to his desk.

Mort snapped to his feet, his face red with anger.

"Baron Richtofen, would you say you enjoyed killing Sergeant Dunn?"

"I took no joy in it. I was not in the habit of killing other men before the war, but such is the nature of combat."

"But afterwards you went to the crash site and took a trophy? Wasn't that your 'habit'? Also commemorating your kills with a silver cup for each plane you shot down?"

Richtofen shifted in his seat. There was a clink of chains as he fiddled with his cuffs.

"I did remove the aircraft number from the tail. It was the only part that wasn't burnt. Hunters keep trophies. This is the German way."

"So that's all Dunn was? Just another deer in the forest?"

"Hardly. Deer don't shoot back."

Someone dared chuckle from the audience and earned a nasty look from Mort.

Mort reached into a briefcase and pulled out a thin paperback book. He flipped it open to a piece of paper with typed words almost two thirds of the way through.

"We must address the inconsistencies in your statements, Baron. You're familiar with this book? 'Der Rote Kampflieger,' which translates roughly to 'The Red Battle-Flyer,' your autobiography?"

"Yes, I am well aware of my own autobiography."

"Something of a best seller in Germany, yes?"

"Would you like me to sign it for you?"

Wells thought Mort was in danger of suffering an aneurysm in the face of Richthofen's arrogance. The prosecutor visibly composed himself.

"No, Baron, I want you to explain why in chapter ten you said— this translation is certified by the Ministry of Intelligence—and I quote, 'When he had come to the ground, I flew over him at an altitude of about thirty feet in order to ascertain whether I had killed him or not. What did the rascal do? He took his machine-gun and shot holes into my machine. Afterwards Voss told me if that had happened to him, he would have shot the airman on the ground. As a matter of fact, I ought to have done so, for he had not surrendered. He was one of the few fortunate fellows who escaped with their lives. I felt very merry, flew home, and celebrated my thirty-third aeroplane.'

"This doesn't match with the testimony you just gave. Why did you lie in your own autobiography? Guilt over killing a helpless man on the ground? Think you could just brush the crime away with a public statement that you knew would never be challenged?"

"There were—" Richthofen paused for a moment, "—some considerations made for that book. Shooting a man on the ground just because he still wanted to fight wasn't considered…sporting by the publisher."

"Since when is murder a 'sporting' event? You couldn't have the truth—that you fired on two soldiers with no means to fight back—before your adoring public so you lied about it in this book. Tell me, if you'd known Lieutenant Warren would have testified against you, would you have double backed to kill him too?" Mort asked.

"I never fired on someone who was helpless. That Warren of yours was smart enough to know when he was beaten; that's why he's still alive."

"You do not deny killing Sergeant Dunn?"

"I do not."

"But you allege that he was shooting at you, a soldier who knows he's behind enemy lines, who knows he's about to be captured with little to no chance of escape. What kind of a fool would do such a thing?"

"A dead one," Richthofen said.

"Murderer!" came from the crowd. A young man in civilian clothes tried to climb over the wooden railing behind Wells but a pair of guards dragged him away.

A judge rapped his gavel several times until things calmed down.

"Lieutenant Warren's testimony is corroborated; you've publically contradicted yourself," Mort said. "I would advise you to throw yourself at the mercy of this court. No further questions."

"Counsel, do you have any questions for the accused?" the judge asked.

"One, your honor," Wells said. "Baron Richthofen, if you had the situation to do over again, would you still have fired on Sergeant Dunn's plane?"

"Of course. I treated defeated enemies with honor, with respect. If Dunn had not kept fighting, he would be alive today."

"Nothing further."

"Bailiff, return the accused to his holding cell," the judge said.

"Your honor?" Wells raised a hand slightly. "The accused wishes to change his plea…to guilty."

There was a moment of silence in the court, then whispers from the audience. The three judges traded confused glances.

"Counsel, you just offered your defense, and now the defendant is pleading…guilty?" the judge asked.

"Baron Richthofen is well aware of the implications," Wells said.

Rusty hinges creaked as the metal bar door closed on Richthofen in his cage.

"The court will adjourn briefly." The judge smacked his gavel against a wooden block and the three left the room.

"As your lawyer, I told you this was a very poor tactic," Wells said to the German.

"I must show contempt, show that I am above this English ruse. I was a tool of the propagandists for many years, and I learned how to play the game."

"When you're walking up the stairs to the gallows, or about to get the hood before your firing squad, I want you to remember these words, 'I told you so.'"

"There goes our friend in the blue suit." Richthofen looked over Wells shoulder. The lawyer got a fleeting glimpse of the man as he slipped into the judge's chambers. "No doubt carrying instructions for the judges."

"This isn't a show trial, Baron; how many times do I have to tell you that? Our judicial system has the highest standards in the world." Wells shook his head. "I don't even know why I bother anymore."

"Yours is a country that starves women and children to gain an advantage at the negotiating table. Do not lecture me on standards. Behind you is a man with a round pin of the Swiss flag on his lapel, recognize him?"

Wells glanced to the side.

"That's Schmidt, from the Red Cross," the lawyer said.

"He has a message for me. Go shake his hand and come back."

"Espionage…in front of peers of the realm, in open court. Are you daft?"

"Go on. I will pretend to be angry with you." Richthofen leaned back and crossed his arms.

Wells went to his desk, pretended to read from a folder, then traded pleasantries with Schmidt as to the status of his winter vegetable garden. The Swiss man slipped a folded piece of paper into Wells' palm when they shook hands. Wells fished out his copy of Richthofen's autobiography and let the paper fall between the pages as he brought the book and a pen to the German.

"Sign it, if you like," Wells said. "I dare say it will become much more valuable if they execute you."

"You have a German sense of fatalism. I like that." Richthofen opened the note, smiled, then signed the book with a flourish. "The German Red Cross received my request to stop all the food packages…and the German delegation will officially return to negotiations at Versailles."

"Officially? You mean they've been talking the whole time?"

"There are pragmatists in every government, Mr. Wells. What is done for the public and what is done in private can be very different things." Richthofen passed the book back with a smile.

"You're acting like this is good news."

"Not all good news; now I have to eat English food."

"All rise!"

Wells adjusted his wig and stood behind his desk as the three judges returned. The man in the blue suit closed the door behind them.

"Clear the courtroom," the judge said. "Everyone out."

A team of bailiffs armed with clubs opened the rear doors and ushered everyone out, to a great deal of vocal protests and foul language Wells didn't anticipate in this most formal of locations. Once the room was empty of all but the defendant, judges, and legal counsel...and the man in the blue suit, the judge rapped his gavel.

"The defendant will rise," the judge said. "In light of the evidence presented and Baron Richthofen's plea, a verdict of guilty is rendered in this case."

Wells fought the urge to bury his face in his hands.

Richthofen gave the judges a contemptuous smile.

"We hereby sentence the defendant to be incarcerated for twenty years. However, given the nature of combat...the sentence is commuted." The judge stopped and adjusted his reading glasses as he read from something out of Wells' view.

"The commuted sentence stands on the following conditions; that a clause be added to the final treaty being negotiated at Versailles forbidding Manfred von Richthofen from ever holding military rank in the German military. That he never flies an aircraft again and that he have no involvement with the aircraft industry. The prisoner will be held until such time as the treaty is ratified by all belligerent parties.

"Further, the finer details of this sentence are classified by the Official Secrets Act. Is that last part clear to everyone?"

Mort nodded his head, while Wells stared forward, his jaw slack.

"Wells?" the judge asked.

"Yes, crystal, Your Honor," Wells said.

"Any violation of this sentence and the full period of incarceration will be enforced. Do you understand that, Baron?"

"I believe I understand everything just fine," Richthofen said to the man in the blue suit.

"Court adjourned." The judge used his gavel a final time.

Wells remained behind the desk, his brow furrowed.

"Another victory," Richthofen said.

"What? You're guilty. Twenty years in prison if you ever look at a plane again. How is that a victory?" Wells asked.

"Before you arrived at my jail, I received a map, a map of Germany's new borders. My home is in Schweidnitz, and my home was about to become part of Poland. But that part was in pencil, it could be changed. A little hint for me to cooperate with this circus before it even started."

Wells looked at his client, mouth agape.

"It was then that I knew there was a game being played, and I was but a pawn. Your government thought it could gain an advantage in Versailles by humiliating me through all this," Richtofen continued, his tone condescending once more. "Instead, it managed to anger a nation. I doubt the final treaty will be as severe now that Germans remember who the real enemy is. That note you brought to the Swiss, it contained a few lines for the right people in Berlin. I let them know that I would play the part of the unjustly accused, and that they should be ready to direct the public's emotions in the right direction."

"So, all that about the starving children in Germany, that was a bunch of bollocks?"

"Hardly. The Red Cross will stop the packages, and the treaty will be signed that much faster, ending the blockade. The innocent should not suffer. But we Germans will remember what you've done, Mr. Wells."

"Why all the secrecy?"

"The headlines. My twenty-year sentence will be known far and wide. Then I will be quietly sent back to Germany once the public has another matter to worry about. The change will be blamed on a last-minute plea from the German delegation, and my release will not make the news."

"You've got this all figured out, don't you?"

"One cannot play the propaganda game without learning a few tricks."

"And you'll abide by the terms? Never fly again?"

A guard opened the cage and stepped aside for Richthofen to exit.

"Mr. Wells, if I ever take to the air again, England had better send her best pilots to stop me."

\* \* \* \* \*

**Richard Fox Bio**

Richard Fox is a Nebula Award nominated author, and winner of the 2017 Dragon Award for Best Military Science Fiction or Fantasy novel, author of The Ember War Saga, a military science fiction and space opera series, and other novels in the military history, thriller and space opera genres.

# # # # #

# The Kaiserin of the Seas
# by Christopher G. Nuttall

It was a cold, clear day.

*Oberstleutnant* Karl Holliston allowed himself a private moment of relief as his Messerschmitt Bf 109T levelled out from its harrowing launch. The young officer and his squadron had trained extensively, ever since the *Luftwaffe* had condescendingly agreed to provide the *Kriegsmarine* with a naval variant of the Messerschmitt. Still, Karl was reasonably sure he'd never get used to flying off a carrier deck. *Graf Zeppelin's* deck was longer than the makeshift structures they'd used for their early training, yet the carrier had a pronounced tendency to become extremely unstable when the seas turned rough. Karl had never really respected the British carriers—or the outdated aircraft they carried—until he'd had to deploy from a carrier deck for the first time.

*A few more takeoffs like that, and I just might ask for a biplane,* he thought. The *Swordfish* might be outdated, a laughingstock compared to the *Spitfires* and *Hurricanes* he'd faced during the Battle of Britain, but she was an excellent design for a carrier. It had taken the *Reich* longer than Karl cared to admit to catch up.

*And we wouldn't have done it at all if the Japanese hadn't helped*, he thought, sourly. There was something fundamentally wrong about depending on advice from the little yellow men, although no one could doubt their bravery. *We'd have been messing around with heavier aircraft until the whole project was cancelled and the ships scrapped.*

He looked down as he adjusted course slightly, heading towards the gap between Denmark and Norway. *Bismarck* was clearly visible as she ploughed through the waves, with the heavy cruiser *Prinz Eugen* following in her wake. *Graf Zeppelin* brought up the rear, surrounded by a handful of destroyers. It was the largest and most powerful naval force the *Reich* had put to sea, yet Karl knew they were badly outnumbered. The British could afford to trade two or three battleships for *Bismarck* and her task force, secure in the knowledge that it would be years before the *Reich* could rebuild. And yet…

*They'll have to find us first*, Karl thought. The ocean was vast and the task force, even *Bismarck*, was very small. *And even if they do find us, they'll have to get word back home.*

His lips twitched. The British wouldn't find that easy. Not at all.

\* \* \*

"Well," Admiral Günther Lütjens said. "So far, so good."

*Generalleutnant* Volker Schulze nodded, stiffly. He hadn't found his sea legs yet, and he was starting to fear he'd never find them at all. *Bismarck* was huge, but she was rolling in the waves like a rubber duck in an active toddler's bathtub. Volker had flown through rough skies—he'd flown in the Great War, back when aircraft were little more than pieces of wood held together by string—and yet, he found the ship's constant movement disturbing. He hated the thought of being trapped in a metal tomb if the giant ship capsized and went under. There would be no hope of survival if the worst happened.

He dragged his attention back to Lütjens, somehow. The older man *was*, technically, in command of the operation, even though Volker himself was in command of the air wing. He should be on *Graf Zeppelin*, watching his pilots take off and fly into the distance, but Lütjens had insisted on a private conference. Volker suspected that the admiral had orders from his superiors to assert the *Kriegsmarine's* dominance at all times. There might be a war on—they might be challenging the greatest navy ever to exist—but politics still came first. His lips twitched at the thought. The British RAF might be the *Luftwaffe's* rival, but the *Kriegsmarine* was its enemy.

"Yes, *Herr Admiral*," he said. "So far, so good."

*And if it wasn't for Goering getting himself in trouble*, his thoughts added silently, *we might never have gotten this far.*

He felt a pang of guilt as the admiral led him towards the chart table. Hermann Goering was a genuine war hero, one of the men who had rebuilt the German military after the shame of Versailles and turned it into a war machine that had crushed France and threatened Britain with total defeat. And yet, he was also so firmly wedded to the belief that everything that flew was *his* that he was unable to see the advantages in inter-service cooperation. If he hadn't managed to disgrace himself, if he hadn't lost most of his influence in Berlin, there would have been little hope of convincing him to support the navy. Even so…it hadn't been easy to complete Germany's first aircraft carrier before the deadline. Volker was all too aware that his pilots were practically making procedures up as they went along.

*Then, of course, there's the Kriegsmarine, which is certain they'd have had the Tirpitz done by now if the Graf Zeppelin hadn't consumed so many resources,* Volker thought.

"The British will have to try to intercept us before we round Iceland and fall upon their convoys," Lütjens said as if Volker hadn't heard it before. "Their ships will already be looking for us."

"And we will sink them," Volker said. It wasn't easy to believe, looking at her, but *Graf Zeppelin* was the most advanced carrier in northern waters. She was easily a match for two or three of the Royal Navy's vessels. "And that will be the end of the war."

"Let us hope so," Lütjens said. "Now, about our plans…"

\* \* \*

The days wore on as the task force ploughed through the rolling waves. Karl found himself spending his time flying, sleeping, or wolfing down quick meals before returning to the cockpit…when they were allowed to fly. The weather seemed unpredictable, shifting constantly between clear blue skies and storms that sent fear shivering down his spine. He was an experienced flyer, but he still found the storms terrifying. It wasn't easy to keep his nerve when trying to land on a constantly shifting carrier deck.

It was almost a relief when the recon flights sighted a British ship, too close to the task force for anyone to believe that it hadn't spotted them. Karl watched from above as the British fought to stay close, even though it meant straying within range of *Bismarck's* main guns. Great plumes of water blasted up, suggesting it was only a matter of time before the gunners got lucky and sent their tiny opponent to the bottom of the sea. Karl allowed himself a moment of admiration, before turning the aircraft away and resuming his flight. The pilots had pressed to be allowed to attack the British ship, to test their Japanese-designed torpedoes against a moving target, but the admiral had refused. They didn't have many torpedoes and they would have to be saved for a bigger target. He frowned as he swept the ocean, looking for enemy ships. The weather was changing again…

*There!* His eyes went wide as he saw a pair of giant ships, advancing steadily towards *Bismarck*. Battleships…he was sure they were battleships. He swung his aircraft to one side as he saw a flash of light—the British were shooting at him, trying to down his plane before he could summon help—and gabbled hastily into the radio, warning the task force of the danger ahead. A shell exploded near his aircraft, close enough to give him a fright. The British gunners were good. But then, they'd have to be. The *Luftwaffe* had been trying to sink British ships for the last two years.

*And yet, you're not ready*, he thought, coldly. He pulled back, far enough to be out of danger while keeping the British ships in view. *You don't have the slightest idea what's coming your way.*

\* \* \*

"One battleship, one battlecruiser," Lütjens said, calmly. Behind him, the captain was issuing orders as *Bismarck* picked up speed. "They'll be in gunnery range in twenty minutes."

"We can strike them now," Volker said. "The torpedo bombers can go first."

Lütjens looked doubtful. "And if they fail?"

Volker felt a flash of irritation. "We spent the last year training the pilots," he said. "They're ready."

"You can try," Lütjens said. "But we will prepare for an engagement too."

"*Jawohl, Herr Admiral*," Volker said.

He picked up the radio and began to snap orders. Lütjens had a point, as much as Volker hated to admit it. The *Luftwaffe* hadn't done *that* well against British warships, even when the targets had been practically stationary. The Royal Navy had taken losses, yes, but those losses had been to U-boats and battleships. Lütjens had every reason to be concerned. If intelligence was right, if the British really *had* sent HMS *Hood* after them, *Bismarck* could expect a *real* fight. Everyone knew that *Hood* was one of the toughest ships in the world.

*But also unprepared for modern war*, Volker told himself. The Royal Navy was strong, but most of its ships were outdated. The British had adhered to the Washington Treaty for years, even after it should have been clear that Germany, Italy, and Japan were blatantly cheating. *Their ships have never faced a real threat from the skies…*

He smiled, coldly, as the first flight of torpedo bombers left the flight deck, falling into a rough formation as they struggled for altitude. The British had practically *invented* the aircraft carrier, but they hadn't bothered to develop the concept. In some ways, they'd done the *Reich* a favour. All the old ships, tanks, and aircraft the British and French had kept were little more than a millstone around their neck, forcing them to modernise their older ships while the *Reich* had built new ones from scratch. The appearance of strength was all around them, but the reality? Volker suspected the British were in for a nasty shock.

"They're on their way, *Herr Admiral*," Volker said. "And the British haven't realised the threat."

"They should," Lütjens warned. "They're the ones who sent torpedo bombers to sink the Italians, are they not?"

"Yes, *Herr Admiral*," Volker agreed. "And if they recognised the threat, they would never have sent two ships to engage us without a carrier of their own."

\* \* \*

The British ships were moving faster, Karl noted, as he kept a wary distance from their antiaircraft guns. They were not short of bravery, whatever else they lacked. And yet, they were utterly unaware of the threat closing from the north. It took them longer than it should have to detect the fifteen torpedo-bombers heading towards them at breakneck speed. Karl altered course, fighting to get a better vantage point as the British ships opened fire. Puffs of smoke and flashes of light flared up, below him. The torpedo-bombers flew onwards, keeping as low as they dared. The British would have problems lowering their guns enough to engage the incoming aircraft.

*And they can't dodge in time*, Karl thought, as the first torpedoes were launched. *They're doomed.*

He watched, coldly, as the engagement developed. It looked as if the battleship had been targeted, rather than the battlecruiser; she twisted and turned, firing desperately as she tried to evade the incoming torpedoes. Her captain had nerve, he admitted sourly; few people would risk turning *into* the torpedo path, even though it minimised the chance of a hit. The torpedoes couldn't alter course, once they were fired. But it was too late. A great gout of water blasted up from where a torpedo had struck the British ship, followed by two more. The vessel hove to a stop, down by the stern, listing, and with a severe fire clearly underway someplace aft.

*Well we've certainly hurt her*, Karl thought after a few minutes. *It will probably take a second strike to…*

To his shock, the battleship suddenly vanished underneath a brilliant explosion that moved from her stern forward. *Mein Gott*, he thought, suddenly heedless of his own safety. A giant battleship, a queen of the seas, was gone. He felt a stab of pity for the British sailors. They'd be lucky to survive long enough to be rescued.

The other British ship started to pull back, but it was too late. *Hood*, he thought, finally remembering the pictures from their vessel identification drills. The battlecruiser had survived the torpedo-bombers simply because the aircraft needed to return to their carrier to be rearmed. However, the brief engagement had given *Bismarck* time to come into range.

It was over quickly. The *Bismarck* and *Prinz Eugen* opened fire and quickly found the range. Perhaps stunned at the sudden loss of their cohort, the *Hood's* crew had difficulty finding the range even as they turned their broadside to bear. Still, the old battlecruiser fought valiantly, scoring a handful of hits, before an explosion ripped through her hull. Moments later, she too was gone.

Karl felt hollow as he altered course, heading back towards *Graf Zeppelin*. He felt nothing for the British—they had tried to fight and lost—but he couldn't help feeling that something had changed. The world had changed, now. And what—he asked himself—would it mean?

* * *

"The greatest victory in naval history," Lütjens proclaimed, as they watched the handful of British survivors being plucked from the waters. "The British will not risk engaging us again."

Volker shrugged. The British sailors seemed to be in shock. They had expected a quick victory, not a rapid and complete defeat. The Royal Navy *really* hadn't understood the threat, even though...he shook his head. There was no point in dwelling on it. Lütjens was right. They had given the Royal Navy a black eye from which it might never recover...or encouraged them to hunt the force with a single-minded fury.

"They'll come for us," he said, flatly. The Royal Navy *couldn't* allow *Bismarck* and her escorts to survive, not now. "They can't let us break out into the Atlantic."

Lütjens gave him an odd look. "We *have* broken out," he said. "And by the time the British catch up, we will be ready."

Volker kept his thoughts to himself as he nodded.

*One cannot make a fool see reason*, he thought.

Hours later, as he complimented his pilots, listened to their reports, and passed on the compliments of a grateful *Fuhrer* aboard the *Graf Zeppelin*, the *Luftwaffe* officer was slightly more optimistic. The pilots were pumped, their morale soaring as they realised that *they* had sunk a mighty British battleship. Even the discovery that they'd sunk the *Prince of Wales*, rather than the *Hood*, didn't dampen their spirits. The battleship had been a bigger target, even though her crew had apparently not been ready for battle. The handful of survivors had admitted that when they'd been questioned. They hadn't had the time to work up before they'd been sent into action.

*The next engagement will be harder*, Volker thought.

He listened carefully to the BBC Home Service as the British reluctantly admitted the loss of both *Hood* and *Prince of Wales*. There were few details of the engagement—the broadcaster seemed determined to at least *hint* that *Bismarck* had been damaged—and nothing beyond a grim promise that both ships would be avenged. Volker had no doubt the British *would* be concentrating every ship they could into a mighty fleet, one that would be brought to bear against the task force as soon as possible. But when would they come? The British had lost them. Even the cruisers that had shadowed the ships ever since they emerged from home waters had been left behind, chased off by *Bismarck*'s guns.

*They know logistics better than us*, he conceded, sourly. *They probably have an excellent idea of our cruising range.*

It wasn't something he'd had to worry about, not when he'd been fighting in France. During the Battle of Britain, Volker had been well aware that parts of Britain had been effectively out of range, if only because the *Luftwaffe* hadn't been able to bomb them without the aircraft running out of fuel on the way home. Still, it was hard for him to believe that a *ship* could run out of fuel and simply *stop*. But it could. *Bismarck* had an excellent cruising range; *Graf Zeppelin* did not. There was no way they could be resupplied either, not until they reached a friendly port. The British would not allow a supply convoy to pass through the narrows and reach the task force, even if the task force *could* resupply in the middle of the ocean. It struck him as an immensely difficult and dangerous thing to do.

He sighed as he turned his attention to the map. The ocean was vast, and the ships were very small. The British would be coming. *But when? And where?*

* * *

The room was brightly lit, but the fog of tobacco smoke hung in the air.

Winston Spencer Churchill stood at the head of the table, smoking his cigar and trying not to let his despair show on his face. He'd been quick to understand the danger presented by *Bismarck*, but slower—to his eternal shame—to foresee the combination of *Bismarck* and *Graf Zeppelin*. The German carrier wasn't anything near as tough as the armoured carriers the Royal Navy had built—or so he told himself—but it hardly mattered. She carried enough aircraft to give any British ship that encountered her a very bad day.

*It was a mistake to send* Prince of Wales *out unprepared*, he thought, cursing under his breath as he watched the WREN moving wooden blocks around the chart table. *Of course, who would have thought she'd prove vulnerable to aircraft at sea?* Churchill realized now that neither he nor his admirals had truly grasped the danger posed by carrier-borne aircraft.

*We hurt a handful of Italian ships, but they'd been at anchor, trapped within the harbour and paralysed by a shortage of fuel.* It just hadn't seemed *possible* that two big ships, with layers of armour and room to manoeuvre, could be brought down by a swarm of stinging gnats.

*Like a hero laid low by a malarious mosquito*, he thought angrily. *Which will encourage every other bugger in the swamp.*

Churchill turned his attention to the map of naval stations on the wall, showing installations from Gibraltar and Malta to Hong Kong and Singapore. The Japanese were restless, damn them; Churchill knew it was only a matter of time before they tried to take what they desperately needed by force. They'd only be encouraged, once they heard that two British warships had been sunk. And who knew what the Americans would do? Churchill had no illusions. Unless the

United States entered the war openly, Britain would eventually be starved to death. There would be no hope of keeping the sea lanes open.

He silently cursed his predecessors as the table was updated, once again. *Bismarck* was fast as well as powerful, fast enough to outrun anything capable of sinking her. The irony wasn't lost on him. He and Fisher had used the same rationale back in the Great War, when they'd designed and launched the battlecruisers. And now the Germans had turned it against the Royal Navy. If Chamberlain had realised what the Germans were doing…Churchill gritted his teeth. The fool had wanted peace at any price. He'd turned a blind eye to the warning signs until it was too late.

*Whatever it takes*, he thought as a naval briefer approached him, *those ships have got to be sunk.*

"Prime Minister," the briefer said. "The Admiralty is assembling…"

Churchill listened with half an ear. Two carriers, four battleships…all outdated, compared to the German ships, and unable even to *catch* her unless she sailed into a trap. Even *finding* her was going to be a problem. Where *were* the German ships?

He ground his teeth as the briefer droned to a halt. It didn't seem fair, somehow. The Royal Navy could sink every ship the Germans possessed, and it wouldn't prove decisive, but if the British took major losses…Churchill had no illusions about that too. The British Empire was teetering on a knife's edge. If they couldn't keep the sea lanes open, if they couldn't keep the Italians bottled up, if they couldn't deter the Japanese…

*Parliament is already demanding answers*, he thought, as he approved the plan. His government, too, was hanging by a thread. A defeat now would mean the end. Britain had lost battles and wars before, but this was different. Hitler could not be trusted. Britain would be overshadowed by the *Reich* until she was no better than Vichy France, a slave state in all but name. *And if Parliament rejects me, they'll try to come to terms with a man who sees weakness as an invitation...*

He cleared his throat. The Royal Navy *had* to win the coming battle. It simply *had* to.

* * *

The last few days had been nightmarish.

Karl had been sick, repeatedly, as the weather grew worse and worse. He'd spent most of his time in his bunk, trying unsuccessfully to keep something down as *Graf Zeppelin* pitched and rolled, plunging through giant waves that threatened to capsize the entire ship. The sailors seemed to find it amusing, damn them. He'd heard them laughing at the pilots, mocking the fliers who'd lost their sea legs as quickly as they'd found them. The men who had sunk a British battleship were helpless, unable to run to their aircraft if the British hove into view. Karl suspected the sailors were right. The pilots were helpless in the face of the storm.

It was a very definite relief when the storm broke and the ship stopped rolling from side to side. He stumbled into the mess, ate a dry breakfast and reported for duty, silently wishing they'd spent more time drilling in the ocean before they'd gone to war. The sailors *claimed* that the pilots would be fine, given time, but Karl found it hard to believe. He promised himself that, if they made it home, he'd seek transfer back to the land-based squadrons. Someone else could fly off a carrier, if they wanted to be brave. *Karl* had had quite enough of it.

*Even though we all got promoted*, Karl thought, as he clambered into his aircraft. The *Fuhrer* had been grateful, very grateful. The task force had been honoured. Everyone who had taken part in the battle had been promoted. *I think I want to go home.*

His lips curved into a smile as he started the engine. They wouldn't see home for a long time, but when they did…

"I'll have a story to tell," he muttered. It would impress the girls, he was sure. Girls loved pilots. He'd lost count of how many girls had opened their legs for him, in the years since the war had begun. "And no one will care if I want to stay on dry land from now on."

\* \* \*

"Radar reports a flight of enemy aircraft, closing from the south," Lütjens said. "The British have found us."

*Because you decided to call home*, Volker thought, angrily. He resisted the urge to point it out, again. Lütjens was an old-school admiral, but he wasn't *that* old. He should have known that the British would intercept the message and triangulate the task force's location, even if they couldn't decipher it. *And now we have a British carrier somewhere within striking range.*

He turned his attention to the map, thinking hard. They were—probably—out of range of British land-based aircraft, unless the British intended to take the risk of ditching in the sea and hoping for pickup before it was too late.

*I wouldn't put it past them*, Volker thought grimly. *But I doubt they're that desperate. Yet.*

"It's either *Ark Royal* or *Victorious*," Volker stated, then added, "if your intelligence officers are as smart as they believe."

Lütjens pursed his lips at the implied insult, but Volker wouldn't be surprised to hear that intelligence had missed something. *Even if that something is the size of an aircraft carrier*, he thought. He'd heard enough intelligence officers be wrong with confidence to take everything they said with a sizable pinch of salt. *If intelligence was always right, I'd be sunning myself in southern Kent right now with some turncoat Englishwoman on my lap. Last fifty Spitfires my arse.*

The radar operator was snapping out updates, directing the task force's fighters towards the British attackers. Volker allowed himself another smile, silently relieved that Goering had rendered himself ineffectual with his overdose during Munich. Given how the man had opposed the use of Japanese technology, what would he have said if he'd realised that Volker and his fellows intended to use *Italian* technology?

*The Italians may throw down their guns and surrender at the first sight of a British Tommy, but strangely they know how to work electronics.* It should not have been surprising that the land which had given the world Marconi had designed and built the best radar sets in the world, but the *Reich* had been slow to believe it. God knew it had taken longer than it should to copy the designs, give them a suitable Germanic name and start installing them across the *Reich*. The early engagements between the Royal Navy and the Italians would have gone differently, Volker was sure, if the Italians had made proper use of their own technology...

He shrugged. It didn't matter.

\* \* \*

**K**arl watched with a flicker of admiration as the British *Swordfish* came into view, shifting from side to side as they approached *Graf Zeppelin*. The British CO was smart, Karl noted; smart enough to understand that the carrier was the *real* threat. If the British sunk the German carrier, it would be years before her sister ship could be completed and sent out to pillage the shipping lanes. By then, the British would have a dozen modern carriers of their own.

He put the thought aside as he closed on his target. The British *Swordfish* was old and slow, but far more stable—and manoeuvrable—than his own aircraft. The British pilot jinked from side to side as he tried to get closer, dropping his torpedo a second before Karl opened fire, putting a hail of bullets through the *Swordfish's* wings. He blinked in surprise as the damaged aircraft kept flying, seemingly unconcerned about the damage. The British had designed the aircraft to take a pounding and keep going. He took aim again, putting his bullets through the enemy aircraft's engine. The *Swordfish* tilted, then cart-wheeled out of the sky. Karl barely had time to note that the pilot had attempted to bail out before he was past and searching for another target.

*Poor bastard*, Karl thought. They were far too low for parachutes to work but high enough that the Atlantic would be unforgiving. With as cold as it was, that might be a blessing.

"*Horrido!*" one of his comrades cried, breaking him out of his sympathy.

*We have to cover the carrier*, he thought, as he saw a flight of British aircraft retreating at high speed. It would be easy to run them down, but *Graf Zeppelin* came first. The carrier looked undamaged, although it was hard to be sure. She and her two larger escorts were evading rapidly, as if they expected to be attacked again at any moment. *We cannot let the carrier be sunk.*

He gritted his teeth as another *Swordfish* appeared, flying so low that she was literally flying *under* the German flak. Karl altered course, flying in pursuit. The British were copying the German tactics—which the Germans had copied from the Japanese—but it hardly mattered. The *Swordfish* was old and slow, but there was a very good chance that she would manage to land a blow on *Bismarck*. Karl had seen *Prince of Wales* die. He had no intention of letting *Bismarck* go the same way.

The British pilot was good, very good. And he knew his aircraft. He seemed to pause, his aircraft hanging in the air as if she was about to stall and plummet into the churning waters below. Karl only realised his mistake when it was too late. There was no way he could evade, let alone stop himself without crashing. He shot past the *Swordfish*, allowing the enemy pilot to draw a bead on him. A hail of bullets raced through the air, narrowly missing his aircraft. Karl pulled away, feeling warm liquid trickling between his legs as he also evaded flak from the battleship. *Bismarck* clearly didn't realise that he was friendly.

*Clever bastard*, he thought, as he twisted around. The British pilot hadn't wasted time. He was already closing rapidly with *Bismarck*, readying himself to drop his torpedo at point-blank range. The British clearly had no intention of giving the German battleship a chance to evade. *Clever, but not clever enough.*

Karl gunned the engine, relying on his superior speed to close the range. The British pilot, intensely focused on the battleship, didn't realise he was there until it was too late. Or he was simply determined to land the killer blow before his inevitable death. Karl shot him out of the sky, just in time. He watched, paying a moment of respect, as the enemy aircraft crashed into the water, then turned to search for new targets. The battleship's guns were still firing. Karl just wasn't sure what they thought they were shooting *at*.

\* \* \*

"That was close," Lütjens said, as the enemy aircraft hit the water and vanished. "A few seconds more and we would have been hit."

"I think my carrier has proved her worth, *Herr Admiral*," Volker noted, his tone flat. He'd ordered his torpedo-bombers to launch, in hopes of finding the British ship, but he had a feeling they weren't going to be lucky. The weather was already worsening again. "The *Fuhrer* will be pleased."

"But we have to make a decision now," Lütjens said. "Do we head for Brest? Or do we try to go home?"

Volker wanted to argue, but he knew it would be pointless. The *Graf Zeppelin* was running short on fuel. He hated to turn around and go home without even sighting a British convoy, but they'd more than proved themselves. They could go home and ready themselves for another operation. This time, perhaps, they could be joined by *Tirpitz* and the remaining capital ships. The British wouldn't be able to face them.

"We can't go to Brest," he said, quietly. "We'd be vulnerable to British land-based air, and they would send their entire air force for us after *Hood*."

"True," Lütjens said. He glanced at the map, then shrugged. "We'll head home."

He barked orders. Moments later, the giant ships slowly turned and headed for Germany.

\* \* \*

"The reports are in, Prime Minister," the briefer said. "*Bismarck* has dropped out of sight again."

Churchill nodded, tensely. He'd hoped that *Victorious* would be able to slow the Germans down, but it seemed as if *Bismarck* had absorbed the damage—if indeed the ship *had* been damaged—and carried on. The *Swordfish* might be elderly—he was painfully aware that Britain had only a handful of modern torpedo-bombers—but they were effective, and their pilots knew how to get the best out of them. And yet, it was starting to look as if he'd sent the pilots on a suicide mission. Only two had returned to their carrier, with the senior of the two pilots a mental wreck.

*And if the weather hadn't turned bad*, he thought, *the Germans might have sent our carrier to the bottom too.*

He forced himself to study the map, barely listening to the naval briefer as he yammered on. What would the Germans do? What would *he* do, if *he* were a German? The German ships had to be running short of fuel by now…the carrier, at least. She might not have enough fuel to do anything, but head for port. And where would she go?

"Sir Dudley believes that the Germans will make for Brest," the briefer said. "They can refuel and link up with their other capital ships there…"

Churchill shook his head, cutting off the briefer in mid-explanation. Sir Dudley was a good man, but he—and his staff—suffered from a lack of imagination. Yes, the Germans *could* go to

Brest—the French port was currently playing host to *Scharnhorst* and *Gneisenau*. However, the damages the RAF and Coastal Command had delivered upon those two vessels were a cautionary tale.

*I don't know how many bombers it takes to hole a carrier, but I'd make sure Portal and Harris understood it was their task to find out*, Churchill thought angrily. Churchill had listened to Radio Berlin, gloating about the sinking of *Hood* and *Prince of Wales*. Such a defeat could not be allowed to stand. So, while logic suggested that the Germans would head to Brest, Churchill's instincts told him the Germans knew it'd be safer to go home instead.

*I wonder if they are aware that Force H has transited the Straits of Gibraltar? If so, then they also have to know if they head to Brest, they risk having us bring them to battle when they're short of fuel.*

"They're heading back to Germany," he said. It was a gamble, with everything at stake, but he knew he was right. "And we'll have to meet them on the way home."

"Yes, Prime Minister," the briefer said. "Ah…the Air Chief Marshal wants to deploy the Seafires…"

"Do it," Churchill said.

\* \* \*

The weather shifted constantly as the task force slowly headed home. Karl slowly grew used to days when he was in the cockpit for hours and days when all he could do was sit in the briefing room and pray that the weather cleared enough for him to fly. He had the feeling that it was going to be awkward to explain, once they returned to regular flying. The sooner they set up a naval air arm, the better.

*And hopefully without me*, he thought, as he took to the skies again. Intelligence had warned that there was a British fleet *somewhere* in the area, searching for them, but the weather had been so bad that the British and German ships could have passed within metres of each other without making contact. *I want to go back to dry land.*

His eyes scanned the horizon for signs of trouble, but the seas were clear. It was easy to understand, at times, why the sailors *liked* being at sea. He could believe—easily—that the world had shrunk to the carrier's hull, that there was nothing outside...he shook his head, telling himself not to be silly. The sailors might *like* to talk about the romance of sailing, of being alone on the seas, but it wasn't for him. A life on the ocean wave was the key to a watery grave...a bit of doggerel he'd heard from somewhere.

*Wait a second, what was that?* he thought, turning his head back around. A thrill of excitement flashed through him as he spied a handful of dark shapes, making their way through the icy waters below. Battleships...*British* battleships. The ships had to be British. There wasn't anyone else who operated so far north, save for the *Kriegsmarine* itself, and he knew where its only operational battleship was. Karl altered course back into the clouds, preparing to make a sighting report. The British hadn't seen him yet, as far as he could tell, but that would change.

*And if they don't realise I've seen them*, he thought, *then we might just be able to catch them by surprise.*

\* \* \*

"They got close," Lütjens said. His eyes flickered over the map. "They're far too close."

"They also don't know where we are,"

Volker said. He was a little disturbed that the British *had* managed to get close to the task force, although it was clear the British *didn't* know precisely where the Germans were. *Bismarck* hadn't detected any radio transmissions from prowling British aircraft—or submarines. "We have the advantage of surprise."

"Four battleships," Lütjens pointed out, his tone cautious. "Do you truly think we can take them?"

*My how quickly you go from arrogant ass to the King of Trepidation*, Volker thought unkindly.

"I think we can cripple them," Volker allowed. He was no naval officer, but he could read a map and knew a little bit about his potential targets. Most of the British vessels were slower than *Bismarck* to start with. If they were damaged, *Bismarck* and her consorts could make their escape before the British rallied. "And we can launch repeated strikes to bring the British ships down."

"At least until we get out of range," Lütjens mused. "Or until they launch aircraft of their own."

"If they have a carrier nearby," Volker said. The recon flight hadn't spotted a carrier, but that was meaningless. The British would be foolish to put a carrier in the line of battle. *Graf Zeppelin* was too close to the enemy battleships for *his* comfort. "*Herr Admiral*, I request permission to launch a strike against the enemy ships."

"Do it," Lütjens ordered.

\* \* \*

The aircraft felt heavy as she lumbered into the sky, the weight of the torpedo dragging her down. Karl braced himself as a gust of wind struck his aircraft, wondering if the weather was about to change at the worst possible moment.

The squadron would have to try to return to their ship, *after* dumping their torpedoes in the water. He didn't want to risk landing on an uneven flight deck if it could be avoided. *And the only alternative is ditching in the sea*, he thought, coldly. *And that isn't much of an alternative at all.*

He used hand signals to organise the squadron, directing them to follow him. The British ships were *somewhere* in the trackless wastes of ocean…they couldn't have gone that far, he told himself, even if they *had* sighted him and changed course immediately. But…he put the thought to one side as he picked up speed, the aircraft whining uncomfortably as another gust of wind battered against the cockpit. They had to find the British before it was too late.

*And before the British bring up another carrier or two of their own*, he reminded himself. *They know better than to send their ships against us without air cover now.*

He winced at the thought. A *Swordfish* had come far too close to shooting him down. He didn't want to meet a *Spitfire* or *Hurricane*, if the British had had time to transfer a squadron to the carrier. Intelligence had warned that the British were producing a naval variant of the *Spitfire*, and they'd apparently operated *Hurricanes* in the Med. Karl had faced enough *Spitfires* over England to know he didn't want to encounter another if it could be avoided. The British *had* to be trying—desperately—to get the aircraft into service. They had no choice.

*They should have done it earlier*, he thought, grimly. *I think…*

He cursed under his breath as the British ships suddenly came into view. Four lumbering battleships, heading straight for *Bismarck*. He frowned, then cursed as he realised something he should have guessed from the start. The British ships had radar. They'd seen him right from the start, then followed his heading back towards the *Graf Zeppelin*. It had been sheer luck they hadn't come into range before it was too late. A puff of smoke appeared, too close for comfort. The British ships had opened fire. If there was any doubt that the British knew they were there, it was gone now.

"Prepare to attack," he ordered. "I..."

A glint caught his eye, coming out of the sun. He yanked his aircraft to one side, an instant before a hail of bullets could tear through his cockpit and blow him out of the sky. For a second, his blood turned to ice. A *Spitfire* flashed past him, followed by two more. He swore out loud as he realised what had happened. The British had flown *Spitfires* to their carrier...perhaps more than one carrier. Karl and his fellows had certainly made sure the British had *room* for the modern aircraft.

He snapped out orders as the British fell on his aircraft like wolves on sheep. Karl saw four of his pilots die before they saw the threat, their aircraft plunging towards the water far below. He twisted and fired back, watching a British pilot swing out of the way with effortless ease. Karl swallowed a curse, then took better aim as another *Spitfire* overshot his aircraft. This time, the British pilot was unlucky. Trailing smoke, the other aircraft dropped like a stone.

Karl forced himself to think as the dogfight spun out of control. There didn't seem to be many British aircraft, but they had an edge. Karl's aircraft was too heavy to manoeuvre properly, at least as long as he was carrying the torpedo. He thought briefly about simply dropping it—it *might* hit something worthwhile, although he had a feeling that was just wishful thinking—before sending his aircraft into a dive instead. The framework protested loudly—for a moment, he thought he'd made a dreadful mistake—as he struggled to level out, bare metres above the water. The manoeuvre worked, a pair of Spitfires breaking off as he hurtled low over the waves. The British aircraft had just started circling back when two shark-like shapes slashed into them.

*They launched the second squadron!* he thought. *Graf Zeppelin* had kept a squadron of fighters in reserve just in case the British had launched an airstrike of their own. Clearly someone had noted the approaching *Spitfires* on radar and launched the hasty escort. Screaming in relief, Karl attempted to take stock of how many of his men had survived.

Seeing two other Me-109Ts circling with their weapons, he waggled his wings for them to join up. Seeing the men slide into position, he turned to look for a target. Ten thousand meters away, a British battleship loomed ahead of him, its guns firing wildly in all directions as it turned away from a flight of 109Ts.

*Nelson* or *Rodney*, he thought. Motioning, he led the three 109Ts down into the attack. In the smoke and haze, the British crew did not see the attacking bombers until far too late. Even as tracers flew around him, Karl slipped past a British destroyer and dropped his torpedo, aiming it towards the enemy ship. His two men followed suit, right before one of them was swatted from the sky by a direct hit.

*Come on, come on...* Karl thought once he was through the cauldron of fire. The British battleship gamely tried to reverse its course but was far from agile enough. There was a spout of water forward and, a moment later, another near the stern. Karl felt a wave of elation as the battleship continued to turn, her bow swinging around in a giant circle.

*Maybe steerage*, he thought. He saw a flash of motion out of his eye; a pair of *Spitfires* chasing a 109T.

"All right," he said. His aircraft was far easier to handle, now that the torpedo was gone. "Let's see how you like fighting me now."

\* \* \*

"Two battleships damaged," Volker reported. "The British aircraft were a nasty surprise."

"Recall the aircraft," Lütjens ordered. "We can get out of here."

"No, *Herr Admiral*," Volker said. "We can finish the job."

"No," Lütjens said. "There's a British carrier nearby. We have to keep our fighters..."

"That carrier has launched all her aircraft," Volker said. It was a guess, but he was sure he was right. "If she had more aircraft, she would have *sent* more aircraft. We can send her to the bottom before she has a chance to escape."

Lütjens hesitated, then shook his head.

"No, we have done enough," he replied firmly. "How many torpedoes does your carrier have left? How much fuel?"

Volker pursed his lips. As annoyed as he was, he knew the admiral had a point.

"Well, *Herr Admiral*, we have won something they will call a victory," Volker snapped.

Lütjens gave Volker a sharp look, as if he suspected Volker of mocking him. The *Luftwaffe* officer coolly returned his look.

"Well, perhaps we will have achieved what you flyboys could not last summer," Lütjens replied. Volker felt colour rising in his cheeks as the admiral continued. "This will be a great shock; the vaunted Royal Navy having lost two capital ships and had another two mauled. Judging from the fact the three undamaged battleships turned away, clearly they have had enough for now."

Volker watched the man turn and look out the bridge window.

"We will return, next time with *Tirpitz*," Lütjens said. "Then we will sink their convoys."

"And then the war will be won," Volker agreed.

Visions of glory ran through his head, of German troops landing in a starving and helpless Britain. Perhaps, eventually, the Greater Reich's *Kriegsmarine* would challenge the Americans and land troops in New York and Washington. Certainly fanciful, but with the Royal Navy vanquished, almost nothing seemed beyond their grasp.

*All that remains is the proper application of force*, Volker thought with a smile.

"*Heil Hitler!*" he said.

\* \* \* \* \*

### Historian's Note

Historically, the Germans were slow to develop the concept of carrier-based airpower. They lacked the resources to experiment with carriers, a problem made worse by scrabbles between the *Luftwaffe* and the *Kriegsmarine* over who would control the naval air arm (and disputes within the navy between the capital ship enthusiasts and those who believed that a fleet of u-boats would be a better use of resources.) *Graf Zeppelin* was never completed and never saw active service, although—if she had been completed—she would have been more than a match for comparable British designs. In this timeline, the Germans have taken the plunge and—with help from the Japanese—completed their sole carrier in time for her to sail with the *Bismarck* in 1941.

It is one of World War Two's little ironies that Italy—yes, Italy—effectively led the world in radar technology, at least until 1943. A team of Italian inventors put together a series of radar sets but failed to interest the Italian Navy in actually *using* them until the Royal Navy taught the Italians the value of radar kits. By then, it was too late. In this timeline, the Germans are less resistant to using concepts from other countries and copied—stole—the Italian designs so they could be used by the *Kriegsmarine*.

Although, on the face of it, the *Bismarck* was hopelessly outnumbered and outmatched by the Royal Navy, she was a very serious concern until she was sunk in 1941. She could—in theory—pick and choose her engagements, making it hard for the British to stop her from either picking off isolated warships or sinking convoys at will. A more successful career might have seriously weakened Britain in 1941, particularly if there were fewer warships available to go to the Far East. On the other hand, this might have worked out better for

Britain in some ways. *Prince of Wales* and *Repulse* might not have been sunk near Singapore if they were needed in northern waters.

\* \* \*

### Christopher G. Nuttall Bio

Christopher Nuttall has been planning sci-fi books since he learned to read. Born and raised in Edinburgh, Chris created an alternate history website and eventually graduated to writing full-sized novels. Studying history independently allowed him to develop worlds that hung together and provided a base for storytelling. After graduating from university, Chris started writing full-time. As an indie author, he has published fifty novels and one novella (so far) through Amazon Kindle Direct Publishing.

Professionally, he has published The Royal Sorceress, Bookworm, A Life Less Ordinary, Sufficiently Advanced Technology, The Royal Sorceress II: The Great Game and Bookworm II: The Very Ugly Duckling with Elsewhen Press, and Schooled in Magic through Twilight Times Books.

As a matter of principle, all of Chris's self-published Kindle books are DRM-free.

Chris has a blog where he published updates, snippets and world-building notes at http://chrishanger.wordpress.com/ and a website at http://www.chrishanger.net.

Chris is currently living in Edinburgh with his partner, muse, and critic Aisha.

# # # # #

# Through the Squall
# by Taylor Anderson

## A Destroyerman Story

*I*n *the years since we came to this mysterious, deadly…other Earth aboard the old Asiatic Fleet "four-stacker" destroyer, USS* Walker, *we've beheld countless wonders, experienced adventures beyond our imaginings, suffered tragic losses, and occasionally celebrated triumphs. Yet never have we discovered a sufficiently satisfactory, (to me), explanation for our arrival on this seemingly alternate world, peopled by representatives of often strange, sometimes very different histories. Still, as that statement implies, we were never quite alone. And even from the beginning, we always had each other aboard our battered, leaky old ship. Such was not the case for everyone, and we sometimes discovered the sad, abandoned relics of other "crossings," occasionally—probably—from the very same world and circumstances we ourselves were drawn. One example of this was the forlorn, half-sunken hulk of a PBY Catalina flying boat that Ben Mallory salvaged off a lonely island beach and which, when mended a bit, gave indispensable service to our cause in the early months of the Lemurian's bitter struggle against the Grik. Yet no one knew how the plane came to be there, and the fate of its missing aircrew remained still another melancholy mystery until a long-delayed account of its ordeal was recently related to me and I was able to record it here.*

Excerpt from Courtney Bradford's *The Worlds I've Wondered*, University of New Glasgow Press, 1956

\* \* \*

*March 1, 1942*

Ensign Mike Hayes was tired, damn tired, and he'd drifted off almost as soon as the big, lumbering PBY-4 flying boat climbed out of Tjilatjap, Java, at dawn. He'd managed this despite the mind-numbing roar of two engines almost directly overhead and the dull, gut-clenching fear that had twisted his insides for the last three months. Oddly, the disaster in the Java Sea and the virtual annihilation of the US Asiatic Fleet—to which VP-101 Squadron of Patrol Wing 10 had been attached— hadn't really made his anxiety any worse. Nor had the departure of the squadron's *only* other surviving plane for Perth, Australia. It was like he'd reached a point where mere dread, regardless how profound, couldn't pass. And the realization *"Big Boobs"* was the last, biggest, slowest prey—in the air, at least—for Japanese planes prowling the south coast of Java, simply couldn't conquer the exhaustion he'd accumulated. Fear and danger, inspired by strange, relentless invaders in an exotic setting, had become the norm for the 22-year-old from tiny Harrisville, Michigan. Only a call to duty or something *un*usual was likely to stir him at the moment.

Mike Hayes got both when he heard the nervous voice of *Big Boobs'* pilot, Lieutenant (jg) Dave Wheeler, murmur "What the hell?" over the interphone headset covering his ears. It was the tone more than the words that jerked him awake. Wheeler wasn't Superman; he was only 24 himself and had to be just as scared on some level as the rest of the hard-used PBY's diminished six-man crew. But he was born to lead, and he'd never, ever, let fear touch his voice before. Mike pushed the brim of his ball cap up and straightened in his co-pilot's seat. Blinking, he followed Wheeler's gaze out forward and slightly to the left. "Whatcha got?" he asked.

Wheeler glanced at him apologetically, and his voice firmed. "Ah? Oh, sorry, Mike. Didn't mean to wake you. I know you, Garza and Pike worked all night just so this turd would fly." Aviation Machinist's Mate First Class Neville (call me "Nev," dammit) Garza was *Big Boobs'* flight engineer, and AMM3c Jed Pike currently manned a .50 caliber in the starboard observation blister in the waist. Both were solid guys, and Mike doubted either—or Radioman Second Class Don Frazee, who'd been up almost as long—had been asleep. He felt especially sorry for the 18-year-old Frazee who'd have to scramble forward from his radio compartment to the nose turret, if called on, and man a gun he'd never fired. He would've been the bombardier there, too, if *Big Boobs* carried bombs this trip. Wheeler and Mike had to fill in for the navigator the plane didn't have.

There was only one other man in the plane, Seaman Third Class Colin Sanford, and it was pointless asking him to take up any slack since "slack" pretty much described the tall, gangly, redhead. He'd come to *Big Boobs* as the sole replacement for three good men killed or injured when the PBY got shot up attempting to bomb a Japanese cruiser. Disgusted and mad, Garza compared the mission to sending a pelican to lay a crap on half a dozen goose hunters. *Big Boobs* limped back to Surabaya, her base at the time, but lost a third of her tight-knit crew. Sanford only added insult to injury. Mike originally thought his surly, uncommunicative manner was his way of coping with a new assignment in the midst of their current predicament, along with the same fear everyone felt, but it went deeper than that. He flat didn't *care* about anybody but himself, and never became part of the crew. Worse, though he wouldn't refuse an order, he'd carry it out with such sullen incompetence that somebody else always had to fix what he screwed up. Jed Pike absolutely hated him, but couldn't cover both waist guns by himself. That was probably the only reason he hadn't thrown Sanford out of the plane.

Mike yawned. "Skip it. I think…" he stopped when he saw what caught Wheeler's attention. A large greenish rain squall loomed ahead like a miles-long, impenetrable cliff, standing as high as they flew. Mike blinked. Squalls weren't unusual here, even sometimes as heavy and dense as this, but most were filmy, insubstantial things, building up to touch the sea with wispy gray fingers before passing away. *Not* seeing a squall somewhere on the horizon would've been remarkable, especially in the afternoon. But this one was different, the color all wrong, and it radiated a disconcerting sense of…energy unlike anything he'd ever seen.

Lt. Wheeler chuckled forcefully, tilting his head behind them toward the rising sun. "It has to be the light."

"Are we flyin' *through* that?" came Pike's crackly, unhappy voice over the interphone. The switchbox in the cockpit had been damaged, and Frazee had to re-wire the interphone so everyone was on the same circuit. Peering through his blister, Pike would see what brooded ahead as well as anyone.

"What the hell is that?" came Sanford's higher-pitched query. "We *aren't* going into that!"

"Shut up, you, or I'll shut you up!" Pike snapped.

"*Everybody* shut up!" roared Nev Garza in his narrow engineer's space up under the wing. Like Frazee, still in the radio compartment, he probably barely saw the weird squall.

"Right, keep the jabber down," Wheeler said, pulling slightly back on the wheel. The one in front of Mike moved too. "We'll see if we can get over it." He paused. "Look, fellas, let's keep it together. We have *one* job left, then we can look out for ourselves. Most of what's left of ABDAfloat is heading south to Australia, and the rest is making for the Sunda Strait and Ceylon. We'll take a quick look to see if the strait's clear, then we're off to Ceylon too. We'll finally be *done* with all this."

"Why do we even have to look?" Sanford whined. "The dope is the Japs're already *in* the strait and sank the *Houston* there last night. Why stick our necks out for a couple of Limey ships? They don't give a damn about *us*!"

"I heard that rumor too, and it might be true. That's why we have to check," Wheeler explained through clenched teeth. "And the British ships, *Exeter* and *Encounter*, have three of ours along: *Pope*, *Walker* and *Mahan*." Wheeler's voice turned sharper than Mike had ever heard it. "But I don't care if they're American, British, Australian, or Dutch. We've all been on the same bush-league team out here, and run through the same Jap wringer, so I don't want to hear any more of that 'us and them' crap." He sighed. "Finding out if the Japs're there or not is our *last* mission for the Asiatic Fleet. Probably Patwing 10, too. Now *cut the chatter*," he added harshly.

Immediately, somewhat hesitantly, Pike spoke up. "Ah, sir? There's a ship down there, almost right below."

"Have a look, Mike," Wheeler said, waiting until Mike raised his binoculars, then banking to the right.

The movement and vibration of the big plane made the binoculars difficult to focus, but Mike saw well enough. "Mid-size auxiliary freighter, single stack, crates on deck, making for Tjilatjap...That's the old *Santa Catalina*, carrying P-40 fighters in for the Army," he declared, then shook his head. "Too late. They'll never...Wow! Damn! Jap planes're working her over. Big bomb splash, close aboard!"

"What kind of planes?" Wheeler demanded.

"Carrier dive bombers. Maybe *Vals*."

Wheeler hesitated, probably tempted to swoop among the bombers to break up their attacks. He'd done it before, when *Big Boobs* was healthier and had a full crew of experienced gunners, even for the tunnel gun "stinger" aft. Finally, he shook his head and leveled out. The peculiar green squall was closer now, and he hadn't climbed over it yet. "Nothing we can do," he said grudgingly, "and we have a final chore. Everybody keep your eyes peeled. Carrier bombers will have fighters around. Frazee, get down in the nose. We might need you on the gun."

The dark-haired radioman reluctantly left his communications gear and squeezed between Mike and Wheeler. Going down on all fours, Frazee slithered under the dual control column and instrument panel to crawl behind the .30 caliber machine gun in the Plexiglas-enclosed turret in front of the cockpit. He was just in time. An instant later, *Big Boobs* was jolted by a stream of 7.7mm and 20mm projectiles, punching bright holes in one side of the compartment Frazee just left, and out the other, blowing confetti-like pieces of shredded paper and aluminum fragments all the way into the cockpit. Mike caught a glimpse of the gray-white belly and red "meatballs" of a Japanese fighter flashing over them from left to right.

"Damn it, Sanford! That one came from your side!" Wheeler bellowed. "If you aren't going to shoot at them, at least call them out so someone else can!"

Sanford didn't reply.

"He can't do shit, curled up on the goddamn deck!" Pike called back in disgust. "Useless bastard!"

"There's another one coming in on the right!" shouted Garza, with only his little window to see. *Big Boobs* shuddered again, from the combination of Pike's .50 caliber firing, and more savage bullet and shell impacts tearing through the fuselage. Frazee's nose gun clattered when the plane roared past, but his tracers followed way behind. "They're eatin' us alive, Skipper," Garza's voice continued, sounding strained. He coughed. "An' they chewed up the port fuel tank, at least. Fuel's sprayin' out like crazy."

Wheeler craned his head around to see, but couldn't.

"He's right, Lieutenant," Pike confirmed. "I just shut the port blister. It was sucking fuel into the plane—an' Sanford's not usin' the gun anyway," he added with a snarl.

Mike watched Wheeler do the mental calculations; at least two fighters, three times as fast and infinitely more agile, had already shot them up pretty bad. And they only had one gunner they could count on. Their attackers had probably figured that out and would simply approach from another quarter. If Wheeler didn't do something fast, they'd soon be falling, burning to the sea.

"Duck into the squall!" Mike urged. "Even if they chase us in, they'll never see us."

Wheeler looked at the looming storm, now almost directly ahead. Regardless of the jam they were in, he hesitated. Mike understood, since he couldn't escape a foreboding sense that the greenish squall was somehow worse. All the same, it took Wheeler less than three seconds to push the steering column forward. The big plane dove, gathering speed as it plummeted down, aiming at a point about half-way up the towering wall of water.

Only one enemy plane came after them, and its pursuit was half-hearted. The PBYs angle was such that it would enter the squall before the Japanese pilot was close enough for a certain kill, and aerial combat simply couldn't proceed when canopies turned opaque from pounding rain. That didn't stop the enemy flyer from sending them some parting gifts. *Big Boobs* shook and clattered again when a long burst of machine gun and cannon fire marched up her spine. The fusillade walked across the middle of her wing between the engines, blowing through and making big holes in the hull when the misshapen projectiles exited. Even so, Mike doubted the noise of destruction would compare to the booming thunder of the squall. And he was right—but not like he'd expected. In the instant before *Big Boobs* roared into the greenish, now almost phosphorescent curtain, he got the distinct impression the raindrops weren't really falling, but just hanging...suspended. He assured himself it was because they were still diving, falling as fast as the rain, and then *Big Boobs* rumbled when she hit it.

For a moment, except for the swirling darkness smeared across the windscreen, blotting out all visibility, everything seemed as it should, and a surge of relief flooded the young ensign while excited voices crowded the interphone. Pike was yelling triumphantly that he'd winged their attacker as it peeled away, and Frazee was shouting that he'd never been so glad to see rain in his life, before urgently requesting to return to his post behind the cockpit. Sanford contributed nothing, of course, but Mike was surprised not to hear Garza—

or Lieutenant Wheeler—tell everyone to pipe down after the first celebratory moment. Looking at their pilot, he was stunned to see Wheeler staring wide-eyed and ashen-faced at the instruments in front of him. That's when Mike realized not only were the instruments going crazy, they were covered with blood.

For an instant he was too stunned by his first discovery for the second to really register. The altimeter needle was spinning like a prop and the turn and bank indicator was doing stuff Mike would *feel* if the plane did them too. The magnetic compass was rolling erratically and the gyro compass had simply quit, but every gauge that relied on air pressure for any reason was rising fast. He did feel that, and gasped when it seemed like his eyes were being mashed into his head and he convulsively retched in the gap between him and Lieutenant Wheeler—right on top of Radioman Frazee, who in his own obvious misery, was crawling back to the space he considered "his."

"Help the Skipper," Mike managed to shout at Frazee. "I think he's hit." On top of whatever other injuries he'd sustained, Wheeler was feeling the same…other discomforts, and as soon as his co-pilot grasped the somewhat flat-topped, oval-shaped wheel, Wheeler groaned and let go, slouching back in his seat.

"I gotta try to straighten us out," Mike hissed at Frazee, who was practically climbing the pilot to look him over, even while retching himself. But controlling the plane in zero visibility without any instruments would be virtually impossible for anyone, even Wheeler. Mike later thought there'd been other unusual phenomena, like a keening, screeching sound right inside his head, but he was so focused on what he was doing, he decided it was just somebody screaming. Maybe him. He also dismissed the sudden, violently upward lurch he felt, but terrified and flying blind, he might've done that himself as well. He had no idea how long he flew like that, fighting the torrent and the bucking, damaged plane, occasionally risking glimpses at Wheeler as Frazee frantically described and tried to patch his wounds. It felt like hours, but was probably only minutes before the battered, staggering plane exploded into sunlight, streaming a rainbow of water mixed with leaking fuel.

"*What the hell was that?*" demanded Pike over the interphone, his normally gruff, somewhat belligerent voice several octaves higher than usual.

"Damned if I know," Mike barked back. "Worst weather I ever flew through." That wasn't saying much, considering his inexperience.

"*You* flew…where's the skipper?"

"He's hit," Mike replied, looking nervously at Wheeler, "but he's okay," he added, as if wishing would make it so. "Keep your eyes peeled for Japs." He had a sudden thought. "And send Sanford to check on Garza." There hadn't been a word from the flight engineer. He only heard one side of the bitter exchange that followed, but eventually Pike reported "He's going."

"How's Mr. Wheeler?" Mike asked Frazee.

"I'm okay," Wheeler replied himself, voice a little wispy.

"No bullets hit him," Frazee reported. "Some chunks of what they threw around messed up his right arm and shoulder pretty bad, though. And he lost a lot of blood before I plugged the leaks."

"Thanks Frazee," Wheeler said with a weak smile. "Go check your radio gear, and help Sanford with Garza." He looked at Mike and nodded sheepishly at his useless arm. "You got her?"

"I got her, Skipper," Mike confirmed, wrapping his fingers more tightly around the vibrating wheel.

"Garza's dead," Sanford practically shouted over the flight engineer's microphone, his voice uncharacteristically animated. "*Boy* is he dead! Couple of Jap cannon shells blew him all over the place!"

"Well…get him out of his seat and tell me what his instruments say," Wheeler ordered, some of his old forcefulness returning.

"No! Hey! That's not my job! I don't know what any of those gizmos mean, and there's blood all over the place!"

"There's blood in here too!" Mike snapped, more annoyed than usual by Sanford's complaints.

"You don't have to do anything," Wheeler assured. "Not yet, at least," he added cryptically. "But we're losing fuel, maybe a lot, and I need you to tell me how much." The flight engineer of a PBY-4 had numerous duties in flight, some of which could only be performed in his isolated, elevated position. Many of his gauges mirrored those in the pilot's compartment, but he could also monitor how much engine oil was in the tanks and send it where it needed to go, as well as the temperature of every cylinder of both Pratt & Whitney R-1830-72 Twin Wasp engines. He controlled the cowl flaps and air intake to the carburetors, and fine-tuned the rough mixture settings the pilot made for best efficiency. Perhaps most important of all, only the flight engineer could monitor the fuel level in both tanks by means of a pair of sight glass gauges—and the wing floats had to be raised and lowered from his compartment. With a new surge of alarm, Mike suspected that was something Wheeler might have to ask the reluctant gunner to do.

Sanford didn't reply, but directly they felt more than heard the heavy thud of Garza's unstrapped corpse striking the deck two compartments back. A moment later, Sanford's surly voice complained there was blood all over the headset he put on.

"What's our fuel level?" Wheeler asked, calm but strained.

"It's…let me see, it's dark up there and the light's…shit! It's *gone*! We're out of gas!"

"That's impossible!" Pike snapped over the interphone. "We had full tanks, and as much as we're losing, it ain't *that* much!"

"Come look for yourself! We're out of gas!"

"Let me look," Mike suggested.

Wheeler shook his head and winced at his shoulder again. "No. If he's right, we'll have to set down in a hurry and I can't do it."

"I can't either!" Mike protested. "I've only done it once, and nearly cracked us up!" Just as the scattered instrument and control layout of a PBY Catalina implied that their designers never imagined they'd lose the services of a competent flight engineer, the Navy must've never supposed the pilot might also be incapacitated. Co-pilots were generally trained to fly—something else—and sent to PBYs to learn on the job. Unfortunately, due to the specific and unique skills required to operate the big planes, especially when landing and taking off, a co-pilot's education in those areas might be unusually prolonged. Particularly after American planes of any sort in the region had become so rare and precious. Mike felt comfortable holding *Big Boobs* straight and level while his skipper took a catnap, but that was about it.

"Sure you can," Wheeler assured him unconvincingly. "And it doesn't matter if you bang her up a little, this time, as long as you get her down in one piece," he added with a touch of sadness.

"The dumb shit's right," Pike confirmed somberly, obviously having gone to see for himself. "Sanford, I mean," he hastened to add. "We *are* out of fuel, or almost. There's a little more in the starboard tank than port, but we better start looking for a place to land."

"Fine," Wheeler snapped back, "now get back where you belong and watch for Japs!" Mike couldn't tell if Wheeler was angrier that Pike left his post, or that Sanford's incompetence, belligerent idleness—whatever it was—had caused him to think he had to.

Frazee stuck his head up between the two pilots.

"Nothing on the horn but static, now," the radio operator said. "Maybe the radio got shot up too? Doesn't look like it at a glance. Maybe the aerial's gone."

Before they were attacked there'd been constant, desperate appeals for aid, mostly from merchant ships trying to escape the Dutch East Indies and falling prey to the Japanese. Frazee displayed a folded map. "But I might have a place we can go to roost. "

Mike looked where he pointed; Wheeler seemed to be having trouble focusing his eyes. "Panaitan Island? That's right in the middle of the Sunda Strait. If the Japs really are there, they'll snap us up for sure."

Frazee shook his head. "All the dope had the Japs up around Bantam Bay—if they *did* get *Houston* and *Perth* last night. That's more than a hundred miles to the northeast. And if they're landing on Java, that's where they'll be. Why would they care about a crummy island on the other side of the strait?" He shrugged. "Besides, if the rumors were hogwash after all, and the guys we were scouting for make it through, we might signal them to pick us up."

It sounded reasonable. It sounded like a chance. But if the Japanese *were* in the strait and *did* sink the two Allied cruisers, the wounded British *Exeter* and her four destroyer escorts were doomed as well. Especially in daylight.

The port engine gasped and sputtered a moment and the battered seaplane bucked. "How far?" Wheeler asked tensely.

"About twenty miles," Frazee replied, tone less confident than before.

Wheeler looked at Mike. "Ok, that's what we'll do. It makes sense. The Dutch'll fight. Our guys too. It'll take a while for the Japs to crawl all over Java and they probably won't much care about an isolated island. We'll head for there. Any planes?" he called back to the waist.

"Nothing, sir, not a speck." Pike's voice sounded vaguely surprised. "Maybe the ones that jumped us were low on fuel and had to turn back."

"Doesn't mean there won't be more," Mike warned. "Keep looking."

The engine coughed again.

"Are we going to crash?" demanded Sanford.

"No," Wheeler said definitively, glancing meaningfully up at the mixture controls next to the throttle levers overhead. He couldn't adjust them with his mangled arm. Mike pursed his lips and leaned the engines out as far as he dared. They started to pop and clatter, but when he looked at Wheeler, the other man only nodded and made a "take her down" motion. At barely a thousand feet, the air was thicker and the engine really started to struggle. Mike figured the cylinder head temperatures were going through the roof, and Wheeler nodded back at the mixture control. Mike fed the engines a little more fuel and they flew like that for ten or fifteen minutes, laboring low above a jutting peninsula on the far west coast of Java. Back over the sea once more, all eyes—except maybe Sanford's—scanning the sky for trouble, Frazee pointed ahead at a low-lying, jungle-darkened shape about the same size as the peninsula they'd just overflown.

"Still no planes?" Wheeler asked, his voice noticeably softer than before. "Anybody see any ships?"

"Nothing, sir," Frazee told him, still leaning over the pilot's shoulder, eyes scanning the sky around them, or comparing the island to the one on the map in his hand. "Place looks…different from what it shows here, but that's nothing new." One of the Asiatic Fleet's—and PatWing-10's—biggest problems all along had been the lousy, sometimes ancient charts the Dutch had provided them.

"Gotta be it," Frazee decided.

"Surf looks pretty rough," Mike worried aloud as *Big Boobs* rumbled across a little spit of land and started over a bay about five miles across on the southwest side of the island. "Could be a little smoother in that northern corner over there," he added without much assurance. He glanced anxiously at Wheeler.

"You're fine," the pilot assured. "Take her down a little lower, but keep your speed up around ninety knots. Nothing fancy, hey? Just take her straight in. Sanford, are you listening?"

"Yeah."

"Are you still in Garza's seat?"

"Yeah," Sanford replied resentfully.

"Good. Right in front of you, to the left, is a lever in a little box with a knob on the end. It says 'up,' 'off,' and 'down,' got it?"

"Yeah."

Wheeler coughed wetly and to Mike's alarm, a little blood flecked his lips. "Move the lever down for three or four seconds, then shift it back to 'off.' Do it now."

"Okay. Hey! There's these two socket-looking things spinning in front of me!" Sanford accused.

Mike sighed with relief and a glance out to starboard confirmed the float was coming down. Lt. Wheeler couldn't have been looking forward to talking the whiny Sanford through the process of manually lowering the floats. Mike had been half afraid they'd have to.

"That's fine, Sanford," Wheeler said. "They're supposed to do that. Means you did it right. Now look out your windows to either side. Can you confirm both floats are down and locked?"

"They're down," Sanford responded. "Don't know how to tell if they're locked."

"Take her down, Mike," Wheeler gasped. The port engine gasped as well, and chose that moment to die.

"Shit!" Mike hissed, reaching for the throttle control box and mashing the button that would feather the flailing prop. Without thinking, he then wrenched the throttle lever to the closed position and flipped the ignition OFF. He might not be the most proficient PBY pilot in the world, but he was a pilot. Pushing the nose down, he started to advance the throttle on the starboard engine, but Wheeler said "Wait. Look at those swells down there. You're going to have to stall her anyway."

Mike looked at him in near panic.

"It's okay. I've done it a hundred times. Just ease her down to about twenty or thirty feet and around seventy knots, then inch the column back until she stalls. I know, sounds crazy, but it works."

With the jungle and white-sand beach quickly approaching beyond the marching surf, Mike nervously did as he was told. Nose down to maintain the speed Lt. Wheeler recommended, Mike waited until he thought the crests of the rollers might actually touch the keel, then pulled back on the column. *Big Boobs* hit the water with a deafening, bone-shaking *boom*, pancaking down in the trough between the rollers.

"*Now* give her the gas," Wheeler cried. "I'll help you with the rudder!"

Pushing the throttle to the stop, they both stepped on the rudder pedals to counteract the thrust and keep them heading for the beach instead of broaching-to in the marching waves. Lt. Wheeler might've done this before—Mike doubted he'd really done it often—but Mike never had, and the thought of one of their floats going under, pulling the wing around and taking a wave across it...

*If we ever reach the beach, it'll be in pieces.*

By some miracle, it didn't happen like that, and *Big Boobs* practically surfed into the relatively mild waves washing up in the shallows. Mike started to retard the throttle but Lt. Wheeler stopped him.

"Just run her right up on the beach." Mike could only nod, doing his best to hold his bucking controls and make the rudder keep them straight. Moments later, the big flying boat bumped the sand for the first time, but her inertia, thrust, and the following waves carried her on, bumping and mushing across the slick white sand. The last big wave finally left her half on shore, it seemed, but she wasn't going any farther.

"Couldn't've done better myself," Lt. Wheeler said, leaning back in his seat, closing his eyes. "Get our people out."

Shutting down the starboard engine, Mike unstrapped and reached up to unlatch the panels on each side of the cockpit roof and slide them back. Spray spritzed him as another wave surged around the plane, shifting it alarmingly.

"Hey!" Sanford called, voice high, "we're sinking!"

Mike looked behind to see water fountaining up through many more bullet wounds than he'd ever suspected the plane had suffered. "Get the ration and medical kits. And weapons," he cried. All the men had pistols, a mix of 1911 .45s and whatever they might personally prefer. Wheeler carried a Colt Army Special .32-20 in a shoulder holster, for example, favoring revolvers, as well as the fact he could carry fifty rounds for the thing in his pockets. There was also a 1903 Springfield and two Thompson SMGs aboard. Pike had gathered them all while Frazee listened to the radio a few minutes more before shutting down the generators and all the electrical switches in his quickly flooding compartment. The plane was resting firmer on the sand, but only because it was filling with water. Pike sloshed forward, pushing Sanford in front of him. They had to wait—Sanford impatiently—while Mike and Frazee helped Wheeler out of the plane, then they clambered out the top of the cockpit and onto the sea-scoured sand. Still helping Wheeler—practically dragging him now— Mike shouted for Sanford to pull the anchor cable out of the access hatch in the bow of the plane and follow them to the trees.

"What for?" grumbled the red-headed sailor.

"So it doesn't wash away, you idiot," Pike snapped, still loaded down with weapons. "Who knows how long we'll be here and we might need it, or stuff in it. The radio, for one."

"We ought to burn the damn thing before the Japs spot it," Sanford retorted.

"And they won't see the smoke?" Frazee shot back. Even the young radioman was getting sick of Sanford's attitude. It might be more than that, though. He'd seemed particularly distracted since his last moments with the radio. Then again, they'd just made a forced landing on a strange island in the path of the Japanese juggernaut. It would be weird if they weren't all a little tense, under the circumstances.

Sanford glumly trudged back to the plane through sand-sifting surf and popped the hatch on the left side of the nose, under the turret. Fishing the anchor out, he tossed away the buoys and unrolled the cable back toward the shade of the trees where Mike and Frazee had laid Wheeler down. Frazee had opened a medical kit and was using scissors to cut Wheeler's shirt while Mike examined the damage revealed, gently sopping blood from torn flesh. Pike had leaned a Thompson and the Springfield against another tree, wrapping a web belt with canteen, knife, holster, and magazine pouches around his waist. He'd extracted one of the longer twenty-round magazines and was loading a Thompson for himself. "Secure that cable to one of these bigger trees," Pike instructed Sanford. He shrugged. "Might as well arm yourself, too."

Like Mike and Frazee, Sanford wore a 1911 Colt in a holster at his side, but looked askance at the Springfield and SMG. "Those things are heavy," he complained, "and I'm no good with a rifle."

Mike sent him a frown, suspecting Sanford objected more to the burden of responsibility to the rest of them that carrying one implied, than he did to the actual weight. "Fine. I'll take the rifle. Frazee, you take the Tommy gun." He looked at the young radioman, sprinkling a packet of sulfa on Wheeler's wounds. "Did you get anything on the horn, there at the last?"

Frazee wiped sweat from his brow and nervously cleared his throat. "Yeah, from *Santa Catalina*…and that was *it*," he added significantly. "No other traffic at all."

"Really? What did she say?"

Frazee shook his head. "Didn't make any sense. The Japs beat her up pretty bad, like we figured, before that squall crawled over her." He looked at Mike. "Weird as it was for us, her radioman made it sound even worse on the water. Really shook the guy up. Anyway, he was screaming his head off for help, scared they'd never make Tjilatjap before they sank, and talking crazy about fish—he said *fish*—eating men *in* the ship who were trying to stop the flooding."

Frazee shook his head again, clearly unnerved by what he'd heard and obviously sorry for anyone who could lose it that bad, but worried about something else as well.

"What got me was, there was nothing—*absolutely nothing else*—out there making a peep," Frazee said. "Before we went through that creepy storm, every frequency was jammed with distress calls; tramp freighters begging for reports on where the Japs were, Dutch fishing boats—or cruisers, for all I know—babbling away, probably asking for the same dope."

The radioman paused, looking out at the water.

"But after it passed, there was nothing but *Santa Catalina* and us. It just isn't possible. If I could still hear her, I should hear the rest, but they were all just…gone. And either I couldn't transmit or *Santa Catalina* couldn't receive, so I couldn't even tell her we were out here."

"That damn squall wasn't right," Pike confirmed, gazing up and down the beach, looking for threats. He poked the muzzle of his Thompson up at some colorful, flitting shapes overhead. "And neither is this island. I'm no bird expert, but I guess I've seen most of the screwy sea birds they got around here. Not these. They look more like flying *lizards* than any damn bird!"

Mike glanced up to see the gunner was right, but was even less an ornithologist than Pike. Wheeler seemed interested, but now that he was otherwise comfortable, his pain was drawing most of his attention. A dose of morphine distracted him from everything while Mike and Frazee bound him up.

The morning passed into afternoon while they quietly discussed their options, increasingly relieved—if somewhat surprised—not to see or hear any aircraft snooping about. Weird birds aside, anything in the air at this point was certain to be Japanese. Just as surprising, even though they had a pretty good view of the main body of the strait through a gap in the jungle on the other finger of land forming the northern barrier of the bay, they saw no smoke of passing ships. *Any* ships.

"So what now?" Pike asked quietly so as not to disturb Wheeler's rest, finally drawing closer to sit in the sand beside all but Sanford. Even now, the gangly malcontent kept himself apart. Mike was flattered but concerned that Pike was so willing to defer to him. He was an officer, of course, but the other man was older and a lot more experienced. He cleared his throat. "Obviously, if the Japs spot the plane, we have to get away from it. Otherwise, we'll stay close to it for the night. Hopefully, Mr. Wheeler will feel better tomorrow and have some ideas."

Pike glanced skeptically at the wounded man, but nodded. "What about Nev Garza?" The two had been friends. "We have to bury him."

Mike nodded, ashamed he hadn't already thought of that. "Right." He glanced at Sanford, but mentally shook his head. "Frazee, you stay with Mr. Wheeler. The rest of us will get Garza out of the plane and give him a decent grave. It'll likely be dark by then, and we'll get some rest. Start fresh in the morning."

"Do *you* have any ideas?" Pike pressed.

Uncomfortable, Mike glanced at Wheeler.

"Well...we'll need water," he said. "And food, eventually. We can't stay here long, that's sure."

Mike looked down the shore.

"I guess we should follow the shoreline and look for natives. Anybody know if there are natives here?"

Nobody answered, the crew all giving each other sideways glances.

"Well, if there are, we'll try to get a boat and sneak out from under the Japs." He shrugged, somewhat helplessly. "That's all I have, fellas."

Pike took a deep breath and stood. "Good enough, and about all there is. Let's get Nev."

Advancing on the beached and flooded plane, now barely shifting as the surf washed around it, Pike stopped a moment. The others did too.

"I liked that plane," Pike murmured. "Me and Nev were in her almost a year. Longer even that Lieutenant Wheeler."

"Why did you call her '*Big Boobs?*'" Mike asked.

"That's easy enough to figure," Sanford grouched as if lecturing an idiot. "Those two big engines sticking out, right up front."

Pike sneered at Sanford, but then nodded at Mike. "Yeah. Never painted the name on her, though. Nev was going to, whether Admiral Hart liked it or not, but always figured there'd be time later. Then there wasn't any."

Mike nodded. "Yeah. Sorry. Let's get this over with. Snag anything you see that we might use while we're in there."

They dug Nev Garza's grave a short distance into the trees, unsure how high the tides ran. The digging was easy, but they were constantly kicking strange, aggressive little lizards away from the mangled, parachute-shrouded body. Frazee, not far away, reported he was having the same problem with lizards around Lieutenant Wheeler. And there were equally aggressive crabs with large, lumpy-looking claws and tails like lobsters. Sometimes they got preoccupied with the lizards and the men accepted the grim humor of the predators fighting each other to take possession of them. The growing number of attackers made it clear they'd have to keep a guard all night, however. Not just to protect their wounded pilot, but themselves as well. It was decided that a small fire was a necessity and a negligible risk. It wouldn't illuminate the plane, and natives would build fires at night regardless of the Japanese.

Mike kindled the blaze—he'd always been good at that—while Pike and Frazee fashioned thin, wooden spears. They didn't want to waste ammunition or draw unwanted attention by shooting the vicious little scavengers, but they could stab them and fling them away. After a while of this, most of the creatures left them alone, apparently to eat the victims. Mike later suspected many also went to hide from things that hunted *them* in the dark. He took the first watch himself while the other tired men went to sleep at once. Pike and Sanford both snored, Pike very loudly, but Frazee and—mercifully—Lieutenant Wheeler seemed to sleep as peacefully as ever. Walking slowly around the camp at the edge of the firelight, Mike spent his time adding wood to their small blaze and spearing the occasional intruder. Larger…things sometimes crashed in the brush out of sight in the jungle, and bizarre screeches and moans erupted from time to time. Scary as they sounded, they didn't bother him much. He was used to the thunderous roar of frogs and toads back home and doubted really dangerous predators would announce their presence so robustly. Sometimes he stopped and stared at the plane, forlorn and awash, glowing dully in the light of the gibbous moon, or gazed at the marching surf or up at the familiar stars. Yet everything about his situation was unfamiliar, from the way *Big Boobs* rested helpless in the shallows, to the utterly isolated and frightening surroundings and odd little monsters scurrying on shore.

Most unfamiliar and intimidating of all, perhaps, was the necessity for him to step up and lead. He prayed Lt. Wheeler would be better when he woke, but even if he was, they'd have to take care of *him* for now and not the other way around. Yawning and glancing at the gently glowing hands and numbers on his watch, he finally went and woke Frazee. Without a word, the youngster picked up his Thompson and assumed his duties while Mike lay down on the folded parachute Frazee left behind. In minutes, he was asleep.

At first, Mike thought he was dreaming the screams that didn't quite wake him, but six rapid pistol shots punctuated the screams and that finished the job. Springing to his feet, he was already fumbling his pistol out of its holster as consciousness returned. He noticed at once that the sky was noticeably brighter so it must be almost dawn, but it was still dark enough that the fire might've aided visibility—if it hadn't been long dead. More screams—and vicious snarls—came from where Lieutenant Wheeler had been sleeping, and Mike staggered that way through the shoe-clutching sand. He barely caught a glimpse of what had Lieutenant Wheeler—long, narrow jaws clamped around the man's throat—but that was enough to confirm to him that it and its several companions *couldn't* belong on this island...or anywhere else.

Pike's Thompson roared beside him, fire spitting from the muzzle, bullets shredding foliage over the heads of the things, but Mike started shooting directly at them. "Don't!" Pike yelled. "You'll hit the skipper!"

"He's dead," Mike shouted back, still shooting. One of the things squealed in pain, and they all thrashed away, pulling the limp man with them. "Frazee! Sanford! C'mon!" Mike called, starting in pursuit.

Pike caught his arm. "How do you know he's dead?"

Mike whirled on him. "Because one of those—whatever it was—had torn his throat out," he snapped. "We're wasting time."

"What the hell?" Frazee demanded, voice high-pitched. He had his own Thompson again, and handed the '03 Springfield to Mike. "What's happening? Is it Japs?"

"Not Japs," Mike ground out. "Some kind of lizards, maybe, like the little ones we killed all night, but as big as a man..." He paused. "And it looked like they go on their hind legs!"

"Did you see that?" Frazee asked Pike.

It was swiftly growing lighter, as it did at that latitude, and the big man shook his head. "Not that, not really. I didn't see much at all," he confessed. "But something...not men...got the skipper."

"And he's dead?" Frazee demanded.

Pike looked at Mike. "Mr. Hayes says so. Sounded like he hit one of the bastards that took him, too." He looked around, finally seeing the faint wisp of smoke rising from the dead fire. "Where's Sanford? He had the last watch!"

"Why am I not surprised," Mike growled furiously. "Who cares where he is? We have to get after those things."

"Just hold on," Pike suggested. "You say Lieutenant Wheeler's dead? Okay. It won't hurt him any if we take a few minutes to get our shit in the sock."

Mike hesitated, then nodded. "Right. And we might as well grab everything we meant to take with us, looking for natives. We may not be back this way."

"At least now we won't have to carry the lieutenant around, too," Sanford said, suddenly appearing from behind them.

Pike actually pointed his weapon at the man. "Then why don't I shoot your sorry ass? Just one *more* the rest of us won't have to carry!"

Sanford looked at Mike. "Are you going to let him kill me?"

"Why not? You obviously conked out on guard, and it cost us a man."

Sanford shrugged. "So? I dozed off a couple minutes and the fire went out. All the crawlies were gone by then. But I was awake again for a while, watching the big lizards before they hit the camp. Come on, I'll show you."

"If you saw them, why didn't you warn us?" Frazee demanded.

Sanford turned to him. "Because they would've heard me shout or seen me move and they would've killed me."

"You're a coward," Pike seethed.

"Yes I am," Sanford agreed. "A live coward."

Nev Garza's body had been dug up and eaten. Practically all that was left were shreds of his flight coveralls and shoes. The only bones that remained were mere splintered fragments.

"Holy shit," Pike breathed, glaring over at Sanford. "Maybe it's time you told us exactly what you saw."

Sanford nodded at Mike. "Like he said. Big lizards that spent as much time upright as they did on all fours. I'd been over this way," he glanced back at Mike, "taking my nap, when I heard them digging and snuffling. Then crunching. I don't know what color they are but there was still enough moon that I saw their shape—and what they can do with their teeth—real well."

Mike turned to the others. "Anybody ever hear of lizards around here walking on two legs?"

"Lizards don't do that *anywhere*," Frazee said, a shiver in his voice.

"Maybe they're some sort missing link between dinosaurs and alligators, or something," Pike suggested."

Frazee rolled his eyes. "And the Dutch have been hiding them all this time? They had to know they were here, and somebody would've blown. It would've been all over the papers."

"Maybe the natives didn't tell them," Mike murmured, thoughts racing.

"Or they *are* the natives," Frazee rejoined, actually mirroring Mike's real thoughts. Ever since that damn squall, things had been screwy. It didn't shoot them down, the Japanese did that, but its effects on them and the plane's instruments, and Frazee's comments about the radio traffic were resurfacing in his mind.

"So…what? *Real* dinosaurs? Now we're on Skull Island or some shit, and King Kong's real too?" Pike berated Frazee. "No way, kid. You read too many of those weird books and magazines. Aren't the Japs enough for you?"

Sanford chuckled, a little hysterically it seemed, all his former bluster gone. "You know, if the kid's right, there aren't any Japs here either."

Mike looked at his three men. Sanford remained useless but the other two were sound. And all were his responsibility, more than ever before. The things Sanford described, that Mike himself had seen, gave him the creeps far more than he could possibly admit. Still, the original plan seemed the only option.

"Okay, like I said, we gather our supplies and head out, weapons ready, after those things that took Mr. Wheeler," Mike instructed, then looked at Frazee. "Sooner or later, we're bound to run into a village, with *people*, and we'll get a boat from them."

"That's crazy!" Sanford objected. "I told you what I saw," he gestured at the shreds of cloth, the shoes, and the bone fragments. "*You've* seen what they did. And you want to follow them? No thanks! Not me!"

"Okay, Sanford, do what you want," Mike said as he turned away. "You can go with us or stay here by yourself. I don't really care. I wonder who'll get you first, though, the lizards or the Japs?"

"If there *are* Japs," Frazee muttered, barely audible, as he and Pike stepped past Sanford. After a moment, Sanford followed.

With all the blood and ground disturbance, the trail the intruders made in the jungle was impossible to miss, leading roughly in an east, northeasterly direction. Staying on it at a relatively brisk pace was hot, grueling, and exhausting, however, and thirst was becoming a problem as they all sweated precious moisture at an alarming rate. It stood to reason the near daily rains, if nothing else, would deposit plenty of fresh water on the island, but all they had for now were a couple packs of emergency tins in Pike's and Frazee's care, in addition to what was in their canteens. Sanford had drained his the previous night and begged the others to share without avail. They were already nearly done in by the time Mike had led them barely two miles, constantly stooping and squirming through and around the mangrove-like roots of unusual trees. And though Mike kept his Springfield up and at the ready, it was impossible for him, or any of them, to pay as much attention to their surroundings as they should.

That's how they wound up nearly face to face with two other "lizards," quite different from those they'd been pursuing. They were bigger, for one thing. If the others were almost as large as a man, these stood more than eight feet tall and might've been twenty feet long from their viciously grinning, blood-smeared jaws to the tips of their feathery tails. Both had what looked like fur, whitish on the belly, and elsewhere a mottled black and tan. Only one wore a colorful, feathery crest, flaring tall down the center of its head. That one advanced several paces, vomiting a thunderous, bugling roar, while the first seized a morsel from the underbrush and stood with the half-eaten, bloody form of what could only have been Lieutenant Wheeler. These larger creatures had robbed the smaller ones of their meal.

"Oh, you bastards!" Pike exclaimed, and before Mike could stop the other man, instantly suspecting the animal was making a defensively aggressive demonstration—like a bear, perhaps—Pike stepped past him and hosed the monster with his Thompson on full auto. The entire twenty round magazine made a clattering reply to the creature's challenge and a wild pattern of bloody spots exploded a downy white cloud in front of the thing's chest. Mike saw no choice but to fire as well, and sent a comparatively much more powerful .30-06 bullet down the beast's throat. It might've dismissed the

.45ACP from the Tommy gun as little more than the nuisance of thorns or sharp, broken branches that annoyed it every day, but the pain Mike's Springfield inflicted was on a different level entirely, and that made it mad.

"Run!" Mike shouted to the others as he worked the bolt to chamber another round. The monster charged. Mike fired again, and turning to flee with the rest, he saw Pike still standing, fumbling with another magazine.

"Forget that! C'mon!"

AMM3c Jed Pike paid no attention, and as soon as the magazine was secure, he pointed his muzzle right at the thing's face and held the trigger back—as the terrible, serrated jaws closed on him. Even over Pikes screams, Mike heard the Thompson spit its last round inside the monster's mouth. He ran.

The expected pursuit wasn't long in coming, though it seemed somewhat hesitant at first. Perhaps the crested beast—Mike still couldn't bring himself to call it a 'dinosaur,' despite what his eyes had seen—was hurt worse than it appeared. Or maybe it merely took the time to finish eating Pike before it and the other monster—Mike assumed it was its mate—came after them. He caught up with Frazee, though, and was surprised to see Sanford, wide-eyed and gasping, still in company with the young radioman. Of course, it was clear by now that Frazee's Thompson wouldn't be any more effective than Pike's against creatures as large as those they just saw, but it was better than Sanford's pistol for other things. And not expecting "other things" equally or more dangerous than those already encountered now seemed even less reasonable than the idea of being attacked by dinosaurs once had.

Mike was breathing hard from his run, the humid air drowning his lungs, and shook his head when Frazee asked about Pike. "Didn't make it," he wheezed. "Honest to God, I don't know if he was so mad at what happened to Mr. Wheeler that his mind just flipped the 'fight no matter what' switch, or he was just too scared to run. I'm chalking it up to him sacrificing himself for us, so let's get the hell out of here."

"Which way?" Frazee asked anxiously. Snapping limbs and heavy footfalls, accompanied by gurgling, huffing sounds were growing closer.

"We have to get off this trail," Mike told him. "Get into the thick stuff and make it harder for them to chase us."

"And harder for us to put distance between us," Sanford snapped.

Mike sighed. "They'll catch us in no time if we go back the way we came. But do what you want. Go back to the plane."

"Maybe we should," Sanford shot back. "There's machine guns there. One of the fifties in the waist would make short work of those lizards."

Frazee looked surprised. "You know, Mr. Hayes, that's not such a bad idea." He shook his head. "But only if we had just a few of those things to worry about. This island's probably crawling with them—and other stuff. We *need* a boat."

"Yeah," Mike agreed, "and back to the plane or not, we have to get off the main trail first." The monsters were audibly closer now. "They can step over stuff we have to crawl through." He pointed southeast. "It's thicker that way. Let's get a move on."

Struggling and gasping through the dense trees and entangling roots, they gained a little on their pursuers. They never lost them though, and it became clear the monsters were trailing them by scent—an odor growing ever sharper as they sweated. But they began to smell things too. Frazee claimed he caught a tantalizing hint of woodsmoke. Mike didn't smell it at first, but soon he did, mixed with the aroma of cooking meat as well. He was sure.

The pursuit was too, and made a redoubled effort to catch them before they reached its source. That implied they generally avoided whoever was making the smoke, and maybe even feared them. Panting and blowing, Mike, Frazee, and Sanford managed to quicken their pace. Utterly unexpectedly, they suddenly flailed their way into a broad clearing around a very strange village, and all they could do for a moment was suck air and blink under the bright, hot sun, as details sank in. A great, dense stockade of sharpened, outward-facing tree trunks surrounded a cluster of wood and thatch habitations high above the ground, supported by sturdy, sometimes still living tree trunks themselves. With all the dangerous creatures around, the arrangement struck Mike as eminently sensible. A hunting roar behind them pushed them forward, and Mike hoped the people here were friendly—and wouldn't be annoyed by the large, hungry guests they were bringing. Thoughts like that quickly vanished when he finally glimpsed the inhabitants they were hurrying toward.

"Now I *know* we aren't where we thought we were," Frazee said, freezing in place.

"God damn!" Sanford cried. "They're not even *people*! What the hell? They look like monkeys—or upright cats . .!"

He was right, in a sense. The beings rushing to gather on the other side of the stockade to stare—many holding slender spears much longer than they were tall—*did* look like monkeys, or cats...or neither one, exactly. Their ears and faces were vaguely feline, though their eyes were disproportionately large. Tails curling up from behind light leather kilts might've looked more like those of monkeys than cats, but their physiques weren't like either. In that specific respect, standing quite erect, they were shaped exactly like short, dark-furred humans, down to the naked breasts of the females. Even as the monsters crashed closer in the jungle, the...cat people jabbered excitedly among themselves, less concerned about the threat as astonished by the apparent novelty of the human aviators.

Sanford whirled angrily toward Mike. "Just where the hell did you and Wheeler bring us?"

"Panaitan Island, as far as I know!" There were a pair of roars, as if of exultant discovery behind them, and one of the huge, furry reptiles—the wounded male—burst into the clearing. Immediately, a dozen or more cat people, all with spears, even the females, sprang out through the gaps in the stockade and rushed past the three men to confront it. In no way did they threaten the men—they actually ignored them now—but Sanford pointed his pistol at any who came too close.

"Put that away!" Mike ordered.

A seeping, damaged eye seemed the only serious injury the men had inflicted on the stalking monster, and it didn't appear particularly alarmed by the long spears of the cat people warriors—until they started ferociously stabbing at it. Infuriated, it sprinted toward them, snapping razor-lined jaws at tormentors darting nimbly aside. Excited, trilling cries evidently signaled a retreat, and the cat people surged back around the humans, urging them into the enclosure past the stockade. Sanford balked, shaking off the pressing hands, but even he retreated when the hot breath of the monster gusted down the back of his neck.

The ground seemed to shake like it would from a mild earthquake, and the monster voiced an ear-piercing squeal of agony. Mike turned to see that, in its obsessive fury stirred by bullet wounds and then deliberately whipped to a heat too hot to contain by the relentless spear-thrusts, the deadly beast had deeply impaled itself on one of the massive stockade spikes. Blood spewed out in torrents to spatter on the ground, and with a final feeble screech, the monster shuddered and died. Its mate replied with a roar of its own, but it didn't advance from the jungle. All they could see was its vicious head peering at them through the trees.

Without a single word of command, cat people swarmed the dead monster with blades of volcanic glass, cutting through its tough, downy hide to remove the flesh beneath. This was something they obviously did fairly often. An unarmed group of cat people had collected to study the castaways, staring and blinking rapidly as they spoke to each other in a language unlike anything Mike ever heard. He sensed no malevolence in their manner, just cheerful fascination. In spite of everything, for the first time since Lieutenant Wheeler told him to land their shot-up plane in the surf, he felt himself start to relax. He didn't know what was going on—and that *something* profound had happened to them, apparently in that weird squall, no longer seemed debatable—but even if giant lizards…dinosaurs…somehow hid in remote places of the world, these people weren't hiding. Their village was open to the sky and aerial observation, and millions of people lived on Java, practically a canoe ride away. Mike decided to worry about the implications of that later, and returned the very human grin of a perhaps somewhat aged cat person—judging only by the white fur on his face—who was suddenly gazing up at him. He chittered something unintelligible and

Mike spoke back, and it seemed the cat man was actually delighted that neither had the slightest idea what the other was saying. Frazee appeared increasingly comfortable too, laughing when a small female groped the back of his flight coveralls as if feeling for a tail. Only Sanford remained visibly ill at ease, even hostile toward these small, strange beings who'd almost certainly saved their lives. He kept slapping their probing hands away, and Mike noticed his pistol was still out. "Put that thing away, Sanford!" Mike ordered. "If I have to tell you again, I'll take it away from you."

"Why don't you *try*?" Sanford asked tensely, waving the gun. "Look, damn it, things are too weird here, and I just want out, see? I didn't sign up for any of this shit. Not giant man-eating lizards, talking monkeys, or even the Japs. They can have this dump, and the whole damn Pacific, for all I care. I just want to go back to the plane—like you said—where there's *real* guns to kill the lizards," he gestured around, "and any of these spooky monkeys that come around, too." Mike noted the village elder—whatever he was—didn't fear the pistol. Maybe he didn't know what it was. But he'd picked up on the friction among his guests.

"We're not shooting *any* of these folks," Mike said carefully. "And what'll going to the plane accomplish, besides getting the guns? We still don't have a boat and we'll just starve or get eaten, without help."

Sanford pointed his pistol at the elder, who looked at it curiously. Mike stiffened, slightly raising the muzzle of his Springfield, but there were too many cat people surrounding them. His bullet would certainly kill Sanford, but probably someone behind him as well. "Maybe *they* have boats," Sanford snapped, using the pistol to poke the elder in the chest. He recognized that for the indignity it was, if not the threat, and many of the villagers tensed. "Even if they don't," Sanford continued, "we've got inflatable rafts in the plane. They'll get us to Java. I don't care where we go after that, or even if the Japs take me prisoner. I'd rather take my chances with them than this damn island!"

"You don't need Frazee or me to raft across to Java," Mike told him, "and I don't want to get caught by the Japs," he added, though like even Sanford said that morning, he wasn't sure there *were* any Japanese anymore.

"You expect me to row all the way over there by myself?" Sanford sneered. "And what if the current takes me out of sight of land? I'm no navigator."

"Tough. If you want to go, go. But we're staying here."

Something happened behind Sanford's eyes and they took on a new, hard, ruthlessness that Mike had never seen as he flipped the .45's thumb safety off with an audible click. "Fine," he said, "then I'll just have to fix it so they won't let you."

"No!" Mike shouted, lunging forward, but Frazee was faster. He wouldn't shoot either, but he slammed Sanford back with the heavy Thompson before the sailor's finger jerked the trigger. Frazee cried out and the natives drew back from the loud shot in alarm. Sanford disentangled himself from the collapsing radioman and fired at Mike, who was now aiming back, but there were still too many natives behind his target. Too many behind Mike, too. Sanford's bullet missed him, but hit the young female who'd been making Frazee laugh.

"Shit!" Mike almost screeched in furious frustration, still unable to safely fire while Sanford spun and sprinted away, shooting another cat person in front of him who blocked a portion of the village and the far palisade beyond. "I'm coming for you, you murdering bastard!" Mike bellowed after the man. He barely heard the hollered "Good!" over the sudden uproar in the village. Mike didn't understand the high-pitched shouting, of course, but it was evident the natives were very angry and afraid. Some were mad at *him*, and seized him roughly as he tried to go to Frazee. The elder intervened. He could have no idea what caused the explosion of violence, but seeing what the thing Sanford pointed at him did, he quickly understood Mike and Frazee had protected him, and tried to protect others. With a few yipping words, Mike was released and villagers raced to inspect their fallen people and the moaning radioman.

Compared to the two cat people Sanford shot—one was stone dead and the little female was bleeding profusely—Frazee didn't look too bad. The bullet had hit him high in his left chest, just under the collarbone, but he was in a lot of pain. Still, he managed to speak. "You gotta stop him, sir," he hissed. "He's cracked his nut, and who knows what he'll do if he gets his hands on those machine guns!"

"I know," Mike agreed, though he wasn't sure they hadn't finally seen the *real* Colin Sanford. The elder was calling out more commands and warriors were gathering with shorter spears, more suitable to the close quarters in the jungle. Mike touched the elder to get his attention. Laying his Springfield down beside Frazee, he—carefully—hefted the other man's Thompson. Pointing at the gathered warriors, he shook his head and made a gesture meant to request that the elder hold them back, then slapping himself on the chest, he pointed at the SMG, then in the direction Sanford fled. Somewhat to Mike's surprise, the elder seemed to understand. He signified so by taking a step back and calling to his warriors, who appeared to slightly relax.

Mike nodded gratefully. "So long, Frazee. I'll be back as soon as I can."

"Just be careful, sir," the kid winced, as a cat man—*hell just call 'em 'Cats,* Mike thought—continued inspecting his wound. "This seems a nice place and all, but I don't want to be stuck here by myself." Mike wasn't worried about Frazee. He seemed in good hands, and he had all their remaining medical supplies. "I hear you," Mike replied, and starting jogging off in the direction Sanford went. He never saw the eyes in the great head of the female monster, still glaring at the village, suddenly focus on him. The eyes narrowed. Easing back into the jungle, she began working her way around the village clearing, sure she'd eventually regain the odd new scent of the prey that had led her mate to his over-aggressive, unthinking doom.

Mike wasn't surprised to discover evidence that Sanford was staying on a well-used trail, and navigator or not, he'd picked one heading roughly northwest, back toward the stranded PBY. Once, Mike heard a startled cry and several rapid pistol shots surprisingly close ahead. He caught himself hoping one of the scary inhabitants of this wildly dangerous island might've done his work for him, not only from a personal danger standpoint, but a moral one as well. Mike didn't *want* to kill Sanford. But the moral sword is heavy, and he'd recognized back at the village that he was the one who had to wield it. He'd never asked to be in charge and didn't want to be, but Wheeler's incapacitation, even before the creepy squall, made him so whether he liked it or not. And being in charge of the men he'd brought to this place also meant he was responsible for them. That hadn't worked too well for Wheeler, Pike, and now young Frazee, (even feeling sorry for himself, Mike couldn't blame himself for Garza), but he'd taken a murderer in among apparently peaceful, friendly folk, and watched him kill them. Now if he didn't stop Sanford, he might return with weapons sufficient to wipe them out. No, the behavior of people he supposedly commanded was just as much his responsibility as their safety, and Seaman Colin Sanford had to die.

Something lunged at him out of the brush and long, narrow claws ripped the leg of his flight coveralls and slashed the flesh of his thigh. Mike instinctively fired a short burst from his Thompson into the thing before he even realized what it was. Now quivering in death, he recognized one of the smaller "lizards" like they'd chased that morning. He'd killed it, keeping most of his bullets in the hideous head, but it had already been wounded by several pistol shots, one of which shattered its leg.

"How did you like my little surprise?" Sanford's voice echoed through the trees. "Did it get you?"

Mike pressed forward, limping slightly, but didn't answer. He also kept the heavy Tommy gun up, muzzle questing in front of him, because in addition to Sanford's voice, he also heard the booming surf pounding into the bay ahead and knew neither he nor his quarry could be far from a confrontation. Most critical of all, if Sanford reached the plane more than a few moments before him, Mike would be a sitting duck on the open beach for *Big Boobs'* guns.

That had doubtless been Sanford's hope, but Mike's nearby shots must've convinced him he needed to finish this differently. Mike emerged at the edge of the trees, moving slow, scanning carefully for any disturbance in the sand near the plane where the waves and tide had scoured away their movements of the previous day. There was nothing.

"Pilots always look ahead too much," came a gloating voice behind him. "Takes a waist gunner to keep his eyes out to the sides. All

I had to do was duck behind some of those big leaves back there and watch you go blundering by."

Mike turned slowly. The first thing he saw was the big, black, .45 caliber hole aimed at his face. Behind it was Sanford, face twisted into the same cold, malevolent expression he'd shown back at the village, only now it was touched by self-satisfaction.

"You were a crummy waist gunner," Mike retorted.

Sanford shrugged. "I didn't care, and I hate flying. Getting busted down to the bottom rung and assigned to *Big Boobs* was *punishment,* and I decided to take it out on everyone around me. Now that's over, and I'm back on top. Don't even need *you* anymore." Sanford's eyes flicked to the Thompson. "Toss that over. Easy."

Mike did as he was told, making sure the weapon landed top down in the leafy sand. "I thought you wanted me to navigate for you," he said as Sanford reached down, never taking his eyes—or his pistol—off him.

"Nah. It occurred to me, with all the guns, and the machine guns in the plane, I can make myself *king* of those dopey monkeys, or whatever the hell they are. If the Dutch never cared enough about this island to scout it well enough to find all the creepy shit we've seen, I bet the Japs never will. I'll sit the whole war out."

A dry root cracked behind Sanford and Mike couldn't help but stare, wide eyed, at the massive dark shape of the female monster, about forty yards back, appear out of the jungle gloom. Sanford half-turned to look and Mike bolted to the side. Sanford shot him. Agony flared behind Mike's left ear and it felt like he'd been slammed in the head with a baseball bat. His vision went neon red, and he sprawled heavily in the mushy soil, but another shot might be an instant away so he rolled clumsily and pulled his own pistol. A gnarly tree-trunk stopped him, and he knew he'd never gain his feet to run, so he raised the pistol and flipped the safety off. His eyes were still blurry, the color all wrong, but he immediately saw Sanford wouldn't be shooting at him anymore. He'd probably tried, but his slide was locked back on an empty magazine. And Mike was no longer his problem in any case. The giant, furry lizard was almost on him and it was moving so fast that Sanford must've instinctively known he'd never even reach the carcass of the drowned PBY before it got him. Snatching up the sand-packed Thompson with an hysterical shriek, he pointed it at the beast and squeezed the trigger. There came only the muffled *Pop!* of a half-chambered round, and not only did the ruptured case not fully eject, the grit-bound bolt never went back far enough to pick up another round. After that, all he could do was scream as the monster's jaws snapped shut and ripped away the Thompson—and both his arms. Still screaming, Sanford turned to run but immediately tripped and fell, face down, less than twelve feet from Mike. Close enough Mike could see his screeching, bulging-eyed face when the giant lizard clamped its jaws on his legs and jerked him up in the air.

*I'm next, I guess,* Mike thought grimly, pointing his pistol at the terrible beast. But he didn't fire. Not only was it pointless, he was afraid to attract its attention. Besides, he was getting woozier by the second and probably wouldn't even hit it. *I'm shot in the head,* he told himself. *I'm done for anyway.* The thing had grasped Sanford's torso in its powerful front limbs, claws digging deep, and quickly gnawed his legs off at the knees amid a spattering spray of blood. All the while, the man kept screaming, and Mike thought he'd never stop. He also began to think he heard a strange trilling sound in the jungle around him. The monster grew agitated. Jealously clutching its wailing meal, it whipped its head from side to side as the odd noise grew louder. Mike lowered the pistol until his arm lay in the sand. Darkness was coming quickly, and he suddenly felt a powerful regret that he'd never learn more about the island, or the people he met there. His last thought was somewhat detached, merely wondering if the big lizard would eat his corpse, or whether the little lizards or the goofy crabs would win the battle for it.

He awoke on his back feeling like he was floating on a choppy sea, bouncing a little roughly, but he wasn't uncomfortable. He felt pretty good, in fact, just really hungry. Sunlight flickered through the dense jungle canopy above and he realized he was moving.

"Hey! You're awake!" Frazee cried delightedly. "He's awake!" he repeated excitedly to some cat people nearby. *So it wasn't a dream after all*, Mike thought. Almost immediately, the 'Cat "elder" was grinning down at him, just a few inches from his face. "Don't try to rise up, yet, sir," Frazee warned. "I can walk, but you're on a travois. A bullet grazed your skull pretty good and they can't put your *head* in a sling. You're healing fast, though. Boy, these folks have way better stuff than Sulfa! I never got a hint of infection!"

Mike tried to talk but only croaked. Frazee gave him a sip from his canteen. He finally managed "What happened? How long was I out—and where are we going?" It had dawned on him as he spoke that he must've been out quite a while if Frazee was already up and around, so the travois wasn't carrying him back to the village. And he also noted there were a *lot* of heavily-burdened 'Cats moving in the jungle along what must've been an even broader, more permanent trail than others he'd seen. *Maybe they're all here, but why?*

Frazee frowned. "I'm not sure how long. I was out a few days myself, doped up on some pretty good stuff. You sort of came to from time to time, enough to eat a little, but you were so loopy I'm not surprised you don't remember." He nodded at the 'Cat elder, still grinning as he walked beside the travois. "Best I can get from him— he's Taa-Roo, by the way, the chief, and some sort of priest, I think—we're moving toward that low mountain in the center of the island. Supposed to meet some other tribes there and fort up."

"Fort up? Why?"

Taa-Roo seemed to get the gist of their conversation and stopped grinning. His new expression never touched his eyes, but something about the set of his mouth, ears, even his blinking, gave Mike the impression he would've looked grim if he could. Gesturing around in all directions, he simply said "Grik!" as if that explained everything.

"What's 'Grik?' Mike asked Frazee.

"They showed me some critters painted on a really old pot—look sort of like those middle-size lizards, you know?—and kept saying 'Grik.' I started to catch on. Seems they come in ships and they're scared of them."

Mike frowned. "And since they're not afraid of the big lizards around here…"

"Yeah," Frazee agreed soberly.

Mike considered. "Well, what if we got the machine guns out of the plane? Use them to defend them instead of hurt them."

Frazee scratched his nose. "Yeah, I thought of that, but the plane's gone. At first I figured it washed away and sank while I was out, but again—as best I can piece together from what they try to tell me—hell, look at this." He fished a piece of bright white rawhide, stiff as a board, out of the emergency pouch he still carried and handed it over. Mike stared in wonder at an amazingly well-rendered charcoal drawing of what could only be an American four-stacker destroyer, down to the big '102' painted on her bow.

"USS *Mahan*," Mike breathed.

"Yeah. She came in and dropped some fellas off. They must've patched *Big Boobs* up well enough to fly." Frazee's expression soured. "After what happened with Sanford, I get why these folks didn't want to risk fooling with them." He sighed. "And that's what they did; they flew her the hell off. But she had to fight her way past some wooden sailing ships with these 'Grik' things on them, which *really* scared the bejesus out of everybody. Seems Grik were just a legend, like the boogeyman, till now. But that's why we're moving. Supposedly, if the Grik come back and don't find anybody near shore—they *eat* folks—they'll just go on."

"Yes! Yes!" Taa-Roo said, and Mike smiled at him while wondering how much English the old 'Cat' had picked up from Frazee. Probably more than the kid realized. He looked back at the sky and watched the sunrays shift as he moved.

"Well," Mike said at last, rather philosophically, "we're all alone, stuck on an island of cat people surrounded by things that want to eat us, and our plane got chased off by even scarier things." Frazee nodded agreement as Mike continued.

"On the other hand, the 'Cats are friendly, and if *Mahan* hung around long enough for her people to get *Big Boobs*—*cared* enough to try—chances are they weren't running from the Japs anymore. I don't know what any of that means, but it's kind of comforting to know we aren't *utterly* alone, wherever that squall spit us out." Mike was quite certain now that this wasn't the Panaitan Island in the Sunda Strait—maybe even the world—he knew. "We might still have friends somewhere out there, and maybe we'll see them again."

\* \* \* \* \*

## Taylor Anderson Bio

Taylor Anderson is the New York Times bestselling author of the Alternate History/Military Sci-fi DESTROYERMEN Series. He's a gun-maker, forensic ballistic archeologist, and technical/historical consultant for movies and documentaries. He has a Master's Degree in History and has taught at Tarleton State University in Stephenville, Texas.

Facebook https://www.facebook.com/TaylorAndersonAuthor/

Website http://taylorandersonauthor.com/

# # # # #

# The Lightnings
# and the Cactus
# by James Young

### Chapter 1: Bouncing *Bettys*

*Red One*

*1130 Local*

*12 October 1942*

*I hate water*, Major Connor Copeland thought to himself yet again. *If I had wanted to fly over water, I would have joined the Navy like Uncle Mike did.*

Copeland looked at his P-38's fuel gauge, then allowed himself a grim smile behind his oxygen mask.

*Of course, unlike Uncle Mike, I'm probably not going to run out of fuel in the middle of the Pacific and die.* Connor glanced around at the fifteen other *Lightning*s behind and the four large aircraft accompanying them. *At least, not unless a whole bunch of people are off in navigation.*

While Connor might have doubted the map reading skills of the two C-47 transport crews trailing the formation, the pair of B-17 Flying Fortresses had made the trip from Espiritu Santo to Guadalcanal at least eight times between them. The two transports were carrying the 94th Pursuit Squadron's mechanics and several drop tanks, while each of the heavy bombers were hauling a full load of high explosives.

*Goddamn Navy*, he seethed, shifting uncomfortably in his seat. *Sink four carriers at Midway and suddenly they were convinced they could take on the whole Japanese fleet.*

Connor looked at his watch, then at the dark shapes of islands that had seemingly just appeared on the horizon. The officer didn't even need to do math to know the insistent pressure in his bladder was going to need relief before he got his large fighter set down. Using language that made him sincerely hope his mother's ghost could not manifest thousands of miles from his Midwestern home, Connor began the intricate dance of holding the *Lightning's* yoke, his penis, and the fighter's relief tube in place so that he did not urinate all over his instrument panel.

*Maybe that crazy Aussie was right when he said don't drink wa…*

"Bogeys! Bogeys eleven o'clock high!"

"Son of a bitch!" Connor roared, whipping his gaze around even as he was torn between clenching things mid-stream or hurriedly finishing Nature's task.

*Figures I've got my dick out in the middle of a cold cockpit when the Japanese show up*, he thought angrily as he continued emptying his bladder.

"Say again, Red One?" someone asked. Connor ignored the query, his pulse racing as he saw the cluster of dots that were most definitely not friendly.

"Buster One…"

"I see them," came the B-17 pilot's laconic reply on the 94th Squadron's frequency. Connor watched as the big bombers turned to starboard, away from the enemy aircraft. With relief, Connor saw that the cluster of dots was headed away from his squadron at an angle. Tucking himself back into his flight suit, Connor began barking orders to the rest of the squadron.

"Green Flight, you stick with the transports and the bombers," he said quickly. "White, Blue, Red, follow me."

His orders finished, Connor pulled back on the yoke, then began moving his hands across the cockpit in a drill he had practiced numerous times in the past few weeks. Contorting himself, he first reached for the valves to prepare the empty drop tanks beneath his wings for release. Twisting the stubborn metal to shut off the flow to his internal tanks, Connor briefly considered attempting to turn towards the Japanese bombers with the precious containers aboard.

*Good way to die, idiot*, he thought. Connor's hands continued to move around the cockpit as he armed his guns, adjusted his fuel mixture, turned on the gunsight, and then punched off the external tanks. Hearing the pair of Allison engines mounted abreast of his cockpit change their sound as they were fed more fuel, Connor advanced his throttle firmly but only with moderate speed.

*Last thing I need is to pop a damn engine right now.* The *Lightning*'s twin powerplants gave the large fighter a tremendous rate of climb and speed higher than anything the Japanese had fielded to date. They were also extremely temperamental, especially at his current altitude. Pulling back on the stick, Connor glanced backwards through the P-38's canopy to check his squadron's status. Eleven *Lightning*s were with his fighter; the red, white, and blue top hats in a red ring standing out against their olive drab paint jobs. Two aircraft, the No. 4 fighters in Blue and White flights, were both falling out of formation with one of their props starting to falter as they lost an engine.

*Goddammit,* Connor thought, *I knew Price and Hardison were idiots.* The two neophytes had likely, in their haste, forgotten one of the steps towards getting their P-38s ready for combat. Now both would be limping into Guadalcanal with their fighters, which hopefully the 94th's ground personnel would be able to fix.

"Red One, Blue One, looks like the escort's going hunting," Captain David McIntyre, Blue Flight's lead, observed. A few seconds later, Connor too could make out the gaggle of single-engine fighters accelerating away from the rapidly growing Japanese bombers. Doing a quick count, Connor tallied twenty-six of the cigar-shaped Japanese *Betty* bombers and a similar number of *Zero* fighters. The latter were diving towards Guadalcanal.

*They don't see us,* Connor realized, blood rushing in his ears. *Of course, why would they think to look in this direction when Guadalcanal is in front of them?* The Navy liaison officer at Espiritu Santo had briefed Connor and his flight leaders that the Japanese tended to strike around noon, from the north. This group had apparently circled around wide, as they were approaching the island from almost due east.

*Those Japanese fighters are going to be running on fumes,* Connor thought, glancing nervously at his own gauges. Even though the P-38s had left Espiritu Santo with ostensibly enough fuel to fly to Guadalcanal and back, combat had a way of rapidly draining the tanks.

*Which is why we have to keep these bastards from hitting the runway*, he thought as his P-38 reached 25,000 feet. Bringing his nose level, Connor advanced his throttles to the firewall. Both Allison engines puffed smoke and vibrated, the *Lightning* gaining speed. In far too little time, he drew slightly ahead of the enemy bombers. Turning one last time to look over his twin-boomed aircraft at his squadron, Connor waggled his wings, then put the yoke over to port and began his dive towards the enemy bombers.

\* \* \*

Connor had been incorrect in his assumption—the *Bettys* had seen his fighters. Inexplicably, having never seen P-38s before, many of the Japanese turret gunners either assumed that the *Lightnings* were either friendly aircraft or Allied bombers that were swinging out to give the *Bettys* a wide berth. It was only when the ten fighters pushed over in what could only be an attack profile that cries of alarm were raised in several of the Japanese aircraft.

\* \* \*

The rapidly swelling green bomber began to fill Connor's gunsight. Swallowing, he fought the urge to open fire as its wings began to fill the inner first ring.

Closer…closer…he thought, time seeming to slow. His stomach clenched, his pulse raced, and he felt a strange sensation that was a mix between the most violent nausea and terrific arousal. Without realizing it, Connor began to bite down on his tongue as he skidded the *Lightning* into a turn to apply deflection.

*Oh shit!* he thought, seeing the dorsal turret swing towards him. The weapon's bright flash startled him, causing him to inadvertently jerk the *Lightning*'s control column as the stream of tracers flew past his P-38. With the *Betty*'s wings extending completely past his gunsight, Connor guessed he was at about two hundred yards. Biting harder on his tongue, Connor simultaneously began pulling the *Lightning*'s nose up and squeezing both triggers on his control stick.

Unlike most of its contemporaries, the P-38 armament of four .50-caliber machine guns and solitary 20-millimeter cannon were mounted in its nose. Whereas the other fighter pilots guessed the range at which to converge their wing-mounted guns into a single area, the P-38's firepower arrived in a single murderous torrent regardless. Thus, even though he actually opened fire at three hundred yards, Connor's initial burst was devastating to the lightly built Betty. In under three seconds, the storm of armor-piercing ball and explosive cannon shells cleaved the bomber's rudder in two, decapitated the tail gunner, then found the bomber's unarmored fuel tanks. The resultant fireball detonated the *Betty*'s bombload in an orange-centered brown ball of smoke and debris that flashed outwards into the rest of the formation.

Connor's arms shook as he hauled back on the stick, debris pounding off the *Lightning*'s frame as his vision narrowed. Fighting down his panic as his engines roared, Connor quickly eased forward on the yoke and brought the throttles back. Glancing quickly left and right, he saw that there were several gouges and dents across his fuselage, but no obvious major damage. It was only when the immediate threat was gone that the squadron radio net burst into his consciousness.

"Green Two get back in formation!"

"Watch those fighters coming up!"

"Red Four, break off, you're losing coolant!"

Connor pressed himself up and looked back behind him at the last report. He saw Lieutenant McKnight, Red Two, behind him, but had lost sight of his second section. A pair of rapidly dissipating brown smoke balls told him at least two other pilots had managed to explode one of the Japanese bombers, and he sincerely hoped all three blazing comets falling towards the Pacific below were additional *Bettys*.

*Well, the old hands weren't lying,* he thought. *Their crates come apart really easy.*

As several pilots called out a warning on the squadron net, Connor saw the angry Japanese escorts clawing back to altitude. The Japanese fighters were a mix of olive green and dark gray single-engine *Zeros*, and Connor noted that their rate of climb was nothing to sneeze at.

"*Don't stay and turn with them,*" Connor recalled the advice of the old hands he'd met en route to the South Pacific. *People who try to turn with the Japanese end up dead.*

"White Flight, break right!" Connor barked, not able to see the fuselage markings but recognizing the white spinners of a P-38 swinging back around to attack a Betty. The *Lightning* was at his ten o'clock and lower, with three approaching *Zeros* slashing in towards the turning P-38. Even as Connor was diving towards the Japanese fighter, it cut inside the White Flight *Lightning*'s turn. In a flash, first with its nose machine guns, then the twin cannons in its wings, the lead *Zero* stitched the P-38 through its center nacelle.

*Dammit*, Connor thought as the other P-38 staggered, then fell away in a stall. The *Zero* continued in its turn, and Connor was presented with a perfect plan view of the opposing aircraft. He kicked his rudder to try and track the Japanese fighter, but the nimble Japanese aircraft turned far too tightly. The two aircraft hurtled past each other cockpit to cockpit, with one of the Japanese wingmen attempting to fire a burst at Connor's aircraft. Shoving his throttles to the firewall, Connor turned and looked behind him just in time to see the third *Zero*'s wing hurtling off.

"Good shot Red Two!" Connor shouted. He saw the two remaining Zeros reversing in his rearview mirror…and watched as the leader exploded from a burst of fire coming from its port side. A moment later, a dark blue, stubby fighter flashed across Connor's field of view, white stars sticking out on its wings.

*Looks like the damn Marines finally made it to altitude,* Connor thought, turning his view back forwards. The sky, full of aircraft before, suddenly seemed empty except for descending smoke trails and a couple of parachutes. Puffs of flak in the distance towards Guadalcanal told Connor that the bombers had passed close enough to the island to be engaged.

*I hope we have a runway to land on,* he thought.

"Army fighters, Army fighters, this is Cactus Base," a voice broke in over the 94th squadron's frequency. "All Army fighters, this is Cactus Base."

"Cactus Base, this is Hatter Leader," Connor replied after a couple of moments.

"Be advised you are to land on the main runway, not Fighter One," the voice stated. "I say again, land on Cactus Main."

"This is Hatter Leader, roger," Connor replied. "Hatters, check in."

Connor winced as the calls came in. He had started the day with sixteen *Lightnings*. It looked like he was ending it with eight, with several of those damaged. In exchange, his men claimed that they had knocked down eight bombers and six Zeros. Connor was somewhat skeptical about that one but resolved to sort it out on the ground.

"All right you yahoos, let's get down to our new home." Connor sighed in resignation. "Flight leaders, meet at my fighter when we get down."

\* \* \*

*The Pagoda*
*1900 Local*

Squadron Leader Ian Montgomery swatted the mosquito on the back of his neck with a muttered curse, then swung and caught the one on his left arm without breaking stride. The squish of Ian's boots and the oppressive humidity spoke to the reason for such a high number of the buzzing insects as the night grew darker. The *whump!* of an artillery shell landing at the far end of the runway made him jump, and the Australian officer shook his head angrily.

*Damn Yanks,* he thought angrily. *Not quite sure how my bloody squadron drew the short straw. Oh, wait, that idiot Curtin has the spine of a jellyfish.* Looking at the looming structure, Ian took a deep breath and fought to control his temper.

"What's done is done, and it's only for a fortnight," Ian muttered to himself. No. 305 Squadron (Provisional), RAAF, had been cobbled together from veterans recently returned from Europe and men who had been based at Port Moresby in response to an urgent request from Admiral Nimitz, the Theater Commander. Most of the European veterans, Ian included, had been looking forward to several months of rest after spending literally years fighting the Germans. To stave off a munity, General Eichelberger, the American area commander, had personally promised the men they would only be on Guadalcanal for no more than fourteen days.

*Of course, those of us who end up dead will still technically meet his agreement,* Ian thought grimly, as another shell landed further away from the runway. *Unless, of course, that idiot shooting the harassing artillery lands a lucky shot.*

"Halt! Who goes there!" a nervous Marine sentry barked, struggling to stand up from his post behind some sandbags. Like most of the men Ian had seen, the Marine's eyes were sunken, his face gaunt. From his shivering frame, Ian suspected the man was standing guard on the headquarters rather than on the front lines due to his being malarial.

"Squadron Leader Montgomery for General Geiger," Ian replied crisply. He felt the American look him over with a skeptical air.

"Look, you can bloody well go get your sergeant of the guard," Ian snapped. "If the goddamn Japanese have created a race of shape shifters who can look like a goddamn Australian, we're all more fu…"

"I'll vouch for him, sergeant," a voice said from the doorway. Turning, Ian recognized the P-38 squadron leader whom he had met in Espiritu Santos the day before. The tall, lanky man's frame was a marked contrast to Ian's own rugby prop build, but his voice held a calm assurance that immediately put the nervous Marine at ease.

"Yes, Sir," the Marine said. The noncom's voice made it clear that he had been more than willing to use the bayonet attached to his rifle to teach Ian some respect.

"Major Copeland," Ian said with a nod. "I am told you've already made your presence known."

The American shrugged.

"Bastards were about to plaster the runway, and I didn't feel like trying to fly back to Espiritu Santo," Copeland replied. "Let's get inside, the Marine generals are kind of impatient about something."

Ian followed his compatriot back into the pagoda, passing through two blackout curtains into a large map room. Ten men, six of them Marines, two Navy, and two other Army majors were gathered around a map of the Solomon Islands. To his amusement, Ian noted that the pilots were all separated by their service.

*Glad to see we're not the only armed services with grudges for one another,* Ian thought. *Although, to be fair, the Fleet Air Arm pilots have a legitimate gripe with the RAF.*

"Squadron Leader Montgomery, how good of you to join us," an American naval officer said snidely. Before Copeland could say anything, the flag officer at the front of the table fixed the man with a glare.

"Until you've actually put a torpedo into something other than some whore in Waikiki, you'll shut the fuck up, Lieutenant Commander Saints," Brigadier General Geiger snapped. "I think our Australian friends have earned some leeway on time."

*Well, that's refreshing, a Yank who actually sounds happy to see us,* Ian thought, giving the general a slight nod. *Maybe three dead cruisers actually buys some goodwill with this lot.* Montgomery's brother had been assigned to the *Perth*, his cousin aboard the *Australia*. The former was still missing in the Dutch East Indies, the latter had come back horribly burned from the *Australia's* sinking during the First Battle of Savo Island.

*At least the recce boys sighted that Japanese task force before they could come down here and catch the entire landing by surprise,* Montgomery recalled, gazing at the map. *Not that it probably would have gone much worse for either side if they had—*

"Squadron Leader Montgomery?"

Ian jerked in surprise.

"Sorry sir," he said. "Just thinking my family has some bad luck about these parts."

Geiger gave him a momentary look of puzzlement, then began resuming his introduction.

"The submarine *Tambor* reported a heavy Japanese force coming down from the Truk yesterday evening," Geiger stated. "Additional sightings confirm that at least two battleships and a carrier are heading our direction."

There were murmurs around the map board as the gathered men looked at one another.

"*Catalinas* are out searching for our friends as we speak," Geiger continued.

*Not a job I'd want, flying around in the dark hoping not to blunder into the enemy*, Ian thought. He'd flown on several night attacks in Europe. The sea had a way of trying to fool a man in the darkness. Vertigo was as deadly, if not deadlier, than most enemy defenses.

"It is not all bad news, men," Geiger said, with a slight smile. "The carriers *Wasp*, *Hornet*, and *Enterprise* are all in the area."

That brought large smiles from the Marine and Navy aviators. Ian noted the Army men were just as puzzled as he was.

*I suppose the* Wasp *is allegedly lucky, even if her consorts weren't necessarily.* He'd heard rumors about the carrier having a seemingly untimely deck crash that had caused her to turn out of the path of a Japanese submarine's torpedo spread. Unfortunately, that turn had drawn two of her escorts into the fatal fan.

"Sir, are we coordinating with the carriers?" one of the American Army pilots, a major, asked. "Because I don't think we have the right radios for it."

Geiger sighed.

"Trust me, I am well aware of the difficulties between Army and Navy radios," Geiger stated, pointedly looking at an Army major standing to Ian's right.

"I know that we certainly don't have the correct radios," Ian interjected, drawing all eyes towards him. "Sir."

"Squadron Leader Montgomery, that's why you're here," Geiger noted. "I'm going to let you, Major Copeland, and Major Leopold work out the details of your strike."

Ian raised an eyebrow at that. The Army major who had mentioned radios had an even more expressive look of surprise.

"The Japanese have no idea that, with your and Major Copeland's arrival, we can reach out almost twice as far as they're used to," Geiger stated.

"Sir, don't carriers have fighters?" Major Leopold asked, his shock slowly becoming obvious fear.

"I thought they called your planes the *Flying Fortress?*" one of the Marine fighter pilots teased. Leopold was not amused.

"Listen asshole, I've been flying halfway to Rabaul every other day just to say hello to our yellow friends," Leopold snapped. "It's one thing to take a Fort up and deal with maybe a half dozen fighters that aren't all that interested in dealing with twenty machine guns. It's another when you've got two dozen of them very angry you're trying to blow up their home."

"I'm well aware of how 'angry' Japanese fighters can get," the Marine replied. "I've shot down twelve of them."

"Major Bauer, Major Leopold, as entertaining as this is, I'd prefer we save our anger for the enemy," General Geiger interrupted. "Major Copeland's *Lightnings* will provide escort for both you and Squadron Leader Montgomery's *Beaufighters*. In return, you'll provide navigation, just like you did for them to get here."

"Sir, I only have ten effective fighters," Copeland reported.

"I thought you brought sixteen up here," Geiger replied.

"We did. Unless you happen to have some Allison engine parts lying around, some of my pilots were a little too eager to start trying to catch Major Bauer."

There was a long silence around the table.

"We have some Allison parts," the third Army major stated. Copeland turned to the man in surprise.

"Major Bannon…" he started.

"Look, my damn planes can't even fly above 10,000 feet and we have to run every time the Japanese come to bomb us," Major Bannon replied. "If you have a chance to go out and surprise those fuckers, I'm going to do everything in my power to help you."

"I can field twelve fighters," Copeland said, extending his hand. "Thanks to the Fighting Cocks' generosity."

"We don't need much of an escort," Ian stated. "Once we're rid of our torps, there's not a whole lot that's going to catch a *Beau* at low level. It's the anti-aircraft fire that I'm worried about."

He felt all the Americans' eyes on him as he continued.

"Truth be told, I'll go out with twelve, I'll probably bring back eight, maybe six," Ian continued, his tone bitter. "But my men will do our job."

"Thank you, Squadron Leader Montgomery," Geiger stated. "We know that your nation has already done a great deal for us on this island."

"Keeps the little yellow bastards from having a go at my sisters, Sir," Ian replied with dark humor. He gestured in the general direction of the beach. "Besides, half our navy's out in that sound. Be good to have some Australian bodies on the other side. Fish will certainly appreciate the new flavors, I'm sure."

The silence in the room told him that his gallows humor had fallen quite flat.

"Right then, let's talk about how we're going to shear this sheep."

\* \* \*

Two hours later, after Brigadier General Geiger had cleared out the Navy and Marine pilots, Ian and the two Army officers had finished their planning. The oppressive humidity had made Ian's shirt collar start to chafe, and he had unbuttoned it to try and ease the suffering. Reaching into the pocket, he pulled out a pack of cigarettes and passed it around.

"I think the best bet is that we let Major Copeland's boys go in and have a go at that…what did you lot call it? Oh, CAP."

"It's what I'd prefer, yes," Copeland replied. "It will give us a chance to get the drop on them, climb out, and then come back before you guys arrive."

"Why climb out?" Major Leopold asked nervously.

"Because having seen what those assholes can do if we stick around, I'd rather use the *Lightnings'* strengths," Copeland replied, his voice without rancor. "They climb fast, but the -38 goes up like a homesick angel. If they're busy trying to chase me, you and your bombers can come right in while Squadron Leader Copeland's boys are setting up for their torpedo runs."

"I do wonder what your navy lads are going to be up to while all this is going on?" Ian observed.

"I suspect they've got plans of their own," Leopold said. "But judging from the way those other guys were talking, the Japanese have a range advantage. At least, that's what happened at that carrier battle last month."

"Whole lot of fighting over an island," Copeland muttered.

"There's been, what, two fights out in that sound, a carrier battle, and a few of our ships blasted between here and Espiritu?"

"People react rather strongly when you try to steal their airfield," Ian noted drily. "I will say I'm surprised at how much support your Army Air Corps seems to be providing."

"Army Air Force," Leopold corrected, then smiled self-consciously. "Sorry."

"Well, with General MacArthur dead, Admiral Nimitz is the only four star in theater," Copeland said sourly. "Bad war for four stars. Or at least four stars that say dumb shit like 'I shall return...' or 'They'll send *Lightnings* out there over my dead body...'"

"What?" Leopold asked, even as Ian grinned around taking a drag from his cigarette.

"Yeah, allegedly that's what General Arnold said the night before his heart attack," Copeland continued. "At least, that's what the lieutenant colonel who handed me orders at the airfield in Oklahoma told me."

"Oklahoma?" Leopold asked.

"Yeah, we were flying cross country to New York," Copeland explained. "I should be in England by now."

"You wouldn't like it much," Ian stated. "Place has a bit of a German problem."

Copeland exclaimed and smacked his leg. Ian saw the blood smear where the offending mosquito had apparently been well into starting its meal.

"Then again, at least most of the *Mosquitoes* there are friendly."

"Damn things have always had a taste for me," Copeland said angrily. "Makes my wife happy as can be when we're out together."

"She's going to be a lot less happy when you have malaria," Ian remarked, drawing a concerned look from the Army major.

"We all have to survive tomorrow for that to be a problem," Leopold observed.

"Your odds are much better than mine," Ian said. "Usually we had a flak suppression flight go in if there were enemy escorts about. But at least now I'm in a *Beaufighter* rather than a *Beaufort.*"

Copeland looked like he was about to ask the difference, but they were interrupted by rapid footfalls coming down the hall. A Marine first lieutenant poked his head around the corner.

"Gentlemen, Brigadier General Geiger instructed me to inform you that the *Catalina*s have made contact," the young man said. "He intends to launch before dawn."

"Well, it would appear we're being told to go to bed," Ian said, stubbing out his cigarette. "Let's see what havoc we can wreak on the 'morrow."

\* \* \* \* \*

## Chapter 2: A Surprise All Around

*Red One*

*0845 Local*

*13 October 1942*

The two radio calls were almost simultaneous.

"Bogeys! Many bogeys! Three o'clock low!"

"This is Basher One! I've got smoke on the horizon, eleven o'clock!"

*Smoke is not my problem*, Connor thought, whipping his head to his right. *Enemy aircraft are.* He scanned and did not see any aircraft, much less many of them.

"Blue One, I don't see anything," he said.

"Red One, Blue One, permission to engage!" came the response.

To his surprise, Connor saw Blue Flight punch off their drop tanks.

*Well that's called begging for forgiveness after the fact*, Connor thought bitterly. They'd already passed the *Catalina*'s last reported sighting forty-five minutes before. While he wasn't sure how far away the smoke was, Blue Flight punching off their tanks meant the *Lightnings* weren't going much further.

"Green, stay with the bombers, Blue engage, Red follow me," Connor barked beginning the complicated dance of readying his P-38 for combat. Blue Flight banked almost as one, following Captain McIntyre into a turn to starboard. Connor reefed his own fighter around and began climbing up-sun in the direction that McIntyre had indicated.

"Well shit," Connor muttered, suddenly seeing the large gaggle of aircraft roughly eight thousand feet below. There were at least forty to fifty aircraft, with what appeared to be a motley crew of olive and grey fighters weaving above light-painted dive bombers and olive drab single-engine aircraft. Connor dimly recalled that the Navy called the fixed-gear dive bombers *Vals* and the torpedo bombers *Kates*.

*This plan just went to hell,* Connor thought, his throat going dry as Blue Flight dived in. McIntyre would surely die if he attacked at 10:1 odds. Five to one wasn't much better, but at least it would keep the enemy fighters divided. With that decision made, Connor punched off his tanks.

"Everyone pick a target, preferably a leader," he said quickly. Then the squadron net became bedlam as Blue Flight engaged. To his pleasant surprise, Connor watched as McIntyre's flight got in a bounce, the lead *Zero* and one other bursting into flames. As Connor had hammered into the pilots one last time before takeoff, McIntyre continued his slashing attack through the Japanese formation to the far side, winging one of the fixed-gear dive bombers on his way through. The craft did not burn, but it lurched out of formation with fuel streaming from its wings.

*Well here we go,* Connor thought, Red Flight coming into line abreast formation as the escorts all turned to pursue Blue Flight. Quickly trying to figure out which was the best target, Connor picked out the lead torpedo bomber, waggled his wings, and began his attack dive from the formation's starboard rear.

Red Flight's surprise was almost total. A sharp-eyed tail gunner in a lead dive bomber saw the *Lightnings* just as they were two hundred yards from the dive bombers, but his initial burst was far behind Connor's slashing fighter. The man didn't have time to correct, as Red Two's fire sawed him, and the *Val*'s fuselage, in half.

Connor saw the front half of the dive bomber's fuselage start to tumble out of the corner of his eye, his own attention focusing on the *Kate* swelling in front of him. As his prey's tail gunner unlimbered his machine gun and started to swing it, Connor squeezed the trigger on what he intended to be a three-second burst. Instead, his spray of fire turned the tail gunner into a rag doll of savaged meat before traveling forward to detonate the underslung torpedo beneath the *Kate*'s fuselage.

*Fuck!* Connor thought, as debris slammed back over his fuselage in a series of loud thumps. He passed through the smoke cloud, a flailing torso passing just over his canopy as he continued his dive. Taking several deep breaths, he began pulling up on the stick as the *Lightning* shuddered from the strain. Taking a quick check over his craft, he saw a large black smear and several gouges on his starboard wing.

*Must have gotten hit by the engine*, he had time to think, putting the P-38's nose skyward to convert his excess speed into altitude. A quick check showed Red Two staying with him, while Red Three and Four were turning after the *Zeroes* pursuing Blue Flight.

*Goddammit*, he thought, standing on his own rudder to begin side slipping his nose around. The *Lightnings* realized the error of their ways when two *chutai* of *Zeroes* reversed course back towards the bombers they had abandoned. Even as Connor got his own nose around, the agile Japanese fighters set upon his second section like hyenas on a pair of lions. Red Three managed to saw one assailant's wing off in a head on run, but swiftly had two more on the *Light-*

*ning*'s tail. Red Four's starboard engine was hit, smoke streaming back from the Allison as a *chutai* leader latched onto the P-38.

"You son-of-a-bitch!" Connor shouted as he lined up on the Zero. As if he heard him, the Japanese leader broke up into a chandelle. Connor did not take the bait, instead thundering past and snapping a burst at one of the *Zeroes* attacking Red Three. The stream of fire was wide, but it was enough to make the Japanese fighter break off its pass. An explosion in his rear-view mirror made Connor's heart stop, whipping around to find Red Two. Seeing his wingman, Connor realized McKnight had smoked the *chutai* leader at the apex of his maneuver.

*That kid is going to get a promotion*, he thought, watching as the other *Lightning* stayed tucked in on his tail. Having gained separation, Connor brought his fighter back around just in time to see Red Four going down in flames, the victorious *Zero* looping around to try and chase Red Three. He frantically searched for Blue Flight, not seeing any of their P-38s but noticing another two smoke trails descending towards the sea in the general direction the bombers had been heading.

"Blue Flight, check in!" Connor barked. "Red Three, dive out and head south!"

"This is Blue One, we've splashed another four bombers but are low on fuel!" McIntyre replied.

Connor checked his own fuel gauge and realized it was getting towards time for him to disengage also.

*If only they'd been at the last sighting position*, he fumed. *Shit. Green Flight and the bombers.*

\* \* \*

*Wallaby Leader*

*0915 Local*

*J*erry *had better flak, but these bloody fighters are persistent*, Ian thought. He watched as a P-38 slashed over his *Beaufighter*, charging the *Zero* pursuing him as he led his squadron on a parallel course to the smoking Japanese carrier off his port wing. Someone, most likely an American scout, had managed to hit the vessel with at least one bomb. If Ian had to guess, the damage was far from fatal, even on what appeared to be a light carrier, but it had been helpful in pointing the path towards the ship.

"What the hell?!" his observer, Flight Officer Derek Davenport, shouted. A forest of waterspouts had suddenly erupted all around the Japanese carrier, her form largely hidden by the sudden explosions. The heavy cruiser following the carrier in her turn had one bright explosion on her forward bow, the impact only slightly lessening the intense fire she was putting out towards Ian's *Beaufighter*.

"Perth Flight in position, Wallaby Leader! Starting my attack run now!"

Ian had split his squadron of twelve *Beaufighters* into two. Perth Flight, headed by an energetic lad from its namesake city, was coming in on the Japanese carrier's port side. Ian's six aircraft had been working their way up towards the starboard bow, the one with a heavy cruiser on it.

*Not going to ask a bloke to take the harder shot*, Ian thought.

"Let's get on with it, Wallaby," he said. Bringing the *Beaufighter* around, he began descending and retarding his throttle.

*The problem with torpedoes is that they are so bloody sensitive*, he thought angrily as his strike fighter slowed. The 18-inch torpedo under his fuselage had to be delivered at roughly 150 knots or less, from a height no more than one hundred feet. As tracers from the heavy cruiser and destroyer began reaching out towards his fighter, he felt the aircraft began to grow sluggish as he dumped speed. A flak burst jostled the *Beaufighter*, fragments pinging off the fuselage as the water grew closer below.

"Blimey, Parsons just augered in!" Davenport bit out. The man's next comment was drowned out by a hailstorm of fragments slamming into the *Beaufighter*. The big aircraft lurched, and for a moment Ian was certain they were going to smash into the waves below. Ahead of him, he saw smoke billowing from a destroyer's stack as she began steaming to try and cut across Wallaby's path. The vessel's gunners began shooting at the *Beaufighter*, their initial bursts high.

*Well two can play that game*, Ian thought, realizing the destroyer was indeed going to get in their way. He squeezed his trigger just as two streams of fire began to converge towards him. There was an explosion and faint cry behind him, hot steel lashing into the back of his flight suit even as his and the rest of Wallaby Flight's own cannon fire danced across the destroyer in a strobe light of explosions. As he pulled back on the stick to arc over the vessel, Ian noted the fire suddenly diminish. As the *Beaufighter* flashed over the destroyer, just barely clearing its mast, he saw bodies slumped over guns and on the vessel's bridge.

"Davenport, are you all right?!" Ian asked, shouting to be heard over a rush of wind stream that was suddenly loud in the *Beaufighter*'s nose. There was no response, and Ian quickly looked over his shoulder, pain telling him that he still had fragments of some sort in his back. It took only a glance to see that Davenport was dead, his observer's chest a ruin from some cannon round that had probably killed him instantly.

*Bloody hell,* Ian thought, glancing left then right to note only four of the six *Beaufighters* remained. Before him, he saw that the Japanese carrier captain had made his choice, the vessel's silhouette growing longer beyond the heavy cruiser.

*Almost there...CHRIST!*

The Japanese cruiser's broadside was a spectacle to behold as it erupted towards Wallaby flight. Ian swore he felt the 8-inch shells' passage as they roared just past the *Beaufighters* to erupt roughly two hundred yards behind them. As futile as the display was, the heavy cruiser's light batteries managed to claim one more *Beaufighter,* bursting Wallaby Five's starboard engine into flame. The dying Australian released his weapon as a final act, the big fighter smashing into the water and cartwheeling forward in a massive spray.

Ian cursed, angry tears running down his face as he lined the *Beaufighter*'s stubby nose up and pressed his torpedo release. The heavy weapon dropped away, and he immediately added throttle and skidded his nose to pass astern of the carrier. The *Beaufighter* skimmed just astern, and Ian saw three wakes arrowing towards the Japanese flattop from Perth Flight's drop.

*Either way you go, you bitch,* he thought. Then it was time to pay attention to his flying again, as he saw a *Zero* turning after one of the Perth *Beaufighters.* The Japanese pilot never knew what hit him as Ian came in with almost full deflection, his four cannon and four machine guns ripping the lighter *Zero* to shreds.

"Wallaby Leader! That's a hit! That's a hit!" he heard Major Leopold's voice over the radio. "Two hits!"

*Glad to see our fix worked,* Ian thought. They'd taken the radio out
of one of his *Beaufighters* and placed it in Major Leopold's B-17. It
required the *Flying Fortress*'s flight engineer to turn off his own squadron's radios, but clearly Leopold had seen fit to take the risk.

"Roger Bomber One," Ian said, having forgotten Leopold's actual call sign. His shoulder throbbed even more, and he felt lighthead-
ed. "Give my regards to Green One, his lads did a good job. We're
going home."

\* \* \* \* \*

## Chapter 3: A *Lightning* Cross

*Red One*

*1400 Local*

*17 October 1942*

"I'm starting to think that our friends are going to concede this island," General Geiger observed.

It had been two days since the last Japanese air raid on Guadalcanal, and three days since the conclusion of what the Navy had dubbed the Battle of Santa Cruz. As Connor looked at the Marine general who had seemingly just materialized in the shade under the *Lightning*'s wing, he thought the man looked positively jubilant.

*Wish I could be as chipper*, Connor thought, a shiver running through him. *But funny thing about malaria; it pretty much performs as advertised.*

"Well, I can't say I blame them," he stuttered out. Geiger gave him an appraising look.

"I think you need to go see the flight surgeon, Major," the man said, his tone making it clear that it wasn't really a suggestion.

"Just as soon as we're sure none of our friends will be coming to visit, sir," Connor replied.

*I hate this place*, he thought. *At least I don't have the shits like McIntyre.* His Blue Flight leader had made the mistake of attempting to share some of the Marine rations rather than sticking with the Army packs that had come up on one of the C-47s. While Connor was all about showing solidarity with their brethren, he'd had the feeling there would be plenty of time for that once they ran out of Army chow.

"I think about another hour or so will do it, Major," Geiger allowed. He turned to his aide, and Connor didn't miss the man's subtle nod.

*While technically I don't work for the man, I guess that's my cue to follow orders.*

"Just how bad did the Aussies plaster that carrier anyway?" Connor asked. "I keep hearing different stories on the radio."

Geiger looked around. Satisfied no one was in ear shot, the general smiled. Connor suddenly felt a chill that had nothing to do with his fever.

"They stopped her dead in her tracks," Geiger said. "The *Wasp*'s strike finished her off."

"What happened with our folks?" Connor asked. He shook violently, feeling as if someone had placed a block of ice on his very soul. Geiger looked prepared to order him directly to the surgeon, but demurred.

"Well, someone interfered with the Japanese's Sunday Punch," Geiger stated. "Which was a good thing, as Rear Admiral Kinkaid is an idiot. *Hornet* and *Enterprise* were both badly damaged, but they'll probably survive."

*Well looks like jumping that strike was worth it,* Connor thought. *Or, at least as worth it as losing four of my men could be.*

"At your request, I'm putting Captain McIntyre in for the Medal of Honor," Geiger said. "General Vandegrift has heartily endorsed it."

"Thank you, sir," Connor replied.

"As for you, I think you're going to be the first Army squadron commander to win a Navy Cross," Geiger continued, causing Connor to look up in surprise.

"Sir, I just did my job," he said.

"Major, you did a whole lot more than just your job," Geiger replied. "You probably saved two carriers and thousands of men with your decisions. I'll never say it again or acknowledge it in public, but your squadron may have saved this island."

"I think there's an Australian who had a hand in it as well, Sir," Connor replied.

* * *

*Espiritu Santo*
*1630 Local*
*13 October 1942*

"You know, I think she likes you," Major Leopold said, watching the slim French nurse walk out of the makeshift aid station. The building had formerly belonged to one of the island's families before being appropriated to serve the war effort. Now it was the Australian forces' rehabilitation center for men wounded badly enough to be off duty, but not so badly as to require further evacuation to the south.

*I'm not one to kiss and tell, mate, but I* know *she likes me,* Ian thought. *Not quite how I expected to use the French I learned during escape and evasion classes, but it works.*

"Noelle is just a friendly woman," Ian replied with a smile. "I'm actually surprised they let you in here, given the rules your Vice Admiral Halsey put in place a couple weeks ago when he took over."

Leopold shrugged.

"I have my ways," he replied. "Most of them involving having been roommates with Lieutenant General Eichelberger's aide and that man being on the island."

Ian raised an eyebrow.

"General Eichelberger's on the island?" Ian asked. "Color me surprised. I understand that Vice Admiral Ghormley and he never spoke. At least, that was the impression I got when they were briefing us on coming up here."

"I don't follow the Navy's dealings much," Leopold allowed. "That also might be why Ghormley got fired."

"Ward, ATTENTION!"

"At ease, at ease!" a male voice stated. Ian had just enough time to look at Major Leopold before the door to his own four bed ward opened.

*Well shit, I guess he is on the island,* Ian thought, starting to struggle to his feet at Lieutenant General Robert Eichelberger strode into the room.

"Please, please, don't get up on my account," the white-haired flag officer stated. He gave Major Leopold a puzzled smile.

"Well, I wasn't expecting to find you both together, but this does make my job somewhat easier," Eichelberger said. Ian saw the man's aide smile behind him as Major Leopold's face briefly flashed realization.

*I think someone's roommate was clearly a prankster,* Ian thought.

"Good afternoon, sir," Ian said with a nod.

"So, I'm told that the Marines are putting you in for a Navy Cross," Lieutenant General Eichelberger said.

*Well that's the first I've heard of it,* Ian thought. Thankfully, the man continued.

"Funny, I just happened to have seen a certain Vice Admiral, and he happened to have a supply of those things on hand."

The man reached behind him, taking the box his aide extended.

"While Brigadier General Geiger thought that a Distinguished Flying Cross would be sufficient for you, Major Leopold," Eichelberger continued, "thankfully the Marines still answer to the Navy."

Eichelberger took the first decoration out of the box. To Ian's surprise, the man was very careful as he placed it on Ian's tropical whites. For a moment, Ian thought of poor Davenport and the rest of his men. He fought back tears as he nodded at the general.

"Thank you, Squadron Leader Montgomery, on behalf of a grateful American nation," Eichelberger said. Ian nodded, too overcome by emotion to speak.

"As for you, Leopold," Eichelberger said. "Good work on being the first B-17 squadron to actually hit something."

Major Leopold colored slightly at that but maintained his bearing as Eichelberger pinned the Navy Cross on him. The general came to attention and saluted his subordinate, a gesture Leopold returned with clear surprise.

*"Now, if you'll excuse me, I'm going to go talk with Vice Admiral Halsey about the next thing the Army can do to save the Navy's ass,"* Lieutenant General Eichelberger said. *"That is, assuming he's done ripping some poor rear admiral's face off."*

\* \* \* \* \*

## Dedication

To the men of the 67th Pursuit Squadron, U.S. Army Air Force. They did their best with what they had on Guadalcanal.

\* \* \* \* \*

## Author's Note

In our timeline, the Guadalcanal Campaign was a stubbornly fought series of engagements that resulted in a narrow American victory. Historically, General Hap Arnold, chief of the Army Air Forces, personally prevented any P-38s from being transferred to the Pacific Theater for most of 1942. When shipped, the fighters went to General MacArthur's Southwest Pacific Theater command rather than to the Solomons. As part of that command, the Royal Australian Air Force employed its *Beaufighters* against the Japanese in the New Guinea area, not in the Solomons.

Astute historians will note that the Battle of Savo Island is not as one-sided as it was historically. This is due to multiple sighting reports of Vice Admiral Gunichi Mikawa's task force actually being relayed in a timely manner to USN forces rather than working through General MacArthur's byzantine staff processes. Allied forces stymying Mikawa's force, even at heavy losses, would have allowed for a more robust development of Henderson Field and the Marine perimeter. The "knock on" effects of this are subtly presented in the more robust strike capability available to the Cactus Air Force.

\* \* \* \* \*

## James Young Bio

James Young holds a doctorate in U.S. History from Kansas State University and is a graduate of the United States Military Academy. Fiction is James' first writing love, but he's also dabbled in non-fiction with publications in the *Journal of Military History* and *Proceedings* to his credit. His current fiction series are the *Usurper's War* (alternate history), *Vergassy Chronicles* (space opera), and *Scythefall* (apocalyptic fiction), all of which are available via Amazon. You can find him at his FB Page (https://www.facebook.com/ColfaxDen/), Twitter (@Youngblai), or by signing up for his mailing list on the front page of his blog (https://vergassy.com/).

# # # # #

# Catching the Dark
# by Monalisa Foster

*achthexe. Nochnaya Ved'ma.* Night Witch.
Maria Mikhailovna Sutreva smiled at how poetic
those words sounded. The Nazis were fascist bastards, but the epithet had a certain ring to it. More than a ring; it had power. A sense of satisfaction too. It meant that Maria and her sisters-in-arms had struck fear and inspired hatred in the enemies' hearts. She leaned back in her office chair. Well-padded and comfortable, it creaked a bit, but she settled into its embrace. Steam wafted out of the cut crystal glasses set in their metal holders. Stirring the pillow-shaped tea strainer around in the hot water sent a few tiny tea leaves swirling around the sugar cube that was still dissolving in the center.

She flipped to the next page of the intel report.

*Ha!*

According to the Nazis, the "Night Witches" were not just criminals sent to the front lines as punishment, but they were being given pills to give them a feline's perfect night-vision. It was fantasy disguised as propaganda. The Nazis, already prone to superstition just like their Führer, needed a way to explain why they only heard the sounds of the wind whistling against the biplane's bracing wires right before her crews dropped their bombs. And the soft "whooshing" *did* sound like a broomstick cutting through the air.

Her unit's official designation was the Tsarina's Own Night Bomber Regiment. But "Night Witches" was oh-so-much better. She was of a mind to order that images of a witch riding her broom be painted on the sides of their Polikarpov U-2 biplanes. The rickety, wooden crop-dusters—which were more like coffins with wings than not—needed a little bit of panache. Decorating their U-2s would raise morale if nothing else.

The sugar cube had dissolved. She sipped her tea and flipped to the next page. A dog-eared German newspaper clipping and its translation were held together with a prong fastener. An analyst had circled the relevant text with red ink: any German airman who downed one of the "Night Witches" would be automatically awarded the Iron Cross.

Maria frowned; her previous amusement doused by what she knew of German culture. The Iron Cross was a huge motivator for Nazi troops.

She set the report aside, uncapped her fountain pen and jotted down a note for the Tsarina's public relations department, suggesting they use the Iron Cross incentive to play up the fear that the women of the Tsarina's Own had inspired. They were all tools on two fronts—the war in the air and the war for the minds and hearts of the people. The irony of it stung Maria as she signed her name.

Maria's family had had to call in far too many political favors owed them and heap them atop her own impressive flying record to convince Tsarina Tatiana Nikolaevna Romanova to grant her an audience. Maria had not wasted her opportunity to make the case for forming an all-female regiment and letting them fly combat missions.

The Tsarina had been more than reluctant. She had worked as a Red Cross nurse in the Great War. She knew what war did to soldiers and how much worse it could be for women. The Bolsheviks had made sure of that, and the Tsarina had never forgotten it. But ultimately, Maria pointing out the public relations coup had been the convincing factor.

Russia had lost a lot of planes in Operation Barbarossa. Planes that had been caught on the ground. Russia was not short on pilots. She was short on aircraft. That's how Maria's unit ended up with U-2 biplanes. The U-2, already outdated by the time the war started, had been relegated to a training and crop-dusting role. It may have been made of linen and wood. It may have been so slow that newer, faster airplanes would stall out before they could match its speed, but the U-2 was maneuverable. Maria intended to take advantage of that maneuverability, that ability to turn on a razor's edge. And there were thousands of U-2s spread throughout Russia. They could be spared.

*We will make do with what we have*, she'd told the Tsarina. *It's what we do.*

As Maria dabbed at the fresh ink with a blotter her gaze fell on the framed picture of her brother, Andrei. It had been taken just before he'd joined the infantry. Fresh-faced, he smiled back at her in the way only a young man with the world at his feet could. Now he was gone, the world no longer at his feet, the future no longer before him. He was a pile of bones—if that—rotting under the soil of some battlefield, feeding her need for vengeance, sustaining her through the cold nights, the pain of loss, the rage she often needed to keep going.

Most of the women in her unit had volunteered because they'd lost a brother or a sweetheart to the Nazis. It was loss that bound them together. When the darkness descended, they rose, shedding their femininity to become killing machines.

Maria pulled Andrei's picture to her chest, squeezing hard enough for the edges to dig into her palm, for the glass to make that soft, warning sound announcing its fragility. Andrei's image, Andrei's memory no longer made her cry. At first, she'd been grateful. Now, it terrified her. Someday the war would be over. Hitler would be dead. The Tsarina would put his head on a pike just like she had Lenin's, Stalin's, and Trotsky's.

On that day, Maria hoped she would be able weep for Andrei— for all Russians—once again.

\* \* \*

Everyone thought that Junior Lieutenant Natalya Alexandrovna Ivanova was seventeen. She'd lied, making herself a year older because she didn't think anyone would believe the number of hours on her flight log otherwise. Her family owned many parcels of land, mostly farms, and Natalya and her older sister had been taught to fly so they could dust the crops. At the small, rural flight school Natalya had found her calling, her reason for being. It was there she had learned that she could have the sky, the endless blue and the feeling of freedom that came with it.

Crop-dusting wasn't glamorous, but after the work was done, she was free to soar to her heart's content. Sweet-talking *Pápochka* into the extra fuel for her thrill-flying hadn't been particularly hard, especially as the youngest. He had given her wings and would not deny his little angel the use of them.

The job of navigator wasn't what Natalya had had in mind, but the pilot slots were full. At first, Natalya had been afraid that she'd overdone her "audition." However, the evaluator, a middle-aged Georgian with thick sideburns, signed off and sent her to a training regiment with one piece of advice: follow the rules. She'd taken his advice to heart. There were far more volunteers than slots. She could behave if it meant she got to fly, because once the war had started, the price of fuel had soared and every precious drop was needed to help grow food.

Following the rules had finally gotten her to the Tsaritsyn airdrome and into the Tsarina's Own. She'd learned what to expect from her training regiment.

It still hadn't prepared her for this!

Natalya stuck her gloved finger into one of the bullet holes peppering her Polikarpov's canvas shell.

"Thirty. *Der'mo!*"

She kept counting even as the Sun rose over the windswept airfield.

"Why do you do that?" Eva broke in sternly as she finished tying down the biplane.

At twenty-three, Natalya's pilot, Senior Lieutenant Eva Spozhnikova, was one of the oldest women of the Tsarina's Own. Two weeks ago, after Eva had lost her navigator to anti-aircraft fire, they had been paired together, veteran and green, unproven recruit.

"To know how often to thank God," Natalya said. "Forty-one. Forty-two. *Tvoyu mat.*"

Pain flickered in Eva's eyes as she pulled off her sealskin cap and trudged off, shaking her head. Ever since Eva's newborn daughter had died in the "morale bombing" of Tsaritsyn—along with her husband, parents, and siblings—she'd not just lost faith. She was angry with God. Probably angrier than she was with the Germans.

Sometimes Natalya thought that the "tempering force" that was Eva was only there because of her need for revenge. The longer they flew, the more Germans they could kill. Ultimately that was everyone's goal, but there was something in the cold efficiency of Eva's flying, the fine line between risk and reward that made Natalya wonder what would happen if they were ever faced with a situation where their two lives could be traded for far more German deaths. *How many Germans would she sacrifice us both to kill? What number would make her do it without hesitation?*

Natalya shuddered, suddenly cold despite the fur-lined flight jacket, the insulated coveralls, and the boots fit for an empress. What the Tsarina could not give them in aircraft, she had at least made up for by making sure they were well-dressed for their jobs. Of course, the clothes did not keep out all the cold, but were the difference between a little numbness and frostbite.

Their two mechanics were already careening the motorized sardine-tin-on-wheels—what their American allies called a "Jeep"—onto the tarmac. Natalya shielded her eyes against the sunrise. Olga Tokranova's blonde head barely peeked above the steering wheel as she swerved left and right again, going all the way off the tarmac with one set of wheels before pulling back onto it again. Still getting used to the steering wheel being on the left, their eighteen-year-old mechanic was more than a few centimeters shy of the height the Ford engineers had obviously had in mind for a driver. Her older sister Vera was in the passenger seat, holding on for dear life.

Olga hit the brakes, kicking up a spray of dead weeds, dust and rocks, and leaving a streak of rubber two Jeep-lengths long. Tortured gears screamed in agony as she backed up like she was retreating from a German battalion, and came to a stop in a cloud of smoke and swirling debris. Vera stumbled out of the vehicle, her otherwise pale skin looking more like the vehicle's green than not and glared at Olga.

"That's it," Vera said, holding her forefinger out like a babushka threatening an errant grandchild. "No more driving for you."

"Not my fault the steering wheel is on the wrong side," Olga shouted back as the Jeep's engine sighed to a stop. The younger Tokranova climbed over the seat into the back. A tool bag landed with a thud beside the Jeep. It was followed by another. Then a third.

Vera circled the Polikarpov, eyes going wide at the number of holes. She patted the propeller's nose gently, like one would a wounded puppy.

"What did Eva do to this poor thing?" Vera asked as Natalya walked over to assess the damage with her. Vera's face soured as they circled the plane. The mechanic also counted bullet holes, although for different reasons. The more holes, the more things she had to check and make sure were working properly.

"Forty-two?" Vera asked.

"A new record," Natalya said bitterly.

Vera patted her on the shoulder. "Don't worry. They may try, but the fascists can't put enough bullet holes in any U-2 to bring her down. Not as long as either a pilot or a navigator can still fly her."

Natalya nodded and gave her an appreciative smile. Technically, Vera was right. As long as the bullets weren't tracers. They'd had a good night. Hadn't lost anyone to tracers. No one had lost height in the darkness or the clouds and crashed.

"Go. Get some sleep," Vera said. "We've got her."

Natalya gave Vera a hug. The mechanic smelled of fuel, motor oil, and sweat. Vera pushed her away and aimed Natalya towards the barracks.

By sunset, their Polikarpov, affectionately called *Malyshka*, would be ready to fly once again.

\* \* \*

Natalya and a dozen or so of her fellow pilots and navigators took their dinner—what most sane people called breakfast—in a converted hangar filled with rows and rows of tables. A mix of chairs, some ancient, some rescued from closed schools, surrounded the tables in a disorderly, unmilitary manner that bothered no one.

On good days, they had blinis with jam and hot milk mixed with cocoa and honey. Today it was a slice of cold bread and *kolbasa*, with a thick layer of butter between the two. Instead of tea, Natalya took hot water with lemon and honey. She wanted to get some sleep. Unlike Zoya and Raisa, who drank black tea all night and could still sleep like the dead.

Natalya looked around for Eva but couldn't find her among the women in the dining hall. For two weeks, she'd been trying to get Eva to talk to her as if she were something other than just her navigator. Professionalism was one thing. This was something else, and Natalya wanted to make it—whatever it was—right.

She scarfed down her sandwich, hardly tasting it at all. Being constantly hungry wasn't the best thing when you were flying all night. She blamed it on being sixteen and couldn't wait to outgrow it, so she could sit down at a table like a lady, all manners and poise, instead of a demon possessed who might forget herself and elbow-shove the women in the food line out of her way.

She finished off the hot water, fished out the slice of lemon and munched on it as she crossed the yard to the barracks. Closing her eyes, she stopped to turn her face up to the sun and enjoy its touch. She missed the sun. When the war was over, she was going to go to the shores of the Black Sea and spend a whole summer doing nothing but lying on the warm sands until she was as bronzed as a Greek goddess. When the war was over, she'd fill a swimsuit like a woman should, and men would court her and bring her flowers and try to steal a kiss. When the war was over, she was going to let them.

A yawn reminded her that soon she'd be up in the night sky again. No more daydreaming.

She opened the barracks door, slipped in, hung up her flight gear and stepped out of her boots.

Two rows of beds lined the walls, separated by lines of rope weighed down with drying laundry. Strictly non-regulation, the arrangement afforded at least some semblance of privacy and meant their clothes wouldn't come back frozen stiff only to have to be de-thawed.

They'd even commandeered a few damaged tarps, patched them, and hung them like curtains. Being one of seven children, Natalya didn't mind the bustle and energy of being packed into a small space with unruly siblings, but not everyone had grown up that way.

In one corner, five women relaxed by listening to music played on a hand-cranked phonograph player. They drew lots for turns at picking the songs. If they weren't too tired, they danced. Today, they were tired. Half-dressed, they just sat back and soaked in the music, occasionally humming or singing along.

Tamara, one of the older pilots, sat cross-legged atop her cot, surrounded by three other women, showing them the intricacies of a complicated stitch. Tamara was adamant that sewing pretty things allowed her to forget about the war for awhile. As the war went on, her circle of sewing enthusiasts had grown. Needle and thread had become the most requested care-package items.

Others read. Half of the pilots and navigators were already propped up in bed, reading books that were falling apart. Anything was game. Even children's picture books and folklore. Anything that didn't have to do with war.

Natalya found Eva at the far end of the barracks, behind one of the tarp-curtains, sitting in the only rocking chair, eyes closed in sleep. She'd shed her flight gear and was cradling the commander of the Mouser Regiment in her arms. The bluish-grey cat, referred to as Her Imperial Highness, was purring loudly in Eva's lap. Very pregnant, the small Russian Blue had grown huge. Someone had tacked a calendar to the wall and was dutifully counting down to kitten-day. On a small table, a jar held strips of paper with names. It was already full, waiting on the big day.

Everyone came off the flight line, off the mission, and dealt with the constant back and forth between tedium and terror in their own way. Some sang and danced. Others read books and wrote letters or poetry or sewed. Eva dealt by nurturing new life in the only way the war had left open to her.

Natalya sighed. She'd catch Eva another night. Carefully, she drew the curtain closed and flopped down on her own cot.

She felt underneath its narrow mattress and pulled out the comic book an American pilot had given her. They'd spent two days together on the train that had delivered her to Tsaritsyn. It had been his parting present to her. She lost herself in the color of the pictures and barely decipherable words. Unlike the novels and magazines circulating around the barracks, the comic book allowed her to make up a new story for the pictures every night.

\* \* \*

The early twilight of winter descended, cutting sleep short. The Tsaritsyn airdrome had been blasted with high winds the whole day while Natalya and the rest of her unit had slept. Eventually, she'd get used to the noise and really rest. So everyone said. Cold air seeped through the barracks' thin walls and chilled them despite the heaters. Most everyone settled for a splash of cold water on their faces before donning their flight gear and heading for roll call.

Major Maria Mikhailovna Sutreva was wrapping up her debriefing in the dining hall as Natalya and her sisters ate breakfast. Their commander was a tall woman, her face lined by the ravages of wind and sun, her dark hair showing touches of grey. She moved with a quiet elegance marred by touches of wear and tear, speaking with vigor, without wasting a single word, always making clear the difference between those things they knew for certain and those they merely suspected.

Between sips of hot, bitter tea Natalya made marks on the map she'd learned by heart, noting the location where the Germans advancing on Tsaritsyn had dug in. Between sunset and sunrise, they'd get at least ten sorties in, if the weather cooperated.

"All right sisters," Major Sutreva said, her voice rising. "It's time for our nightly dance. Time to go cheek-to-cheek with Father Frost."

Laughter rippled through the squadron as chairs scraped away from tables. While no one had yet lost a cheek to frostbite, the unusually cold winter made them feel like they were dancing with the wizard-king of winter every time they took to the sky.

Natalya shrugged into her jacket, patted her flight suit's pockets to verify that she had all the tools of her trade: ruler, stopwatch, flashlight, pencil, compass, sidearm. She tucked her too-short hair into the sealskin flight cap and pulled it down tight until the flaps dangled down to her collarbones. The goggles went snugly over the cap. She buttoned the jacket and hung the clipboard with the map off her belt.

Eva was already pulling her cap's flaps tight and shoving her hands into gloves as she headed out the door. Natalya followed, and they did their pre-flight checks as the wind shuddered around them.

Even tied down, *Malyshka* grabbed at the wind with her wings as though she were eager to be in flight. They had been made for each other. These airplanes. These women. They all lived to soar.

The armorers had loaded two fifty-kilo bombs, one under each wing. Natalya ducked under the lower wings to double-check the release mechanism. With the wind howling, she only caught snatches of Vera's report to Eva, but her pilot signed off on the repairs, and they exchanged salutes.

Eva climbed into the front cockpit, reached into her jacket and pulled out a small picture. She stuck the fading image of her baby daughter under the magnet kept on the instrument panel just for that purpose and strapped in.

The engine came to life, sounding like an angry sewing machine. As the propellers picked up speed they looked like scythes cutting through the frigid air.

Natalya climbed into the rear cockpit, strapped in, and clipped her map to the control panel. Tie-downs were released and stops pulled away from the wheels, and *Malyshka* lined up behind the first and second planes of their trio. She tucked the interphone's earpiece under her cap, pulled the flaps tight and fastened the mouthpiece on. A piece of rubber connected her end of it to Eva's. The system's saving grace was that it kept the wind off part of her face, and it was better than shouting. But not by much.

Moments later they were in the air, flying in formation with the other two U-2s leading them.

Natalya took her red-tipped flashlight and turned it on. She checked her compass and map and double-checked their position against the wooded terrain below and the winding tributaries that fed the Volga.

"Were you ever afraid of Baba Yaga?" Eva asked out of the blue.

"What?" Natalya turned off the flashlight.

"We're third in line," Eva explained. "The third sister. Baba Yaga."

Oh. Natalya frowned at the strange question. "No! I was not afraid."

"Never? Not even when you were little?"

Natalya smiled. "Never! Baba Yaga was afraid of me."

Eva's laughter carried through interphone.

A flare dropped from the lead plane, dangling on its silken parachute, lighting up the German fortifications below.

Natalya blew out a long breath. The flare lit only a small patch of a larger darkness as it fell. The pit of her stomach went hard around her breakfast as the searchlights came up, caught the flare and swept the sky.

The first two airplanes fell into the beams. Anti-aircraft guns responded with jets of projectiles streaming into the night sky, reaching, grasping, for the U-2s leading *Malyshka*.

"Steady on course and altitude!" Natalya shouted into the interphone, confirming that they were in range for their first drop.

Wrapped in darkness, Eva idled the engine and they went into a dive, aiming for the source of the nearest column of light.

"Three…two…one…" Natalya pulled on the bomb-release lever and released 100 kilos of explosives right atop the target.

Eva pulled up.

Behind them an angry flower bloomed, extinguishing the searchlight.

Natalya whooped as *Malyshka* soared.

Another searchlight caught them and would not let them go. Eva was flying blind, banking, drawing the light with her so the other planes could take their turn at catching the dark.

Another explosion and one of the anti-aircraft guns went silent.

*Malyshka* swept the sky, dragging the remaining columns of light with them, pulling up and away. Then only darkness. As Eva circled, light burst as more guns fired. One caught them, peppering *Malyshka* with bullets to her wings.

They dove back into the lights, catching a beam. It flickered—but didn't go out—as one of the other U-2s dropped her bombs.

Eva threaded *Malyshka* through the lights, the streams of bullets, waiting for a third explosion.

"*Tvoyu mat!*" rang out over the interphone.

Against the velvet darkness of the sky, one of the other U-2s fell like a flaming torch. A tracer round had hit one of *Malyshka's* sisters, lighting her up like a box of matches. There was nothing they could do but watch their sisters burn.

Eva dove into the darkness, going so low that it must have looked like they were floating a meter above the treetops.

Natalya ran her calculations and gave her pilot the heading back to the airdrome. Once they were on the correct heading, she took the stick, giving Eva time to rest.

"Who do you think it was?" Natalya asked, voice cracking.

"We'll find out soon enough." Eva's voice was ice-cold. It seemed to reach through the interphone and snake through Natalya. She could not shake off its chill.

It was still there when the airdrome came into view and Eva reclaimed the stick.

\* \* \*

Natalya was stooped under the right wing as she helped Olga hoist the fifty-kilo bomb into its cradle.

Eva busied herself by checking *Malyshka*. She'd already circled the U-2 three times, climbed atop the wings, tugged on all the control wires. But she'd not said a word. She never did. There was too much to do.

Vera came running up to them. "That's it," Vera said. "That's all of them."

U-2s had been landing every few minutes and lining up to be refueled and rearmed.

"How many?" Eva asked as she checked the fuel pump. She'd done her best to hide her tears, but they coated her lashes in a fine layer of betraying crystals.

"Two," Vera said. "Tamara and Nina. Zoya and Raisa."

Natalya crossed herself and said a silent prayer for them and their families.

Eva took a deep breath and looked away, absently patting her sidearm as if she was making sure it was still there.

"Tracer rounds," Vera added. "Both of them."

Silent nods of understanding passed between them. Tamara, Nina, Zoya and Raisa had gone up in flames, a better fate than what awaited them had they crashed. Burning was better than crashing. Burning was better because while they all carried guns so they would not be taken alive, there were rumors of being captured, of being gang raped. To crash, lose consciousness, and wake up to that fate...

Olga swiped at her nose with her sleeve and busied herself with disconnecting the fuel line.

"Here's the new flight order," Vera said, handing Eva a piece of paper.

"Same target?" Eva asked.

Vera gave her a grim nod.

Eva hopped up on the wing and climbed in. Natalya followed.

Later, there would be time for tears, for mourning. They would sing for their fallen sisters, pack their things with reverence to be sent back home, and set a place at the table for them one last time. And in her office, Major Sutreva would write a personal letter by hand, praising each woman's accomplishment's and call them heroines, all in the hope that it would provide their families with some bit of comfort.

She would not write of how they had burned, of how painfully they had died, of how fortunate they had been.

She would not write of the future they would not have, of the love they would never know, of the children they would never bear.

She would not write of the Iron Crosses that would decorate the chests of the men who had shot them down.

\* \* \*

On the second sortie, Eva led. Polina's plane, called *Pobeda*, flew alongside them. They didn't need a flare to find their target. The Germans were waiting, stabbing the dark with three searchlights.

*Pobeda* and *Malyshka* raced into their beams. They deliberately attracted the Germans' attention, courting them, inviting the streams of anti-aircraft fire to dance. When all three searchlights were pointed at them they maneuvered wildly, avoiding the tracers.

Natalya was thrown about the rear cockpit, the harness digging into her shoulders. Gravity pushed her back as *Malyshka* looped and rolled, racing the cloud of deadly fireflies swarming after them.

Irina's U-2, the third airplane of their sortie, must have scored a hit. A searchlight went out. Eva brought *Malyshka* back around and they dove in an eerie silence.

"Three...two...one..." Natalya hit the release.

Eva revved up the engine as their wing caught a stream of bullets. Natalya held her breath, waiting for the canvas to start burning, but either the tracers had missed them, or they'd been lucky.

Maybe those prayers hadn't been wasted after all. Still, the hairs on the back of her neck were standing up in warning.

"Something's not right," Natalya said as she turned in her seat. Behind them, the explosion was too small. She leaned out the side of her cockpit.

"Left-wing is still heavy!" The fifty-kilo bomb was still in its cradle.

Natalya's stomach did a flip as Eva banked. Light and fire followed them, greedily closing the distance.

"Drop it now!" Eva ordered.

Natalya pulled on the lever. Nothing. "*Tvoyu mat.*"

"I'm getting us out of here!" Eva said and took them down.

Natalya gaped at the altimeter as its needle floated almost to zero. They needed the folds of the terrain to stay out of the lights, out of the fire. Eva was taking them away from the target.

"Course and heading," Eva demanded.

"You're taking us back?"

"Unless you have a better idea."

Instinct and trepidation mixed together. "I don't want to blow up on landing," Natalya said. If the mechanism was jammed, the bomb could drop at any time. They'd have no control over when and if it did. They might land safely. Or leave a crater on the flight line. Or worse, the bomb would release on its own over one of the airdrome's buildings as they made their approach.

With no radio they had no way to warn anyone.

Natalya checked her map for a clear area, somewhere far from where their sisters continued their attacks, far from the airdrome.

She shouted the new heading to Eva.

"What are you thinking?" Eva asked as she brought *Malyshka* to her new heading.

"A thousand meters is good," Natalya said. *I think. I hope.*

For a couple of minutes, they remained at their current altitude and Natalya thought Eva would pull rank and insist on taking their chances. Then she rose to a thousand meters and held *Malyshka* steady.

Natalya pulled the interphone off, said a prayer and fought her way out of the safety straps. She crawled over the lip of the cockpit. Even over the wind, she could make out Eva's outraged shouting, but *Malyshka* flew like she was gliding on ice.

Natalya hooked her right hand on the leading edge of the wing, her left on the trailing. She pulled herself forward between the wires and reached down, fumbling for the release.

There.

She yanked. It gave. The bomb fell. *Malyshka* wobbled but Eva steadied her. Wind tugged at Natalya as she let go of the wing's trailing edge and dragged herself back towards the rear cockpit. She pulled herself over as Eva re-gained altitude. It wasn't until she was seated and strapped back in that the adrenaline hit her.

With trembling hands, she put the interphone back on.

"*...sumasshedshaya suka!*" Eva was shouting.

"I'm back in," Natalya said. Her own voice sounded strange in her ears.

Eva took them up. Right into an oncoming Messer. The single-engine fighter did not have time to fire as they were too close, but could not miss the biplane that had appeared right in front of them. *Malyshka* spun and turned back through the low clouds as the German reversed his turn in the darkness.

*We cannot outrun him.*

As if reading her navigator's mind, Eva lifted the U-2's nose and aimed them at the approaching German fighter. One by one, eerily slow, like the frames of a moving picture, holes appeared across the wings and marched forward, up and over the fuselage, nicking the top of the windscreen.

*Oh n....*

A bullet drove Natalya's shoulder back into her seat: a crush of pain; an explosion her body grabbed and held onto. Red splatters appeared across her map, ruby crystals that glittered and melted into the paper. Natalya's hand came away from her collarbone covered in blood.

Acceleration pinned her into place as the sky spun around her. *Malyshka's* engine groaned. She gave a shudder, nose dropping.

The Messer buzzed right past them. Once, twice, three times, leaving a trail of holes in his wake.

Usually the Messers left them alone, unwilling to risk stalling out trying to match the U-2's slower speeds. But not this one. This one seemed to have it out for them. It would swing out a wide arc and come right back at them. Like a predator scenting the blood coming off its prey, it gave chase, relentless.

It was going to run them to ground. Or set them afire. Natalya knew it with cold certainty. And Eva must've known it too. She took *Malyshka* into the fight, because she had no choice. She couldn't fly them out. The Messer wasn't going to allow it.

Know your position. It was a navigator's primary responsibility. But Natalya didn't know where they were. Avoiding the Messer had taken them off course. She could tell from the unfamiliar terrain below. None of it was on the map she knew by heart. Until the sun rose, even a compass wasn't going to help them much. And when the sun did rise, it would be all over. They would be defenseless and naked to the light. If they made it to sunrise.

Again and again, Eva flew up. And every time, the Messer returned, circling back to find them despite the dark, like it had caught their scent and yearned to satisfy its bloodlust.

Ever the predator, the Messer did what predators have always done. It drove its wounded, confused prey hard, giving it no time to recover, no way out.

It was driving them out over water. Over the Volga.

The night went quiet. *Malyshka's* engine had come to a stop. It was a different quiet than when they idled it. With only the wind rushing around them, it was almost peaceful.

"Water or land?" Eva asked, her voice as calm as the placid waters beneath them.

"Do we have a choice?" Natalya asked just as weakly. The effort brought blood up into her throat. She choked it down.

"Not really. You swim, right?"

"I swim," Natalya said.

Eva brought them down on one of the lakes off the Volga, gently setting *Malyshka* gliding across its mirror-like surface. The tail skid bit into the ice, making a cutting noise like metal over glass. They slid for long minutes before the bite of the skid brought them to a stop.

Natalya undid her harness, her fingers clumsy from the loss of blood. It hurt to move, to breathe, but there was still strength of will. Prey she may have become. But she—they—were not done yet. Her pilot had done her best to protect them. Now it was her turn to protect Eva, to grab at any chance of surviving the night. That's all they needed to do. A few more hours to be taken a moment at a time. She pushed up and practically fell out of the cockpit and onto the wing.

Twin rows of bullets rained down. Tiny explosions bloomed on either side of *Malyshka*. The Messer, still intent on its prey, came back around and lined up for another strafing run, this time approaching from the front.

Natalya met Eva's gaze just as the ice gave way beneath them. Eva was still in her harness, the look of her face as harsh as the night. She'd pulled her goggles off her face. They were covered in blood. So was the stick. The instruments. The picture of Eva's dead daughter.

A flare of anger drove the gasp escaping Natalya's tightening chest. Eva's windscreen was nothing but holes. She'd lined up *Malyshka* to take as many bullets as she could with the engine, with the forward fuselage, and her own cockpit.

Between one heartbeat and the next, one blink and the next, the frigid water rushed upward, swirled around them, and sucked them down.

A scream bubbled out of Natalya's throat as the black water drove her up into *Malyshka's* upper wing. Eva stared at her with empty eyes as ribbons of scarlet unfurled.

Caught under the wing, Natalya pushed against it, reaching for Eva. Bubbles still rose from her sister's nose. She was still alive. She could still be saved.

A floe of ice caught Natalya in the back, pushed her out from between the wings. As she floated up, *Malyshka* sank into the dark depths. One instant she was there. The next, she'd sunk too far down to see.

The Volga's dark, cold fist wrapped around Natalya, tightening its grip, pulling her up against her will, sucking out her soul as it forced its essence into her lungs.

Bullets streaked through the water around her leaving corkscrewing tails in their wake. Natalya clawed for the sky within a threadbare cloud of red ribbons that followed her up. She clawed, she kicked, lungs burning as her heart slowed.

Pulse weakening, Natalya could no longer breathe.

Blessed numbness took her at last, wrapping around her like Father Frost's cloak.

The sky floated farther away.

Alone, she caught the dark.

\* \* \*

**Thirty years later.**

Spring in Tsaritsyn was Maria's favorite season. The Volga flowed; her waters finally pristine. Russian Orthodox crosses topped the domed cathedrals glittering in the morning sun. Each day, Maria embraced the new sunrise as the beginning, not the end of the day. Tsaritsyn had been rebuilt, a glittering metropolis full of museums and schools, art and music. Full of beauty and hope. Of the noise and bustle of prosperity.

Along the shores of the Volga, new grass covered Aviatrix Hill and school children in starched uniforms ran around, laughing, pigtails flying, black shoes glittering, school emblems flashing. The breezes drove the scents of flowering apricots, pears, and plums swirling around her.

A Tsar led Russia once again, and the school children dodged around the row of flagpoles flying the Romanov coat-of-arms as they raced to the top, their tiny but strong arms laden with flowers. Their laughter, their joy, was more than music. It was a harmony that drowned out the steady clink of the medals on Maria's chest as she slowly made her way up the steps that had been carved into the hill.

Every year it became harder and harder to make the climb, but she'd pledged to make her pilgrimage as long as she drew breath. She owed her girls—her women—that much.

Maria ascended the steps not just with flowers but with tears. Those terrible tears she feared would never come flowed freely enough here, just as they had flowed freely once victory had been declared.

Ten meters tall, The Aviatrix was rendered in stone, her face young, just like Maria remembered. They had all been so very young.

The Aviatrix looked up at the sky, a serene smile on her face, goggles up over her cap, flaps back, caught in some eternal breeze. Unafraid, she faced the world, ready to do what was needed, with pride, with dedication. She was dressed for winter, in an aviator's jacket and coveralls, pockets bulging. The patch on her shoulder bore the Night Witch riding her broomstick. She bore no rank, no medals, and needed neither.

She had become a symbol, not just of victory, but of sacrifice. She had become inspiration. She had become legend.

No matter how hard Maria tried, there was always one face she saw on the statue—Natalya's—even though the sculptor had deliberately created the face not to resemble any particular woman in the Tsarina's Own.

For Maria, Natalya's letter had been the hardest to write. She had been the regiment's youngest flyer. She had left behind not just parents, but siblings. Maria would never forget the stoic man under his hat and moustache, the hard lines on his face as he'd stood at his youngest child's funeral and laid her bullet-ridden body to rest. It had been a closed-casket ceremony. Bullets and the Volga had ravaged Natalya in a way that no father or mother should see.

By the time that the war ended, Maria had written forty-eight of those letters. Eight women lost in training exercises. Ten had gone down after running out of fuel while avoiding faster German aircraft. Four had lost their bearings when heavy clouds had unexpectedly rolled in and caused them to crash into mountainsides. Twenty had burned when tracer fire had ignited their Polikarpov's canvas shells. Six had drowned.

Maria had wrapped a little bit of her soul into each letter, feeling emptier and emptier each time, but never empty enough to shed tears and find closure. She'd had to wait for that. After the war had ended, she'd found it for the first time here, on this hill. They had unveiled the statue and then…then the tears had come, and Maria had found what she sought—the ability to weep for Andrei, for her girls, for those that had given life and limb for Russia.

These were no ordinary girls she had said in an interview shortly after the unveiling. Ordinary girls didn't get to feel the breath of death on their faces every night.

Yet after the war, it was the ordinary that they had all sought.

Every one of them had worked hard not to make the war the most important part of their lives. They had embraced the better things for which they'd fought, the things that their sisters gave their lives for so their sacrifice would not be wasted.

The days of war had become something they could not allow themselves to forget, for they were present in every breath they took, everything they did. Without those days, they would not, could not be who they had become.

Like the Aviatrix rendered in stone, their post-war lives became about remembering the youth and beauty struck down in its prime, the price of victory, paid in pain and blood, with flesh and with spirit.

It became about remembering their dead sisters because they had died childless and there were no children to remember them.

It became about making a life and living it not just for themselves, but for those who had died.

"Do you wish you could do it again?" another interviewer had asked not so long ago.

Speechless, Maria had merely stared at him. He was a bit younger than her brother Andrei had been when he'd died. But there the similarity had ended. This young man would never face the choices that her brother, that her sisters-in-arms had in order to allow him to ask that question, for if he had truly understood, he would've known that the answer was—

Could only be...

*No.*

\* \* \* \* \*

**Monalisa Foster Bio**

Monalisa won life's lottery when she escaped communism and became an unhyphenated American citizen. Her works tend to explore themes of freedom, liberty, and personal responsibility. Despite her degree in physics, she's worked in several fields including engineering and medicine, but she enjoys being a trophy wife and kept woman the most. She and her husband (who is a writer-once-removed via their marriage) are living their happily ever after in Texas, along with their children, both human and canine.

Website: www.monalisafoster.com

Facebook:

https://www.facebook.com/MonalisaFosterStoryteller/

Twitter: https://twitter.com/HouseDobromil

# # # # #

# Do The Hard Thing
# by Kacey Ezell

## A Psyche of War Story

Technician Fourth Class Pearl Silver raised her chin and stood up with the rest of the room. Though her belly fluttered with nerves, she forced her step and her gaze to be steady as she turned and walked toward the crowd forming in the back of the room. She could feel the eyes of some of the men as they locked on her face, and then quickly looked away.

She didn't need her power to know what they were thinking.

*A Negro girl? Here? Bad enough we're supposed to fly with women in combat, but a colored woman, too?*

As usual when confronted with such a situation, Pearl summoned up the memory of her mother's strong, proud face and her half-whispered admonitions:

*You be who you are, baby girl, and you do the hard thing. No matter what anyone thinks, no matter what anyone says. You are powerful and unique, and you can do whatever you want in this world. Nobody can lay a hand on you to stop you, so don't you let them.*

Athena Silver had passed both her psychic power and her defiant attitudes down to her daughter, and so Pearl lifted her chin a bit higher, squared her shoulders, and prepared to wade into the swirling chaos as the aircrews of the 381ˢᵗ Bombardment Group found their assigned psychics.

Not that "assigned psychics" was a thing that 8ᵗʰ Air Force bomber crews were used to having, but desperate times apparently called for desperate measures. The B-17s' attrition rate was catastrophic, and some man somewhere thought that having psychics fly along could help. It hadn't made much sense to Pearl either at first, but once she'd seen how the aptly named *Flying Fortresses* protected themselves and their formation partners with close flying, she could understand the logic.

If nothing else, she and the nineteen other women in this room could keep them from colliding mid air in bad weather. Maybe. If the crews listened and worked well with their psychic…

Which brought her back to the problem it hand. *Would* her assigned crew work with her? Or would her gender and skin color blind them to the power of her mind?

"Technician Silver?"

Pearl turned to see a slightly older man wearing the gold oak leaves of a U.S. Army Major standing right behind her. He gave her a smile as shiny as the silver pilot wings on his chest and stuck out his hand.

"Major Dan Corder," he said. "I'm your pilot, and I hope you'll forgive my language, but I'm damned glad to meet you."

"Are you now?" Pearl asked, unable to keep her eyebrows rising up in skepticism. Then she remembered where she was, and who she was, and what uniform she was wearing, and added a belated "sir," as she put her hand in his.

His wide grin spread a little wider, and he shook her hand heartily, as if she'd been a man.

"Absolutely. We're getting killed out there, and if you can help us fly closer, that's more of my boys we bring home. Where are you from?"

"Atlanta, sir," Pearl said, consciously trying to keep the Southern out of her voice.

"Huh. Well, I'm from Pittsburgh, PA. Ever been there?"

"No sir."

"You should go someday if you can. Nice town. Come on and meet the guys." He let go of her hand and beckoned for her to follow him, then led her out of the main briefing room into a smaller, office-sized room with a table and four chairs. Three of the chairs were occupied by two captains and a first lieutenant. They looked up as the major walked in.

"Gentlemen," Major Corder said as he waved Pearl past him and into the room. "I'd like you to meet Pearl Silver. She's the psychic that Colonel Rizer told us about."

"Good to meet you, miss," the lieutenant, who was sitting closest, said. He gave her a nod and a friendly enough smile. The other two captains offered similar hellos as well. Pearl nodded acknowledgement to each of them and then looked at Major Corder for a cue as to what to do next.

"Have a seat, Technician," the major said with a twist of humor threading through his words. "You're not in trouble, so no need to stand on formality. Let me introduce everyone. Next to you is our copilot, Lieutenant Zachary White."

"Call me Zipper," the lieutenant said.

"I think I'll stick with sir, sir," Pearl said, unable to keep all of the tartness from her words.

Lieutenant White laughed. "Fair enough, Technician. Fair enough."

Major Corder's smile deepened even further, and Pearl found herself wondering just how the man could be so happy. He looked as if he was going to say something else, but then shook his head and went on with the introductions.

"This guy looks like he's twelve, but he's really our Bombardier, Captain Steven T. Smith. And this string bean of a man is our Navigator, Captain Frank Earl. And you already know my name. We're the most experienced crew in the 381st Bombardment Squadron."

"You mean the oldest," Captain Smith said, his voice dry as a bone, and Pearl had to fight not to let herself smile in response.

"That, too. I wanted to get us all together, so we could reassure you that you're going to be just fine. We'll take good care of you in the air, especially if you can take care of us."

"That's why I'm here," she said softly, her eyes narrowing. "But, pardon me, sir, but why aren't any of you surprised to see me?"

Major Corder's epic smile faded a bit, and a grim understanding crept into his eyes.

"You mean," he said. "Why aren't we surprised to find out that you're black?"

"Yes, exactly."

"Colonel Rizer briefed us," he said. "You have to understand that he personally paired up each psychic with her crew, based on what information we had on all of you. He called me in to his office a few weeks ago and asked if I had a problem with black folks. I didn't, never have, and so I said no. Then he asked about my crew, and I gave the same answer. In my experience, people are people, and if you can do the job they say you can do, then I want you on my aircraft. Can you?"

"Do the job?"

"Yes."

Pearl straightened her shoulders again, this time in pride, rather than defiance.

"Better than any woman alive, save only my mother…and maybe Evie Adamsen…but maybe not. She's strong, but I've beaten her before."

"Good enough for me," Major Corder said. "Well, you heard the colonel as well as I did. We're on the roster in the morning, so what preparation do you need tonight?"

\* \* \*

The officers may have been briefed, but Pearl couldn't miss the widened eyes and raised eyebrows of the enlisted crewmen once they met her. Still, they each took her hand and allowed her to link them into a preliminary network readily enough, and she didn't find anything too objectionable in their surface thoughts…not for most of them, anyway.

The leader of the enlisted crew was the Flight Engineer/Gunner, a sergeant by the name of Eric Henson. He was older than most of the rest of the men, with a grizzled look to his short, sandy hair. His eyes squinted slightly at her, but his smile was genuine enough, and he shook her hand without hesitation. His buddy, and the next highest ranking man, was left waist gunner Sergeant Scott Kuntzelman, a lanky fellow who grinned at her behind wire-rimmed glasses. Corporal Peter Gold, the radio operator, took her hand gravely and gave her a solemn nod, but she could feel how glad he was to have her there. The right waist gunner, Corporal Moorefield, gave her a wide, irreverent grin and a "Bless Your Heart" in a soft Carolina accent. Pearl blinked, then laughed in surprise.

"Don't get cheeky with me, Corporal Moorefield," Pearl said. "I was born and raised in Atlanta; I know what 'Bless Your Heart' means."

"Yes ma'am," Moorefield said with a laugh, taking her hand and giving it a solid shake. "She'll be just fine, boys. Just fine. The lady can hold her own."

"Y'all have no idea," Pearl said, flashing him a bright grin before moving on to the other men. Deep in her mind, however, she felt a flash of gratitude for Corporal Moorefield's easing of the mood.

A stocky young man an inch shorter than she was shouldered his way forward. Not a hard thing to do, considering he was nearly as broad as he was tall, and looked like he was chiseled out of stone.

"I'm PFC Lawrence Koz," he said, taking her hand as soon as Moorefield let it go. "Anybody gives you trouble about anything, you come see me. I'll handle it."

He looked like a bulldog, and sounded like one, too, with a gruff, gravelly tone to his words. Pearl couldn't help but smile at him.

"Thank you, PFC Koz," she said. "But as the corporal mentioned, I can handle myself."

"Yeah, but you're a lady. Shouldn't need to. Not when you've got men around to do it for you."

"Aren't you sweet," she said. "Tell you what. Let's just take care of each other, shall we? That's why I'm here, after all…to help you boys take care of yourselves in the air." She looked around then, and belatedly realized that one member of the group hadn't stepped forward yet.

"And you are?" Pearl asked the young man hanging back with a dubious expression.

"Come on, Lester," Koz said, rolling his eyes. "Don't be a fat head."

"Private First Class Lester," Major Corder said then, his voice holding a steely note of warning.

The last young man squared his shoulders and turned to face her. He carefully blanked his expression, but not before Pearl could see the suspicion and doubt in his eyes. Ah. So maybe not all of the crew was as accepting as the major had promised.

Nevertheless, he stepped forward.

"Why the hesitation, Sugar?" Pearl asked, thickening her accent and using the stereotypical term of endearment just to poke at the young man. "Is it because of my power or my color?"

The young man squared his shoulders and met her brown eyes with his own steely ones.

"Neither," he said, his tone clipped.

"Private Lester, if you can't work with our assigned psychic, you can find another crew," Major Corder said. Lester swallowed hard, his Adam's apple bobbing, and then gave a short nod.

"I'm good, sir," he said.

"Then take my hand, Sugar," Pearl said, reaching out. She watched his face, looking for the moment of flinching, the hesitation before he let his lily-white skin touch her own bronzy-pink palm. The hinge of his jaw tightened, as if he were gritting his teeth, but he reached out and took her hand.

The moment his fingers touched hers, Pearl stretched her power out, using that small touch as an anchor and conduit. She felt Jack Lester's surface thoughts and sent a whispered pulse of request to flutter against them. She felt his mind open to hers, albeit slowly, and then the steely strength of his mental landscape pulled her in, welcoming her in a way that Pearl knew the man himself would not, did he have a choice.

*Jack*, she said. *Can you hear me?*

*Y-yes...you're in my head!*

*Yes,* Pearl said, keeping her thoughts patient during this initial burst of panic. It wasn't that unusual for people unused to psychic contact to feel...well...disoriented wasn't the right word, but it was maybe the closest. With a practiced touch, Pearl reached out and smoothed down the ragged skeins of his emotions wherever she could.

*Yes,* she said again. *I'm in your head and you're in mine. Look, you can see through my eyes if you want.* She eased up on the blocks she'd instinctively put on her visual channels, so that he could perceive his own face, paler than normal, his blue eyes bugging out just a bit as he gripped her hand and stared sightlessly at her face.

*I...I can.*

*Yes, and hear through my ears and feel what I feel. This is a good connection. You're the tail gunner, right? This will let me know what you're thinking and pass it to the other men, so that if you get into trouble back there, you won't be left all alone.*

*How did you know I...*Jack trailed off as he realized that his fear of being abandoned at the far end of the B-17's fuselage was clear to her. Despite herself, she sent him a pulse of reassurance.

*Don't worry,* she said. *I won't tell the others or let them feel it. But I bet you'd find them more sympathetic than you think.*

*No thanks,* Jack said, and his suspicion flowed back in as his panic and disorientation faded. Behind her barriers, Pearl sighed in disappointment. For just a moment, she'd thought she'd gotten past his prejudice. But it didn't matter. He didn't have to like her to let her in, and once she was in, she could do her job.

"I've linked with Jack…PFC Lester," she said out loud, letting go of Jack's hand and reaching out to the rest of the group gathered around. "If you'll each come take my hand, I will extend this psychic link to a full network that will include each of you, and then we'll see what we're working with."

To no one's surprise, Major Corder was next. He gripped her fingers and opened his mind, and she felt herself drawn into the landscape of Dan's mind as well.

*Sorry about that, sir,* she said as she remembered that this was a military organization, not a group of random friends at her school or her brother's college. *When linked in a network, I tend to think of you as you tend to think of you, and you think of yourself as "Dan" not "Major Corder."*

*No…problem,* Dan thought back slowly as he realized how to articulate his thoughts to her. *Just be…careful out…loud.*

*Yes sir,* Pearl promised. *Now can you feel Jack, PFC Lester, there with you?*

*J-Jack?* Dan thought.

*Here, sir.* Despite his problems with her, Jack was obviously very close to his aircraft commander, because the lines of the connection snapped into place between the two of them with barely any input from her. *It's strange, but it's not a bad feeling.*

*It's extraordinary!* Dan replied, enthusiasm building in him, ringing through the lines of their connection. *Let's bring the others in, can you?*

*Certainly,* Pearl said, smiling a little bit. At least *someone* appreciated the things she could do. She let go of the major's hand and reached out to the next member of her crew.

\* \* \*

They worked late. Later than they probably should have done, but Pearl wanted to make sure she could tie everyone into a seamless network before their mission in the morning.

When the knock came at 0400, Pearl rose and dressed with the other women, then made her way to the chow hall to get breakfast. Her stomach still ached with hunger from the previous night's exertions. Psychic work was hungry work, and she needed food to keep her fueled if she was going to be successful.

As she and a few of the other women approached the double doors of the rounded hut that held the chow hall, her consciousness twinged at her, pulling her attention off to the side. She turned to look and surprised herself with a smile.

"Well, good morning, Sergeant Kuntzelman," she said, as brightly as she could manage before coffee. "Corporal Gold, Sergeant Henson…is the whole crew here?"

"Just us three for now," Sergeant Kuntzelman said, answering her smile with his own wide grin. "Koz, Moorefield, and Lester are down at the bird already, and the officers are getting their brief. How are you, Technician Silver? It's been ages since I've seen you."

"Very funny," Pearl said, falling into step with the waist gunner.

"Ain't I just?" he said, nudging Henson in the side. "You want to come with us? We were just going to grab a bite for the other guys and head out to load up."

"That sounds perfect," Pearl said. "As long as you don't make any cracks about how much food I bring. Psychic work is hungry work."

"So's flying. Long as you keep it down in the air, I'm not gonna judge you none."

"He's lying," Henson put in, leaning around his buddy's lanky frame to wink at Pearl. "He's a bona fide gossip queen, this one."

Pearl laughed as they walked in through the doors and entered the chow line. She was enjoying the crew's banter so much that it took her a minute to notice the way the noise gradually died down wherever she went. It wasn't until she came face to face with the man serving bacon that she realized that the whole place had fallen silent.

"Serve the technician, Private," Kuntzelman said, his voice low and dangerous. Pearl glanced over at him in surprise. His open, easy face had taken on a hard edge, and his eyes glinted like steel blades behind his glasses. "We ain't got all morning."

"Yes, Sergeant," the private said slowly. He looked down at the tongs in his hands as if he'd never seen them before, then shook himself and picked up a few slices of over-crisp bacon. He set them on Pearl's tray without meeting her eyes, and then hurried to serve Kuntzelman and the others as well.

"Thank you," Pearl said, her voice clipped. The private ignored her, as she'd expected he would, but her mother had raised her to be polite, and so polite she would be. She lifted her chin higher and pushed her tray down along the rails toward the end of the line.

"Don't worry about that guy," Corporal Pete Gold said, coming up to her as she wrapped up her bacon and some biscuits to take out to the aircraft. "He's a known troublemaker from the weather squadron. That's why he's on KP. Sergeant K and Sergeant Henson will straighten him out."

"It's all right," Pearl said, giving Gold a brief smile. "I'm used to it. At least he didn't say anything. And it's not like I don't stick out like a sore thumb."

"It's not all right," Sergeant Henson growled from behind them as he and Kuntzelman caught up. "But we ain't got time to deal with it right now. We'll handle it when we get back, Technician, I promise."

"Thank you," Pearl said again, meaning it a little more this time. "I appreciate y'all backing me up."

"We're a crew," Kuntzelman said, and the others nodded. "You're going up with us...that makes you one of us. That zombie doesn't have the stones...ah...sorry, Technician Silver. We're not used to having ladies around."

"It's quite all right, Sergeant Kuntzelman," Pearl said. Something warm uncurled within her chest, and her smile grew. "And please, call me Pearl."

\* \* \*

*Y*ou doing all right, Pearl? Eric Henson asked later, as they climbed through the thick layer of clouds that blanketed the English Channel. Their bird was called *One For The Money* and was part of a large formation of Flying Fortresses. Pearl didn't really know just how many aircraft were in the air together. She wasn't sure she wanted to know.

*Y-yes,* Pearl said, then firmed up her mind and tried again. *Yes. Flying just takes a bit of getting used to is all. I've done it before, but never in a network this large. It's a lot to take in.*

*You're doing fine,* Eric replied. Then a thread of dry humor tricked down through the lines of the network. *Leastways, I think you are. I've never been in a network this large while flying either!*

Pearl sent a pulse of silent laughter back to the flight engineer, then reached out down the lines of the network to check on the other men in her crew. They were, of course, old hands at flying, and reassured her as much as she did them.

All except for Jack Lester, out on the tail, that is.

*I'm fine,* he responded curtly to her mind touch. *Nothing to report.*

*Roger,* she said, and withdrew quickly back to the much more welcoming thoughts of the rest of the crew. In the back of her mind, she knew that she and Jack would both prefer it if she left him alone. But she had a job to do, and so she kept him wired into the network, though only by the thinnest of psychic threads.

*Pearl.*

That wasn't one of her men. Pearl blinked quickly in surprise and actually turned her body in the direction of the reaching touch from one of her fellow psychics.

*Evie*

*Yes. Listen, Alice McGee got into some trouble on the lead bird. The clouds made her disoriented, and it disoriented her crew. So, we're going to link up, just superficially, and see if we can't reinforce each other.*

*That's a good idea,* Pearl thought back to Evelyn Adamsen in *Pretty Cass* up towards the front of the formation. *Why didn't we think of that before?*

*Maybe because none of us has ever done* this *before,* Evie thought back with her dry, understated humor. *You're one of the strongest of us; see what you can do to help any of the others who falter, all right? I'm going to reach out to Maude on the other side.*

*You got it, Evie.* Pearl thought back and opened up a channel to let the dark-haired girl from South Dakota establish a superficial link. One by one, the girls on the other *Flying Fortresses* linked in, and the whole formation tightened up significantly.

*Wow,* Dan Corder said from his pilot's seat up front. *I can't believe how much easier this is to fly close. It's like I know what he's gonna do right as he does it.*

*Psychic thought is faster than most people's reaction time from visual inputs,* Pearl said. *It takes most people between three and five seconds to visually recognize a stimulus, process the information, and direct their own response. Psychic thought speeds that cycle up by shortening the stimulus response and analysis processes.*

No one said anything on their network. The silence was deafening.

*Did I say something wrong?* Pearl asked, fear stabbing through her. Other than her fellow WACs, these men were the closest thing she had to friends in England. She couldn't afford to alienate them, especially if she was going to keep flying with them!

*Well, we don't exactly know,* Lawrence Koz—who thought of himself as "Koz" rather than Lawrence—said eventually. *I can't speak for the officers, but none of us Joes is smart enough to know what the hell you said, begging your pardon, Pearl.*

*Yeah, we don't know what she said either, Koz,* Zipper quipped, prompting a growing cascade of laughter that rippled through the network from most of the men.

*I was studying to be a nurse before I came here,* Pearl said.

*Nurse? You sound more like a brain surgeon!*

More laughter rolled down the connections, until Pearl finally gave in and shook her head, chuckling.

*Well, y'all remember that, then. I'm not just a pretty face. I've a brain in my head and the will to use it.*

*We all coulda told you that!* Dan said, and that made Pearl join the men in laughing out loud.

* * *

They broke out of the weather over France, and suddenly the long, droning monotony of flight became something entirely different.

The first thing Pearl noticed was a change in the minds of her crewmen. So far, they'd been mostly fighting a sleepy kind of boredom while they locked away their natural fears. But as the French coast stretched away below them, that boredom melted away as those fears spiked through the men, taking the forms of adrenaline and excitement. The enlisted men all racked their weapons and started scanning their assigned sectors for the tell-tale flash of Luftwaffe wings.

*Fighters are bingoing out,* Jack reported through the network. Pearl looked through his eyes and shared the visual of their fighter escort peeling away from the formation. She saw the lead fighter waggle his wings and knew from the men that it was a wish for good luck.

They'd need it.

*Fighters, Twelve o'clock!*

The first call came from Alice in the lead bird, relayed through the other girls in the formation. Pearl felt Eric Henson in the top turret craning his neck upward to see, just as Dan and Zipper fought to fly their Fort as close as possible to their element leader. She followed his line of vision as he craned his eyes to see…

*There.*

*Fighters! Two o'clock high, I got 'em!* Eric sent his thought sailing through the network, riding a wave of savage glee as he tracked his weapons forward of the pair of diving Messerschmitt's and watched smoke begin to trail off the near fighter's wing. The other Eric, Eric Moorefield, began firing his .50 caliber machine gun off the right waist and picked off the second fighter as the pair of them descended down the right side.

*Fighters, eleven o'clock low, ball turret!*

*On 'em, boss!* Koz answered, and Pearl switched to looking through his eyes as he swiveled his turret around and lit up another pair approaching from the front.

*Flak!*

Zipper hurtled the word back to them as he gritted his teeth and fought to keep in position. He and Dan both had their hands on the Fort's yokes, as the bird abruptly pitched up, then dropped sickeningly down. Far below, the German anti-aircraft artillery kept firing, peppering the sky with dark, ominous clouds of metal and smoke.

The air exploded around them with enemy fighters and their own returned fire. *Teacher's Pet,* the lead bird in the formation, got hit, and Pearl felt the sudden searing pain followed by a stab of loss when Alice McGee's mind suddenly ceased to be there. *Liberty Belle,* too, succumbed to the fighters, and the adrenalized excitement in all of their minds became the white-hot rage of loss.

Pearl felt it, too. The emotions of the crew ricocheted through her mental landscape, multiplying with every touch. She stared through the gunners' eyes at the silhouettes of the German fighters and hated them with all the passion in her soul. Every spiraling smoke trail felt like vindication; every snap of the gunners' weapons brought a savage glee.

She couldn't have said how long they flew like that; buffeted by flak, bristling with fire. The Luftwaffe fighters came at them in waves, seeking to separate one of the Forts from the safety of the formation, trying to send it spiraling down toward the occupied ground.

At some point, Frank Earl, the navigator, announced that they were minutes from the bomb run. Shortly after that, Steve Smith, the bombardier, took control of the aircraft. Through the overall formation net, Pearl felt Evie, now in the lead bird, urging the girls to tie the formation tighter together, in order to get a better drop.

She reached out and pulled Frank's visual and auditory inputs to the forefront of her consciousness and strengthened the connection to Evie and the other ladies. She heard the repeated calls of fighters, felt the spiky fear of her men as they shot their way along the bomb run. When Evie transmitted her bombardier's call, Frank's fingers hit the switch on his Norden bomb sight, and thousands of pounds of destruction fell from the belly of their Fort onto the target below.

*It's a good drop!* Pearl felt Evie's jagged exultation as her thought pulsed through the formation network. The emotions were strong enough that they couldn't belong to Evie alone. She must be feeling the amplification effect of her crew's minds, too. In the back, dispassionate corner of her mind, Pearl wondered what the long term affects of such intense linkages would be.

*Fighters! Four o'clock!* Koz shouted out over the net, spinning his ball turret to spit flame at the hated Me-109s. Pearl locked her idle speculation away and concentrated on backing her crew up, reinforcing their connections, and keeping them safe.

They were deep inside occupied territory, and it was a long flight home.

\* \* \*

In the end, they almost made it. The relentless flak and repeated Luftwaffe attacks began to take their toll, but Pearl kept part of her attention on Frank at his navigator's table, and mentally ticked down the minutes until they'd be safe once again.

*Feet wet!* Frank announced as they crossed over the French coastline and continued north and west toward the sanctuary of the British Isles. *Almost there, boys…and Pearl.*

*Fighters! Five o'clock high!* That was Jack, way back on the tail. *Four of them! Top! Ball! Right waist!*

Pearl felt the simultaneous jolt of adrenaline through three minds at once as Koz and the two Erics spun their weapons to meet this new threat. She felt the pounding shudder of the machine guns' recoil as all four men fired, and felt the sickening series of thuds as a line of enemy rounds traced up the side of the Fort, starting at the tail, snaking up the fuselage, ripping through the engines on the wing.

Crushing, blinding agony punched through her hip, making her gasp out loud. Peter Gold looked up from his radio set at her.

*Pearl?* He took a step toward her seat as she doubled over in pain.

*Not me!* She managed to push the thought out through the net. *Jack! Tail's hit!*

*Bastard got number three!* Zipper thought back, and Pearl got a quick flash of his hands and Dan's flying over switches as they fought to shut down fuel to the burning inboard engine.

*And four,* Dan added, straining to keep the aircraft under control with the sudden loss of power from the right side. *She's only producing half power, but she's not on fire. Get three shut down and divert the fuel, Let's see if we can limp all the way to the coast. Steve, get back to the tail and see what you can do for Jack. Pearl, you go too. You're a nurse.*

*I'm just a student!* She protested.

*Good enough. Get back there!*

Dan's normally cheery tone had gone steely hard, and his impatience hit her like a slap to the face. Jack was his man, his responsibility, as was everyone on the now crippled bird. *He* had to keep them all alive by flying the aircraft. *She* needed to do what she could.

Fair enough.

Pearl unhooked her seatbelt and stood up just as the bombardier, Steve, came up through the hatch from the lower forward deck. She followed him as he worked between Eric and Scott, who ignored them in favor of continuing to fire at the tenacious fighters, then out across the catwalk that ran the length of the now-empty bomb bay. At the far end, Steve stopped and motioned for her to squeeze past, into the tiny compartment where the tail gunner lay bleeding.

She took a deep breath and pushed through.

Jack remained on his gun, his breathing thready and rapid. She reached out a hand and touched his shoulder, causing him to jump in surprise. Pain rocketed through them both, buckling Pearl's knees. She reached out with her other hand to grip the nearest piece of the aircraft's metal frame. The bite of the sharp edge into her fingers helped her focus, and she locked on to that sensation.

*The major sent me back to look at you,* she said, gritting her teeth as she pushed the thoughts in his direction. *I was in school to be a nurse.*

*I'm fine,* Jack sent, the sweat on his brow belying his words. *Just a little shrapnel cut. Nothing to worry about.*

*I'm in your head, you can't lie to me, buster,* she said, her thoughts sharp with impatience. If only he would *trust* her! *I know exactly how bad that hurts, and exactly how hard you're having to focus, so knock off the childish bull and let me help you!*

She felt him struggle, pushing back against a distrust ingrained by his upbringing. He shook his head, his face set in mulish lines. *Don't need your help,* he said. Maybe it was all the adrenaline. Maybe it was the brutal edge of combat amplified ten times. Maybe it was the still aching pain of losing some of her friends, but for whatever reason, Jack Lester's stubborn insistence on clinging to his prejudices ignited a fury unlike anything she'd ever experienced. White hot rage erupted in her mind, fountaining out in tidal waves of anger. She balled her hand into a fist and slammed it down, hard, on darkly creeping stain of blood on his hip.

Jack cried out and recoiled, even as agony threatened to tip him over the edge into oblivion. His mental barriers weakened and thinned, and Pearl seized the opportunity to shove her way more fully into his mind and widen the connection.

Pain raced down the lines into her mind, threatening to engulf her. But she was ready for it and used her searing anger to burn it back.

*Listen to me, white boy,* she snarled into his semi-conscious mind. *I don't care if you like me, but I'll burn in hell before I let you make me fail! My aircraft commander told me to keep you alive and I will do. My. Job. So, you stay alive, Jack Lester, do you hear me? You stay alive, and you let me look at your god damn wound!*

He slumped, and let his hand fall away from where he'd been holding pressure on his left hip. Sure enough, shrapnel from the torn aircraft fuselage had ripped up along his thigh and embedded itself in his flesh. Pearl pursed her lips together and tried to figure what was best to be done.

*Haha!* Eric Henson, the flight engineer, shouted down the lines in exultation. *Lookie who came out to play! God Bless His Majesty's Royal Air Force Fighter Command! Jerry's running for the hills!*

*Good,* Dan responded up front, his tone grim, *because we got the fire out in three, but four's coming apart on us. We're not gonna be able to make the coast. We're gonna have to ditch.*

*Jerry got* Tinsel Time, *too,* Eric Henson said, watching from his top turret. *She just broke from the formation.*

*Can y'all follow her down, pilot?* Pearl asked, a sudden urgency throbbing through her. She straightened up and pushed past Steve, who waited behind her in the narrow space before the tail gunner's station.

*Get him out of there,* she said to the bombardier. *I'm pulling away some of his pain, so he should stay conscious. Get pressure on that wound, and then get him up front as soon as you can. You heard the pilot; we're going in the water.*

*You got it,* Steve said, no hesitation in his mind at all. Never mind that she was enlisted and he an officer, or that she a woman—a black woman at that—and he a man. Steve cared about Jack, and she at least had given the bombardier something to do to help his wounded crewman.

*We don't have a choice, Pearl,* Dan responded then, and Pearl could feel the physical strain as he tried to keep the wounded bird under control. *But I can try to keep us as close to them as possible. Why?*

*If I'm close, I might be able to help them as well,* she said as she half-ran back along the catwalk through the bomb bay. She burst into the waist compartment, where Scott and Eric Moorefield were busy throwing their guns and brass out of their windows, trying to lighten the load. Eric turned and ran to Koz's hatch, popping it open and pulling the stocky ball turret gunner into the body of the aircraft.

*I'll get the lifeboats,* Koz broadcast down the net, his eyes meeting Pearl's for a split second as she kept pushing toward the front. She had to look, she wanted to see *Tinsel Time,* to get an idea of where they were in relation to the rest of the formation.

The rest of the formation! She was still connected to the other women!

*We're going in the water!* Pearl sent out, fighting to project a calm she didn't feel. Jack's pain continued to hammer at her, but she locked it away and focused on the job. She clambered up the short ladder and leaned between the two sweating, straining pilots as they struggled to keep the bird flying straight as she descended toward the water. Out at the two o'clock, Pearl spotted *Tinsel Time,* less than a hundred yards away.

*We're still together,* she reported to Evie and the others, stress throwing her thoughts back into the vernacular of her native Atlanta. *Y'all radio ahead and tell them Brit boys to come get us.*

*You got it, Pearl,* Evie Adamsen replied from what was now the lead bird. Evie didn't sound good either, but Pearl didn't have time to worry about it, as the inky surface of the English Channel loomed closer and closer.

*Can y'all swim?* She sent to Dan and Zipper.

*A little,* Zipper replied. *Enough. Get back to the men and the lifeboats. We're going to make this as smooth as possible, but...*

Pearl nodded, then swallowed hard and retreated back to the waist of the aircraft. The rest of the crew were there, Koz and Frank Earl holding the inflatable lifeboats. Pete Gold made one last "mayday" transmission, then switched off his radios as she passed and followed her down.

*I'm gonna keep this net open, come hell or high water,* Pearl said, smiling grimly at her intentional pun as she joined the men sitting in the waist of the aircraft. *Steve, sir, you've got Lester?*

*I do,* Steve replied. Lester raised his head and looked at her but said nothing and sent nothing. Pearl gave him a small smile and pulled even more of his pain into herself. Nausea threatened to overcome her in response but fought it down and locked it away. Pain was the least of her problems right now. She wasn't a strong swimmer.

The nose of the aircraft pitched up as the pilots tried to bleed off as much speed as possible before touching down into the water. The bump rattled Pearl's teeth in her head, and then she found herself thrown abruptly forward into Koz as the water slowed the Fort's forward motion.

"Go!" Dan shouted out loud, as his hands flew over the switches, shutting down the three engines that remained. The droning whine abruptly slowed, leaving a thundering silence in its wake. "Get in the lifeboats, get out of the aircraft! We've got minutes before she sinks!"

Someone, Pearl wasn't sure who, reached under her armpits and dragged her to her feet. Then she found herself with her hand in Koz's, being drug behind him. Somehow, they got out onto the wings of the aircraft, which had begun to slowly settle in the dark, choppy water.

"Pearl!" someone shouted. She shook herself and turned, saw the men deploying the two small lifeboats.

"Where's Jack?" she shouted back, both mentally and out loud. Where was Jack? Where was *Tinsel Time*? Where was the Air Sea Rescue Service?

*I'm here,* Jack said. *I'm safe, thanks to you. Come on, Pearl, we gotta get you into the lifeboat before* One For The Money *sinks.*

Pearl nodded, then swallowed hard and gripped every ounce of courage she had.

*I don't swim well,* she warned them. *Y'all don't let me drown.*

*We won't.* They answered. All of them. Even Jack.

She took a deep breath and jumped into the water. The cold shock of it drove the air from her lungs and paralyzed her diaphragm. Panic began to claw at the edges of her mind.

*We're here!* Someone said...Zipper? Frank? Either of the Erics? Peter? It didn't matter, really, because they really were there. Strong hands reached out and grasped her flailing arms, hauled her up to the surface.

Her head broke into the air, and she dragged in a huge, gasping lungful of air.

*We got you, Pearl,* someone said. *Don't fight us, just relax. We'll get you into the lifeboat.*

She tried. She let her body go limp and tilted her face back as whoever was holding her began to kick through the water toward the lifeboat. As it turned out, that was exactly where she needed to be, otherwise, she might not have seen the Hudson circling overhead.

*Pearl Silver. Pearl Silver, are you down there?*

It was barely a whisper. It would have been so easy to miss...but she didn't miss it. It was there, like a searchlight in the darkness. It wasn't one of her fellow WACs, but it was a psychic's seeking touch, nonetheless.

She took Jack's pain and her own panic and used that emotional fuel to launch the rocket of her consciousness skyward.

*I'm here!* she screamed. *I'm Pearl Silver, and I'm here with my crew and the crew of* Tinsel Time. *Come get us, please!*

Pearl felt the instant that her supercharged transmission hit the British psychic's mind. She knew that in that Hudson aircraft high above, another young woman flinched from the strength of her mind.

She flinched, but she reached out and locked on, establishing contact.

*Pearl Silver? I'm Esther Walmsley. We've got you in sight and a Royal Navy destroyer is en route. We'll have you home and dry in a jiffy! Have you got wounded?*

*I'm so glad to meet you,* Pearl sent, laughter bubbling up inside her as the men hauled her into the life raft. *Yes. My tail gunner took shrapnel to his hip and side. I don't know about* Tinsel Time's *crew.*

*We've them in sight too. You might not be able to see them, but they're quite close. And here comes the* Sabre. *I'll stay in contact until they've picked you both up, shall I?*

*Yes please,* Pearl said. *Thank you.*

*It's very much my pleasure, Pearl. I hope we might meet in person, one day.*

Pearl tried to form a reply, but her thoughts scattered when the lifeboat started rocking a little more violently. She focused her eyes on her surroundings, and found Jack Lester reaching out for her hand. Without much thought, she took his hand in hers.

*Pearl,* he thought. *I—I owe you an apology. I just…You saved my life, and I treated you so badly.*

Despite herself, Pearl smiled a little smile.

*You did,* she said. *And I did. Do you know why?*

*Why?*

*Because my mother taught me to put good into the world. Because I was raised to do my job. Because it doesn't matter if you're going to be a bigot, I'm here to help you come home from this damn war, and I* will *complete my mission. No matter how I might feel about you personally.*

Jack looked around at the other men. Pearl saw them each look away, but knew that they listened in, wondering how the proud tail gunner would take her rebuke.

*You shame me,* he said, and went to withdraw his hand. But she gripped his fingers and refused to let him go.

*Not if you learn,* Pearl said. *Not if you heal from this wound and learn that skin color doesn't define a person. It's just an aspect of who I am, but it doesn't make me less or more than you. It's just a difference, but difference can be celebrated, right?*

Jack nodded. Pearl squeezed his hand once more and willed him to meet her eyes.

*You want to thank me for saving your life? Do the hard thing, Jack. Be my friend. Be a friend to other men and women who look like me. Show people around you that we're all just people. Find others who think the way you did and teach them the truth.*

He slowly lifted his head and locked his gaze on to hers. She watched his Adam's apple bob up and down as he swallowed hard, and then nodded.

"I promise," he said out loud. "I give you my word."

"Good enough for me," Pearl said with a smile. She squeezed his fingers once more, then let go.

"Hey!" Eric Moorefield shouted, standing up in their lifeboat and waving his hands. "I see a ship!"

*Is that your destroyer, Esther?* Pearl asked while the other man began shouting and hooting and waving.

*It is! Well, it's my King's anyway. May I present the HMS* Sabre? *They've just radioed that they've spotted your two lifeboats, Pearl. My radioman is giving them a course to your sister ship now.*

"I think they've got us, boys," Pearl said out loud as the ship turned and began heading steadily toward them. "We'll be home in time for dinner."

\* \* \* \* \*

**The Crew of *One For The Money:***
Pilot: Major Dan Corder
Co-Pilot: 1Lt Zach White
Bombardier: Capt Steven T. Smith
Navigator: Capt Frank Earl
Flight Engineer/Gunner: Sgt Eric Henson
Radio: Cpl Peter Gold
Left Waist: Sgt Scott Kuntzelman
Right Waist: Cpl Eric Moorefield
Ball Turret: Pfc Lawrence Koz
Tail: Pfc Jack Lester

\* \* \* \* \*

## Kacey Ezell Bio

Kacey Ezell is an active duty USAF instructor pilot with 2500+ hours in the UH-1N Huey and Mi-171 helicopters. When not teaching young pilots to beat the air into submission, she writes sci-fi/fantasy/horror/noir/alternate history fiction. Her first novel, *Minds of Men*, was a Dragon Award Finalist for Best Alternate History. She's contributed to multiple Baen Books anthologies and has twice been selected for inclusion in the Year's Best Military and Adventure Science Fiction compilation. In 2018, her story "Family Over Blood" won the Year's Best Military and Adventure Science Fiction Readers' Choice Award. In addition to writing for Baen, she has published several novels and short stories with independent publisher Chris Kennedy Publishing. She is married with two daughters. You can find out more and join her mailing list at www.kaceyezell.net.

# # # # #

# Tail Gunner Joe

# by William Alan Webb     A

## Story of the Time Police

The first rule of time is simple: Don't mess with the stream. When you visit the offices of the Time Police, that rule is plastered everywhere you look, so I knew better when I did it. But I did it anyway, and I deserved a worse punishment than what I got.

\* \* \*

Sergeant Joe Edwards was a veteran of seventeen missions. He had two ME-109s to his credit, both on the same mission, which was quite a score for a tail gunner. He manned the loneliest position on the plane. To reach his battle station, Edwards crawled down a narrow tunnel to the rear of the Flying Fortress. Being bulked-up in a flight suit, oxygen mask, heavy boots and fur-lined gloves made it slow and sweaty. Once in his seat Edwards never saw where they were going, only where they'd been. If the bomber took fatal damage he was screwed. It wasn't impossible to get out of the plane, but it was close.

There was a splendid majesty to it all, even if it was ancient history to me. During my college days, I had been on field trips to other great events in human history, mainly battles, among them Cannae, Agincourt, Hastings, Waterloo, Gettysburg and, of course, the Somme. So are all the moments of greatest human endeavors painted in blood? Not necessarily. During debates of the Council of Nicea in 325 A.D., when Constantine convened the Christian bishops to decide what was canonical and what wasn't, things got pretty heated. I'm still surprised nobody got whacked by a thrown goblet or wine bottle. I guess they were too afraid of Constantine, who wasn't known for suffering fools.

I've munched figs while strolling through the Agora during the glory days of Athens and watched Plato stare mesmerized as Socrates taught a lesson. I've watched Hannibal's military councils during the Second Punic War. I've stood in the court of Frederick the Great where French was the only language and, thanks to my embedded translator, I understood every word. Regardless of the culture or the era, observing human history is an awesome, humbling experience. Watching the 91st Bomb Group drone towards Germany was no exception and, for a moment, the fact that I was committing a Major Crime against Time didn't register in my mind.

That was my second big mistake.

In the time-stream when I was born Holographic Time Projection with Enhanced Sensory Perception was the hottest new technology. In essence, it allowed all your senses to function during a time-trip, although at a reduced level. How well they functioned was dependent on the power supply; more power, more sensory input. This could be done despite your being a hologram projected through time. So now, in 1944, I didn't only see history unfold, I heard the crackle of the inter-plane radio, smelled the oil of the turret bearings and felt the high-altitude cold. I could taste the second-hand smoke of the last Lucky Strike before takeoff. ESP made history come alive in a palpable way that merely watching couldn't do. It immersed you in the moment, as you were literally right there in the action.

Now you know my first mistake.

You see, it was an historian's dream but highly illegal. My license didn't permit ESP, let alone full visibility; they reserved red cards for government types. Before, I had thought such regulations were nothing more than bureaucratic snobbery. You know, jealous civil servants keeping the scholars in the dark to protect their own little fiefdom. Now I know how wrong I was, but now it's too late.

The bomb group maintained 28,000 feet that day, crippling the performance of most Luftwaffe fighters that might rise to meet them. By that stage of the war the quality of German aviation fuel was poor, making it hard for the remaining fighters to be effective at high altitude.

Flak, however, was not affected by height.

I always envisioned flak as the number one fear of the bomber crews. The German 88-millimeter dual purpose cannon was the deadliest AA gun of its day, with the killing power to rip a B-17 to shreds with one hit. Much to my surprise, most flight crews didn't sweat the flak too much. You couldn't do anything about it, so why worry? They hated it, but there were too many other dangers involved in flying ten-hour missions over enemy territory to lose sleep over flak. This was a revelation to me then.

From his vantage point in the tail turret of the lead plane, Edwards could see the 91st Bomb Group (H) strung out over the North Sea. The B-17s' vapor trails in the ice blue sky marked the route back to England. The dazzling sun could blind an unwary man as it reflected off the wings of the bare-metal plane. Overhead, the occasional glint of sunlight from a P-51 flashed a comforting light as the "Little Friends" kept the remnants of the Luftwaffe at bay. By the summer of 1944 the Germans had precious few fighters left to attack the bomber streams, but even one ME-109 that got through the P-51s could wreak havoc.

German fighters had initially tried attacking from the rear in the early phases of the war. They'd found out quickly that was where the defensive firepower of the group was concentrated, so they'd switched to coming in from the nose. Unfortunately, frontal attacks took a degree of skill no longer prevalent with most Luftwaffe pilots, so now those few who survived the escorts had switched back to tail attacks. At least Edwards' B-17, nicknamed Jumpin' Jenny, was a G model, with a powered tail turret. Before that, the rear protection was a pair of hand-swiveled fifty-caliber machine guns, clumsy to aim and very heavy. Believe me, it makes a difference.

World War Two has always been a passion with me. And, as good historians should, I'd done quite a lot of research on my subjects, Edwards included. He'd been born in 1922 in Olive Branch, MS, and moved to Memphis when he was six, graduating from Humes High School in 1940. Thanks to his father's connections, Edwards landed a great job in a tire factory and worked there until Pearl Harbor rocked the nation. Like millions of other young men, he joined the Army to kill either Krauts or Japs. Edwards had thought he wanted to carry a rifle until he ate the chow in boot camp. Then came a call for volunteers; the Army needed tail gunners and since Air Corps food beat the hell out of K-rations and mess hall slop, Edwards joined without a second thought. He excelled at gunnery school and made sergeant in March, 1944. Then came that incredible June day over Bremerhaven, when he shot down two ME-109's that broke through the fighter cover. In later years, Edwards would have called it the greatest day of his life, if I hadn't committed a time crime scant months later.

Both fighters had been painted with the yellow fuselage bands designating them as Russian Front veterans. My later research informed me this was because their Gruppen hadn't had time to replace them with red Home Defense bands. Edwards killed the first Messerschmitt with a long burst at a high angle of deflection, a tough shot. The other seemed intent on ramming, he'd pressed his attack so close. For one split second that Joe Edwards never would have forgotten, he and the German pilot faced each other over flaming guns. The B-17 staggered as 30-millimeter cannon shells ripped into her tail and vertical stabilizers. Somehow, none hit Edwards and his turret. Then the fighter exploded, and it was over.

Why am I telling you all of this? Guilt, I suppose. What more should you know? Really, he was just your average middle-of-the-century American. After the war, he would have tried college at Ole Miss, dropped out, married Adele Stephenson in 1948, had three kids, a boy and two girls, made shift foreman at the tire plant in 1954, retired in 1983 and died of kidney failure in 1996. Throughout his life, Adele would have nagged him to quit smoking, he would have developed a passion for Zane Grey and Louis L'Amour, hated television except for Jeopardy, liked early rock 'n' roll, especially fellow Mississippian Elvis Presley, and broken his hip at the Grand Opening of the Pyramid in Memphis in 1991 when he slipped off a curb. His great-great-grandson would have been one of the first recipients of the Muscular Dystrophy vaccine in 2036. His son would have played basketball for Memphis State, closing out his career by scoring nine points in a tight victory over UCLA in the 1973 NCAA title game. (Final score: UCLA 71, Memphis State 73.) Joseph Daniel Edwards III would have rotated down to double team UCLA center Bill Walton, stolen the ball several times, and the Bruins would have stopped feeding Walton the ball to their overall detriment. It would have made all the difference and proud papa Edwards would have been in the arena to see it.

And then I came along.

\* \* \*

I wanted to write the definitive history of World War Two, using revelations about the Allied effort that only came to light in the late 21st century. Western histories are replete with acres of books about how brave and noble the war was, which it was but also wasn't. The average American soldier did his part, it's true. And on the surface it was a good war fought for the right reasons with more than enough provocation. Only fifty years after the fact did the government admit to things like testing mustard gas on unsuspecting Navy personnel, then denying them medical care when their lungs disintegrated. The truth of the Philadelphia Experiment was too shocking even then for most to believe it. And the revelation of Hitler's real identity changed everything.

\* \* \*

I wanted to tell the full story, the brilliant strategies and incredible heroics as well as the nasty stuff the armed forces would rather have kept quiet. Sometimes humans make mistakes and do terrible things. And if the Allies didn't execute millions of people for no reason, neither were their hands clean of innocent blood.

My idea was to use technology to interview the people who actually fought the war and let them write the book. While Russian artillery shells rained on the Führerbunker, did Hitler have any regrets? Did he realize what could have been if he had pulled just one panzer division out of Russia and sent it to Rommel before El Alamein? Did FDR know the Japanese were heading for Pearl Harbor, as revisionists claim? Did Mussolini know how bad his army was before he invaded Greece? Did Churchill really like Montgomery, or did he think him a necessary pain-in-the-ass? Time windows could bring answers to some long sought questions.

But accomplishing this meant I had to live the war, know its combatants, and see them fight and die. In short, it meant going Interactive, the worst Crime against Time on the books, short of changing history. Another crime which, unfortunately, I also committed.

The Time Regulatory Commission was cooperative to a point. They issued me a yellow-card, which meant I could watch all I wanted but no visibility, ESP, or Interaction. On penalty of dire consequences, I could most definitely not interfere. Fine, I said. Then I bought two machines. The first was a new HP-2B with optional outboard ESP module, (the TSP issued the actual modules). The second was a black-market, very expensive, you'd-better-not-get-caught-with-this HP-A5-2, with inboard ESP, Visibility, and Interaction modules. When that cash changed hands, I became a criminal. Especially since the cash in question wasn't government issued (paper currency's evils were well known by that point) but actually fizzles, the digital currency of the Dark League. Figuring even owning fizzles was a high crime, I splurged for the Scanchecker option. That allowed me to know which frequencies the TRC monitored at any given moment and would vary my signal to avoid detection. A neat feature which cost me almost every last fizzle I had.

I thought I was being very clever. I left no digital breadcrumbs for my illegal purchases and never said a word to anybody. To cover up the huge power demands of the HP-A5-2, I had my HP-2B repaired four times for excessive power usage. In the end it didn't matter.

\* \* \*

That day's mission was Peenemunde, the German rocket and jet research center on the coast of the Baltic Sea. The air war over Germany reached a crescendo in 1944 when long-range American escort fighters cut bomber losses way down. Germany's piston-engine fighter force suffered ruinous losses of pilots and machines and by August 4th, the day in question, Luftwaffe resistance had grown weak. That put every target in Germany in the crosshairs of Norden bomb sights.

I had dreaded the roar of the B-17's four big Pratt and Whitney's, but to my surprise the noise soon became a muted drone. You got used to it much faster than I had anticipated, and the crew no longer noticed it at all. In fact, for the tail gunner, it could be eerily quiet.

It was bumpy, though. Jumpin' Jenny's fuselage vibrated with something called flutter, which modern aircraft no longer have to deal with. Flutter is an oscillation caused by interaction of aerodynamic forces, structural elasticity, and inertial effects. Add in the inherent torque of the engines, and it rattled you like a monitor lizard shaking a rat. If you were one of the crew, you were also thrown around by air-pockets, winds, and flak. After a while it felt like your brain was sloshing around inside your skull.

Five and a half miles below our feet, the steel blue of the North Sea lightened as we approached the coast of Holland. Edwards knew they would soon be over enemy territory and rechecked his equipment for the thousandth time. I watched him with admiration. What motivated this tire worker from Mississippi to travel thousands of miles from home to fight for his country? I wondered. What was the essence of such a man? Nationalism and its first cousin patriotism were largely gone from my time, so I was genuinely curious about Edwards' motivations.

Passing the coastline, the copilot's voice crackled on the intercom, checking stations. Nearing the European coast was the time to be alert. And Edwards was alert, until I butted in.

"Bombardier, check. Top turret, check…" When his turn came Edwards said the same things he always said, unwilling to break the superstitions that had brought him back from seventeen previous missions.

"Tail gunner check. Permission to test guns?"

"You've already done that, Joe."

"But twice is nice, unless I'm payin' for the ammo."

The copilot chuckled into his microphone. "Shoot away, tail gunner."

When Edwards squeezed the trigger, I watched the twin fifty-caliber machine guns jolt him with their recoil. He fired ten rounds each with no misfires.

"Tail gunner to copilot. Both guns A-okay. I need to piss."

"Permission denied. No pissin' except on the Germans."

"Roger that."

Soldiers' rituals are universal, part of every army that has ever marched, and the Eighth Air Force was no exception. When Ken Waters came aboard Jumpin' Jenny as waist gunner, it took three hours at a local pub to review the plane's do's and don'ts list.

"Pilot to crew. Keep it loose, gentlemen. Short bursts only, if we see any 190's don't lead 'em too much. We're over angels twenty so they can't juke around much up here."

I watched as Edwards nodded, even if no one could see him.

"Remember your briefings on that jet G2 says the Krauts have. If we see one lead it half again as much as a 109 and remember everything you can about it. Count the guns and the boys at G-2 will buy you the biggest steak in London. If you're lucky that steak might even be from a cow."

Edwards shook his head at the pilot's joke. They'd heard all that before, including full briefings on the new jet fighter everybody had expected to see by now. Some veterans even thought it was a hoax to keep them sharp. Except I knew it wasn't. The aircraft was called the ME-262, and if was too late and in too small a number to influence the outcome of the war, it would still kill a lot of B-17s before Hitler finally put a bullet in his brain. An incredible plane, it would be the basis for all western post-war fighter designs. It would make its first appearance on that very day, and the first person to see one would be Sergeant Joe Edwards. He would count the guns, even if nobody believed it had four cannon in the nose. The boys in G-2 would buy him a steak and, as a sign of appreciation, his group commander would even throw in a bottle of Jack Daniels. He would also inflict serious damage that grounded ME-262 flight operations for a month as the krauts tried to figure out what they did wrong. That saved a lot of American lives and was a pivotal moment in the history of aviation. It was the reason I was there.

\* \* \*

I knew it was past time to start the interview. By now German radar was tracking us and vectoring any Luftwaffe squadrons in the vicinity onto our course. Pathfinders had dropped clouds of metal foil called "window" to confuse the radar operators, a ploy which usually worked. The foil reflected radar waves and made the Germans guess which blips on their oscilloscopes were real bombers. That day they guessed right.

How do you start a conversation with someone who died two hundred years before you were born? "Hello, I'm an historian from the future who wants to ask you a few questions. I know I'm semitransparent and six inches tall, but don't let that bother you. Please, go about your business." I reasoned that a man born in 1922 was unlikely to respond to any overture I could make that was close to the truth.

So I lied.

I had taken a few precautions. In the weeks previous I had appeared to Edwards three times, twice at night and once in the morning. I told him I was part of a top-secret government experiment, that he shouldn't be alarmed and that he should definitely not mention my presence to anybody. I recorded his surprisingly calm responses, analyzed them with some commercially available psychology programs, and determined that Edwards was stable enough for my purposes. Did I mention that I had already been through this preliminary phase with three other men and found them not up to the strain? I was trying to be careful.

Anyway, Edwards thought in the beginning that he'd drunk some bad liquor. The American Army of World War Two could make hooch out of almost anything, potatoes being the most common ingredient. After a few minutes of my first visit, he seemed to believe that maybe I really was part of some secret research project. None of our sessions lasted more than ten minutes, I gave him no more information than I had to, then concluded each session by telling him not to panic if I showed up again. He had a healthy skepticism, and I felt good about taking my experiment to its ultimate conclusion, namely, recording his experiences in the heat of combat. With that in mind and while bouncing in the tail-turret of the Jumpin' Jenny, I pushed the button on my hand-held controller to activate full-interactive mode.

"Those jets are real, you know," I said aloud, shivering from the high-altitude cold. I heard my words clearly in the un-pressurized air, which meant my HP-A5-2 was doing its job. "The ones the pilot warned you about, I mean."

Edwards jumped against his seat's restraining harness, startled. He half-turned and saw me standing beside the first-aid kit.

"You again," he said. His face sagged. He turned away from me and stared out the Plexiglas.

"Ummm…yes, me again. Part of our experiment involves studying stress on men in combat. I hope I didn't frighten you."

Edwards didn't reply.

Ever.

In that hot core of his being, what he would have called his soul, my sudden appearance shattered a fragile hold on reality that had gone undetected by me and the flight doctors. The constant stress of flying combat missions over Germany had taken its toll. Without my interference he would have gritted his teeth and made it through, but I pushed him over the brink and into the abyss of insanity. A transparent man six inches tall pried his mind loose of reality. Maybe he knew he had finally snapped and couldn't live with the stigma that mid-twentieth century society attached to such men. I don't know. I'll never know, and I'll bet even the so-called experts don't either. I can only report what happened.

He hunched forward in his seat and continued to stare. The thousand-yard stare it has been called. I tried rousing him for a few minutes simply by talking. When that didn't work I walked around the turret (quite a long way when you're six inches tall). His eyes were locked on some distant object only he could see; he had the glassy, unblinking eyes of a man whose mind had shut down.

The experts in Time Psychology who testified at my trial called it Severe Phenomena-Induced Trauma. Apparently it was a well-known malady that first showed up in the early days of time travel. The public never heard of it because there was no reason they should. People like me weren't allowed to do what I did, only government experts were, and they were trained to deal with all known time-related problems, including Severe Phenomena-Induced Trauma. During the trial they asked me why I thought licenses were regulated in the first place. What gave me the right to meddle in things I didn't understand? Why did I, a lowly historian, think I knew more about the dangers of time travel than the experts? There was only one mitigating factor in my favor and it saved my existence, though not my life.

I'd never seen someone whose mind snapped before, but that didn't keep me from knowing what had happened. His eyes took on a vacant quality that hadn't been there before, like a bottle drained of its water. Immediately upon seeing Edwards' madman stare I realized he was in some sort of shock. What I did next cheated the hangman. First I tried shouting, hoping somehow to wake him. Of course that didn't work, for though I was fully interactive, I was still only a hologram and my voice didn't carry its full weight or volume. Then I clawed my way up his boot to a crease in his flight suit, which I followed to the knee, ran up his thigh and edged along a fold in his jacket as though it were a narrow trail on the side of a cliff, once clinging to the zipper to keep from falling. (Although a hologram, I did have enough physical presence in Edward's time stream to touch or handle things.) Finally I made it to his shoulder where I shouted in his ear, slapped his jaw, pulled at some unshaven beard on his neck and, in desperation, tried biting him. Nothing worked. A six-inch hologram doesn't have much strength to call on. But I did everything I could think of to correct my mistake. I tried, and in the end that was what mattered.

Winded from the exertion I rested a minute, my gaze straying to the fields of Germany far below. The sun glinted from something for a split-second, but I lost it. Was that an aircraft? I looked were it should have been if it was rising to meet the bombers, but saw nothing. I kept staring until my eyes watered. Then my peripheral vision caught another glint and my stomach tightened. It was a plane, all right, but moving much faster than any piston-driven fighter. Edwards was about to keep his date with history...the plane was an ME-262.

I panicked, wasting time trying to depress the Sergeant's throat mike with my tiny, semi-solid hands. I tried firing the twin fifties, striking a match to start a fire, anything to get the attention of the other crew members, to let them know their tail gunner was a vegetable and their worst nightmare was closing fast from the rear. Nothing worked, and I realize now, in retrospect, that nothing would have.

I saw four jets now. They were five miles out and closing fast. I could see their cigar-shaped bodies and blunt, shark-like noses. I slid and tumbled off the sergeant and hit the turret-floor running. I hoped to alert the waist gunner before thirty millimeter shells tore Jumpin' Jenny to shreds. Sweating and stumbling and cursing I only made it to the hatch when the world exploded around me.

Edwards died in the first stream of shells, his body ripped to shreds of bone and flesh that spattered me from head to toe. Shards of Plexiglas and steel filled the air with shrapnel. I crouched behind a hydraulic line as Jenny shuddered under the punishing barrage. And then I wasn't in the turret any more. I was in a chair at the TRC with a grim man standing over me. His name was Gomorrah.

* * *

When Edwards died, history changed. Down-time the Time Police knew it at once. They scanned the appropriate frequencies, cross-checked the findings against abnormal power usages and fingered me as the culprit, all in about 4 seconds. It took seven more seconds to override command of my HP-A5-2 and less than one second to transport me back to my own time. The lead prosecutor was a hardass named Peter Dance. It took him no time at all to prepare the case against me.

What defense could I offer? Because of me a man died who should have lived. Children who should have led wonderful lives were never born, and their children were erased from history. Instead of a two-point victory, Memphis State lost by twenty-one to UCLA in the 1973 NCAA finals. Without Edwards' son there to help shut down Bill Walton, the big redhead hit 21 out of 22 shots and scored 44 points. The TRC prosecutors called it collateral homicide, a specific term for a specific form of murder.

The question then was what to do with me. Prison overcrowding was a huge problem. The best thing I had going for me was that I stayed and tried to right my wrong. The court was inclined to leniency but they couldn't just let me go, so what was to be done with me? Overcrowded prisons certainly didn't need another long-timer on the rolls.

Jurassic Jails were in their infancy then, and they considered it. Strand me in 100 million B.C. and let it go at that. It was a way to make sure I served my sentence without spending much money feeding and housing me, with disease or a giant lizard doing the hangman's job in the end. Then someone brought up indentured servitude on a Roman galley, and somebody else a brick-maker in service of Pharaoh to build the Great Pyramids of Giza. In panic I pitched Mr. Dance on a wild idea that I sold with the passion of desperation. That's why the final resolution of my case was my own idea.

\* \* \*

My name is now Joe Edwards. No relation to Jumpin Jenny's previous tail gunner; it's just one of those weird coincidences you read about. That's my cover story. My superstitious crewmates give me the fish eye, like I'm a ghost or something worse. That won't change until we survive a mission and they can see I'm not a jinx. I don't blame them, though, but I reassure them I'm not a ghost. I don't tell them I'm something worse.

Staring through the Plexiglas of my tail-turret I can see the entire bomb-group spread out above the North Sea, the ice-crystals of their vapor trails pointing the way back to England. The sky is clear, and, as I see the P-51's shining in the sun far above, I am comforted. The Little Friends are on station, ready to escort us to today's target: Berlin. While the other members of Jumpin' Jenny's crew don't seem worried about the anti-aircraft guns, the heavy flak over the capital of the Third Reich scares the hell out of me.

I carry the picture of a girl named Adele Stephenson in my wallet. When the war is over I am going to court her and hopefully marry her and have three children, assuming I survive. With any luck one will play basketball for Memphis State. I've started smoking Lucky Strikes and reading westerns. There's a job waiting for me at a tire factory in Memphis, and it's now my life's ambition to make shift foreman. When I cry myself to sleep at night my new crew mates ask what's wrong, and I tell them I'm weeping for the life I left behind, which is true.

There's turbulence over Germany this day, and, as I'm bouncing against my harness, I remember one of the rituals I'd learned.

"Tail gunner to copilot. Permission to test guns?"

"Granted."

Both work perfectly, the jolting recoil of the twin fifties shaking me to my teeth.

"Guns OK. I need to piss."

The copilot is quiet for a moment. Finally, he says, "That's what Edwards used to say."

"Oh?" I reply.

"Yeah…"

"Weird, huh?"

The copilot paused again. "No pissing, except on the Germans."

"Roger that."

There's no sign of the damage inflicted by the ME-262. Ground crews have replaced the turret and cleaned up the blood and bones. My window of Plexiglas is new and clean. It is time for me to face my fate, to fight for a country that is not mine, all while hoping to survive my sentence.

\* \* \* \* \*

## William Alan Webb Bio

As a West Tennessee native raised in the 60s and 70s, and born into a family with a long tradition of military service, it should be no surprise that the three chief influences on Bill's life have been military history, science fiction and fantasy and the natural world. In 1972 he won the Tennessee State High School Dual Chess Championship, and spent every waking moment playing board games, role-playing games, and naval miniatures. College featured dual concentrations in History and English. Everything after that is anti-climax, except for wife, kids, published books and all that kind of stuff.

Website: www.thelastbrigade.com

Facebook page:

https://www.facebook.com/keepyouupallnightbooks

\# \# \# \# \#

# Red Tailed Tigers
# by Justin Watson

Benny rocked as the C-47's wheels hit the tarmac. Standing five foot eight and a heavily muscled one hundred and sixty pounds, Benny had caramel skin and refined, patrician features thanks to his Creole mother. Until three days ago, he'd also been an Air Force officer with a promising career ahead of him.

The cargo plane rolled for about five more minutes, Benny swaying miserably in his seat the whole way before the roar of the engines turned into a whine and then came to a full stop. Benny ran a hand across his brow and wiped the accumulated perspiration on the gooney bird's canvas seat before lurching to his feet. Benjamin Jakes and Robin Olds were the only passengers; the rest of the hold was filled with crates of .50 caliber ammunition. Benny gave Olds a baleful look.

"What? It's no worse than the Philippines," Olds said, retrieving his duffel bag. "Aren't you from Louisiana?"

"I feel like I'm drinking the air," Benny said.

"Bitch, bitch, bitch," Olds said.

"Gentlemen," the C-47 pilot said as he stepped out of the cockpit. "Welcome to Gia Lam Airport, jewel of Hanoi. The temperature is five degrees hotter than hell and it's humid enough to drown a fucking fish. If you head down the gangway and take a left, the 4th AVG building is right there. No offense fellas, but shake a leg. I can't get out of this hellhole until they come unload all this ammo."

The pilot was a middle-aged man with thinning gray hair.

"Alright, buddy, we're moving," Olds said. "High risk of air raid here, I take it?"

"Nah," the cargo pilot said, tapping out a cigarette and lighting it. "The war is all out on the frontier with Laos and Cambodia. Both sides are leaving the rear areas alone for the moment."

"So why are you in such a hurry?" Benny said.

The pilot took a drag off his cigarette and chuckled.

"Because I fucking hate it here," he said.

The sun was blinding after the dim cargo hold, and it cooked Benny's head and shoulders unmercifully as they trekked across the tarmac. On their way to an over-sized Quonset hut, with a simple wooden sign that read, "4TH AVG," Benny counted sixteen straight-winged, smooth nosed P-80 jets waiting on the flight line, and twice that number, each, of single propeller driven P-51 *Mustangs*, P-47 *Thunderbolts* and fork-tailed P-38 *Lightnings*.

"You had to deck that colonel," Olds said.

Benny glared at Olds. His friend was a solid five inches taller than him and seemed wide as a barn door with a broad, square face that bore no hint of chagrin.

"He tried to deck me," Benny said. "*After* you provoked him."

Olds shrugged. "He shouldn't have called you a nigger."

"That's my fight, Robin," Benny said. "Do you want fly jets or go around punching every bigot in the Air Force? The latter is going to take you a lot of time."

"They both sound fun, to be honest," Olds said. "Look are you going to keep bitching at me or can we check in and start flying jets?"

"You brought it up."

Benny and Olds continued their trek across the tarmac.

"They've got a nice little Air Force going here," Olds said.

"Yeah," Benny said, pulling the door to the hut open. "Wonder what all the French have got on the other side. Besides the 262s, of course."

The clattering of typewriters and static-ridden radio chatter greeted them as they stepped inside. The layout was familiar, with maps and charts dominating large tables in the center of the space illuminated by intermittent bulbs hung from the peak of the arced ceiling.

"Okay, tell the bombers we'll have escort up in five minutes," a deep Texas drawl drew Benny's eyes to a radio set on the other side of a massive map of Vietnam. "They can sortie now, and we'll get ahead of them."

The speaker was a tall, lean man with a broad face and over-prominent ears. He looked up from the radio just in time to see Benny and Olds step through the door.

"Olds, Jakes," he said. "They told me y'all were coming. Good, now we've got a four-ship."

"Sir?" Benny said.

"This ain't the Air Force, Jakes, I'm the boss, David Miller," he said. "Call me Tex. And I'm glad you're in flight suits because we've got a mission."

"Sir, what?" Olds said. "We just got here—"

"And now that I have you, that makes four P-80 qualified pilots between you me and Jesus over there," Miller pronounced the name

*Hey-soos*, and pointed to a swarthy man bent over the map. Jesus looked up and gave them both a toothy grin.

Benny exchanged a look with Olds, who shrugged.

"What's the mission, sir?" Olds said.

"I told y'all to call me Tex," Miller said. "The Viet Minh have a company of Frenchies pinned on our side of the border. We're sending a passel of Jugs to hammer 'em real good. The P-51s will sweep ahead and level, we four are going to fly outlaw high, and surprise them sonsabitches if they show up in their German jets.

"Here, I'll show you the route on the map..."

\* \* \*

Benny applied a bit of pressure to his stick and compensated with the opposite rudder pedal to drop his P-80's left wing while maintaining course. Several thousand feet below he saw flights of P-47 *Thunderbolts* diving on the jungle like piston-driven angels of vengeance. Explosions reverberated through the thick jungle air as the verdant tree top canopy was alternately consumed by clouds of fire from bombs then perforated by hailstorms of .50 caliber rounds. At this altitude, he couldn't make out anything of the enemy ground force, but if the Jugs were even remotely accurate, the French were not having a good day.

"Eight Bandits, ten o'clock low," Hill announced. "Olds, Jakes, you got high flight, we'll take low. Dive in on them, then lay on the throttle and get some distance before you reengage. If you get into real trouble, climb as soon as you can extend, we got 'em beat for speed and ceiling."

Benny saw two flights of four Me 262s staggered in altitude by about two thousand feet, laterally by about five thousand. Rather than the Buck Rogers shape of the P-80s, the Me-262s followed much the same pattern as the propeller driven planes of the '40s. Their graceful lines were marred only by the massive jet engines slung under each wing. The French pilots were boring in on the P-47s, probably intent on relieving their comrades on the ground.

"Roger, acknowledge all. Tally Bandits," Olds answered. "Engaging."

Benny felt his stomach lurch in negative G as he put his P-80's nose below the horizon and followed Olds' dive. They didn't need to talk, automatically sub-dividing their targets as they had a hundred times before in training.

As they came close enough to see roundels on the Messerschmidt's wings, Benny adjusted his approach to a more lateral vector. It added deflection to the shot, which made it trickier, but would allow him to engage the second target more easily.

Applying fractional adjustments on the stick and rudder pedals, Benny put the gunsight piper right over the 262's wing joint and squeezed the trigger on his control stick. Metallic clatter filled his ears, the sky before him burned with muzzle flashes, and the cockpit rocked with the recoil of six .50 caliber machine guns each firing twenty rounds per second. Red tracers lanced through the sky and tore into the first French jet's fuselage. Benny was rewarded with an orange and black explosion followed by the sight of the 262's right wing falling away. The remainder of the jet spun off toward the distant ground.

*That's five,* Benny grinned behind his oxygen mask. *I'm a bona fide fucking ace!*

In his peripheral vision Benny saw Olds' target burst into flames and plummet. The surviving French jets banked hard left then split, one climbing the other diving. Benny yanked his stick until his wings were perpendicular to the horizon to stay on the low man. Acceleration pressed him into his seat and his g-suit constricted around him, slowing the flow of blood toward his feet. He grunted as he fought the pipper out in front of the enemy. Once he judged the lead sufficient, he squeezed the trigger again, sending another burst from his six machine guns arcing toward his enemy. His P-80 was only one hundred meters away from the Frenchman when the 262's canopy shattered from the impact of several dozen .50 caliber rounds, sending glittering fragments all about. The plane inverted less than a second later and began to spin to the ground.

*Six,* Benny thought, as he pulled his P-80 about and climbed to regain his position on Olds' tail. *This is shaping up to be a good war.*

"Benny, get up here," Olds said, his voice calm but strained. "I got a bandit at six."

Scanning the skies, it took Benny precious seconds to spot the 262 on Olds' tail. Olds was maneuvering violently but the French pilot was staying with him, using his lower speed and tighter turn radius to keep Olds in front of him as they scissored back and forth across the sky. Benny opened his throttle to close the gap, his P-80 shooting up into the sky at thirty-five meters per second.

"Break right and climb, Rob," Benny said. "I've got him."

Olds' P-80 banked hard and its nose shot skyward as instructed. This Me-262 pilot had better situational awareness than his friends, though, and after a missed snapshot at Olds, the jet dropped into a split S, falling out of Benny's sight picture just as he pulled the trigger.

*Damn.* Gravity pulled Benny against his restraints as he inverted his jet to get a better look down. Enemy in sight, he pulled his stick back and sacrificed altitude for energy, closing on the 262 in a dive. The 262 was still on his guard, though, and the Frenchman's hard bank took him out of Benny's gunsight again, forcing Benny to level off to maintain pursuit.

*This guy is a good stick*, Benny thought. As he brought his nose up from the dive, the enemy pilot attempted another high-g bank, trying to get Benny to overshoot. Benny countered by pulling his nose up and then into a roll, completing a high yo-yo. It prevented an overshoot, but only barely as the 262 now filled Benny's forward canopy and his plane shook with the enemy's jetwash. At this range, there was no need to worry about the gun sight. Benny mashed the trigger, cutting his enemy to ribbons with a point blank stream of .50 caliber rounds.

There was no time to avoid the resultant fireball and cloud of debris; dozens of chunks of molten hot steel clattered against his fuselage. Something big enough to jerk the P-80's nose hard right impacted with a loud BANG as he cleared the cloud. A bare three seconds later his engine began to sputter, his plane shook, and then the cockpit was filled with deadly silence as the roar of his jet engine died.

Benny gently pulled his stick and pressed the rudder pedals until his nose was pointed east, deeper into Vietnam.

"My engine is dead," Benny reported, sounding calmer than he felt. "I'm on glide path east, going to bail out before I go into a spin."

"Roger, Benny," Tex answered him. "We've got friendlies all over the area. Stay calm, we'll have search and rescue to you in no time."

"Acknowledged," Benny said. "See you later, guys!"

Grunting with effort, Benny worked the canopy release lever. The mechanism gave way with a pop and the glass and steel canopy flew away into the sky. He was buffeted with hot wind as he undid his restraints and clumsily hauled himself out of his seat. A carpet of green tree tops rushed upward to meet him. Heart pounding, hands shaking, Benny made his way out of the cockpit and onto the wing and unceremoniously fell off, plummeting toward the ground like a rock.

*Oh, Jesus Christ!*

Fighting the panic, Benny struggled against swirling atmosphere and his own momentum to get into a flat arched position, arms and legs splayed to each side. It took precious seconds of effort and hundreds of feet of altitude before he stabilized. He tasted bile in the back of his mouth, and he was pretty certain his pants were now soaked in his own piss, but at least he was alive. In the distance he saw his P-80's angle of descent steepen then go nearly perpendicular to the ground as it crashed into the jungle, the secondary explosion lighting up the tree tops.

Benny yanked the ripcord and his parachute harness dug violently into his groin and shoulders, drawing another grunt from him. Dangling from the silk, risers in hand, he finally was able to draw several deep breaths and take stock of the situation around him.

The bombing and strafing had ceased; he could see the P-47s vanishing east back toward the airfields. The dogfight seemed to be over, too; the three P-80s were flying a wide racetrack orbit around him, close enough to see, far enough not to catch his chute in jetwash. Glad to have friends close by, he turned his attention to his next task, figuring out where the hell he was going to land.

Gaps in the jungle canopy were few and narrow. Picking the best of bad options, Benny pulled down on his left riser trying to steer towards something other than solid treetop. Despite his efforts, tree branches pummeled his legs and torso as he fell into the jungle. Benny struggled to keep his feet and knees together. The branches batted and scraped at him, taking scraps of flightsuit and swaths of skin from him on his way down.

Finally, he broke through the lowest branches and crumpled to the jungle floor like a sack of shit. Miraculously, his chute hadn't caught in the trees. Battered from both high g-maneuvering and his descent through the treetops, Benny hit the releases on his parachute and lay back in the thick grass. The humidity and heat were oppressive, but he took a few breaths to enjoy the quiet anyway.

Running feet and voices shouting in a sing-song language shattered his calm. Springing to his feet, he looked around and saw that green palm fronds and bush cut visibility to mere feet in every direction. He was debating whether or not to hide when three short men in too-baggy green fatigues burst through the bushes to his left, rifles leveled at him. They were shouting in the same sing-song language he couldn't understand. He noted that the rifles were M1 Carbines, the fatigues clearly American cast offs.

Benny put his hands in the air. *Now if only I can convince them not to shoot me.*

"Hey, guys," he said. "Same side, I'm here to shoot down French jets."

The tallest of the three men advanced on Benny, almond-shaped eyes wide with anger and adrenaline.

"Hold on, now," Benny said, hands still up. "Just wait—"

The man slammed the butt of his carbine into the side of Benny's face. Benny's vision went white, then black, then puckered with sparkling gold stars as the interwoven branches and leaves of the jungle canopy started to come back into focus. As if through a funnel he heard another voice. This one was definitely American, with a corn belt rasp.

"Goddamn it, Dat, he's an American," the voice was shouting in English before switching to the native patois. "Người Pháp không để người da đen bay máy bay, Thang cho de!"

Benny was only vaguely aware of hands lifting him off the soft jungle floor and carrying him...somewhere. Somewhere in the jungle with a large cloud of yellow smoke, and a...a massive ceiling fan? What the hell...

* * *

The long swim up from the depths started with a dull pain in his lower back, then another sharper one in his head. Light crept in at the seams of his eyelids, then muffled voices that sounded as if they originated on the other side of a thin door. The air around him smelled of ethanol and iron. Cracking a single eye, bright morning sun penetrated his pupil like a lance into his brain, eliciting an involuntary croak from him.

He heard footsteps on tile and one of the voices growing closer, more distinct. The voice was pleasant, feminine and...French?

Forcing his eyelids open and accepting the resultant stabbing pain, Benny appraised his surroundings. He was lying on a hard mattress with rough linens at the end of a long line of beds, about half of them occupied. An intravenous needle was lodged in his left arm, its tube leading up to a glass bottle full of clear solution, and he wasn't wearing anything besides a pair of skivvy shorts.

The first person he saw was a woman who strode rapidly toward his bedside. She was clothed in green fatigues with the sleeves rolled to her elbows. Her chestnut hair was bound up neatly in a tight bun, and she smiled at him warmly. Benny found himself staring into her large, dark eyes; she was such an incongruously lovely vision for a war zone.

"Good Morning, Mr. Jakes," she said, her English clear but heavily French-accented. "I'm so happy you've elected to rejoin us."

Benny tried to straighten up in bed, his expression hardening.

"Bonjour, Mademoiselle," Benny said, his parched throat grating the French words before they could escape his lips. "Suis-je un prisonnier, alors?"

She chuckled as she reached for a pitcher of water and glass from a shelf behind his bed.

"No, you are certainly not," She said as she poured the glass and held it out to him. "Though I understand your confusion. I am one of many free Frenchmen and women here in Indochina aiding our Vietnamese and American friends."

Benny didn't take the glass. Incredulity marred his features.

"You're aiding us against your own people?" He said.

"They are no longer my people," she said, thrusting the glass at him. "They are Nazis. Take this, you must rehydrate. You have been asleep for more than a day and saline solution isn't as good as drinking your fill."

He accepted the glass with a chagrined expression and drained it in one draught.

"Forgive me if I've offended you," he said, handing the glass back to her. "The narcotics must have made me stupid. Is the doctor available? I feel much better, and I want to get back to my unit."

She arched a dark brown eyebrow at him and accepted the empty glass.

"*I* am the doctor, Mr. Jakes," she said. "Dr. Margot Durand, at your service. And no, you are not leaving. You suffered a significant head trauma. Your waking wasn't a forgone conclusion, not to mention the lacerations you suffered. If you don't let those heal up properly you are asking for some nasty infections."

"Oh, sure, give the lazy bastard an excuse to lay about some more," a familiar booming voice interrupted from the door.

Benny turned his head just enough to see Robin Olds' bulk filling the door frame at the near end of the ward. He was dressed in a green flight suit, a grin on his big blunt face.

"Mr. Olds," Durand said. "I will thank you to lower your voice, I have patients resting in this ward."

"Oh, I'm very sorry, Doctor," Olds said, with no discernible change in volume. "I'm just glad to see my friend here awake."

Durand's expression was suddenly much more stern, and she didn't bother to hide her asperity when she spoke again.

"Very well," she said. "I will give you ten minutes to chat, but no more. Mr. Jakes also needs rest."

She turned to leave but before she could go, Benny spoke up.

"Dr. Durand, would it be possible to speak to the chopper pilot who flew me out?" He said.

Durand turned back to him, a slight smile on her full lips.

"This is possible," she said. "What would you say?"

"Well, anyone with the…gumption…to fly that tinker toy into combat deserves at least a drink for it," Benny said. "He's a braver man than me."

"I'll pass that along," she said. Her smile hardened into something more severe when she turned her eyes on Olds. "Ten minutes."

Olds was chuckling even as he spared an appreciative glance at Durand's retreating form. Even the baggy fatigue pants didn't hide her curves and the sway of her hips as she walked. Benny found himself annoyed with Olds and then annoyed that he was annoyed.

"What are you laughing about?" Benny asked.

"She flew the helicopter, buddy boy," Olds said.

"What?" Benny said, sitting up straighter. "Stop screwing with me."

"Cross my heart and hope to die, Benny," Olds said, grinning. "A body like that and she can fly, too. A helicopter, no less. Frankly I'm not sure how it generates enough lift to keep her big brass ovaries in the air."

"No shit," Benny said. "They sent a Frenchwoman to flight school?"

"Not so much," Olds said. "The Agency let her finish medical school and come here as a surgeon. She convinced the head of the whirlybird detachment to teach her to fly. Then she started flying search and rescue with no one's permission. Feldman tried to stop her, but she's rescued sixty-three men, and operated on twenty-six of them so he gave up on that. The guys around here worship her."

"Sweet Jesus," Benny said.

"Yeah, the lady gets what she wants," Olds said. "I mean, do you think you'd have any luck saying no to her?"

Benny didn't answer that. He knew better than to get infatuated with a white woman.

"How did we make out, anyway?" Benny said. "You're here; I assume Tex and Jesus made it back, too?"

"They did," Olds said. "We didn't even lose any Jugs. You're the only one who took a walk. I asked Hill if you counted as your own kill since you basically shot yourself down."

"Ass," Benny said with no real heat.

"Guilty," Olds said. "Regardless, you, me and Tex are the first Americans with jet kills. You've got three confirmed from yesterday, I downed two and a half, Jesus got one and Tex got three and a half. Congratulations, Ace."

"Wow, we really mauled them," Benny said.

"Sure did, half a squadron gone for one of our planes," Olds said. "We can trade eight for one all day, especially if we get our pilot back, anyway."

A Texas drawl interjected.

"Woulda' been eight for ought if y'all had listened to what the hell I told you." Tex Hill stepped through the door. He was dressed in a sweat-stained flight suit and looked tired and exasperated rather than exultant.

"Come on, Tex," Olds said. "We nailed them, didn't we?"

"You nailed 'em because you're both shit hot on the stick," Hill said, his drawl becoming more pronounced as he grew angrier. "But if you'd made one pass, dived and used your speed to create a gap before you reengaged, like I damned well told you to, I'd have sixteen P-80s instead of fifteen."

Benny frowned. It felt wrong getting a lecture after he'd just become an ace, but he saw Hill's point. If they'd listened they wouldn't have had to dogfight the French at all for their kills.

"You're right, sir," Benny said before Robin could speak. "No excuse."

Tex's expression relaxed.

"Oh, can the kay-det crap, Benny," Tex said. "Truth is you flew great, and I appreciate aggression. Just keep in mind, you're about to be taking new guys into combat. They see you taking unnecessary risks, they might put themselves in a situation where you can pull it out of the fire, but they can't."

Olds exhaled, visibly letting go of a counterargument.

"Hell, you're right, Tex," Olds said. "I'm sorry, too."

"Sorry don't kill Messerschmitts, boys. Just learn," Tex said. "And do better."

Movement in his peripheral vision drew Benny's eye away from Tex to Durand who stepped next to his bed, clearing her throat.

"Pardon me, gentlemen," Durand said. "But I need to examine him and then he will need to rest."

"Of course, ma'am," Tex said. "How long do you think he'll be out?"

"At least a week," Durand said. "I need to evaluate the effects of his head trauma and his wounds need to close up properly before he returns to the cockpit."

Tex frowned, but he didn't argue.

"Alright, then," he said. "I suppose a week of vacation for making ace isn't too much to ask. I'll check in on you later, Jakes. Come on, Olds, you heard the doctor."

"See you later, Benny," Olds said.

Durand pulled a small flashlight from a fatigue pocket and sat down on Benny's bed next to him. Taking his wrist in her hands, she found his vein with her fingers and he saw her nodding as she counted his pulse. Benny realized, of course, that she was just being a medical professional, but his body took her touch in all the wrong ways. He took a deep breath, trying to slow his heart rate, and thought of penguins. Apparently satisfied, Durand dropped his wrist without comment and put her left hand on his cheek, tilting his eyes toward her and leaned in close, shining the flashlight in his eyes.

"Your eyes are dilating properly," she said, putting away the flashlight and pulling a fountain pen from her breast pocket. "This is very good. Please now follow my pen without moving your head."

Benny tracked the tip of the pen without issue as she moved it right and left, and up and down in front of his face. The pen stopped in front of her nose and when she dropped it he was staring into her eyes again. She met his gaze for a long moment, her chin tilted just slightly to the side, a hint of mischief tugging her lips into a smile.

"Also very good," she said, unscrewing the cap of the fountain pen and reaching for a clipboard hanging from a nail beside his bed.

"Thank you," Benny said. "For saving my life, I mean."

"For flying my, 'tinker toy,' into combat to get you, you mean?" Durand said, an impish smile blossoming on her face. "It wasn't as dramatic as all that. The boys had the enemy on the run. I didn't even take small arms fire."

Benny snorted and shook his head. *Brass ovaries indeed.*

"What?" Durand said. "Several men tried to kill you yesterday, you don't seem perturbed by the fact, why should I feel differently?"

"You've got me there," Benny admitted. "Thank you, nonetheless."

Durand finished what she was writing with a bold stroke and re-capped her pen before answering him.

"You are most welcome," she said. "Now tell me, where did you learn to speak French so well?"

"My family is from New Orleans," Benny said. "My mother made sure I could speak French. My grandmother didn't even speak English."

"It's an interesting accent," Durand said. "It reminds me of my grandfather. He was a country farmer and always spoke a bit rougher than his cousins from Paris. Tres masculin."

As she reached out to put the clipboard back on its nail, Benny noticed a tattoo on her forearm. It was nothing artistic, just a long series of small black numbers. Durand saw him staring at it, and her smile vanished. Realizing he'd upset her, though not why, Benny dropped his gaze.

"I'm sorry," he muttered. "I didn't mean to make you uncomfortable."

"It's alright," Durand said. "I'll check in on you later. If there's anything you need while I'm out of the ward, just let one of the nurses know, and they'll take care of you."

"Thank you again," Benny said.

"It is my pleasure again," Durand said, making her tone light with visible effort. "Perhaps when you are not my patient anymore, I'll let you buy that drink you owe me."

"Oh, you don't have to—" Benny said, "I mean, I didn't know you were a…that is, I wouldn't want to embarrass you or…"

*Benny Jakes, flying ace and stammering idiot.*

"Embarrass me how? Are you reneging on your debt, Mr. Jakes?" Durand said.

"Of course not," Benny said. "I just wouldn't want anyone to gossip, if you were seen socializing with, well, with me outside of a professional setting."

"Oh, Mr. Jakes," Durand said, disarming smile back in place. "I'm a big girl, and I socialize with whomever I please. You rest now; we'll chat more later."

\* \* \*

Six weeks later, Benny and his three charges were cruising eastward, closing on a final approach back to Gia Lam in a standard finger-four formation. He smiled behind his oxygen mask. Four French Stukas were smoking wrecks just on the Laotian side of the border; they'd been dead before they'd known they were in danger.

The hunting was a lot thinner these days. The French had become careful about how and when they employed their airpower, taking pains to avoid the threat from the P-80 squadron. They sent their Sturmvogel ground-attack Me-262s only for quick bombing raids wherever the P-80s weren't.

On the bright side, American planes and volunteer pilots continued to flow into Vietnam. Between Free Vietnamese Air Force and AVG pilots, they now had sixteen qualified P-80 pilots and eighteen operational airframes. Initially, Tex had divided out the American and Vietnamese pilots evenly amongst the four flights. Each flight got three Americans and one Vietnamese pilot.

As it turned out, though, Benny was the only leader who spoke decent French. The other three flight leads became quickly frustrated by the language barrier, and Tex reassigned all three Vietnamese pilots to Benny's flight. At first he'd found his new subordinates to be competent pilots, but on the timid side and entirely too deferential for fighter jocks. However, three weeks getting to know them revealed they suffered no deficit of killer instinct and, while still scrupulously polite, they each displayed keen and quirky humor the longer they were in the flight.

Earlier that morning, when he'd walked out to the flight line, he'd noted that his four ships had a new coat of paint on the tail. Tex Miller had insisted on shark's teeth on all the P-80s, but only Benny's birds had a bright red coat of paint on the tail.

When he'd asked his maintenance chief, Sergeant Hernandez, about the surprise aesthetic modification, the man had looked at Benny like the answer was obvious.

"Well, sir, you were in the 332$^{nd}$ in the War, and you guys kicked ass," Hernandez had stated. "I figured it would be good luck."

"*Excellent travail aujourd'hui, les hommes,*" Benny told his men. "Now lets give them a show. Keep it tight."

"*D'accord,*" each of his men acknowledged the order.

Switching back to English to talk to the Tower, he announced his intentions.

"Tower, this is Tiger Four on final approach," Benny said. "Stand by for victory loop."

"Tiger Four," the Tower operator responded in a clipped Boston accent. "You are cleared for loop."

Benny kicked his plane into a wide cork-screwing series of turns over the runway, his men following him perfectly. His grin grew wider as the g's pulled him this way and that against the restraints. As the end of the runway passed beneath him, he leveled out for three seconds before pulling his nose hard up, shooting into the air, all the way over into a loop that put them back on approach to Gia Lam.

"Good show, boys," Benny said. "Now let's get into our normal landing pattern. I'll see you all at the O Club tonight. Drinks on me."

\* \* \*

The O Club's turntable was connected to some surprisingly good speakers so they had jazz records piped in with their meal. The décor was all rich browns and golds, definitely an artifact of the Club's previous owners. Robin and two of his guys were mangling a waltz with three of the nurses on the dance floor while Benny and his pilots celebrated the day's victories on the second floor balcony.

"We're tied at four kills, Tran," Ngo Than Duc, the oldest and shortest of the three Vietnamese said. "But you're still a *trinh nữ* in jets."

"Eat shit," Tran Hien Vo, the youngest, replied. "I'll put five thousand piastres against your sister's virtue that I'll be the first Vietnamese ace."

"That's a losing bet," Lee Phi Hung, Benny's wingman and the middle "child" of his pilots said. "No way something as battered as his sister's virtue is worth five thousand piastres."

All four pilots roared at that.

"Ngo, what's a, 'trin new?'" Benny said when they'd stopped laughing. His Vietnamese was improving, but his guys still talked mostly French around him out of courtesy.

"It's…ah," Ngo stopped. "I don't know the French word."

"Sir it means he's never, ah," Lee made a circle with left thumb and forefinger and poked his index finger through it in universal sign language.

"I see," Benny said laughing again.

A figure in a dark red dress caught Benny's eye approaching the bar below. Conversation forgotten, he stared like a moonstruck school boy. He'd thought Margot beautiful from the first time he'd laid eyes on her, but in a red, form-fitting silk dress, she appeared as something from a dream.

Benny frowned. He'd taken lunch several times with Margot Durand, always accompanied by Robin and one of Margot's nurses or another woman for proper chaperonage. Margot seemed amused by Benny's insistence on the propriety, but she was no less charming and interesting for it. They shared an affinity for Victor Hugo and jazz, and they enjoyed their disagreements regarding the merits of Camus and Sartre's works—those published before World War II, or smuggled out following both men's executions in 1945.

*Damn Vichy*, Benny thought. As Margot moved around the room, his thoughts turned back to the French doctor. He was drawn to her, but wary. Miscegenation was still illegal in most of the United States. Openly romancing a white woman could get him arrested; hell, even sharing a table with Margot, as he'd already done, could get him murdered back home in Louisiana. This wasn't Louisiana by several decimal places, but survival habits died hard.

*But women like Margot don't grow on trees.*

When he pulled his eyes off of Margot, he saw that all three of his men were grinning knowingly at him.

"*Dai uy*, why don't you go wish Dr. Margot a pleasant evening?" Ngo said. "We'll be alright up here."

"No, no," Benny said. "I shouldn't—"

"No, sir, really, go ahead," Tran chimed in. "Unless you're afraid…"

"Go to hell, Tran," Benny said. "I hope Ngo does get his fifth kill before you do."

The table erupted in laughter again as Benny stood up, drawing Margot's eye to their table.

*Well, I'm pot-committed now.*

Margot followed him down the stairs with her eyes, all the way to the bar with an inviting smile on her face the whole time.

"Benny," she said, her accent inflecting the y at the end of his name in a manner he'd come to appreciate. "I saw the victory loop; you broke the dry streak today, congratulations."

"Merci beaucoup," Benny said, returning her smile. "You look especially lovely tonight, Margot."

"You are too kind," Margot said, her wide, dark eyes reflecting the warm incandescent light of the club.

"I am too honest," Benny said, shaking his head. "And I must be crazy."

"Why? Because you find yourself interested in a woman? This is a strange definition of insanity, Benjamin," Margot said.

"Do I really have to spell it out for you?" Benny said. "Is France really that progressive, that it just doesn't matter? Or did you miss the fact that I'm black as the as the ace of spades?"

"You are most certainly not," Margot said, lifting her chin. "You are a lovely chocolate and caramel shade; I find it most appealing."

"Oh, for Christ's sake, Margot," Benny said, putting a hand to his face and rubbing his forehead.

A dark line appeared between Margot's eyebrows and something not entirely pleasant flickered in her lovely eyes. She was quiet for a moment, staring at Benny. Suddenly she thrust out her right forearm, palm up to show the ivory skin covering her veins and the series of numbers he'd seen that first day in the hospital.

"You saw this in the hospital," Margot said. "You didn't ask what it was."

"You seemed upset when I noticed," Benny said. "I didn't want to distress you."

"That's very polite," She said. "It is from Ravensbruck. Is this a place you have heard of?"

*It sounds familiar...oh...oh.*

"My God," Benny said. "The camps—"

"Yes, the camps," Margot said, dropping her arm. "I was at Ravensbruck from 1943 until 1945, when your government negotiated our release."

"I didn't even know you were Jewish," Benny said. "I'm so sorry, I can't even imagine—"

"I am not Jewish." She cut him off. "I left medical school to fight with the resistance. I had already killed four policeman and a collaborating mayor. When I tried for an SS Obergruppenfuhrer, it did not go as well."

Benny felt respect conflating with terror as he looked at her.

"I'll spare you the details of everything they did to me," Margot continued. "Afterward, I thought that I was broken by it, that they had turned me into something worth less than a whore. After we were deported, I spent months feeling sorry for myself. One day, though, I realized that I am a survivor. The French fighting for the Reich? *They* are the whores."

She paused, visibly taking an effort to calm herself.

"Your people would not put me in a position to fight them," she said. "So I rescue warriors, heal you so you can kill them for me. Through all that pain I learned to reach for what I want, Benjamin." Benny heard the determination in her voice and could almost guess what was coming next.

"When I say I do not care what others think when we are together, allow me to be absolutely clear: I do not give a single *fuck* what anyone else thinks of us," Margot said. "I have faced much worse than them. I like you, and I think you like me, too. If that isn't true, then by all means, I shall not trouble you further."

Margot took a step back and started to turn on her heel. Benny reached out and put a hand on her arm.

"Margot, wait," he said.

"Wait for what, Benny? You to get a chaperone so we can continue this conversation without offending bigots?"

Benny thought furiously. He didn't know what to say. Five minutes ago he'd thought their relationship impossible; now it seemed nothing in the world mattered more than convincing her to stay. In the background the record changed, and Fred Astaire's voice filled the room to a smooth bass and piano accompaniment.

"Dr. Durand, would you dance with me?" Benny said.

Removing his right hand from her arm, he extended his left hand palm-up in a time honored courtly gesture. Margot's eyes widened for a long moment, then, slowly, she smiled again and the light returning to her eyes seared his anxiety away. She placed her right hand in his left.

"Yes, Mr. Jakes," she said. "I would love to dance."

Benny led her to the dance floor, aware of every eye following them. Only Margot, her hand still warm and gripping his firmly, allowed him to ignore them all. She flowed into his arms, assuming an elegant, strong frame against his. They moved into an easy foxtrot together, gliding across the floor with a stride that was simultaneously jaunty and graceful. She picked up on the rhythm naturally and followed his lead without a missed step.

"You know how to dance," Benny said.

"So do you," Margot said.

Benny twirled Margot into an underarm turn and back into his arms, then a reverse turn to shadow position for a few counts, her back to him with his hand on her stomach. He picked up the floral scent of shampoo on her chestnut hair before she returned to his arms to glide across the floor once again. Everyone else in the world fell away; there was only Margot and the music.

They opened up into a promenade, and Margot's shapely legs flashed as they strode across the floor and as they came back together for the final beat of the song she pressed her body fully against his, drawing a sharp breath of surprise from him.

"That's not part of the foxtrot," Benny said.

Margot batted her eyes and leaned up to whisper in his ear.

"It is in France."

Applause and a wolf-whistle pierced the spell of the dance. He spared a glance for the room, Robin Olds was standing near the turntable, grinning broadly and clapping; upstairs Tran, Ngo and Lee were likewise applauding. The rest of the officers in the club and their dates were torn, some smiling and clapping, some looked uncomfortable, and a handful glared.

*To hell with you, gentlemen,* Benny thought as he bowed to the crowd, and Margot curtsied like a born queen. *For once, you just wish you were me.*

\* \* \*

The next morning as he stepped into 4th AVG headquarters, Benny could hear explosions and gunfire over the radio speakers along with the voices of men doing their best to maintain Laconic professionalism under fire.

"Tiger Main, this is Ajax Main," a static-ridden Midwestern voice announced. "We have one company engaged with a battalion in the hamlets three kilometers to our direct east. Another company has been cut off on the northeast bank of the lake, five klicks out. We estimate at least two enemy battalions. Ajax Main and Ajax North are both under intermittent indirect fire, over."

"Understood, Ajax," Tex said. "We're loading bombs now, eta one hour, over."

"We need you ASAP, Tiger," a note of fear crept into the voice from the other end. "That company on the lake can't last long."

"Roger, Ajax," Tex said. "My staff will be monitoring this net. Send updates. We'll be there as soon as we can. Tiger Main, out."

Robin stepped into the building behind Benny, followed by Jesus.

"What's going on, Tex?" Robin said, his usually cheerful face grim.

"The base at Pleiku and the outpost at Kon Tum are under attack," Tex said. "The French crossed the border in division strength an hour ago. We're loading bombs now, and we're sortieing the whole squadron because we can get there faster than anyone else. Ground intercept radar doesn't report any enemy air, but we'll be cautious. When we get there, Benny and Jesus will take the first bomb runs, while Olds and me fly high cover, then we'll switch. Eventually the prop birds will catch up, and we can rotate out to refuel and rearm. Get to your birds."

\* \* \*

B enny pulled his stick back and leveled out twenty feet above the treetops. Ahead of him, breaking up the green jungle-infested hills of the highlands was a massive blue lake. On the northeast bank of the lake he caught muzzle flashes in between the tiny gaps in the vegetation, but couldn't make out any of the human shapes beneath the canopy.

"Ajax Main, this is Tiger Four checking in," Benny announced over the advisor's frequency. He was answered immediately.

"Glad to hear it, Tiger Four," the same Midwestern voice he'd heard back at the AVG answered. "Stand by for the advisor on the scene. Ajax One-Six, we have air, over."

"Roger, Ajax Main," another voice said , this one with a French accent. "Tiger Four, this is Ajax One-Six, recommend you make your run northeast to southwest, parallel to our position, initial point on or north of Zebra-Baker Zero-One-Zero, One-Five-Two. That pattern should keep you clear of the gun-target line from the artillery at Ajax Main."

*Cool customer.* Benny could hear intense machine gun fire, thuds, explosions, the screams of the wounded, but Ajax One-Six's voice was steady as a rock, and he had the presence of mind to try and deconflict friendly artillery with air. Benny relayed the new plan to Tran, Ngo, and Lee in French, then switched back to English to talk to Ajax One-Six.

"Ajax One-Six, roger," Benny said. "You have sixteen P-80s with two thousand-pound bombs each. We can't see shit through the canopy, can you mark your forward position and the enemy's approximate center of mass."

"Roger, Tiger," the voice answered. "Marking our forward position first."

A few seconds later, a plume of green smoke drifted through the tree-tops, about two hundred meters from the riverbed.

"One-Six, I see green smoke," Benny said. "Confirm green smoke, over."

"Roger, Tiger," One-Six said. "Green smoke, stand by for enemy center of mass."

Even in the cockpit he heard the report of the howitzer from over in Pleiku. Thirty seconds later, a much larger cloud of white smoke billowed into existence *over* the treetops, about four hundred meter north and east of the green smoke.

"Ajax One-Six, I tally white smoke," Benny said. "I say again, white smoke. Be advised target mark is well within danger close of your position."

"Roger, Tiger Four," the same calm tone replied. "I confirm white smoke on the target, acknowledge danger-close."

"I have visual on friendly markings, I tally target marking," Benny said. "I am at the IP now. Four-ship in the initial pass."

"Roger, Tiger Four, you are cleared hot," One-Six confirmed.

"Get small, Ajax," Benny said. "This is going to be close."

Benny dropped down to five feet off the tree tops and throttled back to just shy of stall speed. Dropping bombs without a bombsight was very much an art form. As the lead, his steadiness and judgment would dictate the effectiveness of the planes following him. He kept his eyes on the center of the smoke as he made tiny rudder and stick adjustments to maintain level flight against the turbulence bouncing him around the cockpit.

*Almost there...right...about...DROP.*

Benny hit the bomb release and pulled up and right, opening his throttle to regain airspeed. Even roaring away at hundreds of miles per hour, the detonation of nearly eight thousand pounds of high explosive rattled him in his cockpit.

"Good drop," Ajax One-Six reported. "Keep laying it on."

"Alright, Benny, you head to thirty-thousand feet and keep an eye out," Tex said. "Robin, head for the IP."

"Much obliged Tigers," One-Six said after the last flight, Tex's own, had dropped. "We're still taking fire, but we've got some breathing room."

"Can you make it back to friendly lines, One-Six?" Tex asked.

"We're certainly going to try, Tiger," One-Six said. "We've got a lot of wounded, though."

"Stand by," a feminine voice interjected. "This is Angel Three-Five. We are a flight of three Ravens. Meet me at the clearing on the river bank one hundred meters south by southeast of your green smoke. My rotor cone will fit there. I can take your wounded first, then drop my litters and ferry the rest of your men on the skids."

*Margot?!*

Sure enough, low and to the east he saw three tiny shapes darting over the canopy toward the river. It took every ounce of professionalism in Benny's body not to tell Margot to get the hell out of here.

*Let the woman do her job. You do yours.*

"Roger, Angel Three-Five," the advisor on the ground said. "Thanks a lot, both of you. I take back every unkind word I've ever said about flyboys."

"All elements, this is Ajax Main," the plain Midwestern voice from earlier blared onto the net. "Ground control radar reports sixteen bogeys coming in from the west. Too fast for propeller driven birds, bearing two-eight-three."

"Roger, Ajax, coming to two-eight three," Tex acknowledged, his Texas drawl betraying a hint of eagerness. "Tigers, spread out and climb to thirty-thousand feet and we'll see if we can dive on these bastards."

Benny relayed the orders in French to his flight and pulled his stick back, following the rest of the squadron up to an altitude the Me-262s couldn't reach. He was surprised the French would sortie their limited number of jets when they had to know the P-80s were in play. They must have really wanted this attack to succeed.

*Which means we may be facing a full-scale invasion, not a glorified raid.*

With guidance from the radars, they vectored in on the approaching enemy. Three minutes into the approach, Benny spotted a series of black dots against the horizon.

"Tiger One, Tiger Four," Benny said. "I have visual on eight bandits, ten o'clock low."

"Tally, Tiger Four," Tex said. "Maintain altitude until we get a little closer—"

As Tex spoke, all eight dots shot up into the air, followed by eight more. They climbed fast, faster than any Me-262 he'd ever seen, and as the miles between them evaporated, Benny began to see the profile on the approaching enemy didn't fit the cross of a straight-winged jet, but was more of a V.

"Tiger One, those aren't 262s," Benny said. "Those are swept wing, I say again, swept wing airframes."

"Holy shit," Van Camp, one of the newer American pilots, said. "Those are fucking Me-503s."

"Can it, Tiger Three-Two," Tex snapped.

Benny understood the younger pilot's reaction. Intelligence swore on a stack of bibles that the Germans were retaining the Me-

503, the most advanced fighter in Europe—maybe in the world—strictly for Luftwaffe squadrons. Yet here they were. Worse, they were seconds away from effective range now, and the 503s had out-climbed them.

"Wait for them to dive," Tex said. "Then try a defensive roll. See if you can force an overshoot."

Benny translated the orders once again for his flight. It was a liability having to repeat everything, but it was better than flying three pilots short. In seconds, Benny had the unnerving honor of getting to look right up into a German jet intake and, though he couldn't make them out, he knew the ports for the 503's thirty-millimeter cannons were trained on him.

*Don't panic…not yet…NOW.*

"Roll," Benny said. Matching deed to word, he was thrown against the side of his cockpit as he violently pitched his jet up and out of plane and back down again, Tran, Ngo and Lee following close behind, just as four streams of furious red tracers stitched the sky where they'd been.

The two lead 503s overshot, ending at Benny's one o'clock low. As he pulled his nose violently over, centripetal force and Mother Earth's gravity well cooperated to pull the blood from his brain, opposed instantly by the grip of his g-suit on his abdomen and thighs. Grunting against the pressure, ignoring the gray at the edges of his vision, Benny fought the gun-sight piper onto the lead 503's flight path and fired.

Six streams of tracers erupted from the nose of his craft, lancing through the sky towards the nimble, swept-wing fighter. Benny was rewarded with an orange flash and the sight of the lead Frenchman spinning off toward the jungle below. He gasped in relief as he came out of the high-g turn only to see the trail 503 perform an impossibly fast and tight bank right out of his firing solution.

*Holy shit, those things are nimble.*

A part of his brain processed the radio chatter as he tried to keep up with the Messerschmidt.

"Tex, bandit at your six, break right and dive," Robin said.

"Affirm—ah, shit," Tex's voice cut off abruptly, replaced by Robin swearing briefly and vehemently.

Benny pushed grief away without conscious effort. Nothing he could do for Tex now.

"Two Bandits on our six," Ngo's voice remained steady, if strained. "They're on us tight. Damn it, Tran is down."

Benny spotted the fireball of Tran's P-80 plummeting toward the earth, and Ngo's jet yanking and banking violently, trying to avoid the agile killers on his tail.

"Lee stay on this one," Benny ordered as he banked hard right to try and save Ngo. The 503s on Ngo's six had *both* focused on the kill, the wingman having forgotten, if only momentarily, that his purpose in life was to watch the leader's six.

Benny made that mistake their last. Lining up the gun sight with relative ease, he sprayed the leader's cockpit with .50 caliber rounds, then gave the wingman the same treatment as he obligingly flew into Benny' sight picture.

"Thanks, Tiger Four," Ngo's relief was palpable, but there was no time to celebrate.

"Jesus, watch your six," Van Camp shouted, "Fuck, Jesus is down!"

"All Tigers, this is Tiger Three," Robin's voice said, still steady amidst the chaos. "Let's set up a weave, we've got to get some distance on these assholes—"

"Tiger Three, this is Hellcat One," a new voice announced. "Stand by, we're almost there."

"Two 503s are breaking off," VanCamp announced. "They're headed toward the river."

*Fuck!*

"Angel Three-Five," Benny shouted as he came around, desperately trying to close the gap and get his gun sight on the two runners. "Get the hell out of here, Messerschmitts are closing on you."

"Roger, Tiger Four," Margot answered, but even as she did, the 503s were within range, they started blazing away at the helicopter formation. He saw the far right skeletal machine, two men hanging on each skid, shudder, then burst into flames and spin out of control into the river. The center bird sparked with impacts as well; it skidded on the opposite bank of the river coming to a stop without a secondary explosion by some miracle.

"Margot!" Benny shouted, just as he aligned his nose on the trail 503 and mashed the trigger for his .50 cals. Despite the impressiveness of their machines, a lack of situational awareness killed their pilots all the same. The trail 503 joined its victim in the river. The lead 503 broke hard left and laid on the acceleration.

Benny tried to keep the 503 in his sight, but it was no use. The damn thing was just too fast and agile when aware of a threat. If he split his attention, the bastard would get away, if he didn't maintain situational awareness, he became a target.

As if from nowhere, dozens of tracer streams raced overhead. Benny looked back over his shoulder and saw the sky was filled with sleek P-51s, robust P-47s and fork-tailed P-38s. Superior design or not, the Me-503s now faced the remaining P-80s and several dozen older prop driven fighters. The French pilots exercised the better part of valor and fled west, faster than any of their enemies could pursue.

Which didn't mean they didn't want to.

"This is Hellcat One," the P-51 squadron leader announced. "We are pursuing."

"Negative, Hellcat One," Robin remonstrated. "They'll lure you until you're low on fuel then sortie the rest of their fighters and cut you to pieces."

"Roger, Tiger Three," the P-51 driver sounded pissed, but he wasn't stupid.

"Angel Three-Five, Angel Three-Five, do you read?" *God, please let her be alive.* "Margot? Do you read?"

Several heartbreaking seconds passed in silence, Benny hit the transmit button again, but before he could talk his radio crackled to life.

"Benny, I'm alright," Margot said. "I'm walking out with the boys. I'll see you back home."

"Roger," Benny croaked, his throat unaccountably tight. "Be safe."

"Alright Tigers," Robin's voice cut through. "We're pushing bingo. Return to base."

Benny's heart expanded in his chest, and he took a deep shuddering breath as he formed up on Olds. For the remainder of the flight, he prayed, silently but fervently.

* * *

R obin and Benny stood on the flight line as the sun set on Gia Lam airfield, tallying the butcher's bill and discussing how to proceed. Robin was the next most senior after Hill, now deceased, and Jesus, now deceased, so he would assume command of the entire group. Benny would take what was left of the P-80 squadron, which was really just two flights. The Me-503s had downed eight of the P-80s at the cost of only five of their own. If the prop-driven squadrons hadn't arrived when they did, it would have been worse.

Long after the decisions were made, Benny remained on the flight line, waiting. Knowing there was no point in trying to talk Benny into resting, Robin merely patted his friend on the shoulder and headed for the showers himself. Benny remained standing, stock-still next to the waiting ambulances until after sundown. Finally, the drone of a gooney-bird's twin engines filled the night sky.

Benny waited patiently as the cargo plane landed and taxied, then patients in various state of disrepair and dishevelment hobbled or were carried painfully down the C-47's ramp. He even restrained himself when a familiar mane of thick, dark brown hair poked out of the plane door, and Margot made her way down the ramp. She was talking to nurses and medics about care for wounded men; he would not interrupt that.

He waited until the C-47's engines died, and Margot stood, alone at least for a moment, and then he could wait no more.

"Margot," he called, trying, and failing, not to break into a jog to reach her.

She turned to face him. Even in the moonlight, her relief at seeing him was evident in her eyes as she likewise jogged to him. They stopped mere inches from one another, unsure of what to do next.

"I'm so glad you're alright," he said.

Margot's hands twitched as if she wanted to reach for him, but she kept them at her sides.

"I know," she said. "I was afraid those new jets would cut you to shreds."

They stood for a long silent moment. Benny was lost in her eyes, a depth of feeling he'd never experienced before welling up inside him as the adrenaline dump of combat, his fear for Margot, and his affection for her all washed over him like breaking tidal waves.

"My patients," Margot said, finally. "I should—"

Benny gathered her into his arms and pressed his lips to hers, kissing her intently. Margot did not stiffen—did not protest—but flowed into his arms just as she had on the dance floor and matched his intensity, returning the kiss with a will.

After several blissfully sweet seconds, Margot pulled away from him and took a deep breath, then gave a throaty little chuckle.

"Oh, mon amour," she said, caressing Benny's cheek with her fingers. "You have the worst timing."

She tilted her head back and drew his lips down to hers, kissing him once again just as fiercely, albeit more briefly before pushing him away with both hands.

"Now, go away," she said. "You are very distracting, and I *must* work."

Benny watched her walk away for a few seconds, before turning his steps toward home.

*Well, as far as wars go, it could be a lot worse.*

\* \* \* \* \*

### Justin Watson Bio

Justin Watson grew up an Army brat, living in Germany, Alabama, Texas, Korea, Colorado, and Alaska while being fed a steady diet of X-Men, Star Trek, Robert Heinlein, DragonLance, and Babylon 5. While attending West Point, he met his future wife, Michele, on an airplane, and soon began writing in earnest with her encouragement. In 2005, he graduated from West Point and served as a field artillery officer, completing combat tours in Iraq and Afghanistan, and earning the Bronze Star, Purple Heart, and the Combat Action Badge. Medically retired from the Army in 2015, Justin settled in Houston with Michele, their four children, and an excessively friendly Old English Sheepdog.

# # # # #

# Zero Dark 30
# by JL Curtis

**May 18, 1985**

**Moffett Field, California 0400Z**

The tactical grey P-3 Orion bumped through the night skies, descending over San Jose, California, toward Moffett Field Naval Air Station after a nine-hour flight off Seattle, Washington.

"Charlie Fox 232, cleared to land 32 right," crackled through the radio.

LCDR Randy Hathaway nudged the rudder as Senior Chief 'Scoop' Vessels, the flight engineer, and LCDR 'Fast Eddie' Miller, the copilot, reviewed the lineup. LT 'Tip' Adams leaned forward from his position behind Randy and double checked the cockpit even though he didn't have the landing. Fast Eddie replied, "232, cleared on the right. Say winds."

"260 at 12."

"Speeds are 18 and 21, Randy. Landing checklist complete."

"OK, pilot's power, Scoop."

"You got it."

Scoop looked over his shoulder at Chief 'Hairy' Harris and motioned for him to reset the oil tank circuit breakers. Harry did so and shoved a thumbs up in front of Scoop.

At the TACCO's station, Lieutenant Commander Kevin James "KJ" Martin looked out the window making sure the gear was down, rechecked his harness, looked over at LCDR Barney 'Rubble' Roberts, and received a thumbs up. He keyed the ICS and said, "Five is set in the back, gear looks good."

"Roger that, KJ," Fast Eddie replied.

Randy called, "Short final, flaps to land."

"Flaps to land, speed is 118."

"OK."

Randy finessed the P-3 the last 30 feet down to the runway, but it still flopped down the last fifteen feet.

"6000 remaining."

"Four good Beta lights."

"K, Full reverse."

"Charlie Fox 232, right off approved when able, contact ground 236.8."

"232 switching, night Moffett."

Randy steered the P-3 off the runway and keyed the ICS. "Just another day at the office, guys. Crew's released, KJ, let em know we're home, and get us a spot."

KJ double keyed the ICS in acknowledgment, noted the landing time on his log, and did the arithmetic for total flight time. He waited for Barney to complete the in-report to the ASW Operations Center and switched to the squadron's base frequency. Barney gave him a thumbs up, and KJ keyed UHF2, called maintenance and gave the time, status and asked for a parking spot. The maintenance chief told him to park it in front of the hangar, as the bird was due for a periodic maintenance inspection.

Meanwhile, Chief Iverson, the in-flight technician, strolled up with the first aid kit and his helmet on sideways. KJ smiled and pointed to the flight station; Iverson assumed the persona of an injured person and limped into the flight station. "Anybody up here need this? We only need a couple of ambulances for the guys in back."

Randy shrugged as Fast Eddie, Tip and Scoop laughed. "Sorry 'bout that, I didn't do it on purpose. Any major gripes?"

"Nope, we're up and up in the back, Sir, but this ain't a 747; we're a little closer to the ground. Just saying," Iverson replied.

KJ came over the ICS saying, "Randy, put it right in front of the hangar; no gas, no covers. Scoop, they're gonna do an inspection."

KJ keyed the PA, telling everyone to pick up all loose gear, secure their stations, and clear all codes. Barney and Tip walked through the airplane, clearing all the secure equipment codes, inventoried the communications box, and signed it off.

Chief Clark, the senior anti-submarine warfare operator, asked who had to go to the debrief. KJ replied, "Well, since we debriefed at Whidbey, I don't see any reason for any of y'all to go, Randy and I can handle it."

"Sure about that, TACCO? After all, it took you seven minutes to get the torp off after we told you where the boat was," the chief replied with a smile.

Chuckling, KJ shot back, "Alright Charlie, you can come along and keep us straight."

"Naw boss, we trust you to get it right. We'll be waitin' in the parking lot."

The bird was parked and turned over to maintenance, and Randy and KJ went to the ASW operations center to turn in the operational message blank, debrief with the watch officer, and turn in all the classified material. Chief Clark, the ordnance chief, and the ordnancemen cleaned up the bomb bay and did a walkthrough on the bird. Scoop and the second engineer did their post flight, then went into maintenance to write up gripes on the plane and sign off the daily inspection.

An hour later, the crew gathered at KJ's rental car in front of Hangar Two for the parking lot debrief. KJ started things off by handing out beers and cokes, then did a round robin of each crew-member for comments, complaints, and plans. As a master augmentation unit crew, they didn't work or fly on the same schedule as a standard reserve crew. They flew their own aircraft or one loaned by an operational squadron. Since most of the crew lived and worked in the Bay Area, most of them were headed home until next month, as they had no squadron support flights or operational commitments scheduled.

KJ and Randy walked back into the MAU's space in the hangar and were approached by the ops boss. "Nice flight guys, the Skipper wants to see you both in his office."

"OK, Willie. Hope to hell something hasn't come up, since I just let the crew go," KJ replied.

Commander Furness looked up as KJ and Randy knocked on the door. "Come on in guys, nice flight. Seven minutes from COMEX to weapon is a new record for us, KJ. How the hell do you do it? Especially with a reserve crew? Most of the fleet squadrons can't even do that well."

Randy and KJ looked at each other, and Randy replied, "Shit, Skipper, look at the qualifications and experience we've got here. Fast Eddie and Tip both had crews in the fleet, KJ and Barney were both first tour mission commanders, Chief Clark has seventeen years as an acoustic operator, Henerson and Macklin both have over fifteen, Iverson is a wizard with the gear, Vessels and Harris both are old B-model flight engineers who know ASW as well as or better than we do, and 'Pops' Kanaka did his last fleet tour with PMTC as the research and development ordnance shop leading petty officer before he flipped over to the civilian side. There isn't a fleet crew that could come close to that, much less stay together for five years like we have."

"Guess so, but you guys never cease to amaze me. Randy, what's your schedule?"

"Seven in the morning, here to L.A., layover, then Sydney and back."

"When are you going to upgrade? Or is United holding you back?"

"Hell, I don't know, and no, they aren't. Flying right seat on a 747 ain't bad. Plus, if I upgrade to Captain on the 75 it would mean moving back to L.A., and Julie would shoot me," Randy replied.

CDR Furness laughed and nodded at KJ. "What about you, still looking for a real job?"

KJ rolled his eyes, chuckled, and answered, "Why get a job, Skipper? It would just ruin my social life. Seriously, I finished up a security job yesterday, and I'm headed back to Bradenton tomorrow morning. We're doing pretty well with the FBO business, and Dad's having a ball, which lets me run around and do other things."

The skipper shook his head and said, "I'll never understand how the Navy didn't let you fly."

KJ grimaced and replied, "Shit, they claimed I wasn't 20-20. Said I was 20-25 in the right eye, and you know how that goes; one chance and that's it. I decided to try the NFO route since I was already there, besides which, if I'd gone home, then the old man would've killed me. You know how he feels about doing your time."

"Well, you guys need your rest, so thanks for a great job, and see ya next month. Your crew should be doing an ASWEX with VP-19."

*Reflections: CDR Bob Furness*

*Those two guys are damn good, maybe the best I've seen in 20 years. Too bad we couldn't keep them on active duty. Randy's a known entity—steady, happily married and loves flying for the airlines. KJ's a different story altogether—his record is outstanding from the start. A real golden boy in his first tour, special missions certified and every possible important job. A tactical wizard—that's what his skipper said. I wonder what would have happened if KJ's wife hadn't been killed during his first shore tour, and he hadn't resigned to take care of his daughter. Wonder if KJ will ever get a real job—he's so damn talented it's not funny, but he plays with airplanes, has this KJM Consulting which he won't talk about, but seems to make money, has some connection with his Dad's fixed base operation at Bradenton, Florida; lives in Florida, but drills in California. Ah hell, I guess I shouldn't look two damn good gift horses in the mouth. I'll just take 'em and run.*

Randy and KJ got up and headed out the door, logging out with the duty officer to ensure their drill time was counted. In the parking lot, they coordinated the call tree for next month, said their good-byes, and KJ jumped in his rental and headed back to the Airport Crowne Plaza. He had paperwork to do and was looking forward to a good night's sleep and getting home to his now teenaged daughter, Jonna, who was thirteen going on thirty-one, or so she thought. He just hoped she'd behaved, as Mom had promised to have a 'girl' talk with her.

\* \* \*

**May 22, 1985**

**Washington, DC 1300Z**

Third assistant agricultural attaché and KGB Lieutenant Colonel Sergei Rostov picked up the *Washington Post* and scanned the headlines, immediately focusing on the arrest of John Walker in Norfolk, VA, for spying. He slammed the chair down and hurried down to the secure room to find out what had happened.

\* \* \*

**CINCLANTFLT Compound, Norfolk, Virginia 1500Z**

'Chief' Downs had his feet up on the watch desk, idly watching the staff in the watch center starting their turnovers, when the secure phone on his desk rang. He sighed as he reached for it and said, "Watch officer."

A couple of seconds later, his feet hit the floor, and he was writing quickly on the pad by the phone as the voice on the other end identified himself as the deputy director of the FBI. He said, "Sir, I'm the watch officer. I need to get this information to the chain of command. Will someone be there in the next half hour or so? Yes, sir. I'll have them call you back."

He jumped up and headed for the door, telling the commander on the submarine ops desk, "Shit's gonna hit the fan. FBI caught a spy with classified Navy carrier data. I'm going up to the flag office. You've got the desk."

The commander nodded and got up, moving to the watch desk as Downs banged through the door. A couple of minutes later, he stood in front of the flag aide's desk, "Commander, I need to see the boss right now. We got a problem."

"What kind of problem, Chief?"

Chief glanced around before answering softly, "A spy, caught with classified carrier plans."

"You're not kidding, are you?"

Chief shook his head, "Not in the slightest."

"C'mon." The aide got up, went to the admiral's door, and knocked. "Admiral, Chief Downs from the watch floor with a hot one. Chief, go right in."

\* \* \*

**May 26, 1985**

**Chief of Naval Operations Office, the Pentagon 1400Z**

The CNO turned toward the deputy director of the FBI. "So, you're telling me he's *admitted* they've been passing all our crypto to the Soviets?"

"Yes, sir. He says they've never asked for hardware, only the codes."

The CNO leaned back against his desk, scrubbing his hands over his face. "So...as of now we have to believe the Soviets are reading all our traffic, including the encrypted traffic. And we have no alternative but to destroy all the current crypto in the entire Navy and reissue all new." He glanced at the Vice CNO. "How long?"

"Thirty days, maybe forty-five. Depends on the courier delivery to overseas. What do we do in the meantime about the boomers?"

"Recall them. We need them out of harm's way. We need to do a secure...shit, I'm not even sure we *can* do secure voice either." He pushed off the desk, pointed at the deputy director and said, "You need to come with me, we need to go brief the secretary and chairman of the joint chiefs. I hope you didn't have anything planned this morning."

"No, sir. I didn't. We planned to give the other services courtesy briefs once we found out the level of compromise to our systems."

The CNO looked at the Vice CNO. "Mark, get with your counterparts, figure out what crypto we have in common, and let them know about the compromise. We're not going to downplay this. It is too important."

\* \* \*

### Admiral of the Soviet Fleet Gorchakov's office, the Kremlin 1100Z

"So, we have lost our naval spy," asked Admiral Gorchakov.

"It appears so, sir. Comrade Rostov in Washington was able to confirm he has been picked up, along with his son and other members of his cell."

"So, now we go to work. Are there any units we can pick off before the Americans know about it?"

His chief of staff unrolled a chart on his desk, pointing at an area in the North Atlantic off Norway. "There is one. The USS *Michigan* is on patrol here. *Kursk* and K-324 have been detached from the operations off Murmansk and are en-route, pending your approval. They should be there in eighteen hours. K-123, an *Alfa,* is already in the area and believes she has had a couple of sniffs of contact. We have positioned her in a patrol box southwest of that position."

"Send a *Udaloy* ASW destroyer also. If we can get her up, the *Udaloy* can hold her hostage."

"It will be done, Admiral."

\* \* \*

**May 27, 1985**
**USS *Michigan*, North Atlantic 0300Z**

Captain Thomas stuck his head in Sonar. "What you got, Chief?"

"*Alfa* is still south of us. I think we've got one or two *Victor* IIIs coming down from the north. They're a couple of convergence zones out yet." He pointed to a couple of dim lines on one of the screens.

"So, they're trying to box us. Dammit, we can't go further west; no water. I think we'll move east and see if we can sneak down the coast."

"We gonna stay deep, Skipper?"

"Unless I hear different, Chief. No reason to go up on the roof since we got the orders for recall and to terminate comms. Something bad is going down, and I've got a feeling...our comms might be compromised."

"That Walker thing that was on the feed?"

"Yep. Keep us honest, Chief. I'll be in Conn."

"Will do, Sir."

\* \* \*

**Navy Ops Center, the Pentagon 1700Z**

The various Navy department heads sat around the conference table, empty coffee cups and wax paper cups filling the trash cans as Captain Montfort, the lead planner, asked tiredly, "Any other options? There sure as hell isn't anything in the contingency plans covering this level of cluster fuck."

The LANTFLT rep on the VTC said, "We've got a carrier underway from the Med, but she's a couple of days away at best. And we really don't know where *Michigan* is or if she's still in her patrol box. Everybody else is accounted for and headed home but her, and we've grounded all Naval Air outside the US, for obvious reasons."

Montfort heard a grumble from down the table and said, "What?"

Captain Tobin looked up in irritation, "And that's BS. There is no reason to ground the P-3s. We could have been out there locating *Michigan* and giving her a hand. We routinely communicate with subs at sea."

"You don't work with boomers. And the Soviet's posture right now is to try to provoke a situation. You saw the report where that MIG hit the Norwegian P-3," the SUBLANT chief of staff countered.

"I don't remember anything in the SOPs that says we can't communicate with boomers, and you guys *supposedly* have the same pubs and buoys aboard."

"Well, they aren't allowed to use those."

Montfort made a chopping motion, "Alright, knock it off, you two. Who *did* authorize the grounding of the P-3s and why?"

\* \* \*

**May 28, 1985**

**Test Center, NAS Patuxent River, Maryland 0000Z**

The P-3 taxiing into the transient line with one engine feathered stopped suddenly, then turned and taxied to a hangar on the Test Center side of the field. It came to a stop in front of a hangar as the doors slid slowly open, and a tow crew tractor hooked up to the airplane. Minutes later, the hangar doors rumbled closed behind the airplane. As the crew trooped off, they were loaded on a bus and taken to base housing, with the mission commander being told he would be notified when the P-3 was ready for a test flight.

Once the crew was gone, a group of civilians came out of various offices and started moving equipment into place on the unmarked P-3 in the other half of the hangar. Four torpedoes were pushed from behind a bank of storage containers as the bomb bay on that P-3 whined open.

\* \* \*

**Tactical Support Center, NAS Patuxent River, Maryland 0200Z**

KJ led the rest of the officers and the three anti-submarine warfare chiefs into the briefing room, where they quietly took chairs, staring at each other. Finally, Charlie Clark said, "Still no idea what is going on, TACCO?"

KJ shrugged. "Your guess is as good as mine. We weren't supposed to be on the hook for another three weeks, much less here. I guess we'll find out, since we're obviously going flying somewhere tonight."

The door opened, and a grizzled chief stuck his head in. "I see this is the mushroom locker. Kept in the dark and fed shit as usual."

Randy started up, bristling, but KJ jumped up. "Dusty! What the hell are you doing here?"

They shook hands, and that devolved into beating each other on the back as Dusty said, "Same shit; different day. I'm workin' out of here now. Looks like I'm going with you."

KJ cocked his head. "I've already got—"

"We're taking 323. It's here, and full up."

Charlie walked over, "Hey, you old reprobate. You ain't getting my seat."

They shook hands as Dusty replied, "Don't need to, I got my own. Your ordy will lose, he gets the galley seat."

Somebody said, "Attention on deck!" and everyone popped to attention as two older men in civvies walked into the briefing room.

One was RADM Gallo, the current Patrol Wings Commander, and he said, "At ease. Seats, guys." The second man wearing civilian clothes walked forward, a briefcase in hand, as the admiral made sure the door was locked. "Gents, this is Vice Admiral Mark Kalenberg. He's the VCNO, and he's going to brief you."

The Vice Admiral nodded and popped the latches on his briefcase, pulled two sealed envelopes from it and set them aside. He pulled a third sealed envelope out and slit the end open, extracting a number of pages. "Gentlemen, we are in serious trouble. Our entire encryption system Navy-wide is compromised. We have an SSBN currently trapped off the coast of Norway by three Soviet submarines and an *Udaloy* DDG. The sub popped a position today, and she is not in extremis, but she can't get home without help."

He handed the two sealed envelopes across the table. "You folks are the help. You're off the books so to speak, not tied to any squadron, and apparently pretty damn good at putting torps on submarines."

*  *  *

### P-3 #323, NAS Patuxent River, Maryland 0300Z

The bus deposited a very sober group at the hangar after the brief. KJ and the others were all positively identified before being allowed in the hangar, and the first thing he noted was there were two identically painted P-3s sitting side by side. *So, this is how they're doing this....Shades of the old days.*

Pops Kanaka came out of the bomb bay and waved to him, motioning him over. KJ told Barney, "I'll be there in a minute. Looks like I've got a checklist to run." Barney nodded and headed up the ladder along with the rest of the crew.

"Hey, Pops. Guess you got a surprise, didn't you?"

Pops handed him the checklist. "To put it mildly. These are war shots. And brand-new MK-50s. These aren't even approved yet, but we're carrying four of them?"

"I'll explain at planeside. Let's run this checklist. Gotta admit, it's the first time I've done one in a hangar."

"And I was told no final checker. We do everything in here, then close the bomb bay and go."

"Then let's get to it. Item one—"

*  *  *

**May 29, 1985**

**Tactical Support Center, NAS Keflavik, Iceland 0000Z**

The debriefing officer looked across the table at KJ and Randy. "So, you guys have a mission brief you're not allowed to share with me. And we're laying on three other flights fifteen minutes apart to cover whatever the hell it is you're doing? Is that what you're telling me?"

KJ looked levelly at him. "That's right, Lieutenant. This was tasked by higher than you or I are cleared for. If you've got a problem…"

The DBO threw up his arms. "Oh screw it. At this point none of us knows what is going on. We're not getting shit over any secure circuit, and…oh never mind. You're scheduled for a zero dark thirty go, take off at 0230 local. You are Mike Kilo 21. No tactical call sign since we aren't doing shit. Go forth and do whatever it is you're supposed to do. That's all I've got."

"Thanks, Lieutenant. Don't feel bad. You're not the only one in the dark, trust me on this." As they walked out, KJ asked, "You got our track points and times to give to 22? And remind him to change voices when reporting for us, right?"

Randy rolled his eyes, "I may be a pilot, but I can accomplish something this simple KJ. Don't sweat the petty stuff, and don't pet the sweaty stuff."

KJ laughed. "Okay, see you at planeside."

\* \* \*

**May 29, 1985**

**USS *Michigan*, North Atlantic 0200Z**

Captain Thomas sat in the wardroom nursing a cup of coffee and wracking his brain for a way out of the box they were in. He'd even thought about using a couple of decoys to see if he could confuse people enough to slip away, but that would have given away his hidey hole. So far even the intermittent pings from either the subs or the Soviet destroyer had failed to spook him, but the crew was coming closer and closer to the breaking point. Four days of being constantly on pins and needles was impacting morale and the crew's ability to get rest. Plus, they had to look at possible rationing for food and consumables, like toilet paper. No showers and no laundry for four days were beginning to become apparent, and the boat was starting to stink.

LT Ryerson, the communications officer, came in with the tear sheet from the broadcast they had just copied. "Nothing new, Skipper. But somebody back in Norfolk fucked up the sports again."

"How, this time?"

"Chief caught it; it's item 6 and he circled it," he said, laying the tear sheet in front of the captain.

He quickly scanned the tear sheet, then read item six- "FOR THE TROOPS UP NORTH, THE SUSPENDED GAME BETWEEN THE YANKEES AND BEARS WILL RECOMMENCE AT 0800 WITH THE SCORE YANKEES 5-BEARS 2". "Yeah, whoever did the sports obviously isn't a fan. Yankees would never play the Bears. Two different sports." He shook his head, "Put out the other stuff, but leave that one off." The Supply Officer stepped into the wardroom, and the captain said, "I need some time with SUPO."

The communications officer got up quickly. "Yes, sir." He threw a look of commiseration at the supply officer on his way out, thinking, *Better him than me. I just get fucked up sports, not trying to figure out how to cut rations.*

* * *

### P-3 #323, 200NM Southeast of Iceland 0330Z

KJ keyed the ICS, "Okay, we're out of radar coverage. Time to go see if we get to start World War Three. Randy, make sure 22's got our comms. I'm dropping a fly-to point for you."

He heard the VHF radio key, "22, this is 21."

"21, go."

"We're chopping. You've got our comms."

"Good luck, whatever you're doing. We got it."

KJ came over the PA, "Crew, TACCO, set EMCON, darken ship. We're going down below 1000 feet, floatation gear required. We've got two hours till on station. Pops says breakfast will be?"

He heard a pop and chuckle over the ICS from Pops. "Whatever the flight kitchen packed. No crew box on here, TACCO."

Various boos and hisses were heard, and Scoop keyed up, "I hope there are hard boiled eggs!"

Randy keyed the PA. "Hairy, check the breakfasts, if there are any hard-boiled eggs, *dump them immediately!*" He pulled the power back, looked over at Scoop and Eddie and said, "Descent checklist, let's take it down to the deck. I don't want to depressurize unless we have to go to free fall on buoys." He keyed the PA again, "We're EMCON up here. IFF is off, DVARS is off, lights are off."

KJ noted the EMCON on his log, shook his head, unstrapped and stretched.

*No gahdamn eggs for Scoop! I don't think I've ever smelled anything that vile in my life, and I sure as hell don't want to again.* He looked over at Barney and mimed drinking a cup of coffee, and Barney nodded. Getting up, he headed for the galley and the coffee pot. *At least we got a coffee pot.*

As he walked aft, he checked with each of the operators and got a thumbs up as they completed their systems checks. Dusty was leaning back in the aft observer's seat, sound asleep as usual. KJ laughed to himself and checked the extra sensor station in front of Dusty. As always, there was a sticky with an up arrow on it. *Some things never change. I wonder if anything actually bothers Dusty.* Pops Kanaka was sorting through the boxes of food from the flight line kitchen with Hairy and smiled, "No hard-boiled eggs, TACCO. Looks like omelets and meat du jure in the oven."

Hairy nodded. "At least I can get some sleep before I go back in the seat."

Randy came back, dropped the rack down and climbed in. "I'm down until we go on station. Tim's in the left seat, and Eddie's in the right." He stuck earplugs in and rolled over, away from the galley light, wiggling to try to get comfortable on the thin mat as the airplane bumped down through the light cloud cover.

\* \* \*

### The Battle Cab, the Pentagon 0600Z

The captain and colonel on watch were on pins and needles as the Chairman, Joint Chiefs of Staff, and the service chiefs followed him into the cab and took seats in the back. One of the Army colonels whispered to the current Air Force watch officer, "Any idea what is going on?"

"Not a fucking clue," said the watch officer.

The chairman tapped the microphone at his seat. "This thing on? Focus on the GIUK gap please. All air, surface, and subsurface assets, please."

As the picture zoomed in, the Chief of the Air Force asked, "Status on AWACS and tankers."

The Air Force watch officer used a laser pointer. "AWACS is proceeding to a northern Norwegian Sea patrol, and there is one Tanker, Ploy 87, on a Faroes Island refueling track, Sir. But I have no scheduled ops for that track."

The Chief nodded. "Status of 57th FIS?"

"Four F-4s on Alert 30, four on Alert 60. Weather is projected to be good."

The Chief looked down at his notepad, "493rd?"

The colonel flipped through his notebook, "Four F-111Fs on Alert 30, four on Alert 60, weather is marginal."

The Chairman leaned over, "Russ, can they go if they need to?"

"Yeah, they are zero-zero capable. It'll suck if something breaks. But they can launch."

\* \* \*

**P-3 #323, 1000 Feet, 30NM off the Norwegian Coast 0630Z**

Randy keyed up the PA. "Crew, we're inbound to the first fly to point. TACCO, we're stable at 180 knots, 1000 feet, going to loiter number one. Aft observer, check in."

Chief Isaacson keyed his ICS. "Port aft, standing by." KJ looked out his window as he felt the shudder of the prop feathering, and heard the chief, "Good feather, good X."

KJ looked at the scope and keyed the ICS. "Okay, we're on station now. One minute to the first buoy drop. Mac, you got anything on ESM?"

"Intermittent Top Plate. Some Soviet combatant. Might be an *Udaloy* or *Krivak*. Still points north, no cross bearing available."

"Charlie, Stretch, Dusty, standby for channels 1 and 12, then we're going to run up the channels as we go. Wide spacing as we discussed."

They all felt the thump of the buoy firing externally and the second internally. KJ heard the rattle of the high-speed printer as Barney dumped the position and Pops opened the chute to pull the empty launch container out. "Two buoys away."

The inside of the P-3 filled with the odor of cordite, and Dusty crowed, "Ah, the smell, the smell! Let the hunt begin!"

KJ smiled, remembering when he and Dusty were on the special missions' crew and running all over the Atlantic and Mediterranean doing various operations. "Two minutes to next drop, channel 2."

A half hour later, the entire pattern was in the water, and both Charlie and Stretch were sending data on two different subs. "Which is which, Charlie?"

"TACCO, the one to the south of 9 is the *Alfa*." There was a minute of silence, and he continued, "The one to the west of 12, well between 5 and 12, is the *Victor*."

"Nothing else?"

Dusty chimed in, "TACCO, low poss on an *Oscar* 030 off buoy 2. Sniff on our guy east of 15."

\* \* \*

### The Hot Line, Washington, DC 0700Z

"I have the Kremlin on the line, sir."

"Mr. President, I have a statement to read and will wait for it to be translated and your reply."

"Da."

"Mr. President, we know that you have compromised our secure communications cryptographic systems for now and that you have isolated and are attempting to either capture or board one of our ballistic missile submarines in international waters in the North Atlantic. You have one hour to contact your units and turn them north, removing the blockade on our unit. If you do not do so, I will authorize torpedoes to be used against your units in the area. This is not negotiable."

A simultaneous translation was heard, then a spate of Russian, and the translator said, "We categorically deny that we are attempting anything. We do not admit anything. We are operating in international waters and will continue to do so."

"Mr. President, you know that is a lie. You have one hour. This line will continue to be monitored until 0800 Zulu." He turned to the others in the room, "Come get me if they decide to talk. Otherwise, I'll be in my office," the President said.

\* \* \*

### P-3 #323, 1000 Feet, 30NM off the Norwegian Coast 0705Z

"TACCO, Jez. I wonder if the reason we're not seeing the *Oscar* is they are using depth separation."

"Hold that thought. Flight, new fly-to, gimme a right 270 after this line. Pops, I'll put this pattern out external. Going to put a containment around the *Victor*, then the *Alfa*, then we'll go look for that *Oscar*."

"Flight, aye."

As the third buoy spit, Mac said, "Got another hit on that Top Plate in sector scan. Sending a cross fix. Looks to be about 30 miles north of us, but I think it's coming south."

A fix popped in on KJ's scope and he nodded, "Good call. 32 miles. Flight, let's take it down to 500. I want to stay below his radar horizon, just in case."

Randy keyed the PA. "Crew, going below 1000, floatation required." He dropped back to ICS and continued, "Looks like a sea state of 1 or 2. Winds are probably 290 at around 10. Swells look like they are from about 270."

Barney keyed up. "Got it, thanks. Nav is looking pretty good. Minimal split between the inertial systems.

Chief Iverson came forward with two cups of coffee, handing one to Barney and the other to KJ, "Looking good in the back. I just hope Dusty's shit doesn't break. I don't know jack about it."

KJ nodded his thanks. "Don't worry about it, he's an expert on those and actually is building them in his day job." He took a sip of the coffee and grimaced. "Gah, Maxwell House, again?"

"Sorry, we already drank all the Folgers I brought. And I never got to the commissary." The airplane started bumping and bouncing as they leveled at 500 feet, and the chief sighed. "Once more into the bumps we go. Why can't we *ever* get a smooth flight?"

Barney laughed. "It's a P3, whatta ya expect, Chief?"

\* \* \*

### The Battle Cab, the Pentagon 0715Z

"Fighter launch, Murmansk. Estimate four MIG-25s. Possible launch IL-78 Midas," came over the speakers in the cab.

The Air Force chief spoke into the mic at his chair, "Bring 57th and 493rd to Alert 5 and Alert 15, please. Notify AWACS and Ploy 87 of the MIG launch. Launch the alert tanker from Lakenheath."

The Air Force watch officer spun around and quickly made the calls. Once they were done, the Army watch officer leaned over again, "I wish I knew what the fuck is going on! We're *never* supposed to be out of the loop. *Never*!"

The Air Force watch officer shrugged. "Well, we obviously are in this case. And if we are, I'm not real sure I really want to know."

The chiefs watched, and as soon as the MIGs turned west, the Chairman asked, "Should we launch our guys?"

The Air Force chief spoke into his mic and asked, "Do we have a speed on the MIGs yet?"

The colonel said, "Appears to be supersonic, sir."

"Shit. Scramble the 57th, point them at AWACS. Scramble the 493rd and point them north to intercept the MIGs. Launch the Alert

15s from both locations as soon as possible and point them at the Faroes Tanker." He leaned over to the Chairman. "We...it's going to be tight. Might have waited too long."

\* \* \*

### Alert Barns, Keflavik and Lakenheath, 0728Z

Klaxons blared in both locations as pilots and WSOs scrambled to man their aircraft, and PAs clicked on. "Immediate launch, immediate launch. Alert 5, Alert 15, immediate launch. Standby for coordinates on common after launch." The message repeated twice more, and the klaxons sounded again but were quickly drowned out by the rising scream of jet carts, then the jets themselves.

Six minutes later, the first pair of F-4s lifted off from Keflavik, cleared unrestricted climb to flight level 280 and speed restrictions lifted. Two minutes later, the first F-111s lifted off from Lakenheath and climbed into the low clouds, clawing for altitude in the rough air. In Reaper 01, the WSO was cursing as he tried to get his systems online in the turbulence and suddenly sat back. "Damn, Roscoe, whatever is going on, it looks like it's for real."

Just as he said that, the British controller came on the radio. "Reaper Flight you are cleared unrestricted to FL280, cleared direct the ADIZ heading 000. Speed restrictions are lifted. We are clearing a corridor for you."

Captain 'Roscoe' Booker keyed his radio, "Ah, Departure, Reaper Flight copies all. Passing flight level 180 for flight level 280, coming to 000 at this time." They heard the other three aircraft roger the course change, and he said, "What are you talking about, Mongo?"

"I've got Link 4 with an AWACS that's up. Four MIG-25s coming around the horn of North Cape with their hair on fire, and we've got 1300 miles to intercept point. I don't know if we're going to beat them there. And not a fucking clue why the intercept point is over the water."

Roscoe looked over at him in amazement. "You got to be shitting me!"

Mongo stared back at him and said carefully, "Roscoe, this *is not a* drill. I think the shit is about to hit the fan for real." He glanced quickly down. "And you're about to break our altitude."

They broke out of the clouds and he dumped the nose over, skirting the tops of the cloud deck, as the other three F-111s broke out. Keying his radio, he said, "London, Reaper Flight is level at flight level 280." London acknowledged, and he keyed up on common, "Reapers, pin the wings back. We got a long way to go and not much time to get there. Confirm Link 4 is up and operating."

\* \* \*

### The Hot Line, Washington, DC 0750Z

"Have we heard anything back yet?"

"No, Sir. Not a peep."

"Do we go back to them again?"

"I wouldn't, sir. You were pretty unequivocal in your statement. If you ask now, I believe you would be showing weakness."

"Probably. Dammit! Why do they have to be so damn stubborn when they are well and truly caught out?"

"Bluster and bullshit, sir. It's been that way since Khrushchev. If they back down, they potentially lose control."

"And they don't care if people die, correct?"

"As long as it's not them. No, they don't."

"Do we have comms with the Pentagon?"

"Yes, Sir. They are standing by."

\* \* \*

### The Battle Cab, the Pentagon 0801Z

The Chairman's face turned white as he listened to the phone, then said, "Yes, Sir. I understand. We will give them the launch code, sir. I agree, sir. There will most probably be a loss of life, possibly on both sides. No, sir. Thank you, sir." He hung up and swiped a hand across his face, then turned to the CNO. "It's a go. Do you want to send the message?"

The CNO nodded. "They're my people. It's only fair that I send the message that may get them killed."

The Chairman opened a sealed binder and pulled out one code. "Launch code, correct?" he asked as he passed it down to each chief. They all agreed and passed it back.

He handed it to the CNO, who keyed his mic. "Can I have the secure HF on my phone, please?" A few seconds later, the light above the handset lit up, and he heard the hissing of HF as he put it to his ear and squeezed the handset switch. They all looked up at the big screen as four blue flights sped into the North Atlantic to meet the oncoming red flight as it tracked further and further south.

\* \* \*

### P-3 #323, 500 Feet, 30NM off the Norwegian Coast 0804Z

KJ heard a sudden pop in his ear and faintly heard their call sign. He looked at Barney, who was looking back, both hands clamped over his ears, and keyed the ICS. "Getting a call on HF 1, everybody copy, please." He reached up and killed all the radios except HF 1 and heard, "Mike Kilo Two One, Mike Kilo Two One, this is November Charlie Alpha. How copy?"

He glanced at Barney who pointed at him and handed him the sealed packet from the comm box. He keyed his mic. "November Charlie Alpha this is Mike Kilo Two One. Copy you weak but readable. How me?"

"Mike Kilo Two One, November Charlie Alpha, copy you same. Stand by for code word."

"Mike Kilo Two One, standing by."

Mike Kilo Two One, November Charlie Alpha, code word is fastball, I say again fastball. How copy."

"Mike Kilo Two One, November Charlie Alpha, copy code word fastball." KJ slit the package open as he keyed the ICS. "I copied fastball. Everybody else get that?"

Randy looked around the cockpit and got thumbs up from everyone, "Flight station agrees."

"Jez, agrees."

"IFT, yep. Fastball."

KJ pulled out the envelope that said Fastball across the front, showed it to Barney, who nodded. He carefully slit it open and pulled out the authentication sequence. He showed that to Barney, who nodded again, and keyed the mic, "November Charlie Alpha, Mike Kilo Two One, request you authenticate Romeo Juliet."

"Mike Kilo Two One, November Charlie Alpha authenticates Papa Kilo X-ray." KJ keyed his ICS, "Did y'all get Papa Kilo X-ray?"

A flurry of double clicks answered him, and he keyed his mic. "November Charlie Alpha, Mike Kilo Two One, confirming authentication. Executing."

"Mike Kilo Two One, November Charlie Alpha understands executing. Be advised four MIG-two fives en route your position. God go with you."

"Mike Kilo Two One copies all." KJ looked at the tasking order for a moment, then keyed the PA, "Crew, listen up. Our tasking is to launch our torpedoes against the Soviet subs. This is not a drill. I'm afraid we *are* about to start World War Three. And there are apparently MIG-25s inbound, probably to try to stop us. Pops, gimme a signal buoy in the chute. Code five. Flight take us down to 200. I'd also suggest we think about getting in poopy suits in case this all goes to shit and we end up in the water."

"Buoy's loaded, TACCO." KJ gave the flight station a fly-to point east of where the Soviet subs were and activated it, feeling the airplane bank that way as it bounced lower.

Barney was struggling into his poopy suit, and KJ smiled as he reached behind the seat for his. *Now I will not only be hot, I'll be uncomfortable as hell as I try to get this shit right.* Royster came forward in his suit, carrying Scoop's, and he smiled wanly as he walked by KJ.

"Pops, weapons checklist. We'll go mid depth first for the *Victor*, then I want to go deep for the *Alfa*. We'll reevaluate on the *Oscar* at that point."

Randy said, "Got comms on 243.0, Reaper flight. They want to know where we are."

KJ shrugged. "Handle it. Fifteen seconds to drop."

"Signal buoy away." He activated the first weapons fly-to and said, "Flight, come right. I want you to hit that waypoint heading south."

"Got it."

"Mac, get the MAD warmed up. If we get a hit, I'll drop on it."

"Copy. Be advised I've got Saphir radar in search mode, TAC-CO. Bearing is north."

"Flight, set five. We're about to be in the shit. MiG-25 with look down, shoot down inbound. Only good thing is the *Foxbats* don't have a gun!"

Randy keyed the PA, "Crew, set five, strap in now! Man the aft windows, keep looking for anything coming down on us from above."

Iverson asked, "What is the bottom of the cloud deck?"

KJ looked at his notes and said, "4000. Don't plan on seeing the *Foxbats*. They can stay high and pop off missiles at us."

\* \* \*

### USS *Michigan*, North Atlantic 0811Z

"Conn, Sonar. I've got a code buoy pinging!"

The captain asked, "One of ours?"

"Yes, sir. A code five. What the hell is—?"

The captain suddenly realized what it meant and yelled, "Take us up! Take us up! Keel depth 50 feet! Try not to broach." He ran to sonar. "Chief, let me know if you hear torpedoes."

The sonar chief turned white. "Torps?"

The captain nodded grimly. "And I don't think they are going to be EX-torps. I think they will be war shots."

\* \* \*

### P-3 #323, 200 Feet, 30NM off the Norwegian Coast 0816Z

KJ keyed the ICS. "Two minutes to drop. Come left 160, flight. MAD standby."

"Bomb bay doors coming open," Randy said. "Checklist complete."

KJ saw movement in the passageway and saw Pops crouching over the bomb bay window. He yelled, "What the fuck are you doing, Pops? Get in a seat!"

Pops yelled back, "Gotta make sure it goes. I can roll into a ditching station right here."

Just as KJ started to say standby, Mac yelled, "MADMAN, MADMAN, MADMAN."

KJ punched the button and the torpedo fell free. "Weapon away, 0818."

Mac yelled again, "Saphir in fire control mode. They've locked us up! Bearing north."

Randy already had the bomb bay doors closing, and he rolled the P-3 seventy degrees and pulled almost three Gs, turning to the left and back into the MiGs.

Iverson groaned. "Got a white streak coming down out of the clouds. It's…went over us."

Barney yelled, "*Aphid*? No radar?"

"Probably," KJ yelled back and heard a groan in the aisle.

Chief Clark and Dusty both said, "Torp lit off. High speed screws."

Mac came on again, "Saphir in search mode, bearing 180 from us."

KJ made a snap decision. Rolling his cursor over the suspected track of the *Alfa*, he dropped another weapons fly-to point and said, "Flight, hit that if we have time. Five, six minutes out if you reverse now."

Randy rolled the airplane hard again as Chief Clark said, "*Victor* is running. Got decoys in the water. Looks like he's turning northward."

KJ double clicked the mic and started setting up the second torpedo's programming as Randy stabilized the airplane heading more or less south. He heard a groan again and looked back to see Pops sprawled in the aisle with his left leg going in an unnatural direction. He keyed the PA, "Dusty, Ivy, can y'all come get Pops and put him in the ditching station by the over wing hatch? I think his leg's broken."

He heard, "On it." and seconds later, the two of them were lifting Pops carefully and dragging him toward the back of the airplane.

Randy said, "Reapers are three minutes out, they're going to stay high. Knights are four minutes out, descending. They're going to come down to 3000."

KJ looked at the checklist, made the last selection and said, "Weapon is programmed. All we need is the bomb bay doors. Two minutes out."

He got a double click, and Mac said, "Bearing reversal. Saphir in search mode still, bearing now 000." A minute later he said, "Looks like the *Foxbats* split. One set of bearings now 330, the other…shit! Saphir lock again!"

Randy said, "KJ?"

"Gimme fifteen seconds." He rolled the scale down and said, "Fuck it, weapon away 0823. Your airplane, Flight."

Randy rolled the airplane violently again just as Mac said, "New radar, terminal home mode! 000 bearing!"

"*Acrid*, AA-6," Barney yelled.

Suddenly, Dusty came over the ICS singing, "Fins to the left, fins to the right…"

KJ burst out laughing and glanced over at Barney who was smiling and shaking his head. He keyed the PA. "Yeah, we get it, Dusty." He leaned across and yelled at Barney, "He ain't never been right in the head."

Iverson came on quietly, "Something hit the water a couple of hundred yards 7 o'clock from us."

"Terminal homing radar lost," Mac added. Then he said, "Bearing reversal on Saphir lock up."

KJ looked at his scope. "Flight, keeping heading northwest. Buoy 4, I'm going to put a torp out up there. Maybe we can get the *Oscar's* attention."

Dusty said, "I've got the *Oscar* 330 out of 4. He's fairly close to the buoy."

Randy asked, "How long? They seem to be locking us up every couple of minutes."

"Three, maybe four. Programming now."

A minute or two later, Eddie yelled, "Visual! Looks like…2 MiGs off the nose, high."

Mac chimed in, "Saphir lock up, 330, off the nose. Other set 240, search mode."

Randy replied, "We're going to keep running at them. I don't think they can lock us up and get a weapon off before we...Shit...Missile launch, right down our throat. Hang on folks."

KJ calmly said, "Gimme bomb bay doors." He heard them cycle open and punched the third torp away. "Weapon away. 0828, line of bearing search."

Dusty came on the ICS. "Hey flight, that ship we just went by is shooting at us. It's a *Udaloy*."

Mac said, "Bearing reversal."

Just as Randy and Eddie said, "Missile went high, MiGs just went over us."

"Aphid again," Barney added.

"Flight, gimme a left 270, I'm going to put the last torp on that damn *Udaloy*. Let's see how he likes it." KJ quickly worked through the programming, and as Randy straightened the P-3 on the new course, he hit the weapons release one more time. "Weapon away, torp 4, 0829. And we're Winchester at this time."

"Saphir lock up, bearing 180, Flight!"

Randy rolled the P-3 sharply right saying, "Right turns aren't natural. Eddie, don't let me hit the water, okay?"

Scoop pushed up power, "Ain't gonna happen boss. I'll slap the shit outta you, you crash my airplane."

Randy couldn't help but laugh as he continued pulling almost three Gs to get the airplane on a southern heading. This time Randy saw the two MiGs first. "Visual, off the nose, two MiGs, one of them is in a dive, it looks like. Missile away, inbound!"

Mac yelled, "Terminal homing!"

Charlie said, "Explosion, buoy 11, no other sounds."

"Copy. Don't worry about them right now. Everybody cinch your belts down."

The P-3 was rocked hard left, and it was all Randy could do to keep it from rolling completely over as the missile hit the water and exploded underneath the right wing. "Lost aileron effectiveness, Eddie, we still got a wing out there?"

"Yeah, but number four is on fire."

\* \* \*

**USS *Michigan*, North Atlantic 0830Z**

"Conn, Sonar. Fourth torp in the water, bearing 030 relative."

Captain Thomas whistled softly as he looked at the plot. "Wonder what the fourth drop was on?" He looked at the plot again and smiled slowly. "High diddle, diddle."

The XO, Commander Green, looked over at him. "Sir?"

"Whoever that was opened the middle up for us." Pointing at the relative bearing lines to the torpedo noises, he continued, "Helm, make your course 245 True. Make turns for one half knot below cavitation speed. Weaps open outer doors, prep Mk-48s for snapshot."

"Helm, aye," was the response, and he felt the deck tilt slightly and the thrum of the propulsor increase.

"Weaps, aye."

"We're going to run southwest, right through the middle. I think that was the intent." He stepped over to the scope. "Scope up." He caught it about waist high, spinning around as the tube rose higher, until he was standing straight up. "Close aboard is clear."

He turned toward the bow and increased the magnification to the maximum, moving back and forth. "Might be a P-3 out there. Distant. Some…jets too. And…that one looked like an F-4. Smoke trails. Somebody is catching hell. Just saw an explosion. Bearing, mark! Second explosion, bearing, mark!"

"243 True, 238 True, Captain."

"Tell Sonar to listen down bearing 243." He slapped the handles up and retracted the scope, "XO, you have the conn."

\* \* \*

### Reaper and Black Knight Flights 0830Z

"Reaper, Knight 01, we've got a tally on two Foxbats down here, oh wait, make that *one* Foxbat. The second just splashed itself. One P-3, on fire, it's turning west. We're intercepting remaining Foxbat."

"Knight, Reaper's got two Foxbats turning tail up here. We're at flight level 240 on top. Current heading 000 true."

"And Reaper, Knight. This guy doesn't want to play. He's…in the cloud, coming around on 000. I still have a lock. Coming upstairs, I'll stop at 200. Go air-air 29."

"29."

"I've gotcha 190 at 10. I *think* this guy is going to pop out in front of you."

"Roger. We'll pull it back a bit to make sure."

\* \* \*

### P-3 #323, 200 Feet, 40NM off the Norwegian Coast 0832Z

Scoop E-handled the number 4 engine, and Eddie said, "Good feather."

"Fire light, number 4. Check me, fire bottle selected."

Randy said, "Number 4. Hit it." Scoop hit the fire extinguisher.

Dusty came on the ICS. "Flight, I see fuel streaming out from under the wing between 3 and 4. And I still see fire in what's left of number 4."

Eddie said, "Still seeing flames."

Scoop sighed. "Selecting alternate fire bottle. This is our last shot."

Eddie said, "Alternate selected."

Scoop fired it and watched as Eddie looked out the side window. "No joy."

Dusty yelled, "Flight, lots of flames out from under the wing, outboard of number 3!"

Randy keyed the PA, "Crew, prepare for ditching. We don't have any choice." He turned the P-3 slowly south, paralleling the waves and said, "Fuck it. Send a distress message."

Barney keyed the HF as KJ keyed the UHF on guard. Barney put out the standard ditching message as KJ said quickly, "Knight, Mike Kilo 21, we're going in. How about relaying to somebody to come get us?"

He heard a quick, breathless response. "Knight 02, copy. We see you. SOBs?"

KJ answered, "Thirteen, one three. Souls on board. One injured, broken leg. Time 0834."

"Knight 02 copies."

Randy keyed the PA. "Standby for ditch." One long ring of the command bell followed, and he said, "Brace!"

KJ glanced over at Barney as he put his head down, saying a quick prayer as the P-3 hit the water, then bounced, bounced again, and slewed violently to the right. KJ vaguely remembered throwing up his arm, and then nothing.

He came to as Barney and Tim dragged him down the aisle, and he moaned in pain. Tim asked, "Where are you hurt?"

"My arm. I can walk, I think." Water sloshed back and forth as it bubbled deeper and deeper, and he asked, "Everybody out?"

"Randy's checking. We're the last from up front."

The next thing he remembered was lying in the raft, and Dusty, his face covered in blood, bitching, "I brode by dam node agin. Dam parachood."

He looked around. "Where's Pop?"

Randy leaned over him. "He's in the other raft. We're all out. Iverson broke his foot falling in the hydraulic service center. Here, take this aspirin," Randy said, sticking it between his lips and holding a baby bottle full of water up to his lips.

KJ choked it down and coughed, "Thanks. What happened?"

Eddie laughed ironically. "Right wing outboard of number three came off. Hooked a wave. Six of us in here, the other seven in the twelve man. We're tied together. Knights said they'd notify sea-air rescue. They had to leave; they were out of gas and needed to tank to get home."

KJ propped himself up a little. "So what have we got for radios and rats?"

Hairy replied, "Standard raft fare, and the rate we're drifting, we might make Norway before anyone finds us. So far, five, maybe six working radios, plus the two radios on the raft. One radio watch, one lookout. Two hours at a time."

\* \* \*

### USS *Michigan*, North Atlantic 1230Z

Chief of the Boat Handfield swung the periscope and flipped to maximum magnification, then sang out, "I've got a life raft. Bearing, Mark!"

The navigator said, "243 true."

"Somebody go wake up the captain." He ran the cross hairs down and said, "Range 1100 yards. Second raft sighted." He looked over at the helm, "Make turns for slow ahead. Steer 235."

"Helm, aye."

He had just taken a second mark when Captain Taylor stumbled into the conn, rubbing his face. "Whatcha got, COB?"

"Two rafts. They're drifting down on us. Range 800." He stepped away from the periscope and said, "Bearing about 239."

The captain hooked his forearms over the scope handles, made a quick full sweep, then a second, and finally turned to the heading. "Yep, looks like two rafts. Shall we offer them a ride?" he asked rhetorically.

The COB almost choked trying to keep from laughing as the XO ran into the conn. "XO, you have the conn. Let's get up on the roof and see if these guys want a lift home. Muster the rescue party, and get them ready, if you will."

He felt the deck tilt as he hurried back to his stateroom, grabbing his float-coat off the back of the door. He started back out, then reached back and crammed his ball cap on his head. Five minutes later, he stood on the bridge, bull horn in hand, as he conned the sub between the two rafts, catching the line between them on the conning tower. He turned to the talker, "All stop. Rescue party on deck, please." He clicked on the bull horn and cleared his throat. "Ah, gentlemen in the rafts, may I have your attention." A couple of heads popped out, and he smiled as he continued, "We were in the neighborhood and wondered if you might like a ride."

\* \* \*

### June 9, 1985
### Kings Bay, Georgia 0300Z

The tugs nestled the USS *Michigan* up to her berth at the pier, and the brow was swung over and fastened into place. Rear Admiral Owens, the submarine squadron commander, closely followed by three other officers, came up the brow and stepped onboard before the watch had a chance to challenge them. Rear Admiral Owens told the top side watch, "Gents, this boat is on lockdown. Nobody on or off until you are released. Speak to no one and don't announce us. Understood?"

The three watch standers came to attention and said in chorus, "Yes, sir." As the officers passed, one of the watch standers whispered to another, "Did you see that middle guy? How many stars did he have, three, or four?"

The second watch stander shook his head, "Don't know and ain't asking."

The four went down the ladder and into the passageway, marching forward much to the surprise of the sailors on the ship. A ripple of "Attention on deck," was passed forward as they advanced on the conn.

Captain Thomas was surprised to see Rear Admiral Owens step into the conn, and even more surprised when Vice Admiral Mark Kalenberg stepped in. The VCNO nodded. "Admiral Owens has a brief for you and the crew. Where are the aviators?"

"They're all in the wardroom, Admiral. XO, would you escort the admiral, please?"

As they stepped into the wardroom, KJ looked up and called, "Attention on deck!"

The crew was rising when the VCNO said, "At ease, keep your seats. Gentlemen, I'll make this short and to the point. You were injured by a freak wave while you were onboard a fishing boat off Brunswick. You were brought here for medical treatment. Your luggage is here. Your TAD never happened, you left Patuxent River, flew to NAS Jacksonville and broke the airplane." He turned to his flag aide, who handed him thirteen pink sheets. "Take one, pass them around and sign them. You know what they are. Unofficially, you did a helluva job, even if all the Soviet subs made it back to port. Officially," he shrugged. "Nothing ever happened."

Chief Clark muttered, "Didn't think so. The explosions were all time outs then. Dammit."

Dusty asked, "So, even though we got a MiG, we don't get to paint a silhouette on a P-3, sir?"

The admiral laughed as the flag aide looked at Dusty in horror. "No son. You don't. Not even on a model. Ever."

\* \* \* \* \*

## JL Curtis Bio

JL Curtis was born in Louisiana and raised in the Ark-La-Tex area. He began his education with guns at age eight with a SAA and a Grandfather that had carried one for 'work'. He began competitive shooting in the 1970s, an interest he still pursues, time permitting. He is a retired Naval Flight Officer, having spent 21 years serving his country, an NRA instructor, and a retired engineer who escaped the defense industry. He lives in North Texas and is now writing full time, with two series, The Grey Man and Rimworld published. Find him at his blog: http://oldnfo.org.

# # # # #

# Per Ardua Ad Astra
# by Jan Niemczyk

**7 May 2005. Thorpe on the Hill, Lincolnshire, England.**

*'When Saturday the 7ᵗʰ of May dawned, it was Day 15 of World War Three; it was also Day 22 after mobilisation. Fatigue was beginning to set in on both sides. Today it is not particularly remembered; it was neither a "Hardest Day," nor a "Battle of Britain Day," like the battles of the Last War. It was simply "Another Day at the Office" for the men and women assigned to the defence of the UK, and while the day might not have been remembered or marked as being historic, it would be long remembered by most of those who were there.'*

'Extract from *The Aerial Conflict over the United Kingdom and Republic of Ireland, Volume IV* of the *Official History of the Third World War* (Government Official History Series), (London 2020), by Marshal of the Royal Air Force Lord Foster of High Wycombe, RAF (Retired) and Dr Lawrence Marksman.

\* \* \*

David 'Gambo' Gambon, husband, father, Squadron Leader in No. 615 (County of Surrey 'Churchill's Own') Squadron, rolled over in the bed of the budget travel hotel. It took a moment for him to realise he was not in his Haslemere home lying next to his wife Roberta.

*If I was going to spend a night away from my wife in a hotel, I'd have hoped for better circumstances than this.* The hotel had been requisitioned by the RAF a week ago, after the Soviets had bombed the housing areas of a number of RAF Stations. Gambon was of the opinion that the action should have been taken a long time ago, rather than requiring several dozen dead to be implemented.

*Stupid bean counters will be the death of us all,* he thought, stretching and heading into the latrine for his morning routine. Gambon was the tactical director of a Sentry AEW.1 crew, meaning he was the senior man aboard the aircraft. He also was the Officer Commanding A Flight, No. 615 Squadron, a Royal Auxiliary Air Force (RAuxAF) unit that provided additional air and ground crew for the RAF's Sentry force. As an auxiliary, No. 615 had no aircraft of its own, although No. 8 Squadron had been kind enough to paint one of their *Sentries'* port side with the markings of 615.

*Regulars sure have been a lot kinder to us than I expected,* Gambon thought as he began shaving. *Might be because the fighter boys have gotten them used to part timers.* While 615 Squadron did not have aircraft of its own, most of the other RAuxAF flying squadrons that had reappeared during the late 1990s as part of the strengthening of Britain's defences did. That included seven of No. 11 (Fighter) Group's seventeen interceptor and fighter squadrons—their *Tornado F.3s* flown and maintained by volunteers. As the Americans had proven in the '70s and '80s, the old argument that part-timers could not operate sophisticated jet aircraft had just not held up to reality. The RAF had been glad to realise the cost savings involved.

*Only reason we're still in the war*, Gambon thought grimly. *Would not have been enough fighters to go around otherwise*. With that sobering thought, he headed down to get himself breakfast.

\* \* \*

"Wakey, wakey, everybody!" A gruff RAFP corporal stated from the front of the coach. It seemed like only a couple of seconds after Gambon had closed his eyes after boarding the vehicle in front of the hotel. "Have your passes ready for inspection!"

*Bloody hell. Twenty-minutes gets shorter and shorter every day*, Gambon thought, looking around the shuttle from the hotel. Getting his bearings, he began to rummage through the pockets of his flight suit. Outside his window, other RAFP Snowdrops inspected the vehicle while being covered by the rifles of RAF Regiment Gunners.

*I doubt we'd get hijacked in eight miles, but better to be safe than sorry*, Gambon thought. He looked at the police escort, who were waiting just outside of the base's gate to resume escorting the coach when it returned with the outgoing *Sentry* crews.

*Then again, if they get past all of those police, then a few gate guards probably won't even slow them down*. Gambon handed over his pass while hoping *that* disquieting thought didn't show on his face.

\* \* \*

"I really wish they'd properly disposed of '108, Flight," Gambon observed, gesturing towards a burnt-out aircraft through the crew bus window. "Hardly conducive to our morale."

The Sentry that bore the serial number ZH108 had been destroyed in a Soviet air raid a week ago. Its burned-out carcass had been bulldozed onto a patch of grass between the main hardstand and a taxiway, where it was still visible to all. Thankfully, the RAF had enough foresight to disperse its seven precious *Sentries* around the UK, so only a couple had been on the ground at Waddington when it had been attacked.

"At least nobody was killed aboard her, sir." Flight Sergeant Max Phillips replied as the crew bus pulled up to *Sentry* ZH107. "Shame to lose her though; always thought she was amongst the best of the bunch."

Forty-five minutes later, ZH107 was climbing to take her position over the North Sea. Gambon listened as the flight crew began coordinating with the *Tristar* tanker that would top off her tanks.

*It's going to be a long day.*

\* \* \*

**RAF Leuchars, Fife, Scotland.**

Wing Commander John 'Jack' Foster, RAF, Commanding Officer of No. 43 (Fighter) Squadron, tried to focus on shaving rather than his imminent duties that day.

*I'd rather face a flight of* Flankers *than this lot*, he thought. The Ministry of Defence had authorised a group press visit in the hope of getting some good, morale-raising coverage that could also be used in the propaganda war.

*Here's to hoping it will at least be* partially *successful,* Foster thought uncharitably. He'd never been a big fan of the media. If the correspondent wasn't a blithering airhead who had never served, they were generally officers who had retired so long ago they considered the *Hawker Hunter* to have been the apex of modern fighter technology.

*If I'd known making ace would lead to this, I might have let that last* Fencer *get away.* Air Commodore Forbes-Hamilton—the station commander—had insisted that, as the RAF's first modern ace, he should be the one to show around the print and television reporters. At least some of the print journalists were from aviation magazines, which meant they *should* know what they were talking about. Well, apart from a few individuals who still wrote of the *Tornado F.3* as if it was the same aircraft that had first been delivered to the Air Force in 1985.

"Ow! Bugger!" he said, the thought of the latter idiots having apparently led to him pressing a little too hard on the razor. The *Tornado* pilots had been fed up with 'professional' aviation journalists calling their aircraft 'inadequate,' or at best 'barely adequate for the task' prior to the conflict. In the twenty years since the *Tornado F.3* had entered service, it had virtually become a different aircraft, capable of standing up to the best fighters in the world.

*Some people don't keep up with the times,* he thought, dabbing at the blood welling up from his chin.

* * *

4 3 Squadron's crew room was a different place than it had been a few hours ago. Located in the hardened Squadron Headquarters, it was usually full of pizza boxes and detritus from takeaway ordered from local restaurants.

*Thank goodness they got the 'lad' and 'ladette' magazines out*, he thought, looking at the magazine rack located between the crew couches. In their place were a number of aviation magazines, a few copies of *RAF News* and the latest editions of the newspapers the print journalists wrote for. Pictures on the walls of scantily clad persons of both genders had been replaced by aviation prints and aircraft recognition pictures.

"Because they could be scrambled at any time, I'm afraid I can't introduce you to the aircrew on alert, but I can let you speak to others who are off duty at the moment," Foster told the journalists. "They should be happy enough to answer any questions you have for them."

"Before we start, Wing Commander, can I ask how it feels to be the RAF's first ace since the Last War?"

"It's an honour; however, it's one I share with my navigator, Squadron Leader Wilkinson." Foster replied. "It was also very much a team effort. Without the ground crew, my *Tornado* could never have gotten off the ground in the first place, and without those working in the radar stations and AWACS aircraft, we would never have been able to find our targets."

Foster paused to give some of the reporters time to scribble down what he was saying. "I'm very much a cog in a much larger machine. I also hope you'll remember that there are a lot of aircrew out there doing the same job as me, I'm not anything special," Foster said.

"Can I ask how your aircrew feel about flying an aircraft considered inferior to enemy aircraft?"

There was a rustle of paper and clicking of cameras as Foster turned to look at the questioner. Foster recognised the questioner as the defence correspondent of a national newspaper, a man called Mel Rippert. He was renowned for his opinionated and critical articles on UK defence procurement; the last one Foster could recall had suggested the *Typhoon* was a waste of money, and the RAF should have bought the *Super Hornet* instead. Buying American was something of a theme for him, and Foster often wondered if he was paid by the US defence industry to promote their products and rubbish their British and European rivals.

Foster thought uncharitably as he fixed the man with a hard gaze. After a few awkward moments of silence, the man broke eye contact.

"The *Tornado F.3* is in no way inferior to any enemy aircraft we can expect to encounter," Foster said, his tone precise. "Indeed, last year at an exercise in Nevada, crews from this squadron and Treble One racked up a kill ratio of twelve-to-one against American aggressor squadrons simulating Soviet fighters." Foster replied.

"Yes, but the *F.3* can't dog-fight in the same way as American aircraft like the *Hornet*, or Russian ones like the MiG-29," Rippert persisted, as if he had not heard Foster's previous answer.

Foster gave the man a thin smile.

"Our main enemies are cruise missiles, and *Backfire* and *Fencer* bombers, none of which are agile enemies. However, we have fought several successful engagements with Su-27 *Flankers*. I'm sure you saw in the briefing packet that I've killed two and my squadron has downed eighteen total."

Foster paused, his look making it clear he was expecting a response. When the correspondent murmured something, Foster moved on.

"Yes, the *F.3* is not a traditional agile fighter aircraft; it is an interceptor. Moreover, in my opinion, when you are armed with weapons like the AMRAAM and ASRAAM, you have done something wrong if you are forced into a dog-fight."

He swept over the gathered audience, then went in for the finish. "This is 2005, not 1940; we like to kill our enemy before he can see us or knows we are there. Our tactics essentially make the agility of an enemy irrelevant."

The journalist did not look happy with the answer, principally because it did not fit his preconceptions. He was about to make another point when one of his colleagues jumped in first.

"If I may ask a question, how do the female aircrew cope with living in a male-dominated environment?" she asked.

*Oh Lord, not this again.*

"Perhaps I'm not the best person to answer that, after all, I have the wrong equipment," Foster replied. A few of the journalists—but not the questioner—chuckled.

*No sense of humour in some people.*

"However, I have always been of the opinion that there are only two kinds of aircrew in this squadron—pilots and navigators, or Weapon Systems Operators as we are now supposed to call them. Neither aircraft, nor weapons, care whether someone keeps their reproductive equipment on the inside, or outside."

He looked up to see two of his squadron mates' faces fixed with thin smiles.

*They hate these questions as much as I do*, he thought. *Sorry Bubbles and Mamba.*

"I'm sure that any of our female aircrew will be happy to share their experiences with you. Now are there any more questions before I pass you on?"

A journalist from a tabloid put up his hand.

"I wonder if I might ask a couple of personal questions, Wing Commander? It's just that our readers would like to know a bit more about the people behind the uniform."

"Ask away. I don't guarantee to answer if it's a bit too personal," Foster said with a grin.

"Can I ask if you are married?"

"Not yet, but I am engaged."

"How does your fiancée feel about your job?"

"Well...at the moment, she's eating her heart out with jealousy." Foster said laughing. "She's also a pilot, though at the moment she's on a ground posting because of a back injury she got during an ejection."

There was a slight murmur of sympathy from the gathered journalists.

*You'd be more sympathetic if you knew how much fun it is dealing with the cross between a cornered wild cat and disturbed wasp nest at home*, Foster thought.

"She's a better pilot than me, and I'm pretty sure she would have made ace well before I did if given the opportunity."

Once again, he paused as the reporters wrote this information down. He looked at his watch.

"Given the time, I'll let you loose on the aircrew, because I'm pretty sure you've heard enough of my voice." Foster paused for a moment just in case there were any questions. "Good, let me know when you are done, or if you have any trouble."

Foster sighed in relief once the journalists had dispersed to seek new victims. He knew full well his aircrew had been dreading this visit.

*I'll just have to tell them the same thing they told me when I complained: 'It will give you invaluable experience in speaking to the media and thus help with your professional development.'*

"Bet you're glad to get shot of that lot, boss," Squadron Leader George Wilkinson, the squadron's senior navigator, remarked.

"Where have you been hiding, George?" Foster asked, startled by the navigator's appearance. "I'm pretty sure that our esteemed visitors from the media would want to interview the other half of the first *Tornado* crew to become aces."

"I've got paperwork to catch up on, boss, and then I need to inventory my personal kit and clean my SIG pistol. I'm afraid I don't really have the time, sorry."

Foster laughed.

"Nice try, George. I'm afraid you have to share the misery with the rest of us."

"Ah, well, worth a shot," the navigator conceded.

The door opened as an orderly from Sector Headquarters walked in with a message. Foster noted the red folder.

"Sir, could you please sign for this?" the young corporal asked. Foster nodded, scribbling quickly on the requisite message form. Once that was done, he took the folder and checked to make sure no journalists could see what was inside. A quick scan caused him to purse his lips.

"Clear the journos," he stated. "It looks like we're about to be busy."

* * *

Thirty minutes later, Foster put the journalists out of his mind as his *Tornado F.3* taxied out of the Hardened Aircraft Shelter (HAS). He needed to concentrate on the task ahead.

"Leuchars Tower, Delta One Three Alpha requesting permission to depart, over."

*"Delta One Three Alpha, Leuchars Tower, you are clear to depart; contact Buchan once airborne. Good luck, sir."*

"Thank you, and Good Day, tower."

* * *

### Sentry AEW.1 ZH107, Over the North Sea.

Squadron Leader Gambon was half-way through a cup of tea, and a bacon and egg roll, when his working day began.

"Tactical director, surveillance controller, we have what looks like a possible raid developing over the eastern Baltic," Sergeant Harris, one of the ZH107's NCOs, stated. "Have designated as RAID BRAVO ONE THREE, currently composed of sixteen aircraft."

"I can see it on my screen." Gabon replied. "What makes you think it is a threat to the UKADR? Could be heading for a target in the Central Region."

"The aircraft of RAID BRAVO ONE THREE have conducted what looks like air-to-air refuelling. A raid heading for the Central Region is not likely to need to do that," the controller replied.

"Your assessment would be a raid of *Fencers* or *Fullbacks* then?"

"Affirmative," Harris said. "We also have what looks like a raid of *Backfires* coming out of the Leningrad Military District."

"Well if it rains it pours." Gabon commented.

He consulted one of the other displays to check which RAF fighters were in the best position to intercept, then made sure the data-link system was transmitting the most up to date information to them. While the Sentry could control the air battle, for the moment it would be up to the controllers at the two Sector Operations Centres, RAF Buchan and RAF Neatishead, who would make the decisions regarding aircraft allocation.

*Of course, if they get knocked out, it's on us*, he thought, looking at the *Backfires*.

\* \* \*

### HQ, RAF Strike Command, RAF High Wycombe, Buckinghamshire.

Air Chief Marshal Sir Michael Johnson's day had also started early; he had risen from the narrow cot in the room provided for him in the station's bunker, shaved, eaten a rather spartan breakfast, then taken his daily walk outside. The fact that he was accompanied by four armed members of the RAF Regiment and that even his ADC, Flight Lieutenant Victoria 'Vicky' Jackson carried a sidearm, had not spoiled his enjoyment of the fresh air. Well, not too much.

As CINCUKAIR—the Commander in Chief UK Air Forces—Johnson controlled all NATO aircraft based in, or transiting through, the UK. His job had been onerous enough in peacetime. Now that certain people kept trying to bomb his command, the responsibilities had grown exponentially.

"Let's go to the Air Defence Operations Centre," Johnson said, feeling much more refreshed. "Always good to show one's face before things get too hectic."

Vicky and his security detachment laughed politely at his joke as they walked towards the bunker.

"Morning, Colin, how goes it?" Johnson asked the senior officer on duty as he stepped through the final blast door.

"Good morning, Sir." Group Captain Colin Kenneth replied. "Their day shift has put in an appearance a little earlier. We've got several raids appearing already; Frontal Aviation stuff coming out of East Germany plus Long-Range Aviation *Backfires* out of Leningrad and the Kola Peninsula. Danes and Dutch might get some of the Frontal Aviation stuff, but we can't bank on it given operations over the Central Front."

CINCUKAIR took a look at the large display on the far wall which showed all of the radar tracking information available to the ADOC superimposed on an electronic map before he replied. He was also able to take in the virtual tote board alongside it which showed the readiness state of every squadron under his command. The race-track traces of aircraft on combat air patrol, tanker trails, and AEW positions could also be clearly seen on the big display.

"The *Fencers* and *Fullbacks* will probably be escorted." Kenneth continued. "So, we'll have the *Tiffies* go after them and send the *Ton-*

*kas* after the *Backfires.*" He said using the nicknames for the *Typhoon FGR.2* and *Tornado F.3.*

"Best use for them, Colin, although I do recall that *Tonkas* have still managed to give *Flanker* escorts quite a surprise, just as they did to *Eagles* at Red Flag last year," Johnson said.

*If we ever wanted proof the upgrades were worth it, beating up those American* Eagles *provided it,* Johnson thought. *Still, not keen on having the Tornadoes fight* Flankers *too often.*

"Well, Colin, I'm due to call John Hazel, so I'll let you get on with it. I'll pop in this afternoon though, and see how things are going, but if you need me, give me a bell."

"Will do, Sir."

\* \* \*

*echnology is a grand thing,* Johnson thought. Air Vice Marshal William 'Bill' Hazel, Air Officer Commanding No. 11 (Fighter) Group, stood looking into the video camera at RAF Bentley Priory. The station where Air Chief Marshal Dowding had commanded the previous Battle of Britain, Bentley Priory had seen a great deal of updates since 1940. The Standby Air Defence Operations Centre (SADOC) that Hazel currently stood in was heavily computerized, giving him the ability to conduct a video conference with Air Chief Marshal Johnson as if the two had been in the same room.

*This is all a lot for a former fighter jock to take in,* Johnson thought. Hazel had been a *Phantom* driver, while Johnson had flown the *Lightning.* There was more computing technology in the laptop running the conference than whole squadrons of either fighter could have boasted.

*At least Hazel has remained somewhat current,* Johnson thought, remembering that he'd had to forbid Hazel from flying either *Tornado F.3* and *Hawk T.2* sorties after the man had done both the first day of the war.

"Good morning, Sir, I hope you are well," AVM Hazel stated.

"Morning, Bill, I'm not bad thanks," ACM Johnson replied. "I see it looks like our visitors are arriving a bit earlier today than intelligence suggested. Anything we should be worrying about?"

"They went after a few of my mobile ground radars during the night; Neatishead lost one and Boulmer had an emitter damaged," Hazel reported. "However, replacements are now operational, and I don't have any gaps in ground radar coverage."

Johnson saw the man's gaze shift as he looked at the map that was likely located just behind the SADOC's video feed.

"I'd expect the Soviets to try again during the day. I've ordered that as many of the emitters as possible be relocated to make locating them that bit harder."

"Could explain the extra *Backfires*," Johnson replied. "You need me to shift any fighters or ask the Americans for some of their *Eagles*?"

"No sir," Hazel replied quickly, as if he'd anticipated the question. "The American deep strikes need escorts, and I don't have any concerns about the fighter force and our ground defences. I could do with more of both, but I'm sure every commander has said the same during wartime."

Johnson chuckled.

"Absolutely, Bill. We're lucky to have as much as we do."

Both men shared a grim smile at that one, well aware of the politics that had nearly gutted Britain's defence spending in the past. Thankfully, politicians in the 1980s and 1990s had stopped the rot.

"If today is going to be a maximum effort from the other side, I fully expect them to go after our main HQs," Johnson said. "So, there is every chance that you may need to take over; after all, you are my current designated deputy if anything happens to High Wycombe."

"You don't have to worry on that account, sir," Hazel replied. "We're fully ready to take over here if need be. And as the navy toast goes: 'Here's to bloody wars and sickly seasons.'"

CINCUKAIR chuckled at the reference.

"You'll not be getting a promotion today, I hope," he replied. "Either through disease or AS-6."

"Don't jinx yourself, sir," Hazel replied, drawing an involuntary snort from Victoria.

"That reminds me—no flying operationally," Johnson said. "I know you took a *Tornado* up the other day. I expect to be talking to you in a few hours, not hearing from Gwendolyn that SAR are still trying to fish you out of the North Sea, Good luck to you and your people."

\* \* \*

**Over the North Sea.**

Flight Lieutenant Katherine Catz, known by her squadron mates as 'Katy Cat,' or just 'KC,' loved flying the *Typhoon FGR.2*.

*Still the greatest aircraft ever built*, she thought. *Period*. It was her second tour on the *Typhoon*, and her current tour with No. 74 (Tiger) Squadron was quite different than her previous stint with No. 92 Squadron at RAF Wildenrath in West Germany.

*I don't think it's being a lead, either*, she thought. Her experience at Wildenrath had qualified her to lead a flight. She'd led three other *Typhoons* off the runway at RAF Wattisham in Suffolk, and now the two pairs were split at their station over the North Sea. It'd been about an hour flying a lazy figure-eight pattern before her data link had beeped at her.

*Looks like trade*, Catz thought, her pulse picking up. She glanced over at her wingman, Flight Lieutenant Steve Carr, and saw he was waggling his wings to acknowledge he'd received the message as well. It was time to go engage the formation of Soviet aircraft designated 'RAID BRAVO ONE THREE,' a group of sixteen contacts that could be a mixture of various threats.

*Don't know how they did it with* Skyflash*, never mind* Red Top, on the *Lightning*, Catz mused. Her father and grandfather had both wore the Royal Air Force blue and flown interceptors. She was glad her *Typhoon* currently carried the six *Meteors* with their 300 km range; it was nice to be able to engage and still have 200 kilometres to play with before the *Flankers* could employ their AA-12 *Adders*. With four additional ASRAAM infra-red guided missiles and a 27mm Mauser cannon, theoretically the first two *Typhoons* could take down the entire raid before running out of missiles.

*Oh, to live in a world without ECM and self-protective jammers*, she thought, giving a quick scan of her aircraft's main Multi-Function Display. The Soviet raid was broken down into two formations. One of four aircraft, probably the escort, flew a couple of miles ahead of the main formation of twelve aircraft.

*Probably* Fencers; *hopefully not* Fullbacks. The former aircraft, resembling the Americans' F-111, had only rudimentary air-to-air capability. The latter, roughly analogous to the F-15E *Strike Eagle*, had the ability to carry four AA-12s for self-protection. Catz had not been on the flight that had first found that out, but it had resulted in three dead *Tornadoes* and a badly damaged *Typhoon*. In any case, first priority would be the escort, with the hope that their destruction would cause the bombers to turn around. Although Catz had yet to see this happen since the war had begun, allegedly just such an event had occurred on the war's second day.

*If intelligence is to be believed, that flight commander was executed.* Evidently, Soviet authorities took a dim view of aircrew that turned back, even if continuing on meant certain destruction. She turned her head to port, to see if the second pair of *Typhoons* were now in position.

*Here we go.* Catz turned toward the threat and went to full military power, Carr following. They kept their CAPTOR radars silent for the moment, waiting until they were well within range of their *Meteors*. At 250 kilometres, Catz illuminated the radar. The *Typhoon's* systems quickly sorted the targets, selecting those it assessed were the greatest threat. She armed the aircraft's weapons and waited half a second.

"Select Target One, *Meteor* One," she told the *Typhoon's* weapon system.

*"Target One,* Meteor *One selected."* the aircraft's computerised voice confirmed.

"Fox Three! Fox Three!" Catz announced, her first radio call of the sortie.

The *Meteor* missile dropped away from the belly of the aircraft, its solid rocket igniting once it was clear. She saw the weapon flash away, then become a streak as its ramjet took over and pushed it past Mach 4.

"*Target Two selected*," the *Typhoon*'s computer intoned. Catz pushed the pickle button for a second time, transmitting yet another warning. With four missiles in the air from her formation, Catz and Carr shut down their radars, reversed course and lost height to try to avoid any return fire.

\* \* \*

The lead pilot of the Soviet formation had expected to come under attack at some point—the radar warning receiver (RWR) of his Su-27M had been warning him about several airborne and ground radars scanning his aircraft. Amongst the plethora of warnings, he initially missed the addition of the *Typhoons'* radars; he could not miss the strident warning of missile lock, however. The Soviet officer activated his aircraft's defensive systems and began to manoeuvre hard, but it was too late. The *Flanker* was well within the *Meteor*'s 'no escape zone,' and it blasted the Soviet fighter in half. The pilot managed to eject from his crippled aircraft and started his descent towards the unforgiving North Sea below.

\* \* \*

Catz could see that the four *Meteors* fired by her flight and the second pair of *Typhoons* had all found their targets. 'RAID BRAVO ONE THREE' had lost its escorts and was now vulnerable. To her surprise the bombers did not attempt to evade, instead they broke into two formations and came at the British aircraft, missiles separating from under their wings.

"*Warning! Warning! Radar lock!*"

"Oh my God, it's a fighter sweep!" Catz radioed, even as she fired her own *Meteors* then began to evade.

\* \* \*

### Sentry AEW.1 ZH107.

"**D**ammit!" Squadron Leader Gambon exclaimed as Catz's warning blared across the speakers. He quickly checked the display; if the Soviet formation made it past the four *Typhoons,* there was only a pair of *Tornado F.3*s between them and ZH107. As he watched two of the *Typhoons* and another three *Flankers* wink out, Gambon was well aware the Soviets would happily sacrifice sixteen aircraft in exchange for a *Sentry*. That didn't even account for the two additional raids starting to move out of the Baltic behind Bravo One Three.

"Captain, tactical director, I am designating 'RAID BRAVO ONE THREE' as a direct threat to this aircraft. I'm authorising you to take evasive action as necessary to safeguard us."

"Roger that," the aircraft captain replied.

"Fighter controller, tactical director, tell those two *Tonkas* from CAP position Charlie Three Four to go after anything that gets past the *Tiffies*. We're not going to wait for reinforcements to save us."

"Roger that," the fighter controller acknowledged.

While the aircraft captain and fighter controller were carrying out their tasks, Gambon sent an urgent message to the ground. If his *Sentry* was threatened, it was likely the second aircraft also was.

\* \* \*

**Delta Flight.**

Wing Commander Foster had been waiting to be ordered to intercept a formation of Tu-22M4 *Backfire* bombers when he received a message about the threat to the *Sentry*.

"It's turned into a real fur-ball, boss." Squadron Leader Wilkinson reported from the rear cockpit. He could see that the two remaining *Typhoons* were fighting for their lives against Bravo One Threes' remnants. "Two bandits are heading our way."

"Right, George, got it. Time for us to earn our pay."

The pair of *Tornado F.3*s turned up threat and went to full military power. Like the *Typhoons* before them, they kept their Foxhunter radar silent, there being no point to alerting the enemy to their presence before they could engage. The *Tornadoes* had a much harder task, as their AMRAAMs had around the same range as the missiles carried by the *Flanker*s. The Soviet aircraft would have a small window of opportunity to return fire once the RAF aircraft had engaged.

"Coming up on ideal firing range boss, in…three…two…one…lighting them up now."

"Fox Three! Fox Three!" Foster announced as soon as he had lock.

In normal circumstances, he would have launched a single missile at a target, after all, the *AIM-120C* had a kill probability (pK) of something like .95—at least in theory anyway—against target drones. However, these were not normal circumstances, and the enemy were certainly not target drones, so he fired a pair of missiles at each *Flanker,* knowing his wingman would do the same.

"Hold on to your hat, George!" Foster told Wilkinson as he turned the F.3 sharply away from the Soviet aircraft and put it into a dive, pushing the throttle through the gate and engaging reheat. The aircraft creaked and groaned alarmingly as he pushed it to its limit.

*Whoops, forgot the drop tanks,* he thought, levelling off. The two 2,250-lt Hinderburger drop tanks were not rated for supersonic flight, and he punched them both off the wings just in time. Trading altitude for speed, Foster finally pulled up around a hundred meters above the North Sea. As at this altitude there were very few other aircraft out there that could keep up with a *Tornado F.3,* and the radar warning receiver was silent; the initial danger seemed to have passed.

*Time to take stock of the situation*, he thought, reducing to full military power.

* * *

**Sentry AEW.1 ZH107.**

"Looks like we're got some *Tiffie* and *Tonka* mates to thank for saving our bacon," Gambon commented as he observed the end of the engagement.

The Soviet fighter sweep had been decisively defeated—four Su-27Ms were now fleeing east. On the negative side, three *Typhoons* had been lost, though it appeared that their aircrew had survived. At least, they would if SAR hurried up.

"Well, they achieved something with that trick," Sergeant Harris observed. "We're going to have to dispatch the reserves."

\* \* \*

**Over the North Sea, east of the Bass Rock.**

*T*wo sorties in one day is getting old, quickly, Flight Lieutenant Simon Darkshade, RAAF, thought, stifling a yawn as he maintained formation off the port wing of a No. 43 (Fighter) Squadron *Tornado F.3*.

"…angels…incoming…"

*Damn jammers*, Darkshade thought. Soviet jamming was currently making radio conversation with his wingman, the *Tornado F.3*s the pair of *Hawks* were flying with, or the ground impossible. Therefore, Darkshade was keeping one eye on the rear cockpit of the interceptor.

*Glad we're not doing this at low level*, he thought. A moment later, there was a flashing light coming from the navigator's torch. The Morse code gave an instruction to go to combat spread and where to expect the enemy to approach from.

*Glad to put my arse on the line for Queen and Country*, Darkshade thought sarcastically. *Just what I thought would happen when I agreed to be an instructor pilot over here*. Darkshade was an Australian exchange officer serving with No.79 (Reserve) Squadron. He had nominally come to the United Kingdom to help the No.1 Tactical Weapons Unit train pilots on weapons systems before they were assigned to a specific aircraft type. No.1 TWU's *Hawk T.2*s were similar to the RAAF's *Hawk 127*s, so learning the aircraft had not been a problem.

*Kind of hard for the* Tornado *to point me in the right direction if we can't talk,* Darkshade thought. There were two *Tornadoes* guiding four *Hawks,* and not for the first time Darkshade wished a JTIDS terminal had been retrofitted into his aircraft.

*Too expensive my arse,* he thought. He checked over his four ASRAAM, wishing he had two more rather than the fuel tanks underneath his wing. However, even with the *T.2*'s fuel refuelling probe, the *Hawk* was too short-ranged to carry six missiles and the cannon for any useful length of time.

Darkshade looked up from his weapons display just in time to see the *Tornados* engage unseen targets with AMRAAMs.

*Well, I guess we're in it now,* he thought, following the *Tornadoes* as they descended rapidly and turned to attack the enemy formation from the rear. Darkshade stuck to 'his' *Tornado F.3* like glue until distant puff balls of exploding Soviet aircraft oriented him towards their opponents. At this distance they were little more than specks, but from their actions he guessed they were Su-24 *Fencers,* rather than the more modern Su-34 *Fullback.* Lacking the *Tornadoes'* radars, he closed to visual range, ensured he had good tone as the *Fencer* remained unaware of his presence, then squeezed the trigger.

"Fox Two!" he announced to anyone that could hear his radio call.

The missile raced off the port wing-tip pylon, rapidly accelerating to Mach 3 as it tracked the *Fencer.* The Soviet aircraft jettisoned its weapons load, then began to radically manoeuvre as it spewed out decoy flares.

*I'll take a jettison,* Darkshade thought. A couple of second later, the ASRAAM blew off the Su-24's tail, making it a total loss rather than just a mission kill. The crew ejected as their fighter began to disintegrate.

*Time to find more trade,* Darkshade thought as he looked around his aircraft to regain situational awareness. He spotted a *Tornado* chasing after a pair of Su-24s that were running towards the coast in the chaos of the Soviet-RAF merge.

*Brave lads,* Darkshade thought briefly. He punched off his two tanks and pushed the *Hawk*'s throttle forward to maximum. *We'll see if I can make them dead ones.*

\* \* \*

"Annoying buggers aren't they, boss?" Squadron Leader Wilkinson said from the rear cockpit of the pursuing *Tornado F.3.*

"You can say that again, George," Wing Commander Foster replied, frustrated.

The two *Fencers* were jinking just enough to prevent him from getting a lock-on.

*Only one missile left, and I'd like to make sure it hits so I don't have to go to guns,* Foster thought.

"Looks like we've got a *Hawk* trying to join us," Wilkinson observed.

"Optimistic sod." Foster commented. "Well good luck to him."

The four aircraft raced down the Firth of Forth, causing alarm aboard the ships below. In a few minutes, both *Fencers* would be able to drop their weapons on the dockyard and naval base at Rosyth if they chose to. Finally, Foster got a tone and fired.

"Fox Two! Fox Two!"

"Go! Go! Go!" Wilkinson urged the missile.

The *Fencer* pilot had seen the flash from the pursuing *Tornado*'s wing and turned sharply to try and defeat the missile, releasing flares as he did so. Since he was keeping his eye on the incoming ASRAAM, the pilot did not see the island of Inchcolm looming up in front of his aircraft. His navigator's screamed warning caused him to reverse his turn—right into the ASRAAM.

\* \* \*

*W*ell, *looks like that's one*, Darkshade thought, hurtling past the dark ball of smoke that had been two men and their attack aircraft. Seeing the second Su-24 bank tightly and pass over the coast, Darkshade slammed his stick over to cut the corner.

*Never would have caught him if he hadn't have turned.* Focusing on his target, Darkshade was not paying particular attention to the ground below him.

"Fox Two!" he said on getting a good tone and firing.

As with most of its siblings, the missile ran true, destroying its target. The burning wreckage, minus the crew who had ejected, slammed into the ground.

"Oh, shit!" Darkshade exclaimed as he finally noticed where his kill had come down.

\* \* \*

"*T*hey're not going to thank him for that!" Foster commented as he circled the crash site."

"You can say that again, boss!" Wilkinson agreed.

Below them, a column of smoke was rising from the crash site on the edge of the Mossmorran Petrochemical complex. Mossmorran was home to two plants, the Fife Natural Gas Liquid Plant—operated by Shell—and the Fife Ethylene Plant operated by ExxonMobil. The products both plants worked with and produced were somewhat flammable, so it was unfortunate the crashing *Fencer* had already set fire to one storage tank.

Foster and Wilkinson could already see blue flashing lights belonging to fire equipment hurrying along the nearby A92 dual carriageway towards the growing blaze.

"We're nearly at bingo fuel, so I think it is time we made ourselves scarce," Foster decided, turning away from Mossmorran.

* * *

### Durham Tees Valley Airport, County Durham.

Squadron Leader Gambon jerked awake as the *Sentry* touched down.

*Good God, I cannot keep this up*, he thought. *I can't fall asleep while we're flying back to the airfield.*

"Shame about Waddington," one of the controllers was saying to another.

"How many missiles did they say hit?" the second controller asked.

*Enough*, Gambon thought. *The answer you're looking for is* enough. *Sentry* ZH107 had diverted to Durham Tees Valley Airport due to the damage at RAF Waddington. Gambon was glad the RAF had seen fit to base its auxiliary flying squadrons at civilian airports near their recruiting areas, as otherwise there'd have been no support at their destination.

*Even though No. 607 is based on the RAF Middleton St. George side, there's a lot of difference between supporting a* Tornado *squadron and* Sentries, Gambon thought. ZH107 taxied to where ground crew were waiting to service the big jet. There was also a crew bus with the new crew waiting; once the swap over was accomplished, it would take Gambon's crew to their local accommodation.

"All right then, let's get off her quick," Gambon said. Leading by example, he scrambled through the exit door, taking a deep breath once he reached the bottom of the air-stair. The kerosene filled atmosphere was the closest he could get to fresh air after being cooped up in a metal tube for nearly ten hours. After counting his crew off, he spotted his counterpart from B Flight, No. 8 Squadron, and went across to say hello.

"Hi, Bruce, how are you?"

"Hi, Gambo," Squadron Leader Bruce Cameron replied. "I'm not bad, feeling a wee bit knackered though. You?"

"Same really mate, feeling lucky to be alive too. The Russians tried to kill us today."

"What?" Cameron asked, concerned. Gambon relayed the details of the frontal aviation fighter sweep.

"Didn't feel personal until today; know what I mean?" Gambon concluded.

"Aye, they're just blips on a screen until they are trying to kill you," Cameron agreed with a nod. "They tried to kill some of our tankers today as well. I hear we got lucky, although a few air bases were hit again."

Gambon saw the man look up the ladder.

"Anyway, time I was aboard. I'll catch you later. You get off and get some kip."

"I'll do that, Bruce," Gambon said. "See you in a few hours."

* * *

**RAF Leuchars, Fife, Scotland.**

Wing Commander Foster did not realise that he had fallen asleep as his *Tornado* was being winched backwards into the hardened aircraft shelter until the flight sergeant who served as crew chief tapped him on the shoulder.

"Wakey, wakey, boss," the Senior NCO said softly.

"Oh, sorry, Flight," Foster replied with a start as he woke up.

"Don't worry about it, boss, Mr. Wilkinson was kipping too," the Senior NCO replied cheerfully. "You need my boys to paint any more kills on your plane?"

"Err...yes, I think so, Flight," Foster said, yawning. "I think we got at least four today, but I'll need to get back to you. How was it here?"

"We got hit twice; the Rock Apes got quite a few of them thankfully," the NCO replied, referring to the base defence force. "They hit our peacetime HQ, though...and the buggers killed our cockerels and chickens."

As No. 43 Squadron was known as 'the Fighting Cocks' and had a cockerel on its crest; the squadron had long kept cockerels and chickens as mascots. The fresh eggs the chickens produced was a very welcome side benefit.

Foster felt a single tear run down his left cheek.

*We've lost pilots and ground crew, and it's some damn birds that I'm feeling emotional about,* he thought. Even with that thought, he didn't lose his anger.

"Bastards," he muttered as he climbed down from the cockpit.

\* \* \*

**Over the North Sea.**

Captain Dimitri Komissarov was somewhat surprised to be alive; as he had expected during the transit to his target in the UK, NATO forces on the continent had thrown everything they could at him. So far, he had managed to escape by accelerating up to Mach 2.8, the fastest he could go without damaging the airframe of his Mi-25RBsh, or risking having the four 500lb bombs he was carrying detonating.

*This is insanity,* Komissarov thought. *Reconnaissance missions are dangerous enough without also asking me to drop bombs on a radar station.* From his warning system's constant bleeping, Komissarov knew his aircraft was being scanned by at least one airborne and several ground-based radars.

*So much for surprise.* He had not exactly expected to sneak up on the RAF, but it was clear the British were well and truly agitated. Glancing at his systems, he drew some comfort that the all of the electronic emissions were likely being recorded by the MiG-25RBF that had accompanied him for much of the flight.

\* \* \*

Flight Lieutenant Catz shifted in her Martin-Baker ejection seat as she put her aircraft into yet another wide orbit. Catz was on her third sortie of the day, although this one was somewhat different to the last. Rather than the *FGR.2* model, she was flying one of only six *Typhoon FGR.4*s the RAF had in service. This version had the electronically scanned version of the CAPTOR radar, known as CEASAR, the ability to carry conformal fuel tanks, 2-D thrust vectoring and—crucially for this mission—an extra fifteen percent more power in its EJ200 turbofans.

*Someone is about to get a surprise today*, she thought. *At least this one probably isn't a fighter sweep.*

The task of intercepting MiG-25s was, appropriately enough, referred to as 'Fox Hunting'. The *Typhoons* assigned to the task were only armed with a pair of *Meteor* missiles, carried no other external stores, and had been so thoroughly stripped that even the wings' hard-points were blanked off.

*Glad the Soviets obliged us by waiting a few hours to send this mission.* Pairs of Fox Hunters would be launched only once it was certain that a *Foxbat* was on its way. Even then, success was not certain, as only a relatively small number of the Soviet recce birds had been shot down.

Catz's datalink blipped as the *Typhoon FGR.4* crept past Mach 1.7.

*Thank God for supercruise*, she thought, seeing the vector from the *Sentry*. Catz and her wingman pushed their throttles to the stops, accelerating to the *Typhoons'* maximum speed. Catz energised the radar as she pulled back on the stick. Just as the *Typhoon* was about to stall, she got a continuous tone in her ears.

"Fox Three! Fox Three!" she announced firing both *Meteors*. A split-second later her wingman echoed the radio call as both of them nosed their fighters over and retarded their throttles.

*Now for the exhilarating task of finding a tanker before we run out of fuel*, Catz said, noting just how much avgas the ascent and launch had cost her. Setting up the rendezvous in the navigational computer, Catz turned to watch the intercept unfold.

The lead *Foxbat* turned away and began to accelerate, trying to escape. Four decoys separated from the big fighter, and for a moment Catz was certain that the *Meteors* were going to lock onto them. However, on this occasion the jettisoning and acceleration was just a bit too late. One of her missiles, just about to run out of fuel, got close enough to activate its proximity fuse.

*You poor bastard*, Catz thought, genuinely sympathetic. She could envision the blast-fragmentation warhead tearing chunks out of the airframe of the Soviet aircraft. At the speed the *Foxbat* was traveling, the effect was almost immediate. The contact 'bloomed' briefly as the MiG-25 began to tumble and was torn to pieces in less than a second.

*Too bad we missed the second one*, she thought, seeing her wingman's missiles arc past the rushing *Foxbat*.

As she made contact with the *VC.10 K3,* Catz felt somewhat pleased with herself. She was fairly sure she had killed the target.

\* \* \*

Although the destruction of his aircraft had happened in the blink of an eye, the MiG-25RBF's pilot had still had enough time to scream. Captain Komissarov could still hear the man's final moments, broadcast over the Soviet command frequency, ringing in his ears.

*Well it looks like the people in Moscow who wanted electronic intelligence are not going to get what they so desperately needed*, Komissarov thought. He armed his weapons and started his aircraft's cameras. There would only be a fraction of a second to drop the first pair of bombs at the right time.

*They never should have modified these aircraft to allow supersonic strikes*, he thought angrily. *Even with precision guid—*

His thoughts were interrupted by the incessant warning of a *Broadsword* SAM flight locking on. Quickly pickling his bombs as he entered the delivery envelope, Komissarov immediately activated his jammers and turned out to sea.

Unbeknownst to Komissarov, his flight computer had an error in its navigational routines. As a result, both bombs were already off target as soon as they dropped off his MiG, with their point of impact growing even further afield as they ran into shearing winds while crossing over the border into Norfolk. They passed over the radar station at RAF Neatishead, their intended target, then landed in the nearby Burnt Fen broad. Their twin explosions killed quite a lot of wildlife but had no impact on the nearby RAF station other than causing a great deal of consternation.

*It would not make the Commissar happy, but I have a feeling that someone 'Up There' is looking out for me*, Komissarov thought, seeing the sixth *Broadsword* SAM fall away behind his hurtling fighter. It seemed as if after the destruction of the other *Foxbat* the RAF had 'shot its bolt' in terms of fighters that could threaten him. Just to be sure, he took his MiG-25 well out over the North Sea so that he could approach his second target, RAF Boulmer, from the north.

*Let's hope that was the last* Broadsword *battery up here,* he thought. Intelligence swore the British only had limited numbers of the system, but Komissarov had strong doubts. As he crossed back over land, he once more turned on the cameras and armed his bombs. With no strident warning, he waited patiently to close to optimal release range, pressed his button…and felt nothing. Quickly stabbing the button again, Komissarov began cursing as there was a second instance of absolutely nothing.

"Dammit to hell!" he muttered, pushing a few buttons to reset the computer and begin other troubleshooting procedures. He was halfway through troubleshooting when the fighter lurched from first one, then the second, bomb dropping away.

"Fucking shit!" he exclaimed. Taking a look at his navigational system, he saw there was no way the glide bombs could circle back towards his target.

*Well at least it would land somewhere in Britain,* he thought. *Hopefully either a military target, or at worse some fields.*

If he'd been able to see where his bombs headed to, Komissarov would have lost all of his briefly flickering faith in a higher power. Rather than an open field or even a distant military outpost, the unshakeable laws of ballistics took the two bombs to possibly one of the worst destinations they could reach—the Freeman Hospital. Like all other NHS hospitals, the facility had thankfully been cleared of all non-essential patients in expectation of being needed for war casualties. Unfortunately, that still left a fair number of staff from the night shift, transplant patients, cancer sufferers and, of course, their visiting family members.

The effects of two bombs, each containing over 200-kilograms of high explosives, on the hospital were catastrophic.

\* \* \*

Komissarov knew nothing of what had happened behind him, as he finally turned his big fighter for home.

*I have to run a gauntlet to the tanker,* he thought, thinking of the SAMs and fighters between his current location and home base. There was suddenly a cough from somewhere aft that caused the MiG-25RBsh to shudder violently. He urgently checked his heads down display; to his horror he could see that the temperature of the right-hand engine was rising rapidly. It had just reached the red band when the FIRE light came on, followed by the MASTER CAUTION warning along with several urgent audible alarms.

*Shit! Shit! Shit!* Komissarov thought, shutting down the right-hand engine as he punched the fire extinguisher button. Fear ran through him as the engine's temperature continued to rise despite the engine's RPM dropping down to almost nothing. There was only one explanation—he had an uncontained fire in the aft fuselage.

*I do not feel like going for a swim today,* he thought angrily, banking his burning fighter back towards land. He had no desire to be taken prisoner but bailing out over the North Sea would probably just lead to the question of whether he froze to death or drowned.

The MiG-25 was slowly losing both height and speed, making it vulnerable to interception. Although the MASTER CAUTION and fire warning had now been stilled, they were quickly replaced by increasingly strident tones from the radar warning receiver.

*Well, looks like I'm about to get a* Tornado *pilot a medal,* Komissarov thought angrily, noting he was being illuminated by a Foxhunter radar. Very soon the *Tornado F.3* it belonged to would be able to engage him, but likely not until after he had made a considerable distance inland.

The thirty seconds passed quickly. As the *Tornado* closed into the outer edges of its envelope, Komissarov tightened the straps on his harness, checked that there were no loose objects in the cockpit, and paused for a moment. It was often a difficult decision for a pilot to choose to leave the relative comfort and warmth of the cockpit.

*It is time to go.* With a sigh, he pulled the ejection seat handle.

\* \* \*

D etective Sergeant Freddie Spicer stopped his car as he spotted the figure under a descending parachute. He had been driving to the Freeman Hospital to offer what help he could with crowd control. Like a lot of Northumbria Police's detectives, Spicer was also pulling uniform duty, something that most CID officers had a great deal of distaste for.

*Well, time to figure out if this is a Russian or one of our lot*, Spicer thought, getting out of the car. He was keenly aware of being unarmed, but so far, no Russians had attempted to shoot it out after dropping into Great Britain.

*Three hots and a cot will go far to making the other side come along peacefully*, Spicer thought, placing on his peaked cap. He walked towards the pilot as the man stumbled to his feet, then began gathering up his parachute.

"You one of ours, or one of theirs, bonny lad?" Spicer asked.

"I am Captain Komissarov of the Soviet Air Force, officer. I wish to surrender," the pilot said, handing Spicer his pistol.

"Well, you'd better come wi' me then," Spicer said, gesturing back towards his car. The pilot dutifully got into the vehicle's rear seat.

"Control, I have a Soviet pilot in custody on Freeman Road by the tennis courts," Spicer reported. "I'm going to drive him back to the station. Can you let the military know please, over?"

*What does this bloody lot want?* the Detective Sergeant thought, looking at a crowd that was beginning to head his way. People had begun to congregate shortly after the hospital had been bombed and had continued to watch the fire. Rumours were already spreading as to how many people had been killed, and he'd heard the reports that the Maggie's Centre had been destroyed along with its cancer patients. The mood of the local population was already very black.

"That's a bloody Russian!" someone shouted, pointing at Spicer's car.

*Oh shit.*

"Control, I'm going to need back-up. I've a crowd turning nasty here, over," Spicer radioed urgently. He turned in the seat.

"You're not a bomber pilot are you, lad?"

The Russian hesitated, and Spicer sincerely hoped it was because he was processing the question.

"No, I fly, how you say, reconnaissance aircraft," the Soviet replied. "What you call the *Foxbat*."

The crowd, now a mob, was advancing on the Detective Sergeant and pilot. There was no sign as yet of the promised back-up. Spicer drew his baton and turned to Komissarov.

"I think you'd better run, lad," Spicer said firmly. "I'll hold them back as long as I can."

\* \* \*

## HQ, RAF Strike Command, RAF High Wycombe, Buckinghamshire.

Air Chief Marshal Johnson reviewed the events of the past twenty-four hours as he sat down to record his final log.

*Another day of wastage that didn't seem to move the needle at all*, he thought, scribbling. *The defences held up, but damned if we didn't take some damage to the bases.* He ran his hand over the stricken bases. Wick had been damaged badly enough that Air Vice Marshal Hazel had decided to temporarily relocate operations to Sumburgh Airport in Shetland. The Buncefield refinery, which produced aviation fuel, had been set on fire.

*On the plus side, losses were relatively light for us*, he thought. Three *Tornado F.3s*, two *Typhoons*, and a pair of *Hawks*. The last two had been caught on the ground, something he was amazed had not happened to more of his fighters. A *Tristar KC.1* had also been damaged on approach to Aberdeen Airport when it ran into a flock of seabirds. Although it had lost one of its RB211 engines, the tanker had landed safely.

*More importantly, we're getting better at saving the crews that punch out*, he thought. *Even the enemy ones. Well, the ones in the sea, anyway.* There were reports from Newcastle that a mob had hung a Soviet pilot from the nearest lamppost after blaming him for a local hospital's bombing. The same mob had also badly beaten a police officer who had tried to protect the pilot.

"Victoria, please ask Chief Constable of Northumberland Police if it'd be possible for me to visit the officer who was beaten today," Johnson called out after a moment's thought. "I'll make a statement to the press afterwards; we don't want this sort of thing becoming a regular occurrence."

"Yes, sir," Victoria replied from the outer office.

CINCUKAIR looked over the reports on stocks of weapons, fuel, and spare parts. They were not quite as healthy as he would have liked. Still, they were not at the stage yet of being a cause for concern. It did remind him that he was due to speak to the commander of RAF Support Command about his logistical needs in the morning.

"Sir, you should probably head for bed," Victoria stated from his office door. Johnson started. He looked towards his watch, only to recall taking it off in the gent's toilet.

"What time is it, Vicky?" Johnson asked, standing.

"Five to midnight, sir," she replied, having looked at the wall clock behind her boss.

"You really need to get some sleep, sir," she pressed. "You'll not be any use to anyone if you don't get some rest."

"You should too, Vicky."

"Oh, I'm young, sir," she replied, her voice belying her confidence. "I'll manage for a while yet."

The implied suggestion that he was old made Johnson smile for the first time in several hours. It felt good, and that was a bad sign.

"Okay, Vicky, I'll get away to bed," he said with a chuckle and a nod. "Wake me if something serious happens."

With that, Johnson took off his tie and shoes, and then climbed into the narrow cot. Within a few seconds, he was asleep.

\* \* \* \* \*

**Author's Note:**

Readers of my ongoing online novel, *The Last War*, will notice that this story shares some characters and the general scenario from that work. However, it is not a TLW story. Rather, as the great Arthur C. Clarke said of his '*Odyssey*' novels, it is from a very close parallel universe.

\* \* \* \* \*

**Jan Niemczyk Bio**

Jan Niemczyk was born and brought up in Scotland, where he currently lives. He has long had an interest in military history, aviation, naval warfare, cats and horses. He also has an interest in the Cold War. He is still amazed that anything he has written has appeared in an actual proper book. He has definitely not named a character after his cat!

Mr Niemczyk is the author of the web novel *The Last War*, an alternative history where the USSR has survived into the early 21st Century (https://groups.yahoo.com/neo/groups/jans_fiction/files). He is currently employed in the public sector. He would also like to thank all those who had read his work, helped to make it better and who had bought the first book in this series.

# # # # #

# About the Editors

A Webster Award winner and three-time Dragon Award finalist, Chris Kennedy is a Science Fiction/Fantasy/Young Adult author, speaker, and small-press publisher who has written over 20 books and published more than 100 others. Chris' stories include the "Occupied Seattle" military fiction duology, "The Theogony" and "Codex Regius" science fiction trilogies, stories in the "Four Horsemen" and "In Revolution Born" universes and the "War for Dominance" fantasy trilogy. Get his free book, "Shattered Crucible," at his website, chriskennedypublishing.com.

Called "fantastic" and "a great speaker," he has coached hundreds of beginning authors and budding novelists on how to self-publish their stories at a variety of conferences, conventions and writing guild presentations. He is the author of the award-winning #1 bestseller, "Self-Publishing for Profit: How to Get Your Book Out of Your Head and Into the Stores," as well as the leadership training book, "Leadership from the Darkside."

Chris lives in Virginia Beach, Virginia, with his wife, and is the holder of a doctorate in educational leadership and master's degrees in both business and public administration. Follow Chris on Facebook at facebook.com/chriskennedypublishing.biz.

---

James Young holds a doctorate in U.S. History from Kansas State University and is a graduate of the United States Military Academy. Fiction is James' first writing love, but he's also dabbled in non-fiction with publications in the *Journal of Military History* and *Proceedings* to his credit. His current fiction series are the *Usurper's War* (alternate history), *Vergassy Chronicles* (space opera), and *Scythefall* (apocalyptic fiction), all of which are available via Amazon. You can find him at his FB Page (https://www.facebook.com/ColfaxDen/), Twitter (@Youngblai), or by signing up for his mailing list on the front page of his blog (https://vergassy.com/).

\* \* \* \* \*

The following is an
**Excerpt from Book One of The Psyche of War:**

# Minds of Men

_____

# Kacey Ezell

Available from Theogony Books

eBook, Paperback, and Audio

**Excerpt from "Minds of Men:"**

"Look sharp, everyone," Carl said after a while. Evelyn couldn't have said whether they'd been droning for minutes or hours in the cold, dense white of the cloud cover. "We should be overhead the French coast in about thirty seconds."

The men all reacted to this announcement with varying degrees of excitement and terror. Sean got up from his seat and came back to her, holding an awkward looking arrangement of fabric and straps.

*Put this on,* he thought to her. *It's your flak jacket. And your parachute is just there,* he said, pointing. *If the captain gives the order to bail out, you go, clip this piece into your 'chute, and jump out the biggest hole you can find. Do you understand? You do, don't you. This psychic thing certainly makes explaining things easier,* he finished with a grin.

Evelyn gave him what she hoped was a brave smile and took the flak jacket from him. It was deceptively heavy, and she struggled a bit with getting it on. Sean gave her a smile and a thumbs up, and then headed back to his station.

The other men were checking in and charging their weapons. A short time later, Evelyn saw through Rico's eyes as the tail gunner watched their fighter escort waggle their wings at the formation and depart. They didn't have the long-range fuel capability to continue all the way to the target.

*Someday, that long-range fighter escort we were promised will materialize,* Carl thought. His mind felt determinedly positive, like he was trying to be strong for the crew and not let them see his fear. That, of course, was an impossibility, but the crew took it well. After all, they were afraid, too. Especially as the formation had begun its descent to the attack altitude of 20,000 feet. Evelyn became gradually aware of

451

the way the men's collective tension ratcheted up with every hundred feet of descent. They were entering enemy fighter territory.

*Yeah, and someday Veronica Lake will...ah. Never mind. Sorry, Evie.* That was Les. Evelyn could feel the waist gunner's not-quite-repentant grin. She had to suppress a grin of her own, but Les' irreverence was the perfect tension breaker.

*Boys will be boys,* she sent, projecting a sense of tolerance. *But real men keep their private lives private.* She added this last with a bit of smug superiority and felt the rest of the crew's appreciative flare of humor at her jab. Even Les laughed, shaking his head. A warmth that had nothing to do with her electric suit enfolded Evelyn, and she started to feel like, maybe, she just might become part of the crew yet.

*Fighters! Twelve o'clock high!*

The call came from Alice. If she craned her neck to look around Sean's body, Evelyn could just see the terrifying rain of tracer fire coming from the dark, diving silhouette of an enemy fighter. She let the call echo down her own channels and felt her men respond, turning their own weapons to cover *Teacher's Pet*'s flanks. Adrenaline surges spiked through all of them, causing Evelyn's heart to race in turn. She took a deep breath and reached out to tie her crew in closer to the Forts around them.

She looked through Sean's eyes as he fired from the top turret, tracking his line of bullets just in front of the attacking aircraft. His mind was oddly calm and terribly focused...as, indeed, they all were. Even young Lieutenant Bob was zeroed in on his task of keeping a tight position and making it that much harder to penetrate the deadly crossing fire of the Flying Fortress.

*Fighters! Three o'clock low!*

That was Logan in the ball turret. Evelyn felt him as he spun his turret around and began to fire the twin Browning AN/M2 .50 caliber machine guns at the sinister dark shapes rising up to meet them with fire.

*Got 'em,* Bobby Fritsche replied, from his position in the right waist. He, too, opened up with his own .50 caliber machine gun, tracking the barrel forward of the nose of the fighter formation, in order to "lead" their flight and not shoot behind them.

Evelyn blinked, then hastily relayed the call to the other girls in the formation net. She felt their acknowledgement, though it was almost an absentminded thing as each of the girls were focusing mostly on the communication between the men in their individual crews.

*Got you, you Kraut sonofabitch!* Logan exulted. Evelyn looked through his eyes and couldn't help but feel a twist of pity for the pilot of the German fighter as he spiraled toward the ground, one wing completely gone. She carefully kept that emotion from Logan, however, as he was concentrating on trying to take out the other three fighters who'd been in the initial attacking wedge. One fell victim to Bobby's relentless fire as he threw out a curtain of lead that couldn't be avoided.

*Two back to you, tail,* Bobby said, his mind carrying an even calm, devoid of Logan's adrenaline-fueled exultation.

*Yup,* Rico Martinez answered as he visually acquired the two remaining targets and opened fire. He was aided by fire from the aircraft flying off their right wing, the *Nagging Natasha*. She fired from her left waist and tail, and the two remaining fighters faltered and tumbled through the resulting crossfire. Evelyn watched through Rico's eyes as the ugly black smoke trailed the wreckage down.

*Fighters! Twelve high!*

*Fighters! Two high!*

The calls were simultaneous, coming from Sean in his top turret and Les on the left side. Evelyn took a deep breath and did her best to split her attention between the two of them, keeping the net strong and open. Sean and Les opened fire, their respective weapons adding a cacophony of pops to the ever-present thrum of the engines.

*Flak!* That was Carl, up front. Evelyn felt him take hold of the controls, helping the lieutenant to maintain his position in the formation as the Nazi anti-aircraft guns began to send up 20mm shells that blossomed into dark clouds that pocked the sky. One exploded right in front of *Pretty Cass'* nose. Evelyn felt the bottom drop out of her stomach as the aircraft heaved first up and then down. She held on grimly and passed on the wordless knowledge the pilots had no choice but to fly through the debris and shrapnel that resulted.

In the meantime, the gunners continued their rapid fire response to the enemy fighters' attempt to break up the formation. Evelyn took that knowledge—that the Luftwaffe was trying to isolate one of the Forts, make her vulnerable—and passed it along the looser formation net.

*Shit! They got* Liberty Belle! Logan called out then, from his view in the ball turret. Evelyn looked through his angry eyes, feeling his sudden spike of despair as they watched the crippled Fort fall back, two of her four engines smoking. Instantly, the enemy fighters swarmed like so many insects, and Evelyn watched as the aircraft yawed over and began to spin down and out of control.

A few agonizing heartbeats later, first one, then three more parachutes fluttered open far below. Evelyn felt Logan's bitter knowledge that there had been six other men on board that aircraft. *Liberty Belle* was one of the few birds flying without a psychic on board, and Evelyn suppressed a small, wicked feeling of relief that she hadn't just lost one of her friends.

*Fighters! Twelve o'clock level!*

\* \* \* \* \*

**Get "Minds of Men" now at:**

https://www.amazon.com/dp/B0778SPKQV

**Find out more about Kacey Ezell and "Minds of Men" at:**

https://chriskennedypublishing.com

\* \* \* \* \*

The following is an
**Excerpt from Book One of the Salvage Title Trilogy:**

# Salvage Title

---

# Kevin Steverson

Available Now from Theogony Books

eBook, Paperback, and Audio Book

**Excerpt from "Salvage Title:"**

The first thing Clip did was get power to the door and the access panel. Two of his power cells did the trick once he had them wired to the container. He then pulled out his slate and connected it. It lit up, and his fingers flew across it. It took him a few minutes to establish a link, then he programmed it to search for the combination to the access panel.

"Is it from a human ship?" Harmon asked, curious.

"I don't think so, but it doesn't matter; ones and zeros are still ones and zeros when it comes to computers. It's universal. I mean, there are some things you have to know to get other races' computers to run right, but it's not that hard," Clip said.

Harmon shook his head. *Riiigghht,* he thought. He knew better. Clip's intelligence test results were completely off the charts. Clip opted to go to work at Rinto's right after secondary school because there was nothing for him to learn at the colleges and universities on either Tretra or Joth. He could have received academic scholarships for advanced degrees on a number of nearby systems. He could have even gone all the way to Earth and attended the University of Georgia if he wanted. The problem was getting there. The schools would have provided free tuition if he could just have paid to get there.

Secondary school had been rough on Clip. He was a small guy that made excellent grades without trying. It would have been worse if Harmon hadn't let everyone know that Clip was his brother. They lived in the same foster center, so it was mostly true. The first day of school, Harmon had laid down the law—if you messed with Clip, you messed up.

At the age of fourteen, he beat three seniors senseless for attempting to put Clip in a trash container. One of them was a Yalteen, a member of a race of large humanoids from two systems over. It wasn't a fair fight—they should have brought more people with them. Harmon hated bullies.

After the suspension ended, the school's Warball coach came to see him. He started that season as a freshman and worked on using it to earn a scholarship to the academy. By the time he graduated, he was six feet two inches with two hundred and twenty pounds of muscle. He got the scholarship and a shot at going into space. It was the longest time he'd ever spent away from his foster brother, but he couldn't turn it down.

Clip stayed on Joth and went to work for Rinto. He figured it was a job that would get him access to all kinds of technical stuff, servos, motors, and maybe even some alien computers. The first week he was there, he tweaked the equipment and increased the plant's recycled steel production by 12 percent. Rinto was eternally grateful, as it put him solidly into the profit column instead of toeing the line between profit and loss. When Harmon came back to the planet after the academy, Rinto hired him on the spot on Clip's recommendation. After he saw Harmon operate the grappler and got to know him, he was glad he did.

A steady beeping brought Harmon back to the present. Clip's program had succeeded in unlocking the container. "Right on!" Clip exclaimed. He was always using expressions hundreds or more years out of style. "Let's see what we have; I hope this one isn't empty, too." Last month they'd come across a smaller vault, but it had been empty.

Harmon stepped up and wedged his hands into the small opening the door had made when it disengaged the locks. There wasn't enough power in the small cells Clip used to open it any further. He put his weight into it, and the door opened enough for them to get inside. Before they went in, Harmon placed a piece of pipe in the doorway so it couldn't close and lock on them, baking them alive before anyone realized they were missing.

Daylight shone in through the doorway, and they both froze in place; the weapons vault was full.

\* \* \* \* \*

**Get "Salvage Title" now at:**
https://www.amazon.com/dp/B07H8Q3HBV.

**Find out more about Kevin Steverson and "Salvage Title" at:**
http://chriskennedypublishing.com/.

\* \* \* \* \*

The following is an
**Excerpt from Book One of the Earth Song Cycle:**

# Overture

———————————————

# Mark Wandrey

Now Available from Theogony Books

eBook and Paperback

**Excerpt from "Overture:"**

Dawn was still an hour away as Mindy Channely opened the roof access and stared in surprise at the crowd already assembled there. "Authorized Personnel Only" was printed in bold red letters on the door through which she and her husband, Jake, slipped onto the wide roof.

A few people standing nearby took notice of their arrival. Most had no reaction, a few nodded, and a couple waved tentatively. Mindy looked over the skyline of Portland and instinctively oriented herself before glancing to the east. The sky had an unnatural glow that had been growing steadily for hours, and as they watched, scintillating streamers of blue, white, and green radiated over the mountains like a strange, concentrated aurora borealis.

"You almost missed it," one man said. She let the door close, but saw someone had left a brick to keep it from closing completely. Mindy turned and saw the man who had spoken wore a security guard uniform. The easy access to the building made more sense.

"Ain't no one missin' this!" a drunk man slurred.

"We figured most people fled to the hills over the past week," Jake replied.

"I guess we were wrong," Mindy said.

"Might as well enjoy the show," the guard said and offered them a huge, hand-rolled cigarette that didn't smell like tobacco. She waved it off, and the two men shrugged before taking a puff.

"Here it comes!" someone yelled. Mindy looked to the east. There was a bright light coming over the Cascade Mountains, so intense it was like looking at a welder's torch. Asteroid LM-245 hit the atmosphere at over 300 miles per second. It seemed to move faster and faster, from east to west, and the people lifted their hands

465

to shield their eyes from the blinding light. It looked like a blazing comet or a science fiction laser blast.

"Maybe it will just pass over," someone said in a voice full of hope.

Mindy shook her head. She'd studied the asteroid's track many times.

In a matter of a few seconds, it shot by and fell toward the western horizon, disappearing below the mountains between Portland and the ocean. Out of view of the city, it slammed into the ocean.

The impact was unimaginable. The air around the hypersonic projectile turned to superheated plasma, creating a shockwave that generated 10 times the energy of the largest nuclear weapon ever detonated as it hit the ocean's surface.

The kinetic energy was more than 1,000 megatons; however, the object didn't slow as it flashed through a half mile of ocean and into the sea bed, then into the mantel, and beyond.

On the surface, the blast effect appeared as a thermal flash brighter than the sun. Everyone on the rooftop watched with wide-eyed terror as the Tualatin Mountains between Portland and the Pacific Ocean were outlined in blinding light. As the light began to dissipate, the outline of the mountains blurred as a dense bank of smoke climbed from the western range.

The flash had incinerated everything on the other side.

The physical blast, travelling much faster than any normal atmospheric shockwave, hit the mountains and tore them from the bedrock, adding them to the rolling wave of destruction traveling east at several thousand miles per hour. The people on the rooftops of Portland only had two seconds before the entire city was wiped away.

Ten seconds later, the asteroid reached the core of the planet, and another dozen seconds after that, the Earth's fate was sealed.

\* \* \* \* \*

**Get "Overture" now at:**
https://www.amazon.com/dp/B077YMLRHM/

**Find out about Mark Wandrey and the Earth Song Cycle at:**
https://chriskennedypublishing.com/

\* \* \* \* \*

## ALSO BY JAMES YOUNG

### USURPER'S WAR SERIES

Acts of War

Collisions of the Damned

Against the Tide Imperial

### USURPER'S WAR COLLECTION

On Seas So Crimson

Made in the USA
Las Vegas, NV
15 November 2022

59549109R00262